The Symptoms of my INSANITY

by Mindy Raf

DIAL BOOKS
AN IMPRINT OF PENGUIN GROUP (USA) INC.

DIAL BOOKS

An imprint of Penguin Group (USA) Inc.
Published by The Penguin Group
Penguin Group (USA) Inc., 375 Hudson Street,
New York, NY 10014, U.S.A.

USA · Canada · UK · Ireland · Australia · New Zealand · India · South Africa · China
Penguin Books Ltd, Registered Offices: 80 Strand, London WC2R 0RL, England
For more information about the Penguin Group visit penguin.com

Library of Congress Cataloging-in-Publication Data
Raf, Mindy.
The symptoms of my insanity / by Mindy Raf.
p. cm.
Summary: When you're a hypochondriac, there are a million
different things that could be wrong with you, but for Izzy,
focusing on what could be wrong might be keeping her from
dealing with what's really wrong—with her friendships,
her romantic entanglements, and even her family.
ISBN 978-0-8037-3241-4 (hardcover)
[1. High schools—Fiction. 2. Schools—Fiction.
3. Hypochondria—Fiction. 4. Mothers—Fiction.] I. Title.
PZ7.R10952Sym 2013
[Fic]—dc23   2012024708

Printed in the U.S.A.

1 3 5 7 9 10 8 6 4 2

Book design by Sarah Davis Creech
Type set in Stempel Garamond

The publisher does not have any control over and does not assume
any responsibility for author or third-party websites or their content.

*For my dad, who always loves, supports,
and believes in me and all my insanity,
and for my brave and brilliant mom,
who's always here, even when she's not.*

CHAPTER 1

I'm diseased.

I'm standing inside a large fitting room at Lola's Lingerie. Oh, and there are three hands on my breasts.

Yup, three large Russian hands. On my breasts. I'm not kidding.

One of the hands removes itself and returns, holding a tape measure. There are now two hands on my breasts, each cupping a boob. I wonder if the one on the right feels anything out of the ordinary. Should I ask her? Should I say, *Excuse me, Svenya, I know you're just fitting me for a bra, but do you feel anything strange or lumpy in there—does that one feel cancerous to you?*

I read all about breast cancer on one of my mom's chat/support sites. My mom doesn't have breast cancer, but she *does* have this habit of staying logged into all her stuff after she borrows my laptop. One woman had this lump in her breast and just assumed it was a benign cyst. Nothing to worry about. Well, now she has no breasts at all. So, naturally, I decided to study my own breasts in the bathroom mirror. I'm no medical expert or anything, but I could plainly see that my right breast was bigger than my left.

And then today, as I was sitting in biology thinking about having to go get fitted for new bras at stupid Lola's Lingerie after school, my right boob started hurting (the one that's bigger!) and I started to feel really strange. I know it sounds crazy, but self-diagnosis is totally possible, especially when the patient is knowledgeable about symptoms and stuff. Since I had no bathroom passes left, I had to sit through the rest of biology knowing that, at that very moment, cancer was probably spreading throughout my entire body. I almost raised my hand, but what would I say? *Mr. Bayer, may I please be excused? I'm not totally positive, but I think I might have cancer.* No way. Then everyone at school would know, and they would treat me differently, and I would be known as "Izzy, that poor girl who diagnosed herself with breast cancer during biology."

Oh, and then Marcus totally caught me studying my breast asymmetry in bio instead of working on my Punnett square. I tried to act like I was picking lint off my sweater, but I don't think it worked. What's Marcus Mason even doing in my sophomore bio class? I mean, I know why he's there, but who chooses to work on an independent bio project with Mr. Bayer for *fun* their senior year?

At least it was only Jenna's brother Marcus, though, and not like Jacob Ullman or one of his idiot friends. Jenna calls them "testosteclones," and they would totally torture me if they caught me boobing-out in bio. They've been saying idiotic things to me ever since I got these things in fifth grade. "Hey

Izzy, how'd you do on the math breast?" or "Boom badda boom badda boom" when I walk, or "What did you have for bra-fest this morning?" Which is one of Jacob's favorites, and which he actually whispered to me in temple during our eighth-grade Hebrew school graduation. I don't understand why boobs are such a big deal anyway, but if I'm wearing a top that's not super-duper baggy, the guys in my class just stare at my chest like it's one of those Magic Eye patterns.

So yeah, I'm confident my secret's safe with Marcus. His mother would have him locked up if she caught him even looking at boobs anyway. Cathy Mason loves telling people that other people need to be locked up. Mainly people who do things she considers "inappropriate, immoral, and disgraceful." Almost every gossipy conversation she has with my mom ends with her saying, "Can you believe it, Linda? Isn't that completely inappropriate, immoral, and disgraceful?" And my mom always nods back at her and says, "Yes, completely, Cathy."

Anyway, it wasn't just the asymmetry of my breasts that was worrying me today—I would never diagnose myself based on a single symptom. No, I also felt tired. Not ordinary tired, but alarmingly tired. And then this afternoon in the art studio I broke out in a sweat for no reason at all. The ventilation fan next to me was even turned on high, but I just kept sweating. That's not normal. So later in study hall when I was supposed to be doing web research on the Incas, I typed "spontaneous sweating" and "body asymmetry" into Symptomaniac.com.

Do you want to know what came up for me?

Progeria!

That's when children mature really quickly and then die with the body of like a seventy-year-old. I didn't read all the details, but that's the basic idea. Which completely makes sense since I'm fifteen and already have the body of a "voluptuous" (my mom's friend Pam swears that word's a compliment) twenty-five-year-old. It's true. It's December and I no longer fit into any of my bras. The back-to-school ones! The *size C* back-to-school ones! Hence, why I'm trapped here, after school, in a Lola's Lingerie fitting room.

I'm about to ask Svenya if she feels anything suspicious, when I look down and notice the cavernous cleavage I have from the monster-size underwire the Russians have strapped onto me. Holy cow! If one of these ladies dropped her pen right now, my breasts would swallow it whole. I'm like a living, breathing, busty Bermuda Triangle. Forget high school, I should just get a job for the government hiding top secret documents in my cleavage.

"It's a C. No bigger than C. Round, very good. Not sausagey. C."

The hand on the other side wags its fingers and shouts out a reply.

"*Nyet,* a D. Too big for C. Too big."

"They a C."

"They a D."

"They a C."

The third one chimes in.

"*Nyet! Nyet!* A D, a D. They a DD."

A double D?! Oh my God. I've shot up three letter sizes in three months! I'm about to ask for a recount but am silenced by the tape measure. I watch the numbers fly by as it wraps itself around my chest: 5-10-15-20-25-30—

"Thirty-three one half," three voices proclaim in unison. The tape measure is discarded and all three women stare at me a second before victoriously shouting at megaphone volume, "Thirty-four double D!"

Thanks, ladies.

I should not be here right now with the Russian Underwire Trinity. I need to be working on my art portfolio; I'm more than three pieces behind schedule.

"That looks tight. Is it too tight? Does it fit you? It should fit you." Mom steps into the fitting room. She's holding a bunch of merchandise in one hand and waving the other in the air trying to dry the fuchsia nail polish from the manicure she just got next door.

I check myself out in the mirror. No, it's not possible that I'm this unattractive. Is it? No, it must be the fitting room light. Fitting room light is extremely unflattering. I don't think anybody looks good under a fluorescent glare. Mom sets her stuff down in the corner of the giant fitting room and continues air-drying her nails. I take that back. My mom looks good. But she always does. If there were a Miss Cancer America beauty pageant, she would totally win.

"Izzy, does it fit? Is it too tight? Is it pressing on your

shoulders?" Mom is determined that I be well supported. Before I can respond, she and the Russians start conversing about my breasts as if they're having a deep political discussion.

I watch my mom nod her head at the Russians while checking out her nails in the fitting room mirrors. I try to focus really hard on taking what my art teacher Miss S. calls "mental snapshots." She says we go through life so fast and that a good way to remember stuff is to try and take pictures with our mind. Lately, whenever I do something with my mom, I feel like I'm back at summer camp and it's the last day when everyone's all sad and thinking things like, *This is the last time we'll eat lunch at the mess hall, this is the last time we'll hear the announcements by the flagpole,* which is so stupid because this is not the last time I'm going to go shopping with my mom. She's not dying or anything, she's just sick.

Not that you would know it by looking at her. My mom is really good at hiding things. She can wear tons of makeup and make it look like she's not wearing any at all. She's also really good at keeping herself immaculately put together at all times. Her shoes always match her shirt, her shirt always matches her purse, and her nails always match her shoes, shirt, and purse. Her lips are always perfectly lined, her clothes are never wrinkled, there's never anything hanging out of her nose, and she always makes sure that she has no food in her teeth before she leaves the house, even when she's just getting the mail. I can hardly wake up with enough time in the morning to brush my teeth and make sure I have on matching socks.

"I still think you are sisters every time I see together." Svenya looks from Mom to me and back again.

Mom waves a hand, trying to eat her smile. She's in her forties but doesn't look a day over thirty, so I hear this "sisters" thing all the time. But honestly, I really don't see how anyone could possibly think I'm my mom's daughter, let alone her sister. My older sister, Allissa, is the one who looks like Mom. They both have light brown hair, blue eyes, no curves. I have jet-black hair, dark brown eyes, and—according to my mom's friend Pam, who swears it's another compliment—"God-given birthing hips."

Mom says I take after Dad's side of the family. Which is just great because that means I might have inherited my dad's mid-life-crisis chromosome. Like one day when I'm forty, I'm going to move across the country and marry someone half my age. Yay.

Mom's always saying how I look just like dad's mom, Grandma Rose, when she was sixteen. She dug up and showed me an old picture of her and, she's right, I do. Which wouldn't be so bad except that now Grandma Rose is a four-foot-ten-inch-tall, eighty-three-year-old woman with gargantuan breasts that take over her entire bra-less body. Really, I should just bolt out of Lola's Lingerie right now. What's the point of spending money on bras when I'm going to end up a short, eighty-three-year-old woman with dangle-boobs?

Mom's still fielding compliments from Svenya, who's clicking her tongue against her teeth and shaking her head. "You too skinny now. Never have the weight put on. Every time you here, you look like more skinny."

"No, no, I'm fine, I'm fine," Mom demurs, stepping away from the mirror. Svenya gives her a "whatever you say" shrug and leaves the fitting room to dig through the old-lady bra bins for my size. Mom is digging through her own pile of merchandise.

"Look what I found out there, Izzy. Isn't this cute?"

She holds up a cream-colored, floor-length, flannel nightgown decorated with pink bunnies, as if to tell me that although I may have the body of a grown woman, I'm still going to dress like a six-year-old.

"Mom, no. I'll never wear that."

Twenty minutes later we're leaving Lola's Lingerie with six new double D underwire bras and one floor-length, bunny-covered, flannel nightgown.

CHAPTER 2

I'm suggestive.

There are four seasons in Michigan. Winter with snow, winter with rain, summer, and winter with falling leaves. This is one of those uncomfortably cold, winter-with-more-winter kind of days.

Mom and I are now standing in the parking lot of Lola's Lingerie, and she's reapplying her lip gloss in the car's side mirror with one of the fourteen shades of pink she bought today. Just when I think she's done, she takes out another tube of pink from her purse.

"Can't you put that stuff on inside?" I ask. "Gimme the keys."

"Hold your horses," she manages to say while using her lips to blend.

For my mom, going out in public with un-glossed lips is like wearing dirty underwear or forgetting to put on deodorant. Once I tried to count the number of times she reapplied her lip gloss in the course of an hour. I got up to seven before realizing that collecting lip-glossing data was not the most productive use of my time.

"I think this shade of pink is more festive than this one," she declares, holding up both tubes of gloss like they're paint chips.

"What?"

"For the Dance for Darfur centerpieces. See the difference? This one, the festive pink, is more what I had in mind."

"Yes, yes, let's talk about it in the car."

Mom is one of the co-chairs for the Dance for Darfur Holiday Ball happening at school right before winter break. I think it's great that all of our school dances are combined with fund-raising, but it's not so great when your mom's in charge. My freshman year was the Children's Literacy Luau. I was forced to collect donations from my classmates in giant pineapple-shaped bowls and wear so many layers of leis, I looked like I had on a fake-floral neck brace. So fun.

Mom finally puts the glosses away and checks her lips one last time in the car's frosted side mirror, but then she pauses, catching my reflection.

"Why did I buy you that nice winter coat if you're not going to button it up?"

I'm not in the mood to tell her that my bionic boobs have already made it impossible to keep my coat closed.

"Did you wear that sweater to school today?" she asks with a sigh so big, it smokes the winter air.

No, Mom, I changed outfits in the girls' bathroom before you picked me up to go shopping. It's all part of my master plan to never wear the same outfit for more than six hours.

"Yeah, I wore this to school. Why? What's wrong with this sweater?" *Can you tell my right breast is frighteningly bigger than my left?*

"Nothing's wrong with it. It's cute. It's a little suggestive, but cute."

Suggestive is my mom's all-time favorite word, and due to the arrival of my newly measured 34 double Ds and my God-given birthing hips, I have learned two things: 1) Everything I wear looks suggestive, and 2) When someone looks "suggestive," the thing that they are suggesting is sex.

So yeah, I'm not surprised my mom's calling me suggestive in a strip mall parking lot while we inexplicably stand outside the car in the freezing cold. I hear it all the time. I hear it in the morning before I leave for school:

"You can't wear that to school. It's suggestive."

"Mom, it's a button-down shirt."

"Well, you should have bought a large."

"This IS a large."

I hear it at night before I go to bed:

"I really hope you don't plan on wearing that tiny little suggestive T-shirt anywhere but to sleep."

I even hear it in Yiddish:

"Izzy, what is that?!"

"It's a tank top, Mom."

"Well, take it off. It's suggestive. You look like a nafka.*"*

Nafka, by the way, is Yiddish for "a loose woman." When I was little, I thought my mom was fluent in Yiddish. Turns out she was just using the same seven words over and over again. This is her Yiddish vocabulary: *chazzer, nafka, mishi-gas, vildeh-chiyah, meiskeit, bissel,* and *shpilkus.* They mean (respectively): a pig, a loose woman, craziness, a wild animal, really ugly, a little bit, and nervous energy. I'm waiting for the day she uses them all in one long, ungrammatical sentence: "Ugh, Izzy look at that *nafka* over there eating that donut like a *chazzer* while her *meiskeit,* tattoo-covered *vildeh-chiyah* boyfriend drinks that large coffee and really, I don't see how he stands it—even a *bissel* coffee in this *mishi-gas* mall gives me *shpilkus.*"

I hold my coat closed with my hands. It's starting to snow now. Doesn't she understand that my body is noticeable no matter what I wear? And no matter how I walk? Once my mom told me that she thought I *walked* suggestively, that I stuck out my chest too much, which was just asking men to look at me. But I swear I just walk like any other person.

"Mom, it's not my fault my sweater's suggestive."

"Izzy, people don't see things that aren't on display."

She punctuates that sentence with the same facial expression my sister, Allissa, uses when she thinks she's tapping into the depths of my psyche and telling me I need therapy. (Allissa's in college and she's really into her Abnormal Psych class, so she thinks she's really cool when she says things like, *"You need therapy"* or *"Your behavior is way too self-reflective."* I'm not a big, important college student or anything, but I always thought that self-reflection was the whole point of therapy.)

My mom's still giving me her Allissa-Psych-101 face, even

after I tell her that I'm not trying to be on display. "Why would I want to be on display?!"

"I'm not saying you *want* to draw negative attention to yourself," she explains. "I'm just saying that unfortunately you can't get away with wearing just anything like other girls your age. Your body delivers a very specific message, whether you want it to or not."

Oh God, not the "message" talk.

"Fine Mom, I'll just lock myself up at home and never leave the house."

"Don't be ridiculous. I just want you to be aware. That's why we did this today." She smiles at me proudly. "Once they're supported properly, you won't draw so much attention to yourself. You'll see."

There are so many things I want to say back to her, but I can't. I've lost the ability to argue with my mom. What if I end up saying something really overdramatic and awful, like scream out "I hate you!" and then she dies and that's the last thing I ever say to her? Not that she's dying or anything. I just hate that she thinks I want all that attention from guys. Because I don't. I just want to be left alone.

"What are you doing?" I ask when I see Mom still hasn't unlocked the car door and instead is leaning against it rummaging around in her purse. It's snowing harder now, making her black purse fabric look white and fuzzy.

"Forgot we have to stop at Arbor's and get my medicine," she mumbles, nodding across the parking lot to the drugstore. "Aha," she says, pulling papers out of her purse. "Two new prescriptions, one refill." She hands them to me. "So while you take care of that, I'm going to run next door to Farmer Jack's and get milk. Oh, and toilet paper. Oh, and shampoo. Oh, and we need chicken, ice cream, fruit and . . ." She continues rambling off a giant shopping list as she walks back across the freezing parking lot to Farmer Jack's Grocery, turtling her head down and pulling up the collar of her coat to protect her hair from the snow.

I head over to Arbor's Drugs. This is what I do: prescription pickup/drop-off. Broomington isn't exactly a huge town, and although my mom is anything but antisocial, she doesn't like people knowing her personal business. I always tell her that I don't think it matters which one of us goes, since I doubt Mr. Neil thinks I'm the one taking the estrogen and calcium and the heartburn stuff, and the tons of other pills that have names I can't pronounce and that Jenna says go for more than two hundred dollars apiece "on the streets." I don't really know what "streets" she's referring to since she's never left the suburbs, but she does watch a lot of *Law & Order.* Mr. Neil's been filling Mom's prescriptions for years, from when she first had all her hardware taken out—ovaries, uterus, all her tubes, the whole factory—and had to go on hormone pills when I was too small to remember. All the way up through this past summer, when she had her big stomach surgery for the slow-growing cancer they found. Mom tells me that of course Mr. Neil knows all the medicine's for her. That's why she doesn't go in, so she doesn't have to answer any questions.

I drop off the prescriptions and wander over to the magazines. I grab one and remember that I need to get a new math notebook since I spilled orange juice all over mine this morning. So I'm thumbing through some celebrity tabloid and walking down the aisle, which is probably why I totally collide with someone. The magazine flies out of my hands, does a sideways dive into the shelf, and there's a huge clatter as products rain down around me.

"Sorry," I mumble, squatting to collect everything. When I look up, I'm staring at an epic and very familiar jaw—square, slightly stubbled, with a tiny chin scar-dimple on the lower left side. It belongs to Blake Hangry.

I stand up slowly, and place three overturned boxes of anti-diarrhea pills back on the shelf.

"Hey! Izzy! Aw man, did I get you? Sorry!" Blake smiles at me, takes a swig of what's left in his open bottle of Gatorade, and gestures to my neck and coat, now covered with sticky electrolytes. Then a Celine Dion ballad starts playing from inside his coat pocket. "What the—I'm gonna kill those guys," he says, rolling his eyes and pulling out his cell. "Hey," he says into his phone and then turns to me with another smile and one finger up, as if to tell me to hold on for a minute, like the two of us have more to say to each other.

Blake Hangry and his dimpled jaw are smiling at me. Again. For the past few weeks, I'd been thinking of reasons why. *He's thinking of a funny joke in his head,* or *He's looking at someone right behind me,* or *He's spotted half my lunch stuck inside my teeth.*

"So Izzy, you okay? No injuries or anything?" Blake asks now, putting his phone back in his coat pocket and flashing me another smile as he bends down and picks up a subscription postcard from my magazine.

Holy cow, that smile just now was definitely for me. And I realize—I think Blake Hangry and his manly jaw have been *smiling* at *me* all along. Last Tuesday, when he was picking up some old art supplies from the school's studio—that was him smiling at me too. (I smiled back that time because it was kind of funny watching him try to carry four canvases and all those paints and brushes out of the studio by himself. Then Miss S. told me he was giving them to his little sister, Jillian, for her birthday after one of her drawings won Pine Fall Elementary School's "Top Pic" Award, and I just about swoon-melted into my stool.)

"Izzy, you okay?" he asks again, leaning in slightly, eyes searching my face.

He has sweat stains on his T-shirt, which means he should smell kind of wonky, but I get a whiff of his deodorant, which must be that Blade stick he's holding, mixed in with his gym smell, and the combination . . . Well, I've lost the ability to move my mouth. Oh God, he's looking right at me, still smiling, and I know I need to respond, but I can't because my mouth is not connected to my face right now. *Come on Izzy, get it together. Just say something, anything!*

"You're really sweaty."

No, no, no. Crap. Rewind.

"Oh yeah, sorry. I'm nasty. Been working on my free

throws after school," he says, taking an imaginary one-handed shot. "No less than a hundred a day. Gotta get my percentage up for basketball season."

"Your percentage . . . ?" I do a quick wipe of some of the lemon lime off my neck with my scarf.

"Oh, that's not gonna do the trick," he says, laughing. Then he grabs a package of baby wipes from the shelf behind him, takes one out, and starts . . . baby-wiping my neck.

"Sorry," he says mid-wipe in a teasing tone, handing me the package. "Didn't mean to be so forward."

"No, it's okay, I get . . . baby-wiped by guys all the time."

He laughs.

Holy Mother of Gatorade, I just made him laugh.

"So . . . your percentage? Is that the number of baskets you make?" I ask, trying not to sound like a total idiot.

"Oh," he laughs, "I get it. You're doing that whole, 'I'm a girl, I don't know anything about sports' act."

No. It's not an act. Both those things are true.

"Yeah," I laugh. "I know all about basketball. It's that sport where you wear helmets and tackle each other, right? Duh," I say, twirling my hair.

Blake laughs. Again! Then he pushes some of his thick wavy hair out of his face so I can see his blue eyes, which have little gray flecks in them, and which are really nice and set super-symmetrically above his cheekbones. Come to think of it, he has a great face for sculpting. Not that I'd sculpt him or anything. That would be stalkerish, but . . . wait, what is he looking at? Why is he staring at me and grinning like that?

"Your hair," he says, "it's really crazy curly today."

I want to die. I want to sink into the linoleum floor and die. Why did I let my hair air dry into a big, puffy mess today?

"Yeah, it curls when I don't blow-dry it," I explain. "Well, actually, it waves when I don't blow-dry it, and just a couple pieces in the front really curl. And actually it doesn't really wave, it kind of just frizzes out, like this."

Shut up, Izzy, please just shut up.

"No, I like it," he says. "It's kinda wild." And then he reaches out his hand and TOUCHES MY HAIR! And then he says something else to me, but I don't remember what because I'm fantasizing about Blake throwing his Gatorade bottle across the floor and passionately pressing me up against the beverage fridge to make out.

"So . . ." I say, hoping my face doesn't look as hot as it feels, "you need to get your percentage up?"

"Oh. Yeah, working my butt off. I don't have the height, so I gotta make sure I'm sinking rocks every time, you know?"

"Right," I say, nodding at him like I know all about sinking rocks.

"Sorry, I probably sound all jock-like and douchey. Oh, and sorry for saying douchey."

"No problem." I nod, realizing he's probably reacting to

the face I make whenever I hear a vaginal cleaning method used as an adjective.

"Anyway, Tim's helping me out with my game when he's home too, which is awesome."

"Tim?"

"My brother. He plays at Michigan State. Saw a lot of time his freshman year. He'll probably start this season."

"Wow. So . . . you wanna play in college too?"

"Yeah, I mean I hope so. I gotta get a full ride like Tim. My cousin Will's still paying off student loans, and he's like in his thirties!"

"Well, if you don't play basketball, do you—"

"I gotta play, I pretty much suck at everything else," he says, finishing off the bottle.

"I doubt that." And then he doesn't say anything back and I feel stupid because maybe he meant that jokingly, and so I try and think of something else to say to imply that I don't think he really does suck at everything else, but I can't think while he's smiling at me. I know he's only sixteen, but I swear Blake Hangry has the kind of jaw that grown men would envy. I bet right now he could just effortlessly open that bag of Doritos he's holding with his teeth.

"So I like that thing you did, by the way," he says, knocking me out of my Blake-rips-open-a-bag-of-Doritos-with-his-teeth fantasy.

"What thing?"

"The thing—the one in the hall by the art studio."

"Oh, thanks," I say, surprised.

"It's like a self-photo right?"

"Yeah, it's a drawing. It's from last year. In the fall, actually. So it's not very—"

"It's cool. It looks so real. Like a photograph. How do you do that?"

"Oh, I don't know. It's charcoal. Just shading and stuff."

"Yeah, right. Like it's so simple. Well anyway, it's impressive."

"Thanks."

And now Blake's looking at me in this way that affects every single one of my arrector pili muscles. I think that's what they're called from biology, those tiny skin muscles that make your body hair stand up straight when you're around powerfully potent pheromones. The way Blake's looking at me right now makes every single one of them spasm, like goose bumps times a trillion.

"So my mom," he says, "she works for the DIA."

"Oh, wow, that's really cool."

"Yeah. I saw your name and your picture on their website for that Italy thing."

"Oh, right." The Detroit Institute of Arts is giving six students a scholarship to study abroad at U of M's campus in Italy this summer. Miss S. thinks I have a pretty good chance of being one of them, if I ever finish my stupid application portfolio. "So your mom's involved in that?" I ask. "In the scholarship?"

"Yeah. I mean she's not a judge or anything. She's an events coordinator there."

"Oh. That's cool."

"So yeah the DIA, they're having this grand opening thing for this new wing? Food, music, art and all that. Told my sister, Jillian, I'd take her. She's a really good drawer. I mean, for a seven-year-old. Anyway, I think you'd like it too. Right?"

"Yeah!" I say with a tad too much enthusiasm, especially since there's no way Mom will let me go to Detroit, unchaperoned, with a guy.

"Cool," he says, "so you wanna come check it out? It's on Saturday. That's if you're not busy working on your watercolors. Or your charcoal? You said charcoal, right?"

"Oh, yeah. I mean yes, that one was a charcoal drawing, and no, I'm not busy," I tell him, while telling myself that it's not irresponsible to spend a free Saturday not working on my portfolio. It can be research. With Blake!

"Great. Should be some good stuff there. I mean, I don't know exactly—"

"Yeah. Actually, I read an article on the new wing, and there's this painter, Juliana Roriago—well, she's more of a performance artist, and I've always been curious to see her live. And she'll be there on Saturday. She's a resident all month actually. But yes, she'll be there on Saturday. This Saturday. She'll be there. At the new wing. On Saturday. That same Saturday that you're going, 'cause she's debuting. Performance art. This new . . . performance art . . . piece.

And thus ends my own performance art piece entitled, English? Or Word Vomit?

"Well cool . . . okay then, it's on," Blake says.

"Okay. Yeah, it's on," I repeat, nodding my head.

"Well, I gotta get another one of these"—he gestures to his drink, smiles—"and the guys are waiting in the car, so . . ."

"Okay"—I nod my head again, and again, and again—"nice to see you." *Nice to see you?! Blech.*

"Yeah. Oh, and I hope your shopping went well," he says with a slight grin and walks past me to the front of the store.

I stop mid-nod and look after him, confused, and then realize that, oh my God, I've been holding my Lola's Lingerie bag this whole time.

CHAPTER 3

I'm the assistant director.

I know Mom's asking me to tell Cathy Mason something for her tonight when I go over to Jenna's for dinner, but all I can think about while we fill up the trunk with groceries is Blake, his blond-stubbled jaw, and how his lips would taste if we were actually making out.

"Izzy? Did you hear me?"

Salty maybe? Or no, sweet from the Gatorade? Ick, no. Should I be surprised he was so nice to me just then, so nice in fact that he asked me out on a museum date? Not that Blake's ever been mean to me directly, but he's friends with all those guys who are.

Oh man, he'd definitely touch my hair a lot if we made out. I'm thinking he'd brush it out of my face before he went in to kiss me. And that first kiss would be soft. But then I'd touch *his* hair. I'd take hold of it on the back of his head. And then he'd get this look in his eyes, like he couldn't control himself any longer. He'd pull me into him gently. No, roughly. Yes, he'd grab at the sides of my shirt and yank me in super-close. And then we'd basically go at it like crazy animals until I finally pry myself away and say all out of breath, *"Wait, we have to stop, we can't do this here in the middle of the drugstore."*

"Never mind, I'll call Cathy later." Mom sighs, picking up another bag from the cart, but before she can get it into the trunk, she starts coughing so hard that she has to lean against the side of the car.

"Are you okay?" I grab the bag from her.

"Fine, fine, battling a sinus thing, I think." She straightens herself up.

"Wait, didn't you just go grocery shopping the other day?" I ask, seeing our almost-full trunk.

"Yes, but Allissa's coming in for the weekend."

Allissa's school is less than two hours away. Yet whenever she's coming home, Mom acts like my sister's flying in from a foodless, far-off country.

"We're all going to spend the day together on Saturday," Mom continues. "Have a girls' day, go to the mall." She smiles, as if just saying the word *mall* is an endorphin boost. "You both need winter clothes. And you desperately need a haircut."

A girls' day? On Saturday? I would rather watch the Weather Channel, no, get caught in an actual blizzard, than go to the mall with Allissa and Mom. They're always laughing about things I don't find funny and getting excited about things I would never get excited about, like the fact that you get an ugly bag full of nasty-smelling perfume samples when you spend over seventy-five dollars at the makeup counter.

Plus, when Allissa's around, Mom's always asking her about boys, saying nauseating things like, "So Allissa, you think this one's Mr. Right?" and Allissa's always saying equally nauseating things back like, "I don't know, Mom, but we did hold hands during the whole movie." And then they both talk about *me*. About me being antisocial, and never having a boyfriend. Like I'm not even there!

"I don't really need new clothes. The ones I have still fit me fine." Well, except for my winter coat, and most of my button-down shirts, but she doesn't have to know that right now.

"Well, that's not [cough] the point, Izzy."

"So the point of going shopping for new clothes isn't to get new clothes?"

"What?" Mom asks, looking confused, then drops the bag she's holding back into the cart to let out another cough.

"I'll do the rest." I grab that bag and another one as well. "It's just that I didn't know Allissa was coming in this weekend and . . . I kind of already made plans for Saturday."

"What plans?" she asks, leaning against the car again.

"I was going to go to this thing at the DIA," I say casually.

"The DIA." She whips her head around fast. "With who? [cough] What? How are you getting there? Is this for school? I don't [cough] remember signing anything allowing you to take a field trip this weekend to downtown [cough] Detroit. If Miss Swenson thinks she can just take children into one of the most dangerous cities in the country, without [cough] so much as a permission slip [cough], then she's going to get a call from me [cough, cough, cough]."

"No, it's not for Miss S. or for school," I explain, pushing the empty cart back with the others. "My friend's mom works there and this new wing is opening and . . ." I trail off.

"What friend?" she asks as we finally get into the car.

"My friend Blake."

"Who?"

"Blake . . . Hangry," I say, a little louder as she starts the engine.

"I wasn't aware you had a friend named Blake Hangry," Mom says calmly between coughs.

"Well . . . I do. And he's—"

"I'm sorry, Izzy, but you're not going to Detroit on Saturday with . . . Blake Hangry." She lowers her voice when she says his name, like it's a dirty word.

"It's the DIA," I plead. "It's educational. And they're opening this new wing. And . . . there's food, and drinks, and . . . Oh! And his little sister is—"

"Drinks [cough]?"

"No, no, not like 'drinks,' like . . . refreshments." But it's too late and I know what's coming.

"Remember the girl who woke up naked [cough], in a bathtub, with her organs in a jar?" Mom reminds me, dead serious.

"Yeah, but Mom—"

"A couple of beers. That's all she had . . . and boom! No kidneys."

This overdramatic, "I'm clueless" stuff has got to be some passive-aggressive mom technique. I refuse to believe my mother doesn't know the difference between beer and roofies, and urban legends and actual news stories. But before I can explain this difference once and for all, Mom says how excited she is that we're finally going to get rid of my split ends on Saturday. I guess her kidney story settled it: I'm not going anywhere with Blake.

"Come on, sweetie. Don't look so upset." She turns to me at the red light and reaches over, pushing some strands of hair out of my face and tucking them behind my ear. "Can't you wear a shower cap or something when you're painting? This isn't the best way to present yourself," she adds, picking a piece of dried red paint out of my hair.

I don't respond. Instead I set more dried red strands free from behind my ear.

"Well, good thing we're going to get this cut soon anyway." She looks at my face. "What?" she says. "You're not excited to have a girls' day with your mom and your sister?" She smiles and pushes the strand back behind my ear.

"Just have a girls' day without me!" I plead, pulling away. "Why can't you have a girls' day without me? And then I can go to the DIA and then after . . ." I trail off, seeing the hurt expression on her face.

We drive in silence for what seems like a hundred miles before pulling into Jenna's driveway.

"I'd like to meet him first," she finally says, taking out the festive pink gloss from her pocket and reapplying in the rearview mirror. "I'll meet him. And then [cough] maybe."

"Okay," I say. And that look on her face, well, it's a mental snapshot I wish I hadn't taken.

The minute I walk into the Masons' house, Jenna starts laughing. She shakes her head at me and pushes her chopped-out, wispy blond bob away from her eyes.

"I keep telling you my A-minus girls don't need new bras, Izzy. But so sweet of you to think of me."

Stupid Lola's bag sticking out of my backpack.

Jenna and I head up to her room and she immediately puts one of my new double Ds on over her T-shirt.

"I'm totally wearing this baby during dinner."

"No! God, take that off. It's so ugly."

She cups her hands over the bra.

"I can't believe you fill these things. I'm so jealous! I can't even fill my own two hands." She heads to the mirror to ogle her new air-boobs.

The first time I saw Jenna, all I wanted to do was feed her a giant sandwich. She was so thin and pale, I thought she might be sick. But after watching her finish off an entire plate of nachos and win three events on our middle school track-and-field team, I quickly learned that her pale skin, blond hair, and rail-thin body really *are* due to what she likes to call "my cruel genetic fate."

"So . . . tell me again. You ran into Blake Hangry while buying lingerie?"

I left Jenna a scattered voicemail while I was waiting for Mom outside Farmer Jack's.

"Yeah," I say, smiling. "Wait, no, at Arbor's Drugs. I told you, he spilled his Gatorade on me and—"

"Oh right, so his sports juice is all over you, and then he compliments your art skills, and then?" Jenna grabs another bra out of the bag and slips it on over the first. "Wait, let me guess. You perform fellatio on him in the bathroom of the store like a good little Broomington girl?"

"Ew," I say. "You know I hate that word."

"Fellaaaaaaatio," Jenna sings.

There's a big rumor going around school right now that Meredith Brightwell got caught giving Jacob Ullman a blow job in a girls' bathroom stall last week during sixth period. I still don't even know how Jenna's mom found out, but Cathy Mason always finds out about everything. So of course my mom found out too and totally freaked out on me. She was acting like *I* was in the bathroom stall too, like Meredith and I are still best friends or something, giving tag-team blow jobs.

Mom's uptight about a lot of things, but sex things, oh my God. I think that's why she and Grandma Iris don't really talk that much anymore. Allissa and I usually only see Grandma Iris about three times a year, on all of our birthdays. Except this past July she came in for two entire months after Mom had her debulking, this major mucus-scraping surgery for her stomach cancer. They were civil, I guess. But if you didn't know any better, you'd think Grandma was a hired nurse. I don't know all the details about why they don't talk much, but according to what I heard Grandma Iris say to my aunt Lorraine on the phone one time, "Some things are unforgivable," and I think "some things" refers to Allissa being "irresponsibly conceived in sin." My grandma has a very loud phone voice.

"Fellaatio, fellAAAAAAAtio," Jenna is still singing and fumbling to secure the clasp of her third double D.

I cover my ears and whip my head back and forth dramatically. "Stop, please."

When Mom found out about Meredith last week, she sat me down for the longest, most painful lecture of my life. She kept calling Meredith a "bathroom stall *nafka*" and ranted on about respecting oneself, and making smart decisions, and the difference between being social and being taken advantage of, and the worst part was that she kept using the phrase "pleasuring boys" over and over again and asking me if I knew what it meant.

Hello? I think a girl who's used the Internet to find out the details of almost every rare cancer in existence is definitely able to Google "blow job" when she's dared to by Cara Larson in sixth grade. DISGUSTING! I would NEVER ever do that EVER. I couldn't believe it when I heard about Meredith doing it. I thought that was only something women do when they're absolutely desperate for money to survive.

Of course I just shook my head when Mom asked me about it, acting like I had no idea what it meant. Not Jenna, though. I was here when Cathy Mason barged into Jenna's bedroom ranting about blasphemy. The Meredith news must have interrupted her cooking, because she was holding a giant bottle of olive oil, which she unknowingly used as a prop, twice. And when Cathy grilled Jenna for more information, Jenna didn't just shake her head like I had. She looked right up at her mom, and with her usual sugar-sweet, wide-eyed sarcasm, her hands pressed up against her chest and eyelashes batting, she said, "Yes Mom, it's true. All the girls at school pleasure boys in bathroom stalls. How else are we supposed to get them to like us?"

But Jenna's always been able to say things like that and get away with it.

"Okay, okay, sorry," Jenna says, seeing that I'm still covering my ears. "So Blake compliments your art, and then he just asks you to go to the DIA with him?"

"Yup."

"And your mom's letting you go?"

"Well, she has to meet him first, but—"

Jenna snorts and gives me an overexaggerated head nod and a double thumbs-up.

"I know." I fall back traumatically on Jenna's book-covered purple bedspread.

"You should just say, 'Mom, why do you have to meet the guy I'm going to be getting it on with in dimly lit corners amidst important art?'"

"Jenna!"

"What?"

"His little sister is going with us," I say. "And, God, not everything is about . . . sex, you nympho."

"What do you mean by that?"

I frown. "Nothing. I'm just kidding."

"Oooh, is that new?" Jenna asks, plopping down next to me on the bed, now wearing five of my bras at once.

"What?"

"Your ring," she says pointing to my silver band, partially caked in paint.

"Oh. No. Allissa ordered this online in like July, but it ended up being too big for her skinny fingers, so she gave it to me. I just found it again in one of my smocks. I had it on all summer, though. I'm sure you've seen . . . it." I trail off, knowing what's coming next.

"Uh, no," Jenna says. "You were cooped up in your basement making love to your art supplies all summer. Remember?"

I nod, and chip some paint off my ring with my thumbnail, reminded again how totally behind I am on my portfolio. I'd hoped to have most of it done already, but I didn't get much accomplished over the summer. Allissa's on-campus summer job answering phones for some psych professor was more important than me having time to do my art while taking care of post-surgery Mom. And the house. And her office. And acting as a human Grandma-Iris-the-Nurse buffer.

"I'm sorry. That was . . ." Jenna turns her face from me toward her mirror. "Of course you were dealing with your mom and everything."

"No, it's okay. Besides, it's not like you weren't . . . busy partying with your writing group friends in Ann Arbor, so—" I cut myself off.

"I wasn't partying." She whips around fast. "I was—I was around. You were the one who—"

"Sorry, sorry. Right, forget it."

"So . . . Oh!" Jenna says now, bounding up and heading back to the mirror. "I have to tell you what Blake did in drama class today."

"What?" I say, happy for the change in subject.

"Okay, well, he was doing a scene from *A Streetcar Named Desire*—do you know that play? It's wonderful. The set design alone, if it's done right, evokes so much in itself. We so need to watch the movie together. You think Blake is hot? Please. Wait until you see Marlon Brando—"

"Jenna—"

"Okay, so he's doing a *Streetcar* scene with Emily Belfry, who by the way had the worst Southern belle accent ever. It was like a Valley girl with a twang and every so often she sounded Scottish. I told Mrs. Fredmeir that dialect training is essential to good acting, but she never listens to any of my suggestions—"

"Uh-huh. And?"

"And okay, so he's about to start the scene when all of a sudden Mrs. Fredmeir is like, 'Mr. Hangry, I think Stanley here would be shirtless, no?' And Blake's like, 'What?' Looking like he's going to upchuck on Emily's shoes. And Mrs. Fredmeir's like, 'Mr. Hangry,' you know, with that proper voice she has? And she basically tells him that he needs to have his shirt off in order to fully get into character, and she's like quoting Stanislavski and stuff, which, okay, kind of makes sense, but—"

"Wait, are you telling me that Blake—"

"TOOK OFF HIS SHIRT!"

"No!"

"Yes!"

"What?"

"Yeah, and he looked so embarrassed."

"That's like harassment."

"I know! And I swear Fredmeir was checking out his abs the whole time because you know, this is how so many of those nasty student-teacher fling things start and—"

"Unghhh," I groan, "please don't ever say *Fredmeir, nasty,* and *fling things* in the same sentence ever again."

"I'm just saying that during the scene, she looked professional . . . yet aroused."

"Jenna!"

"Sorry, sorry. So anyway, Emily, who can't act in a Tennessee Williams play to save her own life, got to spend the next seven minutes sounding like a Southern Scot doing a scene with a shirtless Blake Hangry!"

"Wow," I say, sitting back.

"Yeah. I told you. Take drama with me," she says, fishing through my Lola's bag again.

I shake my head. Thank God I was able to fill our creative elective requirement with art and not be forced into taking drama or lip-synching my way through a choir class.

"So . . . you're not going to start dating Blake, are you?" Jenna asks.

"Yeah, right."

"Good! I forbid you to get a boyfriend this year and start acting all couple-y on me. Besides, maybe it's not even a date on Saturday."

"Yeah, maybe. Wait, what do you mean?"

"Well, his mom's the one who put your info and stuff on the DIA website, right? Maybe it was her idea to invite you, like an art buddy for his little sister."

"Oh. Yeah. Maybe. So . . . no, you don't have to worry about me having a boyfriend. I'm sure you'll have one before me anyway, hands down."

"What? Why would you say that?"

"Because, please, you always have someone after you. Like Nate Yube. I know you're still totally—"

"Wow! Izzy! This is very cute," Jenna interrupts, finding the pink bunny nightgown in the bag. She tosses it to me like it's a hot potato.

"Unghhh," I groan again, throwing it back in the bag.

"So," Jenna says, "judging from your hot new pajamas, and all my brand-new bras, it looks like you had some fun girl time with your mom."

"It wasn't girl time, it was . . ." I pause, thinking about the girls' day with her and Allissa I tried to blow off. "I just needed new bras."

"No. I think it's good you're spending time together. It's important."

"Yeah. Well, I just needed new bras."

"I know," Jenna sighs, ripping the tag off the top bra she's wearing. "Oh! I can't believe I almost forgot to ask you this! What are you doing after school tomorrow?"

"I don't know. Not too much," I say, watching her pull more tags off more bras. "Actually, I should stay in the studio and work on my portfolio—"

"Good, then you're free." She grins mischievously.

"Well, not exactly . . . Wait, why?" I already fear the worst.

"Okay, so don't flip out—"

"Jenna, what did you do?"

"You're the assistant director-slash-set design helper for the winter musical. Congratulations!"

"Jenna! No!"

"Isabella! Yes!"

"No! No way! I don't have time! I have to finish my portfolio, I have all this dance stuff to do for my mom, and I have to maintain at least a B-plus average to even get to go to Italy. I have no time for this."

"Come on, it's not a big deal. It'll be fun."

I shake my head at her. It's not a big deal for someone like Jenna to direct a play, but to be honest, the thought of assistant directing, of telling everyone what to do, makes me want to vomit repeatedly all over myself. Plus, and I'm sorry if this sounds rude, but all the people who do the plays are kind of crazy. They're really loud and they gesture a lot when they talk, and sometimes they just spontaneously burst into three-part harmony.

I continue to shake my head. "No. Absolutely not. No."

"Come on, Izzy." Jenna grabs my hands, air-boobs swinging. "We're in the final stretch. It'll be easy. And now that

Blake and all those basketball guys are there too, and I have to watch all the girls—and a very horned-up Mrs. Fredmeir—drool-swoon all over the place, I desperately need one person around who doesn't utterly nauseate me. And Ryan Paulson needs major guidance with the set, and you're so good at that stuff."

"Wait, all those guys are in the play now?"

"Yeah, apparently we need bigger guys to lift the girls in the dance numbers, and since they're all required to fit in one non-sport extracurricular anyway, Mrs. Fredmeir's like, 'You're just going to have to make them dancing trees!' It's so stupid. So . . . please say yes."

"I don't know. I'm sorry, but—"

"Come on, you have to do it! I already told Mrs. Fredmeir you would."

"Jenna!"

"What?" she says, as if she didn't just sign me up to do something without asking me first. And then her poorly painted purple bedroom door opens a crack, and a worn white sneaker peeks through.

"Dinner's ready, and Mom wants to know if either of you two wants—"

"Marcus, don't be rude." Jenna singsongs over her brother's low and steady tone. "Come in and say hi to Izzy."

Marcus appears from behind the door, locks his gaze on me through black-rimmed glasses, and says, "Hey."

"Hey," I say back. Then he turns and sees Jenna, who's still decked out in layers of my double-D bras. I think both his face and mine turn as red as my mom's painted nails.

"What the . . ." he starts, then glances back at me, turns even redder, and glances away again, almost tripping over a laundry basket as he escapes to the door. "Dinner's ready," he repeats, and disappears around the doorframe. I sigh.

"Marcus, tell Izzy to work on the musical with us!" Jenna calls, shimmying all my bras down her hips, and then stepping out of the undergarment circle around her ankles gracefully, like she does this all the time.

"Work on the musical with *us*?" I ask as we head down the hall.

"Marcus is stage-managing," Jenna says, flapping her hand like I should know this already.

"No, no, no, I'm just doing light cues for you," Marcus says. He's paused at the top of the stairs. "I have stuff of my own to work on, Jenna."

Marcus is graduating this year and probably going off to some Ivy league school in like New York, or New Haven . . . or some other New-named city where super-smart people go. He actually took a college course last summer on freshwater organism chemicals or something.

"Lights, sound, curtain cues, line prompts," Jenna says, squeezing past him and bounding down the stairs, "it's all connected."

Marcus sighs and I follow him down. Then he stops abruptly in the middle of the stairs. He takes off his glasses to wipe the lenses on his shirt, turns to me, and says, "You should do it, Izzy, keep me company among the crazies." I give him a knowing laugh, always surprised at how big his eyes are without his glasses. He puts them back on and hides the stems behind his hair, which is dark and sticks out in all directions, but still manages to look okay.

"She's already in!" Jenna calls up.

"No, no, I'll . . . I'll think about it."

"Rehearsal goes until seven," Jenna adds.

"Oh, you know what? I have to be home by five tomorrow," I remember, joining her at the kitchen table and saying hello to Cathy, who peeks her head out of the oven long enough to triumphantly inform me that my mom called earlier and told her about finding the perfect shade of pink for me to re-create when I paint the Dance for Darfur centerpiece vases.

"So many shades of pink, so little time," Marcus says under his breath in such a mock solemn tone, I almost spit up the water I'm drinking.

"Oh, that reminds me." Cathy reemerges, both oven-mitted hands pointing at Jenna. "Did you get the dance flyers up and those ticket envelopes stuffed yet?"

"I did all that last weekend," Jenna says, and then shakes her head *no* at me as Cathy swivels back to the oven, "and I was busy at Soaptastic all weekend too. So . . . you're welcome, Mom."

Soaptastic is this vegan-friendly soap store at the mall where Jenna works some weekends. I love visiting and watching her keep a straight face while saying *"Organic scents, just make sense."*

"So why do you have to be home tomorrow?" Marcus asks, sitting down next to me.

"Oh, I have to help my mom. We need to finish cleaning out the attic so the carpet guys can . . . carpet it. We're turning it into an office for her."

"I didn't know your mom was leaving her office." Cathy's forehead scrunches together, matching the crinkle-cut carrots in the salad she sets down.

I nod.

"But she's doing okay, though," Marcus says, "I mean—"

"Yeah, no, she's great. The rent went up a lot on the space she was in, so . . . And she's got a bunch of new projects she's working on, so she'll be really busy working from home."

"Well, that's great!" Cathy says, forehead relaxing.

"Yup." I nod.

Okay, so I exaggerated: Mom actually only has one new project she's working on now, since the surgery over the summer kind of slowed her down, but I'm sure things will pick up once she starts feeling better. I really hope so, because last weekend she came into my room holding all this lacey floral fabric and asked me the most horrifying question I've ever heard: "Do you want a canopy bed?"

"Okay," Jenna talks through her salad mouth, "I guess I'll let you leave our first rehearsal early."

"*Our* rehearsal?"

And that one word makes it official. I'm now the assistant director/set designer of the school musical.

CHAPTER 4

I have knockers grandes.

I wake up the next morning determined. *Four hours, just four more hours.*

That's how long till I can get to the art studio. I psych myself up while brushing my teeth. Today I'm going to start something new, and I'm going to get this portfolio *done*.

I pick up the pace on my walk to school. *Just three more hours.* The Advance Studio Projects kids, we get the small art room all to ourselves since there're only five of us. The 101 class stays in the main art room. The spaces are joined by Miss S.'s office, which is more of a junk closet hallway, but we hardly see or hear the other class, which is fine by me.

If you get here early, come to drama room, need help with tix! I get a text from Jenna and pick up the pace even more, tucking my chin down to cover as much of my face as I can with my scarf. We only live about a fifteen-minute walk from school, but last year Mom made Allissa drive me there and back. My sister drives as if she's both drunk and blind, so I'm more than happy to walk to and from school in the cold this year.

I usually meet Jenna at her U.S. history class to say hello and make fun of what Mrs. Kerns's animal-themed sweatshirt says. "I'm crazy fur you"? "Eel'd with a kiss"? I pass by history on my way to the drama room and peek in quickly. Wow, today's the best one yet: "Polar Coaster!" And yes, it's an image of a screaming polar bear riding a roller coaster.

Jenna's sitting on the drama room floor among piles of envelopes, tickets, and flyers when I walk in.

"Guess I should do this for Cathy now," she says, licking an envelope, "since tickets go on sale this week and she already thinks it's done. Oops." She laughs, and shoves another ticket into a tiny "Dance for Darfur" envelope that I recognize, because Mom made me do the designs and calligraphy last month.

"Polar Coaster!" I say, plopping down and helping Jenna stuff envelopes.

"No! Wait, like a cup of hot coffee resting on top of a polar bear?" Jenna closes her eyes for a second, imagining it. I shake my head imagining it too, and then we burst out laughing.

"So." Jenna picks up a clipboard from the floor. "Meredith Brightwell just signed up to help Cara finish the choreography for the musical." She makes a gag face usually reserved for when I'm eating our cafeteria tacos in front of her. "I think it's great that Meredith's trying to get involved in something at school that's so far away from Jacob Ullman's crotch, but please. Hopefully she won't sign up for the dance committee too. She probably thinks Darfur's an acronym."

I roll my eyes and smile, and then shrug. "We could use an extra person," I say, thinking maybe I could give some of my dance committee tasks to Meredith and get more work done on my portfolio . . . though it would surprise me if she actually did any work on the dance herself, since all she does is ask other people to do stuff for her, like copy notes from class, or borrow someone's computer 'cause she forgot her charger, again.

"We don't need her or any of her bobble babe friends." Jenna makes her gag face again, and then starts bobbing her head up and down, going, "Uh-huh [bob, bob, bob] uh-huh," like Cara Larson and those girls do.

"Yeah, but I haven't even *started* the decorations yet, and our moms want this perfect combo of . . . what does it say in the binder again?"

Jenna thumbs through it and then reads aloud, "*A hybrid of informative and culturally stimulating visuals on the Darfur crisis that evoke an overall festive appearance.*"

I shake my head and toss her another sealed envelope. Then there's a thump. I turn to see Nate Yube leaning up against the entrance of the room, one long, muscle-y arm stretching across the open doorway, his gym bag dropped on the floor beside him.

Jenna springs to her feet, clutching the pile of tickets she's holding to her chest. "Can we help you?"

"Yes, I'd like one ticket please," he says in that Nate Yube voice, like he's always talking through a laugh or something.

"Sorry, not on sale yet," Jenna replies, still weirdly guarding the tickets.

Nate slowly moves his damp, dark hair out of his eyes like he's posing for a photo shoot and then speed-walks toward Jenna. She swiftly zigzags in the opposite direction. He pivots back around toward her. She sidesteps him. He swivels back around. They're face-to-face for a split second before she does a quick 180. Then just as she moves her right arm out, safeguarding the pile of tickets between her and Mrs. Fredmeir's desk, Nate reaches his much longer arm around her and swipes the whole pile from her hand.

I don't watch a lot of basketball, but I feel like Nate just did some fancy slow-motion man-to-man defensive coverage on her.

Jenna turns to snatch the tickets back, but Nate's really tall and starts waving them around over his head like he's teasing a dog with a treat.

"Jenna, I'm not gonna ask you to the dance until you stop being so mean to me," he laugh-talks. The top of his collar is damp from his hair.

Jenna responds by marching over to me and resuming her spot on the floor.

"Jenna's not any fun. Izzy, why isn't Jenna any fun?" he laugh-asks me, which I think is the first time Nate Yube's said anything directly to me since "Your sister's hot" at my bat mitzvah brunch. He drops the tickets on the desk, grabs his bag, and walks out.

I look from Jenna to the door and back again. "What—?"

"How should I know?" Jenna shrugs and starts packing the dance stuff into her backpack.

"Did Nate just try to ask you to the dance?" I say in my art-camp counselor voice.

"No." Jenna's adding an unnecessary amount of tape around and around the ticket envelope box.

"Um, yes. I think he did," I singsong.

"Well, who cares. We're boycotting anyway." She flings her backpack over her shoulders and hands me the ticket box.

"We're boycotting, what? We're . . . what?"

"The whole concept! Having to get *asked* to attend something at your own school. It's such dung, right?"

"Um . . . well, we can't just boycott the dance." I follow her out, awkwardly trying to balance the box and the binder she left behind.

"No, not like boycott the *whole* dance, just the 'dates' part. Or no, actually that's not a bad idea. Yes, we should boycott the whole archaic shebang."

"What? Okay, sure, right. Because our moms won't be upset or anything after we've helped them plan the whole dance."

"Oh," she says, stopping at her locker as if that just occurred to her. "No, you're right. Fine. We'll go, but no dates."

"But . . . okay, but . . . why no dates again?"

"Because it's stupid! Like being all fake, and posing for pictures, and having to talk to some moronic guy all night just because he's your 'date,' right? Let's just get some girls together and go as a group."

"But . . . I think a lot of people already have dates . . . or are hoping to . . . get ones, you know? And Nate was practically asking you just now, so why don't you—"

"Yeah. No," Jenna says, grabbing the binder and box from me and shoving it inside her locker.

"Hm . . . I think . . . maybe someone still has a thing for Nate Yube?"

"Please," she says, slamming her locker shut.

"Don't deny it," I say sweetly.

"I'm not, and I don't." She walks past me.

I race behind her and poke her in her side. "Aw, come on! Remember you used to say, 'Me and Yube, me and Yube. It sounds so good together.'" I laugh.

"Nate Yube"—she stops and turns to me, her eyebrows practically touching—"is a waste of space."

"That's not what you used to say. You used to say that Nate was—"

"PLEASE can you STOP talking for, like, one second! God!"

I stare at her, then down at the ugly green carpeting.

When I look up again, Jenna's eyebrows are back to their naturally separated state and "Sorry" slides out of her half-opened mouth, which then turns up into a small smile when she tells me that she thinks some of her mom's menopause meds might have gotten mixed in with the allergy pills she took this morning.

"... that's why I feel so hormonally imbalanced," she concludes, her eyes looking thrilled with this new epiphany.

"Oh ... well ... wait, when's the last time you got your thyroid checked?" I ask. I just read an article on the thyroid and hormones.

Jenna's small smile turns into a full-out snort-laugh. So I fake a snort-laugh too.

"Dr. Izzy," Jenna manages to snort out at me, "she strikes again."

I turn to her, my face now still. "What?"

Jenna laugh-sighs, shaking her head. "You realize I'm going to be visiting you in a mental hospital someday?"

I just nod at Jenna, and then manage to force-smile out a "Yup."

"I just meant that ... I think my thyroid's fine, that's all," Jenna clarifies.

"Of course it is," I confirm, mustering a nonchalant shrug. "But stop taking your mom's menopause meds," I faux scold her, wagging my index finger before we part for opposite ends of the hall.

On my way to Spanish, I try not to focus on the fact that my best friend thinks I'm going to end up in a straitjacket. Instead I wonder about Jenna's semi-healthy thyroid glands, and my own possibly unhealthy ones, and then all of Blake's glands, which are probably perfect, and how no, I definitely don't want to boycott dates for the dance.

• • •

My ears are completely immune to the speed Spanish firing out of Señora Claudia's mouth.

I'm thinking about Blake, his perfect glands, and how maybe it's a real DIA date this Saturday, and how maybe that real DIA date will lead to a real dance date. Then I can convince Jenna to go with Nate, and we can all go together. Because I know Jenna wants to go to the dance with a date and not just as a PTO mom helper. This whole date boycott thing is just another one of her random tirades.

"*Señorita Isabella? Hola? Señorita Isabella?*"

I wish I wasn't hearing Señora Claudia calling me up to the front of the room to talk about what I did yesterday "*en español*," but it's kind of hard to ignore a woman in a giant sombrero shouting your name. *Less than two hours until I'm in the studio.*

"*Hola. Me llamo Isabella. Y ayer . . .*" I try. Great. There's nothing I did yesterday that I know how to say in Spanish. "*Ayer . . . ayer . . . miré la television.*"

"*Bueno, Isabella,*" Señora says, and I start to head back to my seat, happy that at least the buttons on my suggestive shirt didn't pop open in front of the whole class. But Señora soon stops me, saying, "*Y qué más?*"

What else? What do you mean what else? Um . . . okay, Señora. *Como se dice,* I was up all night worried about play practice, my pathetic art portfolio, and breast cancer, *en español*?

"*Y qué más?*" Señora Claudia is repeating. "*Y qué más?*"

"Um . . . *nada,*" I reply. Señora is not happy with that

response and says, "*Nada*?" and then starts blasting me with more speed Spanish:

"*Trabajodelaescuela? Comerlacena? Ustedlimpiasusitio? Elhablareneteleé fonoconsusamigos?*"

What? What? What about my friends? And then Jacob Ullman whispers really loudly, "*Miré la television con mis knockers. Mi encanta mis knockers, son grandes.*" His freckled cheeks lift in approval as people start snickering, and I know Señora hears them, because she says, "Okay. *Bueno*," and gestures for me to go back to my seat.

I slide back against my chair, pretending not to hear Jacob's guttural, seagull-like laugh, and the boys whispering "knockers" in bad Spanish accents, and wishing I was small enough to fit inside that open pocket of my backpack.

See Mom, I'm wearing my new bra, they're supported properly, but it doesn't change anything.

Why did I think for a second that Saturday was going to be an actual date with Blake? It's obvious that guys are interested in me for a good laugh and that's all. Jenna's right, Blake just asked me to go with him because his mom made him. She probably said, "Blake you should invite a real art student, somebody up for the Italy scholarship. Wouldn't that be nice for Jillian?" Yup, I'm just an art buddy for his sister.

Señora announces that we'll be spending the rest of class working in pairs on our cultural research projects. Meredith Brightwell's my partner—well, my silent partner, since I do most of the work—and we're doing our project on this

Colombian artist named Botero and his awesome, colorful paintings of people who are . . . well, really fat.

"Hey, Izzy."

Meredith's dragging her desk over to mine carefully, as if not to chip her nails, which are done in that French style Allissa tried to do on me once. My nails ended up looking like I was attacked by a bottle of Wite-Out. Meredith's nails look pretty, though, and I see she's still wearing that tiny gold ruby ring she got for her thirteenth birthday. I was always amazed how the red in the gem was almost the exact same strawberry shade as her hair. I wonder if she's grossed out by the paint manicure I always have on my nails.

"Hey," I say back. And then we flip through our Botero books in silence.

I'm not super-sad about not being friends with Meredith anymore. We just kind of naturally grew apart. It's strange seeing someone every day though who used to be your best friend. I met Meredith in first grade, when I was desperate to try out this new prank kit I got for my birthday with fake vomit and snot. So I sat down next to her and faked a huge sneeze, making tons of gooey prop snot appear in my hands. She started crying so hard, she had to leave class. When my mom made me go over to her house that night to apologize, I showed her how to fake vomit, ended up sleeping over, and we were basically inseparable until about seventh grade. That's when she made lots of new friends who didn't seem to want to include me in anything. Also, that's when I got more interested in art than whose lunch table at I sat at.

"You should tell Jacob to just shut the hell up. That's what I do."

Meredith's smiling at me in such an unusually friend-like way, it impedes my motor skills; I drop my Botero book to the floor.

"Don't let them get to you, they're such idiots," she adds.

Okay, why is Meredith Brightwell half whispering and smiling at me? Where's the *Twilight Zone* music? Where's the celebrity host and the camera crew to tell me I'm being pranked?

I manage to nod back at her and pick up my book. Is she buttering me up to ask me to officially do this whole Botero project by myself? I ignore her and go back to my research. But just as I'm learning that Botero's subjects aren't of "fat" people but rather "inflated" people, Meredith half whispers to me again, "So, what are you up to this weekend? You doing anything fun?"

Okay, seriously?

"Um . . . I don't know. Are you . . . up to anything fun?" I full whisper, trying to avoid the penalizing shade of Señora Claudia's giant sombrero, since we're only supposed to be speaking in Spanish.

"I don't know . . . maybe."

Wow. The last conversation I had with Meredith was the other time we were paired up in Spanish. It was for an oral presentation using food vocabulary:

Me gusta los bacalaos. Y tú?

No me gusta los bacalaos. Me gusta los cacahuetes.

Which I think roughly translated to:

I like cod fish. And you?

I don't like cod fish. I like peanuts.

I realize now it was my turn to talk and I didn't. So I just go back to studying Botero's happy, inflated families.

One hour and twenty-five minutes, and then I can go from looking at pictures of paintings to actually painting them. Yes, I am definitely going to paint something new today. I never had a moment to really sit down and figure out what I wanted to do for my portfolio this past summer, so I ended up doing all these drawings and paintings of my cat, Leroy. My cat! It's beyond embarrassing. I mean yes, Miss S. asked me to go next door and talk about one of my cat paintings to the 101 class last month, and she went on and on about how I realistically captured the movement in my lines and how great it was and all. But the thing is, Miss S. is always talking about how art is supposed to say something about you, and about how you know you're doing the right work when you're "whispering your secrets to other people" and stuff. I mean, my cat? No, I can't use anything I have in my Italy portfolio. I can't have a *cat* theme.

Unghhh, and now today I'm losing a whole afternoon of studio time, and a night of studio time too, because of Jenna's musical and cleaning out the attic for Mom. So I really need to use my studio time today.

"Actually, Izzy," Meredith half whisper-smiles to me,

"I'm thinking of going to this party this weekend. In Ann Arbor."

"What?"

Meredith drops her book onto her lap and blinks her gold-shadowed eyelids at me. "There's this party on Saturday night that a bunch of us might go to that Cara's older sister Becca is going to in Ann Arbor. It's at her boyfriend Phil's house."

"Oh. Um. Cool."

"Yeah. And Becca said invite whoever," she continues, actually twirling a strawberry strand of hair, "so do you wanna go?"

"What?"

"To the party? You wanna go?"

"Um . . . well . . . wait what?"

"And Jenna's invited too. See, the thing is that—"

"Psst, Izzy!"

We both turn toward the door. Oh, no. Pam Rubinstein is standing in the doorway. Meredith picks her book back up and mouths to me, "We'll talk later."

We'll talk later? Since when do we talk ever?

"Psst, Izzy!"

Pam's still standing in the doorway, now waving and smiling at me. She does administrative stuff in the main office, but she's also Mom's best friend, so she always finds a way for our paths to cross. Once she came up to me and Jenna in the cafeteria and said, really loudly, "Izzy, are you eating? What are you eating? Go grab a donut, or a quiche. There

53

are no carbs on your tray?" Then she turned to the table of boys next to us and said, "Will you guys tell my Izzy to eat a slice of pizza please, oh my God, she's so gaunt!" And Pam grew up in New York, so what we heard was, "Oh my Gawd, she's so gawnt!"

I was called "Gawnt Girl" for at least a month after. But that wasn't nearly as humiliating as the time she called me a "Botticelli babe" in front of a bunch of senior guys. And hello? Botticelli didn't paint gaunt women, so Pam really needs to make up her mind.

"*Hola.*" Pam waddles over to Señora Claudia, whose pupils dilate upon hearing Pam's East Coast Spanish accent. "*Lo siyento, necessito hablwar con Izzy. Tiyene correo*," she delightedly gets out, holding up a small postal box. I immediately know what's inside.

Pam shuffles over to my desk. "Izzy," she whispers, "is this one of the birthday presents for your mom?" She shakes the box slightly with a grin.

"Oh. Yes. Thank you." I forgot I'd had my latest two purchases sent to Pam to avoid Mom finding out what I'd ordered, or how much I'd spent.

Pam hands me my package, then fishes around in the pockets of her sweater jacket and produces a small object wrapped in a napkin that hits my desk with a thud. "That's a blueberry scone for you," she whispers loudly. "It's a little on the dry side, but not so terrible. Save it for later, keep your blood sugar up."

I notice that Meredith is smiling down at her Botero

book. "Thanks," I say to Pam, putting the scone in the side pocket of my backpack, reserved for Pam's food presents. Pam looks at me and then at my package, which I've placed on the floor next to my desk, her eyes swinging back and forth like that scary kitty cat clock on her kitchen wall.

"So what did you get her? What is it?" she finally says.

"Oh . . . um . . . well . . . I'm in the middle of Spanish—"

"You know what?" Pam thankfully interrupts with another loud whisper. "I was thinking of ordering her some organic ginger."

"Ginger?"

"You buy it online. It's from this farm. I forget where. It's a ginger of the month club! Fresh farmed ginger every month."

"Oh. Wow." I glance over at Meredith, who's now listening to this exchange with confused interest. "I didn't know Mom was . . . that she even liked ginger—"

"Well, you know those ginger candies she's always eating aren't real ginger," Pam responds, as if that explains everything, "but real ginger is good for nausea and healthy digestion. That's what I read. Maybe you can ask Mr. Bayer in bio if it's true, he's so smart. He almost went to medical school, you know. Anyway, since she's been dealing with it so badly lately, poor thing, I thought raw ginger! Perfect, right? She can make tea, or just chew on it when she's not feeling so hot . . ."

I look sharply at Pam. "Oh. Yeah . . . right. Wait, so—"

but before I can ask more about Mom, Señora is shouting, "*Adios, hasta mañana!*" Pam waves good-bye, and me, my postal box, my stale scone, and my knockers *grandes* head off to try and find a casual way to ask Mr. Bayer about the effects of raw ginger on nausea.

CHAPTER 5

I'm having a slumber party.

I have to stop sneaking out of class to go to the art room. It's not right. Even if I do have a nineteen-year-old substitute who basically takes a nap while I'm writing out the Krebs cycle. Even if it does mean I get the art room all to myself.

I practically skip to the drying rack to grab one of the canvases I primed last week. After throwing on my smock, I take a deep breath. I love the way it smells in here, like paint and glue and dust and old clothes.

I squirt out some red paint and some blue and lots of white, then dip some paper towel in a little water and use it to blend the colors across the canvas. I didn't intend to ditch the last half of bio, but when I was writing out my Krebs cycle and trying to remember what happens when plant cells are respiring, I kept thinking about human cells respiring and about glucose and our conversion systems, and what a big deal it was last summer when my mom's system wasn't . . . converting. But it is now. So I decided Pam was definitely overreacting about Mom being so nauseated that she needs constant organic ginger. Still, I couldn't stop thinking about my cells, and my mom's cells, and then it was like a furnace turned on inside me and I started to sweat. I didn't even try to wake up Mr. Nineteen-Year-Old Substitute to tell him I needed a bathroom pass. I just left. And came here.

I'm feeling better as I add more red to the top left corner and swirl it around with my towel. I glance at the canvas and blink my eyes because all I see is a mental snapshot of Meredith dealing me a totally out-of-left-field party invite. What, does she want to be best friends again all of a sudden? More red. I need lots more red. And I can't go to that party anyway. I mean, it's not like I *can't* go. It's not like I should feel guilty for going out to a party now that Mom's basically better. And Jenna would probably be excited; happy I'd finally go with her to an Ann Arbor party. I need to make more purple.

I get up and open the tiny, dust-covered window and stroll back to my section, grabbing new paint tubes on the way, and then stop so abruptly, my sneakers squeak on the floor.

Cara Larson is sitting on my stool. She's leaning over my canvas. Her backpack is on my table. And why is Nate Yube strolling in, sitting down at Ina Lazebnik's table?

I actually rub my palms over my eyes, but no, they're still here. In fact, the whole art room, *my* art room, is filling with more and more 101 kids.

"We are invaded."

Ina Lazebnik is now standing at my side, eyeballing the

new bodies like she's watching mice eat her dinner.

"What are they all doing here?"

"Didn't Miss S. inform you?" Ina's mouth barely moves when she talks, kind of like a ventriloquist without the dummy. "The roof in 101 is leaking, so we are to combine."

"No." My mouth, on the other hand, drops wide open. "No, no, no. For how long?"

"Indefinitely," she informs me with limited mouth movement.

"Helloooooooo, newly combiiiiiiined creators." Miss Swenson dance-walks out of her junk hallway closet office and makes her way around the two large tables to the front of the studio. She swivels her head quickly from left to right. One of her pinned-up braids comes loose and whips down around her ear. Miss S.'s everyday hair looks like mine does after my campers use me as a beauty salon model. "Soooo I know it might feel a smidge cramped in here for a little whiiiiile . . . but let's maaaake the best of it!" She ogles the now packed room like we're all newborn puppies she wants to pick up one by one. "We are not to be segregated by experience nooooor ability, because really"—she clasps both of her hands together—"what a blessing this is for our 101ers to be working side by siiiide with our more advanced creaaaaaaators . . . ." Her air-filled voice always extends her vowels, but today they seem extra-long as she plans her next words. "And ASPers," Miss S. adds, looking directly at my moping face, "I hope you'll embrace your new studio-mates, and perhaps even provide some technical assistance as weeeeeell. Okay, so breathe, and creee-*aaa*—"

The door bursts open, hitting the wall with a crash. In walks Meredith, who waves to Cara and mutters what I'm sure is a reoccurring "Sorry I'm late" to Miss S. She spills her books across my table and takes the stool on my other side, giving me a tiny smile. Then she whispers, "Can I borrow some sketch paper?" and proceeds to rip a page out of my sketchbook. She and Cara start doodling all over it.

Miss S. tries again. "Welcome, welcome. And now breathe, and creee-*aaate . . .*"

I immediately move my canvas away from Cara before the gum she's cracking falls out of her mouth and becomes a part of the painting. Then I survey the room. This is my hour. The one hour I have today all for myself, and now Nate's talk-laughing, Meredith's giggling, and the fifteen or so extra sketchbooks flipping and pencils tapping are all— Unghhh. I can't even think, let alone paint.

I fish my earbuds out of my bag and put them on.

Sunshine, lollipops and rainbows / Everything that's wonderful is what I feel when we're together.

I find some of the Gregorian chants Miss S. plays a tad sleep-inducing, so Mom made a few recommendations. "Lesley Gore's got pep," she told me.

Brighter than a lucky penny / When you're near, the rain cloud disappears, dear.

"Hey again, Izzy."

And I feel so fine—

"Izzy—Izzy." Tap tap tap.

No Meredith, sorry. I will not let you interrupt me with your shoulder taps.

"Hellooo, Izzzy?"

Does she not see that I'm trying to actually do something?

"Hey!" Tap tap tap. "Hey, Izzy! Izzy! Helloooo."

"Yeah?" I say, turning abruptly, attempting to pull my earbuds out with my elbows since both my hands are smudged with paint.

Meredith scoots her stool closer to mine, but keeps her body a good distance from the table as if not to catch its art-germs.

"Wow," she says as she eyes my canvas, "what's that supposed to be?"

"I . . . I don't know yet."

"You don't know yet? So you just like paint and then you know?"

"Yeah, I guess."

"But then how do you know what to paint?"

Ugh. Stupid roof with its stupid leak.

"We're doing figure drawings," Meredith says, putting on what looks like those thin plastic gloves from bio lab, and holding up a small canvas with what looks like a stick figure man on it. She lowers her voice and says, "This was supposed to be an easy elective, but it's kind of kicking my butt."

"Yeah, well, you should be okay. Miss S. grades mostly on effort for you guys anyway."

"Oh," Meredith says, looking down at her drawing, and

I feel like a total jerk. "Am I that bad?" she asks.

"No, no," I say, backtracking and feeling even more terrible. "Not bad, no. You just need some more um, shadow . . . ing."

"Hmm," she says, looking down at it some more.

"And it would be easier to draw without those gloves, I think."

"Yeah, you're probably right. I hate this stuff." Meredith gestures to the charcoal. "It kind of stays under your nails for weeks. My drawings aren't good enough to sacrifice my manicure," she says, and then makes a face and starts laughing.

I shake my head at her, but can't help laughing too. "That was—"

"Oh my God, that was so pathetic-sounding, I know. I just wanted to take photography, but it didn't fit into my schedule. But Marcus says he can help me work on something digital for my final project."

"Oh, wait, what do you mean?"

"Like with my photos? Mostly the ones that didn't make the cut from yearbook last spring. He's doing all the graphic stuff for yearbook, you know? The fancy stuff."

"I know."

"Well, anyway, he said he liked my pictures a lot, that they're pretty good."

"He did?"

"Yeah. He's like so super-nice."

"Yeah, he is."

"Yup, yeah totally." We both turn to Cara, who is apparently a part of our conversation now.

"We should be drawing without the gloves," Meredith informs Cara.

"Yup, yeah totally." Cara stretches her long arms above her head and rhythmically removes her own gloves finger by finger. She's clad as usual in sweatpants and leg warmers as if she's in the middle of teaching a dance class and not at school. Cara used to do competitive gymnastics. She was actually the teacher's assistant in my after-school gymnastics class in third grade. Well, I only lasted two classes because I would rather scream for a full forty-five minutes than walk across a high balance beam.

"Doesn't that look cool, Cara?" Meredith nods her head toward my canvas.

"Yup, yeah totally."

I'm slowly learning that Cara still expresses herself chiefly through movement.

"Hey, do you paint your own nails?" I ask Cara, now eyeing her bright red polish as she brushes her thick bangs to the side of her face.

"Yup, yeah."

"Do you have that color with you?"

"Totally."

"Oh! Great! Can I have it? I'll buy you another, I swear."

"Why do you want her nail polish?" Meredith asks, looking at my ragged fingernails. Allissa and Mom call them my "art claws."

"Can I have it? Please?" I ask Cara again, nodding at my canvas.

Cara shrugs and then one-handedly fishes through her bag for the nail polish, which she sets on the table. I examine the color and then shake it up a bit.

"Awesome! Thank you," I say, seeing the clock and giving both her and Meredith an "I'm going back to work" look. I put one earbud back in.

My life is sunshine, lollipops and rainbows / That's how this refrain goes, so come on, join in / everybody!

Man, this is cheesy. I brush in my new red texture, which to my satisfaction gives off a really nice depth and shine.

"Hey so, Izzy . . ." Meredith glances up at me and then back down at her canvas. "You think you might want to come out, to that party?"

"Oh. I . . . I don't know." I mix some white into the nail polish to add some pinkish tones.

"Well," she says, looking at Cara, then back to me, and moving in even closer, "I think you should. We'd like you to come."

"Oh. Wait. You would?"

"Yeah." Meredith nods.

Cara nods back. "Totally."

Okay, so Jenna wants to boycott the dance, the 101 class is ruining my portfolio chances, and now apparently Meredith actually wants to be friends with me again.

"And I was thinking," Meredith continues, "if you wanted to, we could, you know, maybe hang out, like beforehand?"

"What?" I say, half turning.

"Yeah, I was thinking," Meredith goes on, "that I could come to your house before and then maybe like . . . sleep over that night? Like old times?"

I shake my lone earbud out and drop my brush to my side, turning to face her fully.

"You want to sleep over at my house Saturday night?"

"Oooh, Izzy, gruesooooome," Miss S. says, catching my eye and nodding approvingly at my canvas as she makes her rounds.

Meredith sighs. "Okay, sorry, so here's the deal. Cara told her mom she's staying at Kim's, and Kim told her mom she's staying at Sari's, and Sari told her mom she's staying at Cara's, but my mom has basically banned me from sleeping over at any of my friends' houses ever since Jacob—"

"Yeah, yeah, I know, no need for details," I say, cutting her off before she mentions her famous bathroom-stall feat.

She gives me a funny look, and then continues. "So see . . . my mom loves you. She thinks you're über trustworthy. She's always like, why don't you hang out with Izzy anymore, and—"

"You want to use my house as a cover while you go to a party at U of M," I finish for her.

She looks at me sort of embarrassed, but not really. "If I tell my mom I'm with you, she won't even check up, and I promise it'll be a no-brainer."

"Hey, can you do me a favor and get my bio book out

of my backpack?" I ask through clenched teeth. Not that I should be aggravated right now at all. I should be laughing. Laughing at the fact that I actually thought Meredith was trying to rekindle our lost friendship. Of course she's just using me; of course she just needs a favor from me.

Meredith fishes out the book from my backpack and places it on the table. "So I'll come over for dinner . . ." She runs her fingers slowly down the spiral binding of her sketchbook as she lays out the plan. "I'll sneak out after, and I'll be back the next morning. And see, you don't even have to go to the party. We figured you wouldn't want to go anyway, so . . ."

"Oh. Well . . . yeah, of course. But . . . but what if you're not back in time? What do I tell my mom when you're not there? And why would you figure that . . . Can you just flip to chapter seven, please?"

Meredith looks deep in thought as she riffles through the pages of my bio book. "You can just tell your mom I left early in the morning for . . . Oh, I'm assisting Cara with the choreography for the musical, so you can say I had an early-morning dance rehearsal."

"Oh. Right . . . but—" I dejectedly hunch over the bio book, reminded of my newly assigned musical duties after school.

"Come on, Izzy. I'd do it for you if you asked. I'll so get you back, I will. I'll owe you."

"Meredith, there's no way that my mom—oooh, stay on that page," I tell her, studying the way those ridges look like little mountains.

"Wow, that's kind of nauseating." Meredith eyes my canvas, her shiny lips going horizontal.

"Yeah," I say with a small smile.

"So hey, remember in, like, fifth grade when we used to play 'college party' and walk around my bedroom carrying plastic cups of apple juice, pretending we were drinking beer and dancing with boys?" she asks. I can practically hear her eyes sparkling.

"Yeah . . ." I say, still studying the bio image, fully realizing now that Meredith never expected me to say yes to going to that party. It wasn't even a real invitation.

"We were such dorks," she giggles.

"Yup, we were."

"And what's so great," she goes on excitedly, "is that I already told my mom I was sleeping over, that we were working on our Spanish project together, so it's not a total lie."

"Right," I sigh.

"So . . ." She holds out the word, looking at me like I hold her entire life in my paint-covered hands. "Are you cool with it all?"

"Well . . . maybe. I don't know. I guess . . ." I give in slightly, turning back to my canvas.

"Thank you, thank you, thank you, Izzy!" Meredith bursts out and then jets across the back of the room to Cara, who's now aimlessly fishing through a stack of particle boards.

I step back to study my canvas, comparing what I've just added to the shapes in the text book.

"Soooo, this is neeeeew . . ." Miss S. is leaning in over my shoulder eyeing my work.

"Yeah," I confirm, glad Miss S. has wandered over, feeling for a second like it's my studio again.

"So you're noooot . . . continuing with your animal theme?" She points to a page in my portfolio and fingers for her glasses, which rest on top of her head and are connected to a long beaded chain that, today, is actually woven into her hair.

"I don't . . . I don't know if I want to have an animal theme," I admit, making circles with my fingers along the bumpy table, caked with layers of paint and dried clay.

"Okay, well, that's okaaaay. I don't want to put the pressure on, but I have to submit everything to the DIA by the end of the moooooonth"—another one of her braids comes loose and hits me in the face—"so now would be the time to think about tying all your amazing stuff together, you knoooooow . . . ?"

"I know, I know." I nod, and then I feel my stomach drop—in a good-bad way—thinking about my non-date DIA outing with Blake on Saturday.

"Maybe you just need to mix it up with some new materi-aaaaaals . . . ? Have you rummaged through the junk trunk?" she asks. I shake my head. "Weeeeeell . . . that might be fun." She's pointing to a tall broken mirror beside a giant pile of stuff that's slowing taking over her hallway office and the back wall of the studio. The mirror is one of those skinny ones, the kind that's stuck with putty to the wall of Allissa's dorm room. Great, a broken mirror. Isn't that like twenty-five years of bad luck?

Miss Swenson's fallen braids dangle in my peripheral vision. I look over to find her studying me, her hazel eyes clear. "Don't think so hard, Izzy," she says, squeezing my shoulder, "you'll scare your inspiration away." Then she blinks at me once, and heads back to her hallway junk drawer office.

Don't think so hard? Okay, fine. I won't think so hard about not really being invited to that party by Meredith, and about not really wanting to direct Jacob Ullman and the rest of the basketball guys in a musical while they potentially humiliate me in Spanglish, and how Pam's convinced my mom has a nausea problem, and about how the only thing I really have to look forward to right now is a date with Blake on Saturday that I'm pretty sure is not even a date at all.

I circle around my unfinished painting and focus on diminishing the outlines of my new shapes, blurring all the details together. I float my brush across the canvas, wishing I could blur together all the details of this day too.

CHAPTER 6

I'm a pushover.

I'm sitting in the first row of our auditorium, staring down at a clipboard with nothing clipped on it, hoping it looks like I'm doing something important. Jenna's in full-on director mode, running around, trying to get people seated onstage. "Okay everyone—hello?!" she shouts, tapping her faux animal-print boot on the stage floor.

It's after school and everyone's huddled in noisy groups— Meredith is sitting with a bunch of dancer girls stage left who are being entertained by Ryan Paulson duct-taping himself to his seat. The basketball dancing-tree boys are sitting in the back row of the auditorium, as if to let everyone know they don't belong at a rehearsal for a Rogers and Hammerstein musical. And there's Cara on the floor near the music pit, thumbing through her dance binder, in the splits.

"Izzy, are *you* in the play?" Emily Belfry is holding a pink highlighter and staring up at me with her magazine-ad face. Well, except for its expression, which unfortunately always looks pained, like the air she's breathing tastes bitter.

"No, I'm not in the play," I tell her. "Just helping Jenna with directing. Are you . . . performing?"

She looks at me as if I've just asked her if she pees sitting down.

"I'm a lead." She shifts in her seat to pull the pant leg of her khakis down over the ankle of her shiny brown boots.

Of course. Emily's captain of Broomington's all female a cappella handbell choir, The Bellerinas. She sings first soprano. I only know that because in health class last year during a warning lecture on the effects of cigarette smoke, she kept raising her hand to mention that she would *never engage in an activity that would sully the tone of her expansive first soprano range.*

I have lots of reasons for not smoking too, but I'm not about to start brag-sharing them in health class.

"I really like your jeans," she adds.

"Thanks," I say, even though I sense she means the opposite. Mom got me these jeans and they have embroidered flowers on the pockets and up the side of one leg. I didn't put up a fight when she brought them home because she looked so happy when I tried them on, like she was a stylist to the stars who just found a hot new look. Or at least that's the mental snapshot I remember.

"Can I borrow those and wear them in the show?" Emily asks. "They're very . . . western."

"Sure you can, Em. If you supply the extra denim we'll need to cover your ass, you can most certainly wear them in the show." Jenna swoops in to my rescue and then, without missing a beat, goes right back to trying to corral everyone onto the stage.

Emily makes a bitter-air face and then buries her head in her binder. Still on the floor, Cara's laughing so hard, she falls into an unintentional forward bend stretch.

"Thanks." I climb up with Jenna onstage to help her sort the rest of the dress rehearsal calendars while she furiously staples packets together.

"I *love* those jeans," Jenna says without looking up from her work, which makes us both burst out laughing.

"So by the way"—she hands me a finished packet to add to the pile—"I need you to rescue me and let me hang at your house Saturday night. It's Cathy's turn to host her 'Ladies Who Read Aren't Ladies in Need' book club."

"Oh no. What are they reading this week?"

"I think some memoir about these women who found God after knitting the same scarf in six different countries."

"Nice. Is she making her famous book-shaped brownies?"

"I really hope not."

"Yeah, those ones she made last month tasted . . ."

"Like we were literally eating paperbacks?"

"Yes," I say, laughing. "So on Saturday actually—"

"Oh, last time when the group was over, oh my God, did I tell you? Mrs. Hendricks was wearing one of her famous 'I bought this twenty years ago' jumpsuits, and her camel toe was a work of art. It should have been in a museum. Even Marcus couldn't take his eyes off it."

"Gross!"

"Yeah. I tried to sneak a picture of it on my phone, but there was no way I could hold my cell at a non-obvious angle, and I would get in major trouble if Cathy caught me paparazzi-ing Mrs. Hendricks's crotch."

"What? Whose crotch?" Meredith asks, walking up the stage-left stairs.

"Nothing, nobody's." Jenna stares at Meredith like she just started talking really loud during the serious part of a movie, and then makes a silly face at me.

"Um . . . okay," Meredith relents. "Cara wants to know if you have copies of the calendars, and she also changed the can-can choreography, so we need at least an hour to go over it sometime before we do a full run-through."

"Putting the calendars together now," Jenna informs her, and then turns around and continues to staple.

Meredith looks like she's about to say something else to Jenna, but instead turns to me with a big smile.

"So Izzy, I was just thinking, your sister's in town this weekend, right? Is she going to be there Saturday? I mean, she'll probably be up late and see me leave. Do you think she'd be cool?"

Jenna's hands freeze mid-staple.

"How did you know that Allissa's in for the weekend?" I ask, feeling Jenna's eyes burning a hole through the back of my neck.

"My mom," Meredith says, as if that explains everything. Which it doesn't at all. Why would Meredith's mom know about Allissa coming in this weekend? It's not like Meredith's mom and my mom talk or anything. They used to be friendly, but only because their daughters were best friends. Stacy Brightwell owns Brightwell Interior Energy Designs. She'll be the first to tell you that she's an expert who studied feng shui in China. And my mom will be the first to tell you, "Eh, so what?"

"What do you mean Allissa will see you leave, from where?" Jenna asks Meredith.

"Izzy's. I'm *sleeping over*," Meredith says breezily, using air quotes and all. Then she explains to me that her mom is meeting up with Allissa this weekend.

"Meredith, what are you talking about?" I say.

"What are *you* talking about?" Jenna asks, looking at me.

"She's going to a party at U of M. She needs to tell her mom she's at my house," I explain, and then turn back to Meredith. "Why would Allissa be meeting with your mom?"

"What? Come again, what? I think my ears just shriveled up and fell off my head," Jenna says.

"For your mom's birthday coming up. My mom's giving you guys a bunch of overstocked furniture for your mom's new office. In your attic? Oh, no. I'm sorry. I just assumed you guys were doing it together."

"No. Wait. Wow, what kind of furniture?"

"I think a desk, a couch, an armoire . . . My mom has lots of extra stuff. I guess she knew your mom was leaving her office and that the expensive trendy stuff in there was rented or something 'cause I guess they have the same landlord?

And then she ran into Allissa at the mall and—"

"Seriously? You're going to let her sleep over at your house just so she can leave and go to some party?" Jenna asks, all big-eyed and stifling a laugh. "Izzy, such a pushover," she adds, now full-out laughing and shaking her head at me.

"Well, you're both invited to the party . . ." Meredith adds softly.

"Yeah, like Izzy would even go"—Jenna makes another silly face at me, her brows half raised—"but thanks for the invite."

"Okay, I get it, Jenna," Meredith says a little louder now. "I get why you have no interest in going with *me* to a party at U of M, but—"

"Izzy, will you hand me the rest of that pile." Jenna bolts up fast, turning to me, and accidentally kicks over her full cup of tea. "Crap!" she says as it spills across the stage and all over the newly stapled schedules. "Crap crap crap crap crap!"

I kneel down and start mopping up some of the spill with—oops—I think somebody's scarf, while Jenna runs offstage to grab some napkins.

"I'm sorry." Meredith cringes at me, attempting to shake dry some of the ruined pages. "I really shouldn't have said that."

"No, no, it's okay. Allissa and I sometimes get separate gifts for my mom, so that's why I didn't know anything about the furniture and—"

"Here." Jenna runs back in and hands me some napkins.

"You okay?" I ask her now, because Jenna looks like she's seriously about to bite a hole through her lower lip.

"Yeah, yeah fine," she says, mopping up the tea and then grabbing some papers from her bag. "Do me a huge favor and make more copies for me?" she asks. She hands me the pages and then zaps back into director mode, putting both her hands on her hips, and looking frustrated as she scans the crowd.

"Okay everybody, listen up! Listen up, everybody! SHUT UP! SHUT UP!"

There is a split second of silence and Jenna takes this as her cue.

"Okay, we're heading into the final stretch here, people, and—okay, will everyone come up front so I don't have to yell!"

I weave awkwardly through the oncoming crowd, trying to get to the back of the auditorium.

"Hey," I hear, and feel a tug at the bottom of my shirt just as I'm about to push through the doors.

I turn. Oh. "Hey," I say to Blake, "what's up?"

"Not much, how goes the art?" he asks.

"Um . . . it goes . . . okay, I guess." And then I realize he's still holding on to my sweater. And then he realizes he's still holding on, and realizes that I realize, and then abruptly drops his hands. I see now that he must have just come from practice, because he's got his basketball shorts on, but with a . . . button-down shirt? And wait, why is he wearing boots? He catches me staring at his ridiculous ensemble.

"I know, I know, don't ask." He shakes his head.

"Well, now I kind of have to," I say, laughing.

"Seniors. Hazing."

"Hazing?"

"Yeah, they haze us during workouts. Well, during everything, actually. And more like torture us because that's what it is basically. Anyway, they took my T-shirt, and my jeans, and my sneakers while I was in the shower and they rubbed them all over their . . ." He grimaces and shakes his head remembering.

"You know what? I don't want to know anymore."

"Sorry. Yeah, so anyway . . ." He trails off, gesturing to his shorts, shirt, and boots in a fashion model way that makes me laugh.

Then we hear Jenna shouting, "Does everyone understand? Are you all with me?" and Blake makes a silly face like I got him in trouble or something and heads up front to join the rest of the guys.

I feel a huge smile spread across my face as I head to the computer lab, thinking out my non-date DIA date with Blake. Maybe it's not a mom setup after all. Then I realize Blake is probably going to that U of M party too . . . though I'm the last person he'd expect to see there since apparently I'm a non-party-going pushover. Not that Jenna meant to be mean or anything. Even Meredith assumed I wouldn't want to go. Still, it's annoying that Jenna's blowing off a party invite now, after all those times she's pressured me to go up with her to U of M.

I wait for Jenna's copies to finish, hoping she doesn't have a lot more for me to do today, that maybe I can sneak out to the art room and keep working on that new painting, or maybe just hide out in the back and get to talk to Blake some more and fantasize about—since Jenna has put the image in my head—making out with him amidst important art on Saturday.

Except when I get back, the theater is empty. I can hear the cast through the walls of the connecting choir room singing multi-note *oh*s and *ah*s. I can also faintly hear Jenna's voice coming from backstage, lecturing someone—probably Meredith or Cara—about Oklahoma's territory struggles, and how they should be more "deliberately represented through symbolic choreography."

I tiptoe the photocopies to the stage, and then speed-tiptoe up the aisle to the auditorium doors. But before I can escape, I see one worn white sneaker and the top of a bright red cowboy hat peeking around the half-open door. The cowboy hat lifts to reveal Marcus's face.

"Izzy! Thank God it's you," he whispers. "Are you alone?" His voice sounds strangely urgent.

"Yeah," I say, and then jump back as Marcus pushes his way through the door—with his elbows since his arms are piled high with stuff up to his chin. Before I can ask if he needs help, Marcus is stumbling to the nearest empty row. The bright red, one-size-too-small cowboy hat slides forward on his head. He keels over the armrest, cowboy hat falling onto the seat along with some decorative fans, floral bonnets, two pairs of—I can't believe I know what these are called—pantaloons, and a slew of other random items.

"Man is it good to see you, Izzy," he says, turning to me.

"Um, good to see you too, Marcus." I smile. "Um . . . you still have some . . ." And I can't keep it in any longer and burst out laughing as I pull some pink ribbons and another pair of pantaloons off Marcus's left shoulder.

His cheeks go a pale pink as I throw the items onto his pile.

"Yes, what you're thinking is correct," he says.

"That you're suddenly into eighteenth-century cross-dressing?"

"Oh, um." His cheeks go an even brighter pink and he laughs. "Well, I was going to lie and say a one-man *Oklahoma!* prop table-slash-rolling rack, but yes, you see right through me."

"No, I just see bonnets and pantaloons."

"Don't forget these." He produces a brown, high-heeled, lace-up boot from the pile and grins at me cross-eyed. Then he throws it back, wearily slumping into a seat in the next row.

"What happened to you?" I plop down next to him. "All I've had to do so far is make some photocopies."

He looks at me like I've just told him I've won the lottery.

"Jenna happened to me." He shakes his head and thrusts one hand into his newly matted cowboy hat hair, making it stand on end. "She dragged me to this practice room and started burying me alive with props and costumes. Then I was trapped there listening to Andy Mulvarose, or no, excuse me, Jud Fry, plunk out and sing the same line of his Jud song over and over again." Marcus's fingers fly to his temples and he circles them, repeating, *"Poor Jud is dead, poor Jud is dead."* He drops his hands, and then, as if he's seriously contemplating, asks, "If Jud is dead, why is he *singing*?"

I grin, but then nod my head solemnly. "Don't make fun, that's actually a really beautiful song."

He responds by reaching back to his pile and throwing a plastic flower bouquet at me.

"Here, I got you some flowers to cheer you up," I say, throwing it back at him.

"So"—he tosses the flowers back to his pile—"how are you? What happened to you this afternoon? I mean . . . everything okay?"

"Wait, what? Yeah, everything's fine."

"Oh. It's just that . . . when I was coming back to bio after dropping some tests off in the main office, I saw you running down the hall."

"Oh. Yeah . . ." I trail off, remembering my emergency bio exit. "Yeah . . . I . . . I left."

"Wow." He laughs, and then stops, squinting at me slightly with that eyebrow-shifting face he makes with Mr. Bayer when they're comparing subjects in one of his scientific method experiments. "Really? You just . . . left?"

"Yeah. You know . . . learning about the Krebs cycle and the ground tissue of plants has never really . . . done it for me."

"What, you don't find parenchyma, collenchyma, and sclerenchyma exciting?"

"Yes, of course, when *you* say it I do. Say it again, please."

He makes a show of taking off his glasses in slow motion, then looks into my eyes, freezes his face in a comically amorous expression, and takes his time saying, "Parenchyma, collenchyma, sclerenchyma."

I swoon, pressing my palms to my heart.

"Actually . . ." Marcus clears his throat, his voice returning to normal. "I probably still have a lot of flashcards and notes and stuff from that class at home. You want them?"

"Really? Yeah, that would be great." Better than the textbook anyway. "Thanks."

"And also," he adds, putting his glasses back on, "if you're going to keep running away from class, you'll need help studying, so I'd be happy to help. At rehearsal, maybe, or at study hall . . . I should be there tomorrow . . . or not, I mean if you just want to—"

"Yeah, no at ISH tomorrow would great."

"Marcus?! Is that you?" Jenna shouts from backstage.

"Oh God, she's found us." Marcus cringes.

"She's found *you*," I whisper. "I'm sneaking out to the art room."

He nods, and then grabs my wrists. "Go! Save *yourself!*"

I rise from my seat, clutch my hand to my heart, and say, "Will you survive without me?"

He reaches out to me like a saint in an old renaissance painting, and I play along, giving his hand a reassuring squeeze. But when I turn to leave, he tightens his grip, pulling me back toward him. "Izzy, please don't leave me here."

I don't know if it's the tone of his voice or the crazy expression on his face, but I can't help it—I burst out laughing.

"Oh fine." He laughs too. "Just leave me here to die."

"Marcus! Backstage! I need you!" Marcus releases my hand. He cocks his head to the door. "Get outta here, I release you." He smiles.

I mouth a thank-you, still laughing as I push through the auditorium doors.

I'm bundled up and speed-walking home since I totally lost track of time and should have started work on the attic for Mom about ten minutes ago. I'm halfway home when I hear a car honk, and a "Get in, snow bunny!"

Allissa is waving at me and sticking half her head out the car window. Still driving at full speed, of course. She jerks the car to the side of the road and slams on the brakes, skidding in the slush.

"Do you not check your cell, Izzy? Are you blocking my calls?" she shouts out the window.

I attempt to trudge safely to the passenger's side of Mom's old red sedan that Allissa inherited when she turned sixteen and then promptly dented on three sides.

"I called you to tell you I was coming in a day early, and I was picking you up," Allissa says as I pull the car door closed.

"Oh shoot, sorry. I guess my phone's off."

"How do you function?" she teases.

"I don't," I say, turning my cell on and stripping off my coat since Allissa has the heat up to at least ninety-five degrees.

"Please tell me you did not wear that to school?" she mutters, sounding so much like Mom, it's scary, and grimacing at my sweatpants, old T-shirt, and hoodie combo.

I explain how I was in the art room and decided not to change out of my paint clothes since I knew I'd be working on the attic tonight anyway.

"Oh, yeah, wish I could help you with that"—Allissa veers back into traffic with a lurch—"but I can't lift too much. I strained my lower back in yoga."

"Come on!" I say, stomping the snow off my boots onto the car floor. "You're here tonight and not helping me?"

"I have a fragile lower lumbar. Ew, that snow is yellow!" Allissa looks in horror at the now snow-covered floor mats.

"Allissa! You can't be in both lanes!"

"Don't you have friends to drive you home from school?" she asks, swerving back to the left. "Who walks? It's like so far."

"It's only a mile."

"It's snowing."

"I know. Unlike you, I'm dressed for winter."

"I'm not outside right now. I layer," she says, plucking at her Bedazzled tank top.

"Plus I need the exercise," I add. "It's good for my blood pressure."

"Oh my God, you sound like an infomercial."

"Well, everyone needs at least twenty to thirty—"

"No, please don't go into a rant about your blood pressure," she laughs, "or your thyroid again. It's fine. You're fine. Let's talk about something interesting."

My sister thinks talking about anything other than pop culture is disturbing. Meanwhile, she watches soap operas and refers to the characters in her everyday conversations. What's more disturbing, a conversation about my potentially diseased fate, or one about why Mark poisoned his wife Jill's wine because he impregnated her second cousin Samantha, the recovering alcoholic schizophrenic? I'm sorry, but I've got absolutely nothing to say about *All the World's Children Turn the Minutes of Our Lives* or whatever stupid show she's obsessed with now.

"You know, Allissa, the thyroid controls my hormones, and my hormones affect my organs, so—"

"God, spare me. Enough about you, how's Mom looking?" My sister glances at me, her face serious.

"She's looking the same . . . good, but . . . not a huge appetite still, but—"

"Well, she never really was a big eater to begin with, so—"

"STOP!" I shout as Allissa runs a yellow light and almost ends the life of a slow-walking man and his Portuguese water dog.

"Izzy, don't shout! You can't scare a driver like that."

Allissa leans forward to turn the radio up, and I check to make sure my seat belt strap is at its shortest length.

I debate asking her why I'm not included in Mom's birthday furniture surprise scheme, but decide against it. I guess it's good that Allissa is picking out furniture for Mom's attic office, because they do like the same stuff. She'll probably get her some kind of lacey throw. Or maybe a floral couch cover. And I'll just give Mom the stuff I ordered online and make her another birthday painting, a still life of a vase of flowers, or maybe if I don't have time to paint her something new, I'll give her all my portfolio rejects, my trinity series of paintings: *Leroy the Cat: Stretching, Sleeping, Boring.*

We turn into our driveway and then Allissa jerks the car to a stop. "Whose car is that?"

I look up and see a black Jeep blocking our path, parked at the end of our circular drive. "I have no idea," I say as Allissa reverses. She pulls into the other end of the driveway and, after three attempts, gets the car into the garage without clipping off the side mirrors.

We walk into the house and—

Oh, holy cow.

Blake is there. In our house. Sitting at the kitchen table. Smiling. With my mom.

CHAPTER 7

I love cleaning out the attic.

Blake Hangry is sitting at our kitchen table. He's sitting at our kitchen table looking just so . . . so . . . *good-looking*. And I'm . . . well, I'm in a pair of old sweatpants and a raggedy T-shirt with paint stains on it.

"You're back," he says, bolting up with a cheerful, somewhat desperate smile. And, oh no, wait, he's still wearing his mesh shorts and boots outfit. "I ran into your mom at the gas station on my way home and I tried to call you to let you know, but—"

"She never turns her cell on," Allissa says, looking him up and down, and then turning back to me with an amused smile.

"Oh. Hey, I'm Blake."

"Allissa," she says, and then walks *slooowly*—God, Allissa—by him to give Mom a hug.

"Hey, sweetie! Why are you dressed for Florida? Where's your sweater?" And then Mom's ushering all of us into the living room, where she's already put out appetizers.

"Hey, sorry," Blake says to me quietly, hanging back.

"I'm pumping gas, and I drop my credit card, and this lady picks it up and she says, 'Blake Hangry from Broomington High?' And I'm like, 'Yeah.' And it's your mom! And she asks me to follow her home for a snack and a chat, and then she starts heating up all this food, and she says to hold tight, that you'll be home soon, and so, I do . . . I did."

"Wow," I say, feeling a little shell-shocked, but realizing—after listening to how fast he's regurgitating this info—that Blake's much more nervous to be here than I am about him being here.

"So Blake," Mom calls out to us from the living room, "you were just in the middle of telling me about your sister, Jillian?"

"Yes," he says, hurrying into the living room. "My sister, Jillian. She was actually one of Izzy's campers a couple summers ago, I think. At art camp. She's totally good. Like Izzy is. A lot younger but, you know, has potential. Anyway, I thought it would be great for Jillian to hang out with Izzy, and also pretty sweet for Izzy to see the new wing of the museum. Oh, and also"—he pauses to wipe what I can only guess are sweaty palms on the sides of his mesh shorts—"also Izzy had mentioned to me, earlier, that there was this artist she wanted to see by the name of . . . Rora— Rura—"

"Roriago," I chime in.

"Yeah. So she's going to be presenting this kind of crazy, like whacked-out performance piece she does. I don't really know much about her . . . maybe Izzy, you could . . ."

"Um, oh, well, she's a performance artist and . . . I can show you a video later, Mom."

"Yeah, so anyway," Blake says, nodding, "that is, the plan . . . ma'am."

I see Allissa biting her nails really hard, probably to keep from laughing when Blake called Mom *ma'am*.

"Well, all right . . ." Mom says, scanning Blake with her eyes like she's trying to extract his bar code or something. "Oh," she adds, "and who will be driving?" But before we can answer, Pam bursts through the door, talking a mile a minute, shuffling over to us, her nose buried inside a book of fabric samples.

"Linda, I'm loving this color for my kitchen. I've made up my mind. And let's just go with it, because you know how indecisive I can be. If you like *Salsa Dancing Red*, then I like *Salsa Dancing Red*. Okay? Good!" She kisses Mom hello and then almost drops her book of fabrics when she sees Blake.

"Mr. Hangry, well, hello there," she says to Blake and then looks back at Mom with a "Well, what do we have here?" face.

"Hey, Miss Rubinstein," Blake says. Which is kind of funny to hear, because Pam has always just been Pam to us.

"Allissa! I didn't even see you sitting there! Hi, sweetie pie, gimme some love!"

"Hey, Pam," Allissa says, disappearing into Pam's bear hug.

"Look at your little chicken legs! Look at your thin little chicken legs!"

"Aw, thanks!" Allissa says, even though I'm pretty sure Pam didn't mean it as a compliment.

And now we're all just standing here, in the living room. I don't know what to do, but I have to do something, so I bend down and grab a once-frozen stuffed mushroom off the coffee table. Pam takes my cue and grabs two. Then I catch Blake looking at Leroy, who's pouncing around our box-covered foyer, his fat droopy white belly dragging across the tops of the boxes.

"Are you guys moving?" Blake asks, gesturing at the boxes.

"Oh no, no, not at all," Mom says. "We're just doing a little winter cleaning — cleaning out our attic."

"Actually, *I'll* be cleaning out the attic since Allissa apparently is yoga injured." Allissa verifies this with a sad nod in Mom's direction and a shrug at me.

"Well, I'd be happy to help if I'm needed," Blake says. And this must really impress my mom, Blake offering to help, because she says, "Sure, we could use a guy around to lift the heavy things," and then she turns around and winks at me! What?!

One minute my mom's unhappily lecturing me about being suggestive, and the next she's my wingman?

Mom's smiling at the two of us now and nudging Pam, who finally gets the hint and says, "So Linda, why don't we discuss my new kitchen . . . in your kitchen. Allissa" — she gestures wildly — "come on, I need youth perspective."

Mom and Pam drag Allissa with them to the kitchen so I

can have Blake all to myself to . . . watch me slovenly eat a stuffed mushroom.

"So . . ." I pause with an awkward gulp. "I guess we should . . ." Make out right here, right now, in my living room, on the couch, on the floor, against those drapes?

". . . get to work," Blake finishes for me, clearly needing to polish up on his mind-reading skills.

Ten minutes ago Blake smiled at me in this way that was just . . . *girlfriend.* But then he mentioned his sister and how his mom's thrilled that I could potentially be her new art mentor in a way that was totally, well . . . *art friend.*

I'm in the attic, taping up a dusty cardboard box, and playing my new favorite game: *Art Friend or Girlfriend.* I've also been testing my lung capacity by holding my breath sporadically because I'm sure there have been mice up here and I really want Mom to have a nice office and all, but there is no way I'm dying of hantavirus for it.

"Man, I'm not good with parents," he says, coming back from bringing boxes downstairs.

I gasp out a short breath, surrendering to potential mice bacteria. "No, you're fine."

"I still feel like I might puke."

"Come on," I laugh. "It's just my mom."

"She's very . . . serious," he says, wiping the sweat off his forehead with the back of his hand. "Man, I'm getting a full workout today." He picks up the bottom of his button-down shirt and uses it to wipe more sweat off his face. And when he does, I get a small peek at what apparently his whole drama class has already seen. Yowza.

"No, she's not all serious," I say, turning my head away from Blake's abdominals. "She's just . . . organized." I stretch my box-taping arm up over my head. My T-shirt has a large hole in the armpit. Awesome.

"Yeah," Blake says, looking at the row of seven paint chips pinned up on the wall in slightly varying hues of cream. "Your mom, she's a spreadsheet."

"A what?"

"That's what we call some of the . . . um, you know, more, serious kids at school. Like . . . all data entry, no fun?"

"Oh. Yeah well, no, my mom's fun. She's just so busy and has so much . . . on her plate so she has to stay—"

"No totally, I didn't mean to rag on your mom or any-thing." He fingers the paint chips. "So, are you hired to paint this place?"

"No, no, Mom's hired professionals."

"You're not a professional?"

"Well, no. House-painting is different. Plus I don't have time. And I'd probably mess it up." I look around at the sloped ceiling and all the doorframes, and then all the win-dow trims. Yeah, no way Mom would ever let me tackle this. God forbid I get some cream on what should be a totally ivory doorframe or something.

"You get along with your mom?"

"Yeah. For the most part."

"Yeah, you're probably good like that, running errands, doing favors. You're . . . what's that word . . . ?"

"Um, I don't know. Wait, what do you mean?"

"You're like . . . dependable."

Dependable? Wow. That's something I've always wanted a cute guy to say to me when we're alone in my attic after dark. *Art friend.*

"Dependable?" I repeat back to him.

"No, it's a good thing," he says, and then just stares at me in this way that's like . . . *girlfriend.*

"Do you want some pants?" I blurt.

"Excuse me?"

"I mean, um . . . that box in the back is full of stuff that Mom's collected from people to drop off at Goodwill, so I'm sure there's a pair of men's jeans in there. It's freezing out."

"Oh. Um, okay, thanks." Blake walks sort of haltingly around the boxes to the back of the attic. I watch him rummage through, pulling out pairs of jeans. What is Blake Hangry doing here at my house?

I found this self-help book in our basement last summer that talked about how good things can happen to you if you just think really hard about what you want to happen and then send all those thoughts out into the universe. I didn't believe it, though. It's hard to believe stuff in a book that's called *Say Y-E-S to Y-O-U!*

But I don't know. Last night after Lola's Lingerie and Jenna's, I sent a *lot* of thoughts out into the universe about hanging out with Blake, like one on one at someone's house, like couples do. I know we're just cleaning out my attic, but still, I think it's a pretty good return on all that power-thinking.

"So, I think I'm gonna stick to my shorts," Blake says, walking back over to me and holding up a pair of jean overalls with little hearts painted all over them.

"Yeah, that's probably wise." I smile. "So, thanks for sticking around and helping," I say, throwing what I think were once baby toys into a donation box.

"No problem. One day I'm gonna be like, oh Izzy Sky-men, the famous artist? Yeah, I totally knew her. I helped her clean out an attic." He flashes me a sideways smile. *Girlfriend*.

Then Britney Spears's "I'm Not a Girl, Not Yet a Woman" starts playing from the pocket of Blake's mesh shorts.

"Come on! I am going to murder those guys! Sorry, hold on," he says when he looks at the call. "Hey, Dad."

I continue taping up my box, trying not to listen to his conversation, but it's kind of hard because he gets increasingly louder with every word he says.

"I will—I'll be home later . . . No, I already told you I'm at a friend's house studying— Well, tell Mom I already ate . . . History . . . It's fine . . . No, we're just scenery— I told you last night, we're just lifting up the girls and stupid crap like that— Don't use that— Don't use that word— It's not fa— It's not being gay, Dad, all the sophomores have to— I will— I did, I did already at practice— I am— I *am* working hard!

"God," is all he says when he shoves his phone back in his pocket.

"Not that it's any of my business or anything," I say, "but you could . . . um . . . you could tell your dad that doing the play will look great on your college transcripts."

"Yeah, that's a thought." He picks up a flattened box from the stack and starts aggressively assembling it for me. "I just don't need him stressing me out. I got enough of it with training, and these initiations."

"Initiations? Like the hazing stuff?"

"No. Well . . . yeah that too, but we also have all these things, these tasks we have to do and—" He shakes his head, and when he does, some of his hair flops down onto his forehead. Annoyed, he pushes it back behind his ears. "It's just all so stupid, I know." He sighs. "But the thing is, if you don't do the stuff they ask you to do, it's worse. Ben Rossman, they made him wear a thong all last week, and he didn't have it on when they spot checked him, and now at every practice he has to wear Mike Westley's underwear."

"Who's Mike Westley?"

"He was a student like fifteen years ago. Those things have been worn by about a hundred guys now, and I'm sure never washed."

"That disgusting." I'm thinking about my mom lecturing us when we were little about the importance of clean pants and underwear and the horrors of what she called "crotch rot."

"Yeah, I'd rather wear a thong than that underwear to

practice." Blake bends down to get another box.

"Wait, are you wearing a thong right now?" I smile.

"Not today, are you?" he answers back.

"Oh, um . . ." His quickness catches me off guard, and then I realize that my window of time to come up with a witty response has closed. So I just half smile and sit down on a large box of books.

"So yeah," Blake says, clearing his throat and trying to push through our awkward thong moment. "It's just, you know, I have to do these things, stay on top of it all. It's like my dad thinks I'll just get on varsity and get play time next year for scouts, no problem. Just because of Tim. Like they owe me because of Tim. But that's not how it works. If anything, I get more crap because of him, you know? It's all just a pain in the ass."

"Well, if you don't like it, why don't you just not play?"

"No, I like it, sometimes," he says, sitting down next to me on the box. "And anyway, that's not an option. Like, you can't just quit art, right?"

Our knees are touching.

"Well, I could if I wanted to, I guess."

"But wouldn't your mom flip out? Doesn't she make you do it?"

"No, not at all. I'm sure she likes that I'm good at it, but she doesn't really force me to do it."

The whole right side of my body is touching the whole left side of his.

"Well," he says, thinking it over, "I guess you just end up

doing what you're good at, right? And hopefully . . . you like it."

"Yeah," I say, and then I don't know what possesses me to bring this up, maybe the warmth of Blake's outer thigh through the fabric of my sweatpants, but suddenly I hear myself saying, "So, you going to that party at U of M on Saturday night?"

"Oh. Yeah, I think so. Are you . . . you're going?"

"Thinking about it. Maybe."

"Cool." He smiles and turns his head in, and his breath smells like cinnamon gum. "Then I'd get a full day and night of Miss Izzy Skymen." He tugs at a strand of my hair. "I like the work you've done here. You're very talented." He grins, holding a crusted yellow tip.

"Well, you know, I've been hair-painting for years. I could get to work on yours, but I don't think you could afford me." He laughs and I start to reach for a strand of his when all of a sudden we're on the floor because the box has collapsed. I bolt up, and wave my hand in front of my face to try and ward off all the dust. I look down and there's Blake, lying on his back over the now-flattened box, covered in books.

He starts laughing, like these huge belly laughs. And then I'm laughing too. "I didn't really want to carry this down anyway." He's still laughing as he gets to his feet. But he does help me repack the books, and another box of old clothes, and then his dad calls again and he says he should probably get going.

Mom, Pam, and Allissa are on the second floor, engrossed in comparing bathroom tiles or something, and don't even look up when we head down.

"I'm gonna need you to walk me to my car," Blake says matter-of-factly, dropping the last box on the pile in the foyer, almost crushing poor Leroy, who was in the middle of a power nap in his new cardboard village.

"Oh. Okay." I try to maintain some feeling in my legs as I grab my coat from the kitchen. "Oh, wait," I say on instinct, and take out a bottle of mini hand sanitizer from my coat pocket. "It's just so much dust and old stuff."

"Thanks, Izzy." He laughs, and holds out his hands.

And, holy germ-balls, I'm hand-sanitizing Blake Hangry in my foyer.

I walk him to his car thinking, *Girlfriend, definitely, girlfriend.* He seemed genuinely happy that I was thinking of going to the party, and that's not something his mom would ask him to do. Maybe now that Mom's met Blake, I can negotiate a party out of Saturday too, and not even have to sneak out. Although Meredith will be here, and that will send Mom into a protective, puritanical frenzy. But if Jenna went with us too . . . yes, I'd have to emphasize that I'd be going with Jenna.

We reach the end of the driveway and Blake gestures for me to follow him around to the back of his car. So I do. I'm standing there, leaning up against Blake's trunk, and concentrating on making sure I've positioned my body in what one of Allissa's magazines says is "an angle that shows off your best and hides your worst." I don't know what that means, or what that angle would even be if I knew what it meant, and I don't think it applies to girls who are wearing bulky winter coats that they can't button closed, but I guess it doesn't matter, or maybe I'm doing it right, because all of a sudden Blake pulls me into him and kisses me.

And it's not like one of those crazy, tongue-fight kinds of kisses. It's a long, soft, closed-mouth kind of kiss. *Girlfriend. Girlfriend. Girlfriend.* And Blake's pulling me closer to him, his arms pushing into my lower back, and I feel like everything inside me is melting together. And just as I'm thinking that this feels so good that I hope maybe it turns into one of those crazy, tongue-fight kinds of kisses, I pull away slightly. Which is SO stupid of me. Why did I just pull away? What is my problem? But by the time I realize what a colossal idiot I am, it's too late and we're already not kissing anymore.

"Hey," he says, his arms still locked around me.

"Hey," I say, a little breathless.

"So . . . Saturday will be fun," he says. "Nate and I were helping my mom carry some stuff into the space last week. It looks pretty cool."

"Oh. Good." And I then think about Nate and Jenna and the dance and her boycott and find myself saying, "So Nate . . . does he . . . is he seeing anyone?"

"Um, no . . . why? You interested?" he gives me a sideways grin, which accentuates that dimple on his chin.

"No," I laugh. "I was just thinking of Jenna, actually."

"Oh. Wait, you want Jenna and Nate to—"

"Yeah! Well, I don't know, I just thought I'd try and play matchmaker, and that maybe—"

"Wait, you're kidding, right?"

"What? No . . . I . . ."

Blake laughs a little to himself. "Aw, well . . ." He starts rubbing my back a little. "I think it's cute you want to play matchmaker, but—"

"So do you think that—" But I don't get to finish because Blake moves in to kiss me again. Before long, all of my organs have completely liquefied and— Oh my God, I'm vibrating!

It's my cell, I realize, pulling it out of my coat pocket.

"Hello?" I say, a little out of breath.

"Hello, and who am I speaking with?" The pitch and inflection of my grandma Iris's stratosphere-high voice quickly re-solidifies my internal organs. I'm pretty sure Grandma Iris is able to lure packs of dogs to her side every time she opens her mouth to speak.

"I said, hello, who is speaking, please?"

"It's Izzy, Grandma, this is my cell phone you called."

Blake, hearing this, gives my arm a squeeze and nods his head toward his car. I give him a smile . . . and then almost drop the phone when I see Cathy Mason's car parked on the other side of our circular driveway.

CHAPTER 8

I'm not pretty.

What is Cathy Mason doing here? When did she pull up? Oh my God, please tell me that Cathy Mason did not just see me making out with Blake. Please, please, please!

"Hello? Isabella?"

"Yes Grandma, hello."

"I said I'm sorry to call at this hour and I hope I didn't interrupt your studies."

"No, no, you didn't interrupt my studies, Grandma," I say, and then, remembering who I'm talking to, immediately want to change my answer.

"Why aren't you studying? You should be studying at this hour. What do you have of more importance to do at this hour than study, Isabella?"

"Nothing, Grandma, I just . . . I'm taking a break from studying right now, that's all."

I mouth "Sorry" to Blake and he mouths "No problem" back, and heads around to the driver's side. My eyes flick back to Cathy Mason's car. Oh my God, why is she here?! She probably saw us kissing and now she's going to run into our house to tell my mom wildly exaggerated tales of my new-found promiscuity.

"I'm sorry to be the one to break the news to you like this, Linda. But that's what I saw."

"Oh, Cathy, are you sure? This is just awful. I can't believe Izzy fornicated with that boy in our driveway."

"I know, Linda, it's inappropriate, immoral, and disgraceful. *She should be locked up."*

"Isabella, did you hear what I just asked you?" Grandma Iris screeches and then speaks very slowly. "Is your house on fire?"

"What?!" I say, turning to the house. "No, Grandma." Then I hear a "Hey," and thank God, it's just Marcus standing in front of Blake's car.

"Well, if there is no fire or any other kind of household emergency, then can you please tell me why it is that no one is able to pick up a phone in your house?" Grandma asks, sounding more than a little irritated.

"My mom sent me to drop this off to your mom," Marcus says quickly, holding a huge white binder up in the air, looking at Blake and then back at me now with the same expression my mom has when she thinks I'm walking too suggestively. "It's dance planning stuff. Jenna was supposed to leave it with you today. I guess she forgot," he adds, his eyes sliding back to Blake. I hold a finger up, like just a sec, and then point at the phone.

"Oh, sorry," Marcus whispers, and then turns to Blake and says, "Hangry," somehow conveying a hello, nice to see you, and good-bye all from just saying his last name.

Blake responds with an equally packed "Mason," and then waves bye to me. I watch him pull out of the driveway, semi-listening to Grandma Iris ramble on about household emergencies and fires, and wondering when exactly Marcus pulled up. Then Grandma Iris shouts, "Isabella, do you understand what I'm trying to say?"

"Uh-huh," I say into the phone, and gesture for Marcus to follow me back to the house.

Mom and Pam are sitting in the living room, and I make sure to talk loud enough for them to hear me when I say, "No, no Grandma, the house is not on fire. I'm sorry that nobody picked up the phone."

Upon hearing this, Mom bolts up from the couch and rests her hands against her head as if she's sleeping.

"Well, fine. That's fine," Grandma Iris says. "So where is your mother? Is she there? If she's able to talk, please put her on."

"I'm sorry Grandma, but she's um, taking a nap." Mom shakes her head at me. "Actually, she's totally asleep . . . probably for the night."

"All right fine, yes, she needs to rest. All right then. Listen, Isabella, please tell your mother this: I've received Dr. Madson's new invoice and have taken care of it in full. Please don't send me any money. Did you locate a writing utensil? Shall I repeat it?"

"No Grandma, I got it. Thank you."

"Fine. Now get back to your studies, stay well, wear clean socks," she says, hanging up.

"Sorry sweetie," Mom says. "I don't have the energy for Iris tonight."

"You guys got a lot done." Pam is surveying all the new boxes.

"Oh, Blake had to head home," I tell them. "He says good-bye."

"That was very nice of him to help out. He seems . . . on top of things," Mom says. She's nodding and looking at me, as if waiting for me to contradict this.

"He has a healthy appetite too," Pam chimes in. "I've seen him at lunch. Not a terrible student, good athlete, really nice hair." Pam stops rambling when she sees my mom's face. "What?" she says. "Can't I be excited for her?"

"Are you two going steady now?" Mom asks.

"No!" I say, laughing, and then glance back at Marcus, who looks so uncomfortable, it would almost be funny, if we weren't talking about me going steady.

"What's so funny about going steady?" Mom asks, coughing a little.

"They don't go steady anymore, Linda, they just date," Pam says, smiling knowingly. "Well, the good ones date, and the bad ones just—"

"We're not dating," I interrupt Pam. "We're not going steady, we're just . . . hanging out. That's all," I say. And kissing. We're kissing. We kissed. We kissed and we're kissing. I need to sit down.

"Sorry to, um, interrupt," Marcus says now. "Just wanted to drop this off." He holds up the giant Dance for Darfur binder.

"Oh, hello Marcus! I didn't even see you back there! Thank you, thank you," Mom says. "I just talked to your mom and I was frantic because I left a flash drive in there with all my spreadsheets. Izzy, you have to help me decide on food. Remind me about that. Speaking of, are you hungry, Marcus?"

"Oooh, a tuna melt, make him a tuna melt. You make such good tuna melts, Linda!" Pam says, looking like she might want one herself.

"Oh, no I'm all right, thank you," Marcus says.

"Marcus." Pam turns to him and says in a very serious top secret tone, "Linda makes the best tuna melts."

"Oh, Izzy." Mom is looking me up and down now and shaking her head as if she's seeing me for the first time today. "Look at you. You're dressed like a homeless person."

"No, that's okay, Linda. The homeless look is trendy now," Pam assures Mom. I catch Marcus smiling a little out the corner of my eye.

"I can't believe this is what you were wearing this whole time!" Mom eyes my art studio clothes again as if my wearing them today will have catastrophic effects on both of our futures.

I don't care, though. I just kissed Blake Hangry in our driveway. I just *kissed* Blake Hangry in our driveway. I repeat this to myself over and over again as Mom picks me apart from head to toe. But my mental "I just kissed Blake Hangry in our driveway" shield is penetrated when I hear Pam say out of the corner of her mouth, "I knew she liked boys, I just knew it!"

"I know," Mom says back to her in an equally terrible stage whisper, as if they've discussed this before. "Allissa and her theories. Not that I wouldn't support it if—"

"Of course, no. Both sides of the pond are fine and dandy, but I knew, I knew she liked boys!" Pam rasps, grabbing a cold stuffed mushroom from the coffee table.

Allissa and her what? Oh my God! And now Marcus is outright laughing.

"You guys!" I burst out. "I'm standing right here!"

"What?" Mom says as if she didn't just imply that she's had a talk about my sexual orientation with both Allissa and Pam. Great, so up until tonight, my mom thought I was a homeless-looking lesbian. That's just great. Sometimes my mom lectures me about spending too much time thinking about boys, how they have one-track minds, and how not to lead them on or give them the wrong idea, and then other times I hear her on the phone talking to Pam and saying how worried she is because I'm not social enough, or ever talk about boys with her. I never know what I'm supposed to do. I'm either too suggestive or I'm not suggestive enough. I'm about to go upstairs and strangle my sister, when I remember, *I just kissed Blake Hangry in our driveway,* and everything around me goes mute as I smile and cling to that incredible mental snapshot.

"So what did Grandma want?" Mom asks, zapping me back to the present.

"Oh. She said she paid another doctor's invoice, a new one, and she says don't send her any money."

"Right," Mom says. "You know, I really could scarf down a whole tuna melt right now!"

"Oh," Pam says, turning to Mom, "really?"

"Yes, but . . . we really should finish with the tiles upstairs before it gets really bad outside."

"You're right, yes. Okay, I'll choose one, I promise," Pam says, leading Mom back upstairs.

I watch them go. Since when does my mom ever scarf down tuna melts, or anything else for that matter? She's more a re-arranger when it comes to the food on her plate.

"Hey," Marcus says, and I turn around as he's putting the binder down on the coffee table.

"Hey. Sorry. I'm . . . I'm so sorry you had to witness all that," I say.

"No, I didn't see anything."

"Oh, no, I was talking about . . . Oh. Well . . . Oh." I look back at Marcus, his face slowly turning a familiar nail polish pink. "I was um . . . talking about . . . my mom and Pam and all their crazy—"

"Right. Yes, well . . . right."

"Do you want a pop or something?" I ask.

He nods and walks with me to the kitchen.

"You know, I thought you were your mom." I hand him a can and an empty glass.

"What?"

"When I saw the car in the driveway, I almost had a heart attack."

"Yeah? Well, if my mom saw you with Blake like that

she would've probably dragged you into the house and . . . hosed you down with hand sanitizer or something."

"Exactly!" I wipe my mouth from almost drooled juice, and then, "I knew you saw!"

"Oh. Yes. Guilty." He takes a large gulp from his glass. "Actually, I kind of had this urge to punch Blake in the face."

"What?!" I sit next to him, resting my elbows on the table.

"No! I mean . . . it's just 'cause . . . I mean, if I saw a guy groping Jenna in our driveway I would want to punch that guy too."

"Wait, what do you mean?" Then I look down at my cup, getting it. "Oh, right."

"So, not that it's any of my business, but why was your grandma calling about your house being on fire?"

"No, she was just being overdramatic," I explain, heading to the sink to wash out the pulp from my glass. "She was calling about Mom's doctor."

"Right." Marcus nods, getting up to bring his glass to the sink as well. "So why . . ."

"Well, my grandma's helping us out a little because insurance doesn't really cover Mom's visits with her specialist, and there were a lot last summer, so . . ."

"Hmmm," Marcus says, and then, "So what exactly does your mom—"

"I'm in Broom tomorrow, Friday, and head back Monday morning," Allissa practically shouts into her phone, strolling into the kitchen on her cell. "And prob next weekend too to help move the office stuff out, but let's do lunch on

Wednesday. I feel like I haven't seen you in forever!" She pauses when she sees what looks like Marcus and me doing the dishes together. "Uh-huh," she says into the phone, opening the fridge. "I know, me too!" She grabs an apple from the drawer and waves at Marcus. He returns the wave and walks over to the fridge, grabbing us a couple of apples too. "Well, tell her she's being cheap. Or next time you go out, just make sure she has cash on her." Allissa fades out as she goes back upstairs.

"Here," Marcus says, handing me an apple.

"Thanks. So . . . you're alive."

"What?" he asks mid apple bite.

"You survived the rest of rehearsal without me." I keep a straight face, taking a bite.

"If you call crawling under the auditorium seats and curling into the fetal position for two hours 'surviving,' then yes." He smiles at me with all his teeth, and I laugh so hard, I spit out a piece of my apple, which lands on his shirt.

"Classy," he says, picking the apple bit from his collar. "Yeah it wasn't that bad. And I remembered I had ice cream in my bag from Steve's Freeze during my free eighth period, which I successfully used as a peace offering when mediating a fight between Emily Belfry and Sara Ronaldson over who had the more perfect, perfect pitch. So really, I was a hero." He shrugs one shoulder.

"Well, wow. I don't have perfect pitch, but you should probably bring me a pint of Steve's ice cream tomorrow anyway."

"Oh, I should? Huh, one play rehearsal and you're already a diva."

"Strawberry, please. Um . . . shouldn't you be writing this down?"

He raises his eyebrows at me.

"Actually, make it vegan ice cream. Real dairy might sully my vocal cords."

Marcus chuckles and sits back down at the table. "So . . ." he says, "you and Blake, huh?"

"Oh. Yes." And soon I succumb to another driveway-kiss mental snapshot that sends me sitting back down too.

"So you're, ah . . . you're going steady now? Congratulations."

"Thank you, yes, I'm wearing his pin on my sweater right here." I point to my T-shirt. "Kinda weird, right?"

"Yeah, I guess he is kinda weird." Marcus smiles.

"No, you know what I meant . . . him interested in me and stuff?"

"No. I don't think that's weird."

"It's just that guys are always paying attention to my sister . . . or Jenna—" I stop, seeing his expression. "Sorry."

"Moving on," he says, waving his hand.

"I'm just saying that when guys talk to me, it's usually just comments and stuff, or being jerks, and that doesn't really count."

"Hmmm . . ." is all he says, and then, "So you have a date for the dance now, that's good."

"Well no, not yet."

"Oh. Well, maybe you have to hit a bunch of house parties with him first before you can go to an official school dance."

I can't tell if he's joking. "Yeah, maybe," I say, thinking about this Saturday night. And I guess I make a weird face or cringe or something, because then Marcus asks, "What? You don't like parties?"

"Oh. No . . . I like them fine. I just . . . I mean, I'm not antisocial or anything, but I sometimes don't see the point of hanging out with a whole bunch of people at a party if all you really want to do is hang out with just one person."

"Yeah, I know what you mean. I think I would rather hang out with that one person, but have a party on speakerphone. That way we could still have an audio party vibe and not feel like total losers."

"That's a brilliant idea. We should make an app—*Party Sounds: For People Who Just Want to Stay Home.*"

"We could branch this out, you know, beyond parties," Marcus adds. "Maybe make a whole series of audio apps. Like *Restaurant Noise: For People Who . . . Just Want to Order In.*"

"Perfect," I say, and am about to suggest *Mall Noise: For Online Shoppers* when we hear Allissa scream out, "Shut up! What? Why did you call him back?" from her bedroom upstairs.

"Hey, did I ever tell you I saw Allissa a couple times around the U of M campus last summer? I think she was dating a guy in the class I was taking."

And I immediately know he's talking about Spray-Tan

Bill. That's what my mom and I called this guy Allissa went out with last summer when she showed us his rather orange-faced picture.

"Yeah," I say, "I think that relationship lasted about five minutes." I smile thinking about how many pictures of Allissa's college "boyfriends" I've already seen since she graduated from Broomington last year. "Allissa's relationships tend to be very . . . um . . ."

"Transient?"

"Yeah, she dates a lot."

"Well, she's pretty and all," Marcus says, but kind of more to himself than to me, and then he looks right at me and says, "It's amazing how little you guys look alike."

I freeze in his gaze for a second, and then look down at my apple, focusing on the brown outline forming around my last bite. After what seems like a nine-hundred-year pause, Marcus blurts out, "Oh! Oh, no. No, that's not what I meant. Ah, I didn't mean that you're—"

"No, whatever, it's fine." I wave my hand to signal the end of the whole exchange, but Marcus keeps talking.

"No, no. See . . . ah . . . you're pretty too."

I look down desperately at our cream-colored kitchen floor, wishing it was quicksand, while Marcus continues fumbling for words.

"You're both pretty. I didn't mean to imply that you're not pretty, Izzy. You are. You're not ugly. Neither is your sister. But see, ah, I would categorize her as really pretty and you as more of a . . ."

Large-breasted, potentially diseased, frizzy-haired freak.

". . . a classic . . . a classic . . . beauty, you're more of a classic beauty type."

I continue to squint at the floor, and then look up, humoring him with a small smile. "Good save, Marcus." But Marcus doesn't crack a smile. He looks like he's about to say something else, when, thankfully, Pam wanders into the kitchen.

"Oh my Lord, it looks colder than a witch's broomstick outside." Pam peers out the window. "Don't make me go out there!"

"Stay. It's snowing. The roads are probably terrible," Mom says, following in after her.

"No, no, gotta get home." Pam is already grabbing her coat off one of the chairs.

"Marcus, you sure you're not hungry?" Mom asks.

"No thank you, Mrs. Skymen. I should . . . um . . . I should get going too," he says.

"Oh good." Pam shimmies into her coat. "Walk me to my car, sweetie. If I fall on this ice, I'll never get up."

So Mom and I walk Pam and Marcus to the door, and then just before they head out, Mom turns to Marcus and says, "Oh, and great idea by the way."

"What?" Marcus asks.

"For the sculpture. Your mom said you came up with it. We really want something prominent to display in that front lobby window and, Izzy, you can handle a map, right?"

"What map?" I ask.

"Oh, well, my mom was pressing me for decoration ideas," Marcus says, "and I thought maybe some kind of map."

"Of Darfur, a sculpture!" Mom adds.

"I'd forgotten I'd mentioned it, and that's of course if Izzy even wants to—"

"It's such a great idea," Mom says, nodding rapidly. "A festive map."

"Uh, sure," Marcus says, avoiding my gaze. "I guess Izzy could make it . . . festive."

"Yes, of course," Mom declares, nodding at me.

I shake my head at her.

Finally we say good-bye and watch as Marcus leads Pam down our driveway. Mom's still nodding enthusiastically, repeating, "A festive map." Then she lets out a huge yawn, stretching her arms above her head, the large sleeves on her top hanging low.

"What's up with that top, Mom?"

"What do you mean?" She looks down at it as if she doesn't remember what she's wearing today.

"Nothing, it's just so . . . flowing. I didn't know you were into . . . What are those things called?"

"Tunics. It's a tunic. They're very comfortable. And they're in fashion."

"Of course they are." I humor her. But since when does Mom wear something because it's "fashionable" anyway? She's all about being tailored and fitted. She hates looking "unnecessarily sloppy."

"It's just . . . so big."

"It's supposed to be, Izzy. That's the style."

"Oh. Okay." I nod. "You hungry? Should I heat up dinner?"

"Well . . . Allissa's not eating because she's doing this new diet thing and apparently lasagna has too many stars or not enough hearts? She had an apple earlier. And I'm still full from all those appetizers, a little nauseated, actually. I think the stuffed mushrooms didn't quite agree with me."

"Oh. Okay . . ." I look at her.

"And I'm just wiped, so I think I'll head to bed. You okay with heating up the food?"

I nod. Mom starts up the stairs and soon Leroy, who has supersonic stair-creak ears, bolts awake from his pre-bedtime nap to her side. "Hey, Mom," I call to her. She stops and half turns, Leroy stops and half turns as well. "Everything okay?" Then this weird, worried look comes over her face for a second and I find myself rushing to add, "I mean for Saturday and the DIA, now that you've met Blake and—"

"Oh. Yes." She closes her eyes for a second. "And I realized today I've met his mother." She opens her eyes and smiles. "We worked on a toy drive last year."

"Oh . . . okay, good."

"So, you think you two might go together, to the dance?" Mom asks, using her forced-casual-because-I'm-really-very-excited voice.

"Um . . . well." And I try and use my forced-casual-because-I'm-really-very-excited-too voice when I say, "Maybe. I don't know," but I'm not as skilled as my mom and think

I unintentionally flash my "I kissed Blake Hangry in our driveway" smile. Why else would Mom just start grinning wildly, nodding her head up and down, and start rambling about corsages, and dresses, and haircuts as she and Leroy make their way upstairs.

I walk back to the kitchen and heat up a lone piece of lasagna, still wearing that smile. But then I realize: How in the world am I going to have time to make a whole map sculpture of Darfur *and* the rest of the decorations *and* three more new pieces for my portfolio? Unghhh.

I stress-eat everything in sight and go back for seconds, positive I'm already off the charts of whatever system Allissa is using to track her calories. As I open the fridge, I catch a glimpse of my reflection in the shiny silver doors. *A classic beauty?* What does that even mean? Allissa made me take this magazine quiz once called "Do you have what it takes to be a hottie?" and I didn't. My results fell into the "Well, You're Not Ugly" category. "Beauty" is not even near the same category as "Well, You're Not Ugly." I stare back at my fridge reflection. I arch my back, flinging my arm over my head all Dionysus-like. Yeah, Marcus definitely does *not* understand what "classic beauty" means.

As I head upstairs for bed, I start my art studio count-down, telling myself that I'm going to focus and finish that new painting tomorrow, even if means ditching a little of play rehearsal again. I get into my pajamas, wondering how I'll tell Jenna about Blake and suddenly feeling jittery with excitement. But only for a second, until a mental snapshot of her disapproving face pops into my head with a thump of anxiety. I shake it off. I'll convince her to come out to the party. I bet Nate will be there too, and Blake can help set them up so he'll ask her to the dance, and we can all go together. I know she doesn't want to go alone. Not that Blake's officially asked *me* yet, but maybe he will at the DIA . . . I do my body check for any new lumps, bumps, rashes, or red flags, and then collapse into bed, still wearing my secret "I kissed Blake Hangry in our driveway" smile.

Girlfriend.

CHAPTER 9

I'm a terrible listener.

I'm frantically running around the studio, clutching my bleeding thumb in my paint smock and looking for the first aid kit. Oh my God, this smock is so dirty it's like instant infection. I wonder how much blood I've lost already. I read somewhere that fingers and thumbs bleed a lot more because the blood is thinner near your appendages. Or was it the mouth that bleeds more? *Wait, then what did I read about appendages?!*

I finally find the first aid kit underneath a stack of dusty magazines, and vigorously sterilize and bandage my small wound. Okay, good. That's good.

I put some work gloves on and move the damaged mirror to another table. I should just give up on my Italy portfolio and go back to my papier-mâché map sculpture for the dance, but that's not going so well either. I've already sketched about a dozen maps from the images I downloaded, but the Wi-Fi signal in the art room is so bad, I might as well have chartered a plane to fly over Africa and taken the pictures myself.

"Heeey . . . Izzy. You're baaack . . . Whatcha working on now?" Miss S.'s whirring voice fills the small studio as she emerges from her junk hall-of-fame office. "And where are you suppooosed to beee . . . ?"

"Um . . . study hall. But I was able to get out early," I mumble, glancing over at her. Not adding that I told Marcus today was not a good day for studying bio and instead snuck out of the library when Miss Larper was involved in another Steve Drankin and Roopa Sheti trying-to-make-out-quietly-in-the-back crisis.

Behind her glasses, Miss S.'s magnified hazel eyes see right through me. "Okaaay . . . well . . ." She starts to head back to her office and then turns and says what she usually says when she sees a student in here who's supposed to be somewhere else. "I was here, you were here, but *weee* were never here."

I smile and bend over my latest map sketch, which after about ten minutes of work actually looks pretty good.

"That looks pretty good."

Marcus is peering at my table from the doorway.

"Hey." I shift in my stool to face him, smiling. "What are you doing in here?"

"Well, I figured you might be in here and . . . I just think . . . um, it's important you do well in bio because, well . . . I grade your quizzes, and right now . . . you're not. Doing so well, I mean. And I don't want what I said yesterday to affect your grades or your studying or anything because—"

"Wait, what?"

"It's just, if you're mad about what I said last night, I understand. Still, you should really be prepared because—"

"Oh, no I . . . I didn't skip out on our study session because of what you . . . no I just . . . I'm really behind on my Italy portfolio and with the dance décor now, I just need more time in here."

"Oh. Right. Well . . . okay. Still, though, I just . . . I wanted to tell you that . . . well, I felt bad and didn't want you to think . . . and I just want to apologize for what I said because see . . . I wasn't intending for the thing I said about your sister being pretty to juxtapose with what I said about you guys not looking . . . alike and well, I just wanted to tell you in case, you know, you thought . . . um . . . that I thought that you weren't—which I don't, but in case you think that I thought—"

Before I can stop myself, I just start laughing. And then I feel bad, laughing while Marcus is being so nice and trying to apologize. But then he starts laughing too.

"Sorry, was that even English?" he asks.

"I'm not sure," I say, wheezing.

"Okay, well . . . what if we went over some stuff while you work in here at least?"

"Yeah," I say, grateful, "that works for me. Thanks."

I move a stack of old newspapers I stole from Ina's sacred papier-mâché pile down to the other side of the table to make room for him.

"Okay, explain the second law of thermodynamics." He's leaning over me now and peering at his notes, balancing himself with his hand on the dirty table. He smells sweet. Not like a girl smell or anything, but like fresh sweet, like a bar of fancy soap.

"Okay," I sigh. "The second law . . . it's something to do with disorder always . . . increasing or something?"

"Well, pretty much. Do you remember the whole ice-cube-in-the-glass example?"

I stare at him blankly.

"Okay, well, basically disorder—entropy—will always increase over time. So say for example you're really cold and I come over to you and put my hands on your arms like this to warm you up." He puts his hands on my shoulders and rubs them up and down. "Oh sorry, forgot you're drawing," he says, and stops.

"No, that's okay." I put my pencil down.

He doesn't start rubbing again, but he keeps his hands on my shoulders while he continues explaining. It feels nice, and not in a "Yay, I'm learning about thermodynamics" kind of way.

". . . well, so the heat from this work is why there's an increase rather than a decrease of entropy. Make sense?" he asks.

"Yes," I lie. And it feels like a whole year goes by after he's done explaining, with him standing behind me, his hands on my shoulders.

"Ew, stop molesting Izzy on school property, Marcus," Jenna shouts, peeking her head into the room.

Marcus bolts back to his stool. "I'm not— We're studying. I was explaining—" But Jenna doesn't let him finish.

"Where have you been all day?" She drops the giant cardboard box she's holding on top of my stack of notes and newspapers, then dusts her hands on her pants. "Figures I'd find you in here."

"Yeah, needed to multi-task," I explain a little guiltily. "Sorry I didn't come meet you this morning—I wanted to work on a painting."

"Well, when you have time, can you finish calligraphy-ing these ticket envelopes? There's like fifty blank ones in there still. Oooh, I love papier-mâché." Jenna's eyes widen as she points to my map. "Can I help?

"Yeah, you can ball up paper." I move the box of dance invites off the newspapers and onto the floor.

"Yay!" Jenna plops down across from us and starts ripping and crumpling bits of paper.

I had planned to wait until rehearsal to talk to Jenna, but now I'm dying to tell her about Blake and ask her about the dance and get it over with. And it's not like Marcus doesn't already know. But still, there are details I want to share with Jenna that would just be weird sharing with Marcus too. I decide to wait.

"So, did Marcus tell you about last night?" Jenna asks me, shaking her head.

Marcus and I quickly turn to her, and then to each other.

"About Cathy's latest plan? She wants to fix me up with the son of some woman from her book club."

"Oh, no, I didn't tell her." Marcus sifts through his flashcards.

"Fixing you up?" I assess my map template, almost ready to cut it out now.

"Yeah. Cathy wants to fix me up with this guy named Jenson. Jenson," she repeats the name at half speed. "Sorry, Cathy, but Jenna and Jenson? I mean what was she thinking?"

"So we *did* say the art room!" Meredith rushes inside, her strawberry blond ponytail swinging, a laptop bag over her shoulder. "I was in yearbook. I couldn't remember if we said art room or yearbook."

"Oh, sorry!" Marcus jumps off his stool. "No, we did say yearbook, but I totally forgot that I—"

"No worries, we can work here, it's fine." Meredith plops her bag down on a table, waves at me, and gives Jenna a small smile.

"Work here on what?" I ask, heading to the back shelves to grab some plywood.

"My photos, remember?" Meredith then turns to Marcus. "Miss S. was saying I should make some sort of mosaic, but we're gonna mess with them a little, right, Marcus? You're going have to show me how to—"

"So Jenna and Jenson," Jenna repeats to Marcus and me as if Meredith never arrived. "What was my mom thinking?"

"What?" Meredith blinks her long lashes at Jenna. Marcus fills her in.

"Our mom," he tells her, "she was trying to set Jenna up with a guy named Jenson."

"Oooh. That's so funny." Meredith grins and opens up her laptop.

"Ugh, Jenson." Jenna shakes her head and crumples a piece of newspaper in her hands as if she's trying to disintegrate it. "He's probably one of those annoyingly annoying people who says things like 'That's so funny' instead of actually laughing."

Meredith snaps her head to Jenna, who turns to Marcus and me as if we should back her up on that observation. Marcus just rummages around in his bag for something, and I turn to Meredith, who remains straight-faced, pretending she didn't get the jab.

"Are those yours?" I ask her. "Those are really good." And they are. My eyes catch the slide show of photos loading on her computer.

"Thanks," Meredith says, her smile returning. "That means a lot coming from you."

"Oh, well, I'm not a photographer. Wow, you must have taken pictures of almost everyone in our class."

"Yup, more or less. Oh look, there you are." Meredith points as the slide show pauses on a picture of me sketching in one of the study alcoves. "That was last year, and the light . . . I just had to snap it. You looked so pretty."

Pretty? My hair is in a wonky bun and I have charcoal all over my nose. My mom is right—I do go to school looking like I just rolled out of a cardboard box.

"You're so photogenic, Izzy," she adds.

I whoop out a laugh, and then clear my throat. "No. I'm not."

"Yes, you are. It's not fair."

I respond by getting up and heading to the storage closet.

"And you have the best body," Meredith calls out.

"What?!" I almost drop the mini hand saw I'm carrying back.

"Shut up, don't act like you don't know. I'd kill for your boobs. You'd look hot in this top." She gestures down to the purple scoop-neck she's wearing.

"I would look . . . obscene in that top."

"No way. You would look gooood in this top. You always wear such big stuff. It's such a complete waste, right? Jenna, don't you agree?"

"Nope, I like Izzy's clothes."

"No, I'm not saying I don't like her clothes." Meredith turns back to me. "I'm just saying you have such a hot body, you should show it off more. Right? Marcus, doesn't Izzy have like the best body?"

Marcus's head pops up from behind the newspaper stack and he clears what sounds like a Leroy-strength hairball from his throat before saying, "Um . . . yeah it's . . . the best."

I turn around to clip my template onto the plywood, feeling like the skin on my cheeks could melt marshmallows.

"So, we should probably work on some of your photos before the hour's up," Marcus tells Meredith, clearing his throat again and gathering his binder and flashcards. "We should go to yearbook, though—we need their computer."

"Okay." Meredith nods, closing up her laptop.

"Sorry Izzy, I forgot that I arranged to—"

"Oh no, go ahead. Bio can wait," I say in a way that I

guess is funny because it makes Marcus laugh. I watch them walk out, the studio door closing behind them with its usual dull crash.

Why is Meredith still being so friendly? I already agreed to our fake sleepover on Saturday, so why is she complimenting me on my boobs, and telling me I'm photogenic? I turn to Jenna, shaking my head, half laughing. "That was weird, right? Meredith being . . . so nice?"

Jenna just looks up at me, raises one eyebrow, and answers, "Please don't start wearing tacky scoop-neck shirts."

I laugh, and then see that she's taken a break from her newspaper ripping and is now doodling in Robert Stern's sketchpad.

"Don't forget to rip that out," I tell her, and then not being able to keep it in a second longer, I burst out with, "So, don't you want to hear my news?"

"Oh. Yes, please. Your text this morning was very cryptic. 'Blake update! Ahhh!'" she reads back to me, laughing, but cutting her eyes back to Robert's sketchpad.

"Yeah . . . well . . ." I can't suppress my grin as I start carefully sawing through my plywood.

"Ooooh. Wow, wait, I can tell just by looking at your face. You had sex."

"What? No! What are you— Are you serious?"

"No, I was kidding. Relax, calm down your scrunch face."

"We kissed, though."

Jenna snaps her head up to me, and then goes back to her doodling with a "Wow."

"Yeah. Last night. We kissed in my driveway." I hear my voice rising in pitch but I can't help it. "Well, he kissed me. But I kissed him back. We kissed!"

"Wow . . ." Jenna repeats, ripping out her doodled page. "Is that all?"

I'm not sure what kind of reaction I expected from her, but this wasn't it. "Um . . . well yeah. I guess that's all."

"I thought it was gonna be something indecent like . . . you had sex in the attic."

"Yeah, like I'd have sex with Blake, who's not even my boyfriend, in my house with my mom a floor away." I grab some balled-up papers from the pile and start to tape them onto the wood.

"Oooh, I'm Izzy, I'm so perfect I don't have sex with boys unless they're my boyfriend-slash-soon to be husband." She giggles and I throw a ball of newspaper at her. "So are you coming over Saturday night or not? I have to let Cathy know which brownies to make."

"I can't, remember? Meredith's coming over to go to that party."

"Oh, right," Jenna says, now making her own scrunch face.

"But I was thinking maybe . . . of maybe going too, actually." I add some more paper dimension to my map, trying to match the shape on my laptop screen.

"No way. Really?" Jenna's features wrinkle further.

"Yeah. And you're coming with us! You're always wanting me to go out to parties, so now we can—"

"Yeah no, no thanks."

"Come on. Why? I know Meredith can be a little—"

"No thanks. Not really into those parties anymore." Jenna shrugs as if that's something I should know already.

"What does that mean?" I pull my computer closer, about to zoom in again on my map when something blinks in the corner of the screen. My mom's left one of her support group chat rooms open again.

"I'm just not interested in hanging out at U of M . . . after what happened with Amy."

"Who?" I open up Mom's support group window and start scrolling through the conversations, scanning for any new vocabulary, or topics that I haven't seen covered. I'm just a lurker, like Mom. That's what they call web people who are members of groups who don't ever chat or post things. Which is why I almost fall off my stool when I see a recent post from *LindaSky46*.

"Amy, my cousin?" Jenna moves her hands across the tabletop gathering the balls of newspaper into a neat pile. "I've definitely mentioned her before. She's a sophomore."

"At U of M?"

"Yeah, she transferred in from Wisconsin this year. She was up here last summer getting settled and stuff and I stayed with her a few times. Remember?"

"No, but . . . I guess I didn't realize you were hanging out with your cousin. I thought you were going up there with your creative writing class."

"I was, but I stayed with Amy."

"Oh. Okay. So . . ."

And then Jenna starts telling me something about how Amy was set up with this guy by one of her friends, and that she ended up going to this orientation party with him in September and they ended up having sex in a basement. "But she liked him, and she wanted to do it, you know?" Jenna adds.

"Uh-huh," I say, but I'm not really listening because I'm reading my mom's post and right now I can hardly speak, let alone translate the sounds coming from Jenna's mouth into English.

LindaSky46 Re: Gastroparesis?

Hello All: For the past couple of months I have been experiencing some difficulty in digesting my food and keeping things down. Has anybody else experienced these symptoms after their debulking surgery? Any suggestions and/or information would be ever so helpful. Much luck and love, LindaSky

The past couple of months. Difficulty in digesting my food. I keep scroll-ponging back and forth between those two lines. I need to get up, to pace, but instead I just sit here calmly, hoping it still looks like I'm studying map images.

". . . so I was up on campus the weekend she was with the guy, 'cause our writing class had our showcase that night at Motts Café. Remember? I was reading that prose poem I wrote about if Samuel Beckett made Maya Angelou dinner?"

I struggle to get some words out to Jenna. "I'm sorry I couldn't go to that reading."

"No, whatever, you had your mom and stuff. Anyway, I stayed with Amy that night, and the next morning she was . . . crying and stuff . . ."

What the heck is gastroparesis? Trouble digesting her food? What does that even mean? She's not supposed to have trouble yet; the whole point of the surgery last summer was to stop the trouble, so she could get stronger.

". . . because it was all a big joke . . . Izzy?"

"Yes. What?"

"It was all a big joke," Jenna repeats.

"What was a joke?"

"The guy. Liking her. Sleeping with her. Everything, basically. Are you even listening to me?"

"Yes, yeah, your cousin Amy, sex, in the basement, joke." I nod at Jenna, trying to focus.

"Um . . . yeah, okay. So, it turns out he just had some bet going, some game he was playing with his friends, like sleeping with girls, getting them to do stuff—like this list— checking girls off lists like they're things that you need to pick up at the store."

"Oh. Wow." And I'm looking right at her, but all I see is that post from my mom.

"Yeah, so, I'm still just really disgusted with the whole thing, you know? And I haven't really wanted to go to any stupid parties up there anymore."

"Well . . . yeah, that makes sense . . . okay." I nod.

"Okay? That's your whole response, 'okay'?"

"What? No, I'm sorry. I—"

"God, Izzy, it's like you're not even listening at all."

"No, I am! I'm sorry I'm . . . I'm just a little distracted. There's just . . . there's a lot going on right now and I just saw this—"

"Yeah, yeah, you're always distracted. There's always something going on."

"I'm sorry. And I am really sorry about what happened to Amy. That's so terrible and I—"

"Forget it, it's fine. It's not even a big deal really." She picks up her box of invites and heads for the door.

"Jenna, I'm sorry," I call after her. She turns around and gives me a small smile. "No worries, flaky girl. Get your work done. I'll see you at rehearsal." The studio door closes with a clang-thud. I sit there, very still, staring at the door for I don't know how long. Then I pick up my half-finished map. Then I set it back down on the table. Then I walk to the table next to me. I lean forward slightly, studying my fractured reflection in the mirror. Then I turn back to my computer screen, clicking back and forth between the map image and my mom's support group screen.

The rest of the hour passes, but kind of without me. I don't finish the foundation for my map, or figure out what to do with that mirror. I just sit there on my stool. I just sit there, and read Mom's post over and over and over again.

CHAPTER 10

I'm having trouble breathing.

I'm trapped in a lighting booth trying to go over cues with Derrick Hunter, who's working the spotlight. Except he's in the middle of a love spat with Emily Belfry that's making my lunch come up. Or maybe reading about how one's lunch comes up via gastroparesis on Syptomaniac earlier is the real cause of my queasiness.

"Babycakes, I have to kiss Curly in the show, but I'm only acting," Emily says again for the trillionth time.

"I know, Sugarmuffin. But I have to sit here, night after night, watching you suck face with that moron and it makes this Babycakes very jealous."

"Aw Pumpkinnugget, you're so cute when you're jealous."

Nope, it's them. I'm pretty sure they're solely responsible for my nausea.

"Sorry to interrupt." I finally step between them.

"We're kind of in the middle of a talk," Emily informs me, her upturned, girlfriend-smile souring into its I'm-tasting-bitter-air shape.

"So Derrick," I continue, turning away from Emily and

handing him a binder. "I have these new lighting cues for you. Jenna wrote them all down again because I guess you've been missing a bunch. She wanted me to go over them with you, so—"

"Oh, sweet." He runs one hand through his greasy black hair and takes the binder from me with the other. "Yeah, there are too many cues in this show," he informs me, as if that's an excuse to just not light someone while they're singing a solo on a darkened stage. Then he starts talking about how the lighting system in the theater needs an upgrade and something about flimsy gel frames and how it's not his fault the equipment isn't working. I nod at him, my head feeling especially heavy, full from reading about gastroparesis and all the concerned, informative, but mostly alarming support group responses from my mom's post.

"Emily, get down here, we're doing a vocal run-through!" Jenna pops into the booth and hustles Emily outside. Derrick follows after her, leaving his new binder behind. Jenna pops her head back in. "So is he all set with this?"

"Yeah," I lie. "I think he knows which ones he's missed now."

"Awesome, thank you. You gonna head to the choir room now?"

"Why?"

"The set. We just talked about this, I asked you to help paint earlier?"

"Oh, right. Yes, sorry, I'll head over."

"Great. And if you need me, I'll be onstage listening to the vocal run-through and giving the tenors a thumbs-up, even though they sound like a bunch of dying cats in heat."

"How kind of you." I smile.

Jenna whips around fast to head out of the lighting booth and knocks into Meredith and Cara, who are on their way in.

"Let's try and walk with our eyes open, girls," Jenna says shortly.

Meredith shakes her head as Jenna dodges around them and down the auditorium stairs. Then she turns to me. "So, where should I go?"

"Um, for what?" I suddenly need to lean back against the booth window.

"The square dance. I have to teach the basketball klutzes how to do the basics."

"Can't do it in the choir room 'cause of the set," Cara adds, bending over to pull the fabric down on her dance leggings.

"I want to work on a real dance," Meredith says, almost whining. "Can't I just help you with the ballet?" she asks Cara.

"No, totally, no," Cara responds.

"So . . . Izzy?" Meredith prompts me for a solution.

"Um . . . I guess you could go into the vending machine alcove. Jenna's using the stage for music rehearsal so—"

"Ugh, Jenna is being an extra nightmare today," Meredith says, pulling her hair out of its loose ponytail and shaking her head back and forth a couple of times before attempting to pull it back up again.

"Uh-huh, extra nightmare, totally," Cara agrees, bobbing her head up and down.

"Right, Izzy?" Meredith blinks at me.

I blink back at her, wanting to respond but instead reloading all those support group responses into my brain; words like *blockage*, *scar tissue*, *complications*, all flashing under my eyelids.

"Oh, sorry Izzy, I know she's your friend and she's in charge and all, but she's making it difficult for us to do our jobs. I just think . . . Whatever, I'm pretty sure she still hates me."

"Yeah, she does, totally."

"Thanks." Meredith rolls her eyes, poking Cara.

"I think she still blames me, you know? Izzy?"

I snap back to the conversation, looking around the tiny lighting booth, then at the two of them, willing my eyes to unblur. I don't think there's enough oxygen to go around in here.

"Do you think she still hates me?" Meredith asks.

"Wait, what? Who?"

"Jenna! God Izzy, are you alive in there?" Meredith mimes knocking on my head. "You know her the best. Should I just call her, smooth things over once and for all?"

"Yeah, yeah, call, sure, that sounds good. And . . . um . . . yeah . . . square dance, fine, in the hall, no problem."

"Okay . . . thanks," Meredith laughs and pats me on the head like I'm a little kid who's just uttered her first sentence.

Then I say something about going to the bathroom, or

painting the set, I don't know. But I'm pushing past them, out of the tiny booth, down the balcony stairs, and out the theater doors.

I should be heading to the choir room to help with the set, but my legs take me to the studio. I'll just work on a painting for a half hour and then go to the choir room. I just need to sit at my studio table. I need to sit in the studio all by myself: no Miss S., no 101ers, no Jenna, no laptops with topographical maps or support group sites popping up, no . . . Marcus Mason? Why is Marcus rummaging around the studio supply room?

"Can I help you, sir?" I say in my best customer service voice and tap him on the shoulder. I don't mean to startle him, but I guess I do, because his shoulders twitch, he turns around fast, and then drops four of the wide paint brushes he was carrying in his arms.

"Hey," he says, scrambling to pick them up and dropping them in the bins next to us. "Didn't see you."

"Sorry." I bend down to grab the one by my feet and toss it in the bin. "So, you're stealing from the art room, huh?"

"Nooo," he says in this exaggerated way, as if that's the most ridiculous thing he's ever heard. And then, without missing a beat, he whips his cell phone out from his pocket, covering the mouthpiece with his other hand as he speaks into it in hushed tones. "Abort mission, busted with crusty old paintbrushes, don't come back for the wood glue."

I'm not trying to encourage his antics, but I can't help smiling when I ask, "Seriously, what are you doing here?"

He puts his phone back in his pocket without taking his eyes off me, and then, only moving his arms, grabs the first thing he can reach from the top of Miss S.'s junk pile with one hand, and pulls out a paintbrush from his pocket with the other. He backs away from me slowly, pointing a teeny-tiny paintbrush at me like a gun, and holding a scary decapitated baby doll up in the air as his hostage.

"So . . ." I saunter closer to him, trying to play it cool. "Did Miss S. say you could take this stuff for set painting?" Then I surprise jump him, trying to grab his hostage.

"Nice move." He ducks away, recovers, raises his eyebrows approvingly. He laughs and then his face and voice go cold. "You come any closer, Izzy, and this baby loses her head." Then he looks back at the doll, feigning shock as if he's seeing it for the first time. "Oh crap, too late!"

"Okay," I laugh, and even though set painting isn't the mentally soothing artistic activity I had in mind right now, I find myself saying, "Come on, I'll help you get this stuff to the choir room."

When we get there, I see what Cara meant. The choir room is stuffed. The velvet curtain that usually flanks the mirrored wall is closed, with risers, set pieces, and rolling racks of costumes pushed up against it. The grand piano in the corner seems small compared to the giant set pieces surrounding it.

I get to work on Aunt Eller's house while Marcus adds green to what we hope is a bush and not a tumbleweed. We paint silently for a long time. I almost forget to think.

"You're probably so bored right now," Marcus calls over after a while.

"No, not really." I pop up and turn to face him.

"I just mean this kind of painting is probably torturous, not getting to do anything . . . artistic."

I take an exaggerated breath in. "You don't think this looks artistic?"

"No, I do. I absolutely love how you've multi-layered the brown paint on the stairs."

"Thanks." I gesture to my last freshly painted plank. "I call this piece *Brown on Brown on Brown . . . on Wood*."

He grins. "You should at least sneak something of your own into those stairs—some hidden work of art?"

"I'm sure Jenna wouldn't want me turning her *Oklahoma!* set into one of my paintings."

"It could be something small. Or . . . oh, you could use that invisible paint that only shows up with UV light."

"Black light?"

"Yes. I'll just have to rig Derrick's spotlight with a black lightbulb . . ."

"Okay, so what should I invisible-paint—dirty pictures?"

"Um . . . oh. Well, do you . . . often paint dirty pictures, Izzy?"

"Yeah. Wait, you didn't know that hidden-black-light-dirty pictures are my niche?"

"No, but now I'm very interested in getting a look at your portfolio."

I laugh.

"What if you painted messages on the set, like . . . you know that TV show where they play a music video and then random facts pop up?"

"Yes! I should invisible-paint random facts all over the set—"

"And then I'll black light them at key moments of the show."

"Perfect! It would be like . . ."

"*Pop-Up Musical*!"

"Exactly," I laugh. "*Look closely at the back row in all the dance numbers, those are the singers who can't dance.*"

Marcus offers, "*Did you know that Emily Belfry has five-point-seven percent more perfect, perfect pitch than Sara Ronaldson?*"

"Or how about a meta one like . . . *Guess what? The person sitting next to you didn't wash their hands after using the bathroom at intermission!*"

"Genius!" he laughs, and then adds, "But gross." Marcus stands and wipes his hands on his smock shirt. "You hungry?"

"Nice transition," I point out.

"Oh . . . yeah . . . but I almost forgot!" He goes to his backpack and presents . . . a pint of ice cream!

"What are you doing with that?" I feel myself break into a huge smile.

"Didn't you say you wanted ice cream?"

"I was kidding!"

"I know, but I figured, why not? It's, um, kind of melted by now, but it'll still be good."

He hands me a plastic spoon and sits down, leaning against an unpainted part of Aunt Eller's porch.

"Thanks, Marcus. Wow." I drop my brush, sit down across from him, and go in for a big spoonful, making sure to get a strawberry chunk.

"So"—I talk with slight ice-cream mouth and hand him back the pint—"you do anything fun with Meredith's photos today?"

"Messed around with them a little," he tells me, taking a giant spoonful.

"They're good." I'm remembering the slides I saw on her computer. "I was expecting them to be just . . . the stuff that's in yearbook, but they're not, they're really good."

"Yeah, I agree," Marcus says through his own ice-cream mouth and hands me back the pint.

"Maybe I should just forget about my paintings and submit her photos for my portfolio. You think she'd mind?"

"Nah." He laughs, and then all of a sudden I realize that's exactly what I'm going to do—well, not literally submit them for my portfolio, but use them if Meredith will let me.

"What's up?" Marcus asks me. "You disappeared there for a sec, and you look . . . very serious all of a sudden."

"Nothing, I was just . . ." And I mean to tell him about my new Darfur map sculpture idea, but instead find myself saying, "Have you ever heard of eating ginger to help with nausea?"

"Oh. Um . . . yeah, I have. Why?"

"No reason, just curious" would be the correct response,

and is what I plan on saying, but instead I ramble out, "Well, my mom, she's been . . . I think having some stomach issues lately—it's not a big deal or anything, but if there's something natural like ginger or, I don't know, then maybe . . ." But then I pause with this thought: How long exactly has Pam known about Mom's digestive problems? Clearly long enough to research organic ginger and the effects it has on nausea. So Pam knows more about what's going on with Mom than I do. Does Allissa know stuff too? Am I the only one who is completely out of the loop?

"So your mom's stomach issues . . . are they related to her . . . What exactly does your mom have again?"

"Oh. No, I think it's just indigestion, probably." I focus on the pint and digging out another giant strawberry. "Sorry, what else did you ask?"

"The name . . . of what your mom has?"

"It's called PMP. Psuedomyxoma Peritonei."

"Stomach . . . something?"

"Yeah, it's just a fancy way to say a rare stomach cancer . . . thing."

"It is pretty fancy," Marcus agrees, and then says, "Peritonea," in this squeaky, snooty voice. I laugh and say, "Epithelial mucus," back in the same way.

He looks at me questioningly.

"Oh"—I wave my hand—"it's just . . . it comes with the cancer. Weird cells and this mucus stuff . . ." I smile, but Marcus's expression has gone serious. "Mom's always saying how lucky she is that the surgery last summer went well," I continue quickly, "and that there's actually a PMP specialist that practices in Michigan . . . And I guess so, but . . ." I wave my hand again.

"But?" Marcus asks.

"What? Oh. But . . . I don't know. I don't . . . I guess I don't think having a rare stomach mucus growing inside you is, you know, very lucky."

Silence.

"But she's in remission now?" Marcus asks.

"No . . . well . . . no," I say, getting up to mix a new can of paint, "not really."

"Oh," is all Marcus says, but with that tone, that same tone that Mr. Neil at the pharmacy uses when he makes small talk with me as I'm waiting for Mom's prescriptions.

"There are different strains of PMP. Like speeds. And my mom has a really slow one," I explain, pushing the paint around in circles against the can walls. Then I pause, mid-stir, because I feel like I can't catch my breath. "She's had it for almost thirteen years now, undiagnosed for most, though." I sort of gasp this out. "They thought she had ovarian cancer for a long time." What is going on? Maybe it's this window-less choir room; poor ventilation combined with these paint fumes can't be good. I need fresh air, but I stay where I am. "So yeah she has . . . a slower . . . speed of it," I finish.

"Hmm," Marcus says, and then, "Well, slow speed—that's good, right?"

"Yeah." I try to suck in a deep breath as I start to swirl the paint again, gripping the wooden stirrer as if my life depended on it. "Dr. Madson, that's her specialist, he says she'll probably be fine for a long time more, so . . ." And now it feels like there's something pushing down on my chest, stopping me from taking a deep breath. I stop stirring and try to subtly put my head down, needing to get a full breath in without the chest pressure.

"You okay?" Marcus asks, getting up.

"Yes, yeah, I'm fine."

But Marcus walks up to me anyway, putting his hand on my back.

"You sure?" he asks as I stand straight and lean back against his hand, feeling a little wobbly.

"Yeah, yeah," I say.

Why am I so dizzy? Why can't I get in a good breath? I shuffle through what I know. Hypoglycemia? Lyme? Or no—oh, no. Breast lumps metastasizing? If I feel this sick, it has to be in advanced stages. *Okay no, just relax, breathe. You can breathe.*

"Hey, listen." Marcus turns his head toward mine. "I'm sorry if . . . I didn't mean to ask all those questions if—"

"No, no I think . . . I just . . . I'm fine." I manage to walk away from him, taking a seat on the steps of my half-painted porch.

Marcus stares at me with his scientific method, eyebrow-shifting face. He nods sort of uncertainly in my direction, and then walks back to his almost dry, green shrubbery piece.

"You know what? I think this was a tumbleweed," he finally declares.

I laugh, and manage to suck in a semi-good breath through my nose. I push through another long inhale-exhale. Wow. Yes, I'm definitely inhaling too many potent paint fumes, but I guess that's okay, as long as I'm still breathing.

And I'm still breathing by the time I get home for dinner that night. Which is important in a general "I'd like to stay alive" sense, but tonight specifically because I need to focus on my mom. She has this way of stealthily moving her food around on her plate so that a novice observer would be fooled into thinking she's actually eaten something, but I've fallen for this too many times already.

"And he said he still wants to hang out with me, but like not 'romantically,'" Allissa says, munching sadly on a cucumber from her salad.

"Well, that's okay." Mom reaches over and rubs Allissa on the back. Then she says something to us about how boys don't mature as fast as girls do, and uses the terms "fickle-minded" and "emotionally under-stimulated" a lot. Then she slowly moves a piece of her lasagna from the right side of her plate to the left.

"Not hungry?" I ask.

"Eh, I'm too congested," she says. "This damn cold."

"Oh. Right. But, you're feeling okay, though? I mean, besides the cold?"

Allissa pops a cherry tomato in her mouth, studying me.

"Besides this cold? Yes, I'm feeling pretty good actually."

Mom flashes me a perfectly glossed smile and then executes one of her signature moves, the slow traveling fork. Tonight's destination is a mountain of ricotta cheese.

Great, Mom. So you're not having digestive problems? Digestive problems which you're sharing with PMP strangers, and not your own daughter? And then I don't mean to do it, but I find myself rolling my eyes and sighing.

Mom's too busy doing her fork move to notice, but Allissa does, and her squinty "leave it alone" eyes get extra squinty.

But I can't leave it alone because watching Mom stealthily manipulate the food on her plate is making me so angry, I can barely get anything down myself. *So no, I can't leave it alone, Allissa, because a body's digestive organs not working correctly is kind of a big problem.* How many other big problems has Mom just not told us about? Or at least not told *me* about? And I was actually feeling guilty for wanting to sneak out to a party Saturday night. I was even ready to be honest about it, and ask her permission, but now I don't see the point. Why should I tell Mom every detail about what's going on in my life when she can't fill me in on one, vitally important detail about her own?

"I'm having a friend sleep over Saturday night," I find myself saying.

"Oh, okay, that's fine." Mom nods, twirling some cheese onto her fork and then scraping it off with her knife, and probably assuming I mean Jenna.

"You okay, Mom?" Allissa asks as we watch her now slowly rubbing the right side of her head.

"Yes, I'm just . . . so tired and I have this awful sinus head-ache and . . . I think I'm going to head up." She sets her cheese-filled fork on her plate and gets up slowly. "Make sure to put the leftovers in the fridge. Okay?"

We both nod.

"I told you. She's not eating," I say, as soon as Mom's out of earshot.

"She's got a cold. Leave her be."

"No. She says she's got a cold, but I think—"

"Lemme guess, Disease Louise, you think it's a brain tumor?"

I wince. I hate that nickname.

"You know, Allissa, just because you come up here on the weekends doesn't mean—"

"Oh, and when you and Jenna have your sleepover," my sister interrupts, "I can't drive you guys anywhere 'cause I'm going out with—"

"Jenna's not coming over. Meredith is."

"What? Why?" Allissa looks at me over her fork.

"Because . . . we have to work on a project for school, so we're hanging out and studying so . . . yeah, no need to drive us anywhere."

Allissa flashes me a "yeah right" look, like she's sniffed out Meredith's whole plan already. And then she says all detective-like, "Um, since when do you hang out and study with Meredith Brightwell on a Saturday night?"

"Since when do you plan elaborate Mom birthday gift surprises with Meredith's mother and not include me?"

I give Allissa a small "I know your secret" smile.

But Allissa only sighs and looks down at her plate. "It's not elaborate. Just some furniture. Don't worry about it."

"Well . . . I won't. I'm not. I'll probably give her a painting again anyway, so . . ." I trail off, hoping she doesn't hear my voice crack.

"I just wanted to do something by myself, Izzy. It's no big deal."

"Sure, yeah fine. Well . . . well, make sure you put the food away, okay?" I push my plate toward her and walk quickly upstairs to my room, where I lay my head down on my faded multicolored-tulip pattern comforter. I try closing my eyes, but a day's worth of mental snapshots—Mom's post the biggest of them all—pops them open again. I try sitting up, but I can't because I'm having that "can't get a breath because there's a weight sitting on top of my chest" feeling again. The pressure is actually *around* my chest this time. It feels like, oh God, like I'm wearing an invisible corset and two invisible hands are pulling it tight. I roll over onto my side, then slowly sit up and lean my body forward, feeling a little release as I drop my head toward my knees. I exhale slowly, trying to breathe the corset away.

My phone is on my nightstand. I really need to talk to Jenna. Maybe I can send her Mom's post and see what she thinks. Yes, Jenna will know exactly what to do, and plus she'll tell me exactly what to say to Mom next time I ask her how she's feeling and she tries to evade it. I can already hear Jenna lecturing me about how my keeping quiet and watching my mom not eat is a terrible strategy.

Sadly though, after only a ring, I hear Jenna's *Please try not to say something idiotic [beep]* message. I end up leaving her a super-long and potentially idiotic message, telling her that I really need to talk, and that she can call me anytime tonight. Then as soon as I hang up, my phone rings. It never fails. Jenna always manages to call me back a split second after I've left her a rambling voicemail.

"Hey, I just left you a novel on your voicemail," I say.

"I'm sorry, what?"

And oh, that's not Jenna's voice at all. It's Blake's.

"You what on my voicemail?" he asks.

"Nothing, sorry, I thought you were . . . Hi," I say, sitting up a little straighter, as if Blake can see my bad posture through the phone.

"Hey," he says, "what's up?"

It's really nice to hear his voice, and it immediately takes me back to the driveway, and his lips, and his cinnamon-flavored mouth. But all I say is, "Not too much. You?"

"Yeah, not too much. So . . . I didn't see you at rehearsal today."

"No, I was in the lighting booth and then helping with the set in the choir room, so . . ."

"Oh, yeah . . . I was hoping to see you."

"Yeah?" And I feel like I'm giving my cheeks a workout, I'm smiling so big. "Well, I'll see you tomorrow at school. And then on Saturday for the DIA. And then . . . maybe after that at the party, so . . ."

147

"Yeah," he confirms.

And wow, just the way he says that one-syllable word makes me want to sleep right now so it can be tomorrow and then Saturday already.

"So, Izzy, I actually wanted to say thank you."

"Oh? Um . . . for what?"

"The suggestion you made about what to say to my dad, you know? About the musical? And about how, like, extra-curricular stuff would look good on my college apps."

"Oh, right. That helped?"

"Yeah, you know what? I think it did. So yeah, thanks."

"Well, hey, no problem. You're welcome."

And then, oh no, we are fully having an awkward facial expression phone moment. In a face-to-face conversation we'd probably be exchanging a smile or a glance or something. But on the phone right now we're just exchanging embarrassingly long breathing sounds.

"Okay, so . . ." Blake finally breaks in. "I'll see you tomorrow. And hopefully . . . more than I saw you today?"

"Yeah," I laugh, "hopefully."

After we hang up, I practically glide into my pajamas. I'm feeling so inspired, I decide to set my alarm early so I can get to the studio and work for at least an hour before Spanish, reminding myself to talk to Meredith about using her photos. I am definitely going to make a bigger dent in my portfolio by the end of tomorrow. Definitely. And if I work fast, I can finish the dance map sculpture thing during studio time and get that out of the way too. I'm sure Miss S. won't mind me taking some portfolio time to work on it.

I fall back onto my pillow again and I close my eyes. This time they stay closed because I'm fantasizing about the when and where and how I might kiss Blake again. Then this voice creeps into my head, telling me I should be thinking about Mom. *I know, I know,* I say back to the voice. But it doesn't get a chance to respond, because Blake's lips, and his cinnamon smell, and his dimpled chin have overrun my brain space, loosening up that invisible corset, and allowing me to fall asleep.

CHAPTER 11

I can't get loose.

It's finally Friday morning. I slept well. If I could bottle the getting driveway-kissed again fantasy, it would totally cure insomnia.

My giant smile from last night stretches even wider, my non-date DIA date is less than twenty-four hours away, my portfolio deadline is less than three weeks away, and Blake Hangry is less than three feet away, leaning against Nate's locker.

I've been at my own locker waiting for Jenna, but I guess she's not coming. I called her again this morning to tell her about Mrs. Kerns's StrawBeary Fields sweatshirt, and ask her to drop off the blank envelopes with me now. I'd do the calligraphy before we had to start selling tickets at lunch. Her voicemail must be full, though. She would have called me back otherwise.

I open my locker and out falls the package Pam delivered to me on Wednesday. With everything else going on, I'd kind of forgotten about it. I pick it up from the floor and gently shift the contents around, confirming, thankfully, that the handcrafted, artisan, sinus-irrigating neti pot inside is still in one piece.

I put the package back and am about to slam my locker shut when Blake and Nate walk past.

Blake waves at me and smiles, but then Nate stops, spins around, and says, "So Izzy, is it true?"

"Um . . . what?"

Nate's now leaning against the locker next to mine. He flips his dark hair out of his eyes and looks at me. "Is it true," he laugh-talks, "that Jenna wants me?"

I don't know what I was expecting Nate Yube to say, but it wasn't that.

"Oh, um . . ." is all I manage in response as I stare back at him. He's grinning now and nodding his head up and down, I guess answering the question himself.

"Yube, give it a rest," Blake warns.

"But right, Izzy? Jenna *so* wants me."

"No. No, I just . . . I thought you guys would maybe make a . . ." I turn to Blake, thinking now that maybe it wasn't such a good idea to tell him I wanted to set them up.

"Ignore him, he's delusional," Blake says.

"You're right." Nate smirks, shifting his weight from the locker door and standing up straight. "Jenna and me, not important. What's really important is that you two have a great time on Saturday and—"

"Yube," Blake cuts him off with the kind of glare that usually precedes a punch.

"Sorry, sorry." Nate throws his hands up in the air, mock

protecting his face. "I'd just really love for you and Izzy to have a *great* time when you hang out on Saturday. A greaaaaaaa—" He stretches out that word for so long that I'm starting to think Blake might *actually* punch him. But then we hear, "Izzy!" and see Pam rushing over from the other end of the hall.

Pam's got a postal package tucked under her right arm. Her left hand is clutching her chest, which is visibly heaving up and down. You'd think she completed the final stages of a triathlon and not just walked quickly down the hallway.

"I'm late for a meeting, glad I caught you. Here you are and so here you go." She hands me this second package. "Is it for your Mom's birthday?"

"Oh, thanks, Pam, yeah." I light up and tuck the box under my arms. I'm so excited they've finally arrived. So excited, in fact, that when Nate says, "Oooh, what's in the box? What did Santa bring us?" I almost accidentally blurt out, "Mom's color therapy glasses! Mom's color therapy glasses!"

Thankfully, Pam pants, "Hello Mr. Yube, Mr. Hangry," giving them both a friendly nod. Then she fishes out a mysterious, napkin-wrapped item from her back pocket, bends down, and sets it on top of my backpack on the floor.

"It's a baby quiche. Spinach and feta. A little cold, but totally fine."

"Yum," I say, and set down my new package to place the quiche in my backpack's zipper Pam pocket.

"Cold, but delicious," Pam cries again, now sprint-marching down the hallway to her meeting. Then something flies past my head. I look up in time to see Jacob Ullman catching it from farther down the hall, his freckled face grinning as he almost shakes off his baseball cap doing a pseudo touchdown dance. I look down. My box is gone.

I turn to Nate, feeling the muscles in my face stiffen. He ignores me, signaling Jacob by raising his arms in the air.

"Give it, guys. Stop being douches." Blake charges at Jacob, lunging for my package. Jacob just laughs his congested seagull laugh and sidesteps Blake, throwing the box back to Nate.

"You're going to break them!" I shout.

"Oh no, so sorry," Nate says, backing a good five feet away from me. "Here you go—" Then he winds back his arm as if to throw the box to me, but turns at the last second and heads down the hallway in the other direction. Blake just stands there, his mouth open, then mutters, "I'll get that back for you—promise," and takes off down the hall after Nate.

Great. Nate Yube just stole Mom's color therapy glasses and completely ruined what could have been a potentially good Blake moment. Maybe Blake would have stopped to talk to me, asked me to the dance. Now I kind of hope he does punch Nate.

I put my Spanish books in my bag, hoping Nate's at least passed the package to Jacob. That way I can steal it back when Señora Claudia is eclipsed by her huge sombrero in Spanish. Yes, I'll steal my glasses back, I'll talk to Meredith about using her photos, and then all I have to do is get through bio before I can be in the studio again.

I can't wait to show Miss S. what I did this morning—note to self: Buy Cara new nail polish—and the map too. If I work fast enough I can finish the sculpture, and maybe even get started on something new for my portfolio.

I re-secure my fragile neti pot between a couple binders and gently slam my locker shut, slumping against it. I need to get those glasses back. I spent way too much money on them, and I'm pretty sure WearapyTherapy.com doesn't give full refunds.

In the studio, I'm suddenly seized with a sharp pain in my right butt cheek and I shoot up from my seat. The wooden center of my stool is embedded with glued-on macaroni shells. Cute in the projects the elementary school kids do here on weekends, but lethal at the wrong angle. I switch out my stool and study the bits of mirror in the patterns I've laid out on the table.

"That is looking really great." Ina Lazebnik ambles in, her ventriloquist mouth smiling as she passes my table and heads over to the pottery rack.

"Thanks." I smile back my first real smile since Spanish this morning and shift onto my macaroni-less stool.

I forgot today was cultural immersion day in Spanish. So instead of getting to talk to Meredith about the photos or stealing my package back from Jacob, I had to sit there and listen to music while Señora Claudia danced and translated lyrics that had verb tenses way above our comprehension level. Then in bio we got our quizzes back and I got a C minus. Which is basically a D. Marcus gave me pained look when he handed it back to me and offered to help me study again at rehearsal today. Which I think is futile, but nice of him.

"So close, yet so far away," Ina closed-mouth mutters to herself as she cautiously places her latest piece on the table.

"Wow, that looks amazing," I tell her, because it really does. She's been working for the past two weeks on this really awesome clay sculpture with this crazy intricate etched-in pattern.

I study my almost dried papier-mâché map that I fleshed out this morning and sigh.

"Izzy, Izzy, listen to this!" Meredith and Cara giggle their way into the studio and throw their stuff down on my table, almost disturbing my mirror chip patterns.

"Do it!" Meredith prompts Cara, who then sighs and starts full-out singing the chorus to one of the songs we were listening to in Spanish.

Okay, watching Cara dance and sing off key in a terrible Spanish accent doesn't totally lift my mood, but it does make me laugh a little.

"Doesn't she sound just like the recording?" Meredith laughs.

"That's amazing," I say, shaking my head, while Ina closed-mouth chuckles.

"What's all this?" Meredith asks, getting her supplies out and eyeing my map and mirror fragments.

"It's just for the dance—I'm helping my mom with decorations, and . . . well, actually. . . I know Marcus is helping you do something digital for your final project, but since you have so many photos . . . are you using them all, or—"

"Oh, no way. I'm picking a couple photos and will"—she riffles through her notebook and reads back—"'will employ one to two techniques on each, or tie them together in a thematic way.'"

"Hm." I nod. "Do you think I could . . . maybe use some of the rest? I'd give you photography credit, of course, and—"

"You'd make them part of your painting?"

"No, actually, it's for this . . . sculpture for the dance and—"

"Oh, cool. Yeah, that would be awesome!"

"Oh. Okay, great. Can I copy them to my drive?"

"Totally." Meredith whips out her laptop and I grab my thumb drive.

Meredith cheerfully chats to me as the pictures are being copied to my drive. She's going on and on about which of them she likes best and is telling me how excited she is to be part of one of my art projects, "even thought it's just dance decorations," and then she tells me how much she's always liked my stuff.

"What? Really?" I look up at her from the computer.

"Yeah. I remember in like third grade when we had to draw our self-portraits in crayon or something, and yours actually looked like you."

"What?" I stare back at her, trying to remember.

"Yeah! Remember? And Miss Middlesrat was like, 'Everybody come look at what Izzy did!' and I was thinking, 'That's my best friend, she's going to be in museums, so get her autograph right now.'"

"You did not think that," I say, my morning smile returning again.

"Oh before I forget, let's go over a game plan for tomorrow. Ryan's got his dad's van, so he's driving. He's picking me up around the corner from your house around nine, so I figured if you'll be on the lookout—"

"Well, I was thinking of actually going now . . . to the party, if that's okay," I add.

"Oh, cool! Yeah, that's so great." Meredith claps her hands under her chin. "Okay, well, then we're going to have to re-strategize."

"Wait, what do you mean?"

"Well, the party is actually not at Phil's house anymore. It's at his cousin Steve's fraternity, so it won't really get started until later, but that's okay, because—" And Meredith starts to go over our new plan of action, and I'm fully nodding along but only half listening, thinking, *Oh God, a frat house*. Not that it's a big deal or anything. It's just that, so far, I've yet to actually attend an official frat party. It's one thing just sneaking out to go to Cara's brother's Phil's regular house. But now I'm sneaking out to go to a total stranger's frat house. People go to frat houses to drink and have sex. I don't drink, and Blake and I have only driveway-kissed. Plus, I have no desire to be in a *Babes Gone Bananas* video.

Not that there would be skeezy *Babes Gone Bananas* people in Ann Arbor at this particular frat party, on this particular weekend. But what if I somehow end up flashing a video camera? My mom would officially disown me for the rest of my life. Well, first she would disown me for sneaking out.

Maybe this isn't such a good idea.

"Helloooooooo . . . ladies." Miss S. circles our table. "Everything going okaaaay . . . ?"

"Uh-huh, yeah, totally," Cara says, while Meredith confirms it with a nod and goes back to her photography notes.

"Ooooh, and what's this little mirror medleyyyyy . . . ?" Miss S. circles my table, her pupils dilating as if they're literally absorbing what they're seeing. "And a new sculpture? Aaaaand . . . some multi-mediaaaaaa . . ." she adds, noting the open laptop.

"Oh, well, actually this is for the Dance for Darfur. For the decorations."

"Mmmm," Miss S. muses, her eyebrows shifting down and then up again.

"Yeah, my mom—she's on the planning committee—she wanted some kind of sculpture. It's going to be for the entry-way. Actually, I had this idea yesterday to—"

"I seeeee . . ." Miss S. cuts me off as she curls her lips inward the way she does when she's problem-solving or when it takes extra effort to be constructive.

Wow, her lips are tucked in so far right now that it looks like there's an incision where her mouth should be. That's not good.

"Weeeeeell . . ." she finally sighs, "I think it's great that you're helping out your moooooom . . . This dance is important, I knooow, but Izzy"—she says my name in this "I don't know" tone—"I'm a little concerrrrned . . . about your priorities."

"Oh."

"It's just that we're heading towaaaaaard . . . this deadline and you still have hooooow . . . many full pieces to do?"

"Three," I mumble.

"Yes, well, I think it best to not work on dance de-coooooor . . . during studio time, yes?"

"Yes, of course. I can . . . I can do this on my own time. Yes. Sorry."

"Good." She places a hand flat on my arm, drumming her long fingers across my shoulders. "No worries now, loosen the chest, loosen it all, and deeeeep breath, remember? Stay loooose . . ." she reminds me.

I nod and start to take a breath as Miss S. sway-walks over to the other side of the studio. But it's not a good, loose, deep breath. I don't let the air flow to all my muscles the way Miss S. always tells me I should. I gulp the air down instead, thinking about how I just lied.

I just lied to Miss S. because I can't do this dance map sculpture thing on my own time, because I don't have any of my own time. I have Jenna-time for play rehearsal, Mom-time for getting the attic together, Mom-time for designing and selling dance tickets, Mom-time for doing medical research and reading everything I can—most of it going over my head—about the stomach muscle and all the things that can wrong with it, and—

I rapidly start picking up my bits of mirror, putting them piece by piece back into my plastic supply bin. And if I don't have any of my own time now, I definitely won't have any of it going forward either. I clear the last pattern of mirror shards off the table. Especially if everything I'm reading turns out to be true, if Mom really hasn't gotten that much better from last summer. If maybe she's even gotten worse.

I seal up my storage bin and shove it underneath the table, using my knees to push it farther back and out of sight. My mental snapshots from last summer are back now, mechanically moving through my head like a kid's View-Master. All that sick-Mom-time, click. All that me-not-working-on-my-portfolio-time, click, click, click.

I can't believe I was willing to spend the one official portfolio hour I have today to work on dance decorations for my mother. My mother, who blatantly lies to my face, and who will probably hate this whole sculpture anyway. Or ask me to make what she thinks is a one-minute change, but that will probably take me eight hours.

I rise up from under the table and stare down at my map sculpture. I stare and gulp down three more breaths, feeling anything but loose. In fact, the more I stare at that stupid map, the tighter every single muscle in my body feels. Which is probably why my hands immediately clench and clamp down onto the edge of the table when I hear Jacob Ullman's repulsive seagull laugh. I grind my fingers into the table, trying to ignore that honking, throaty sound. But then I can't help it and turn my head because it's not just Jacob laughing, it's a whole table of boys and they're all—

Oh my God. The whole table of 101 boys are all wearing my mom's color therapy glasses.

I snap my head back around fast, my forearms aching from gripping the table so hard. Then I slowly pivot my body back around so I can sneak a look at the boys.

Yup, there they all are, all seven colored lenses. If they weren't *my* stolen glasses, if they weren't meant for very important medical purposes, then I guess a ROYGBIV spectrum of boys engaging in an unintentional color therapy session in the art room would be kind of funny. Which I guess is why Robert Stern laughs as he walks by and asks what's going on.

"Izzy got these for us," Nate replies, taking off his indigo pair, and reading the little card attached to the frame. "These are supposed to aid in 'sinus and pituitary gland function.'" He strokes his chin with his fingers, feigning an "I'm impressed" face.

"What?" Robert snorts. "Lemme see."

"Okay, ha-ha, very funny, Nate." I hope I sound casual. "Just give them back to me."

"Oh my God, what are they wearing?" Meredith giggles in my direction but then stops when she sees my face.

"They're mine. Nate stole them from me this morning," I say, trying to hold it together. "They're for my mom. They're really expensive and—"

"Give them back, asshats!" Meredith turns to the table.

"Relax, Meredith." Jacob seagull-laughs at her, and then makes a fist with his hand, moving it back and forth toward and away from his face. "I miss you," he adds, making the rest of the table laugh even harder.

"You wish," Meredith snaps at him, the color draining from her cheeks a little, but her voice getting louder.

"Just give them back," I say, louder now, riding on Meredith's energy.

"Okay, okay." Nate laughs and then throws the pair of indigo glasses at us. I follow their trajectory as they fly past Meredith and me, landing on the floor next to the table behind us, skidding a little, then coming to rest still in one piece. I sigh. And then a second later, Roopa Sheti walks through the tables holding a canvas over her head and steps right on them, shattering both lenses and the frames as well.

"Jesus, what the—" She looks around, annoyed.

I stare at the crushed pile of indigo. Then every muscle in my body tightens together like I'm some kind of human spring being pushed all the way down, and then suddenly—"Give me my glasses! Give them back!"—I release, springing at the table of boys, barreling toward Jacob Ullman and trying to snatch my red lenses right off his face. But Jacob manages to get up and books it away from the table, his seagull laugh ringing.

I chase him around the table, reaching out my arms. All I can see is Jacob Ullman and my red glasses. And then—

CRASH.

It's the first time I've seen Ina Lazebnik's mouth open so wide to speak. Except she's not really speaking, she's just swearing, and now . . . crying.

"Sorry, sorry, sorry, sorry," Jacob repeats to her, his voice going soft.

I rush up to them both, stopping at Ina's broken sculpture on the floor.

"I'm so sorry. I'm . . . I'm so, so, sorry." I don't know what else to say, so I bend down to help her pick up the pieces.

"No, don't! I got it." She shakes her head at me, sniffling, and shooing me away.

"Oooooh, oooooh." Miss S. rushes over to us. She picks up one of the clay pieces and cradles it in her hands like a small, wounded animal. She puts one arm around Ina, and then turns to Jacob and me, her hazel eyes hard.

"It was an accident," Jacob mumbles, relinquishing the red lenses to the tabletop.

"Izzy?" Miss S. turns to me, most of her braids now tumbled down around her shoulders.

"Jacob was . . . running from me because he had my glasses and—" I stop because it just sounds so utterly stupid.

"It was Jacob's fault," Meredith chimes in. "He stole Izzy's glasses and then he starts running around the room and—"

"Okay, enough," Miss S. says. She seems to gather herself together. "Jacob, let's go to my office and discuuuuss . . . how we can try and help Ina replenish and re-creaaaate . . . going forward."

She gestures for Jacob to follow her and then gently tells Ina to go take some time and get cleaned up. "Izzy . . ." She pauses, turning to me again with a severely inward-lipped mouth. "You know better."

I watch them walk away, wishing I could rewind it all.

"This was so not your fault," Meredith reassures me, bringing over and then holding open a small garbage bag.

I toss in the pieces of what was once Ina's awesome sculpture and my mom's indigo color therapy glasses, thinking that maybe I belong inside that bag as well.

CHAPTER 12

I'm a clueless cyberchondriac.

I can't get to the main lobby and the ticket-selling table fast enough. Not that I'm looking forward to selling dance tickets on my lunch hour, but I *am* looking forward to finally seeing Jenna.

I throw my backpack on the floor next to the folding table. Jenna's already got it set up in the lobby with the display sign I made weeks ago taped to the front. I drop my battered box of glasses, sans indigo, on top of the table and scan the lobby. Here's the table, but there's no sign of Jenna. I take a seat on one of the folding chairs, trying not to replay the snapshots of the day—Robert Stern's laugh, the crunch of Roopa's shoe, Ina's dazed, sniffling face.

I should offer to help Ina with whatever new project she'll be working on now. Or maybe I should offer her money for more supplies. I should write her an apology note. Miss S. is right, I should know better. What is wrong with me? And why was Robert Stern laughing at those glasses anyway? He's smart. He should know how expensive color therapy glasses are. Ugh. Where is Jenna? I slide the box of tickets on the table closer to me and open it up. Then I see, sitting right on top of the assembled tickets, the pile of blank envelopes I was supposed to decorate. There's a Post-it stuck to the top one that says "Still blank . . ." in Jenna's handwriting.

"Two please. Thanks, Izzy."

I look up, say hello to Derrick, and then quickly check my wallet for bills since there's no cashbox here to make change.

"Would you like to donate any of the following amounts in addition to the price of your ticket?" I add, mimicking Mom's client smile and handing him a donation form. Derrick declines with a "Nah," and so I give him two tickets, but in one of the blank envelopes, which I've suddenly decided to reserve for non-donators.

I watch as Derrick disappears through the cafeteria doors across from me, and then I scan the lobby again.

Twenty minutes later, I've decorated ten envelopes, arranged them in multiple flower patterns on the table, sold three pairs of tickets and gotten two very small donations, and texted Jenna four times. I really think you should let a person know if you're planning on just not showing up for something. Especially when that person is spending their free evenings showing up for you. And especially when they need you—logistically, I mean, because I'm almost out of change. Really, at least leave a person a cashbox.

At that very moment, a metal box lands, rattling my flimsy folding table. It's not the universe hearing me and making cashboxes fall from the sky. No, it's Marcus Mason, smiling at me and saying, "Try not to spend it all on art supplies."

"Hey. Thanks. Where's your sister?"

"I don't know. She texted me to get this to you and help out if I'm needed."

"Oh. She texted you? Is she okay? Is she sick?"

"Nah, I don't think so." He joins me behind the table. "Sorry, you look . . . disappointed that I'm your co-seller?"

"No, no, it's not that. It's good that you're here." I gesture to the nonexistent line of people in front of us. "As you can see, I'm swamped."

"Yeah." He smiles. "Good thing I came along when I did."

Marcus and I do end up pretty busy and selling tickets nonstop for a while near the end of the hour. After our last big rush, I plop down in my chair, doodle-decorating one of the blank envelopes, wondering why Jenna never bothered to text me as well.

"So I have to ask"—Marcus turns to me, closing up cashbox, and gesturing to my package on the far edge of the table—"what's in the box?"

"Oh. Some . . . glasses." I pop open the cardboard flap so he can see inside.

"Wow. All for you?"

"No. Well . . . um, they're not mine. I mean, I ordered them, but they're not mine. I mean, they're mine, but they're for—"

"Wait a minute." He sifts his fingers through the contents, looking at me now the way Allissa does when I tell her about a new symptom. "Why did you order glasses in every color of the rainbow?"

"Um . . . it's actually . . . it's for color therapy," I mumble really fast.

"What?"

"Color therapy," I repeat, taking out a pair—the green ones—and handing them to him. I watch as he holds them up by the stems, like a lab specimen. Maybe Marcus can actually tell me more about how color therapy works since he knows so much already about science and anatomy. Maybe he even knows the details about what certain colors do, or the best ones to use.

"Color therapy," he repeats. "Really?"

"Yeah," I say, frowning.

"Is this for class? Did Bayer cover light refraction or . . .?"

"Oh. No, no, I read about it myself. I was on Symptomaniac and this guy commented on a thread and linked to this site and . . . anyway, then I read about them and how certain colors can balance out certain organs and—"

"Oh. But why did you— No wait, first, why were *you* on Symptomaniac?"

"Oh, um . . ." Crap. *Well Marcus, I go on Symptomaniac for a lot of different reasons. For instance, I had a headache last week that wouldn't go away even after I took three Advil, and I read this article once that said headaches that don't go away can be a sign of a brain tumor. Then I saw on the news that they think now cell phones give you brain tumors, and I use my cell phone a lot. Also, one of my breasts is oddly bigger than the other. Have I ever mentioned that? No? Oh, and did I tell you I'm aging prematurely? Or that, most disturb-*

ingly, I've recently had trouble breathing? "I don't know," I say at last. "I'm just bored sometimes, I guess."

"Oh. Well, I think it's more fun reading medical journals. They're more reliable than the websites and sometimes they have really detailed pictures too."

"Really?" I ask, excited about the detailed pictures.

"Yeah, my dad has tons of them in his office."

"So you really check to see what kinds of diseases you have in medical journals?"

"Check to see—no, no, I don't think I have any diseases. Just interested in anatomy, medicine . . ."

"Wait, I thought you wanted to go into engineering or something?" I ask, hoping for a subject change.

"I don't know. I'd like to end up doing something with computers, but medical school isn't completely out of the question. I guess it just depends— Wait, you look up diseases and stuff for personal reasons? Because you think you have them?"

"No, of course not. I mean sometimes I do, sometimes I think I may have a symptom or something, but I'm not sure, so I look and . . ." I stop myself and trail off.

Marcus looks at me for a long second. And then he starts to laugh. He starts to laugh at me, and it feels like someone heaved a bowling ball into my stomach.

"Izzy, that's hilarious."

"Well, good," I mumble, "I'm glad you find me so amusing."

"Oh," Marcus says, his face going still. "No, I didn't mean to laugh. I don't find *you* amusing. I mean I do, but not in a bad way. It's just I've never met anyone who thinks that they have things, things other than a cold or the flu, things that they actually have to . . . look up."

"Uh-huh." The bowling ball sinks farther.

"Izzy, you're a hypochondriac," he says to me, smiling.

"What? No I'm not."

"Actually, no, you're not. You're a cyberchondriac."

"No, no, I'm not a . . . I'm not one of those either." Note to self: Look up *cyberchondriac* on Symptomaniac later.

"Right." He nods. "No, you're definitely not. Listen, next time you're on Symptomaniac, do you mind looking up some symptoms for me? I think I may have the Black Plague. The late 1600s London strain."

"Okay, I get it." I fake smile. "You think I'm insane and that I'm going to end up in a mental hospital or something. I get it, trust me."

"Oh. No, I don't. I don't think you're insane." He stares at me for another long second and then looks down at the green-tinted glasses in his hands. "I do think that color therapy is insane, though. As if seeing a color would just magically zap energy through the eyes, to the hypothalamus, and on to the pineal gland to mess with our hormones and heal an organ." He chuckles again, and says "Color therapy" in this amused way that makes my bowling ball stomach turn.

"Well, then I guess you think I'm pretty stupid for getting them for my mom." I snatch the glasses out of his hands.

"No, no, it's just that—no, Izzy you're not. For your mom?"

"It's fine, really. I'm used to this by now, so—"

"Used to . . ."

"People . . . just not . . . not really understanding that—" I cut myself off. "Forget it."

"No, I understand. I mean . . . I do. I guess it all kind of makes sense."

"What makes sense?"

"You being obsessively interested in illness, diseases, and such, you know, because of your mom being sick and—" Marcus stops speaking, seeing the expression on my face. I'm telling myself to look unfazed and nod casually, but I can't because it's like I can see Marcus's last words floating in the air between us. I can't stop seeing them. I shake my head, trying to make the words go away, surprised at the shaky sound of my own voice when I say, "I . . . I'm not obsessed with illness and disease. I'm—"

"No, I didn't mean . . ." He holds up a hand, palm circling toward his chest, as if trying to propel his sentence to a close.

"—and my mom being sick doesn't have anything to do with anything."

"Sure, no, let me rephrase—"

But I don't let him rephrase, I just keep talking, moving my face closer to his, my voice wobbling more but rising in volume. "You know, Marcus, some people are just interested in being as healthy as they possibly can."

"Of course. No, Izzy, I didn't mean to—"

"And some people think that the truly crazy people are the ones who close their minds to everything you can't . . . *test* with Mr. Bayer's stupid scientific method!" I grab my backpack and my glasses, and take off, not sure where I'm going till I see the sign for the girls' bathroom.

I charge through the door. *Stop it, Izzy. What are you doing? Stop crying!* I open my eyes wide and look toward the top of the mirror. What is wrong with me? So what if Marcus thinks color therapy is insane, and that I'm insane? Why am I so upset about one more person thinking I'm mentally unstable?

I splash some water on my face and pat my palms to my cheeks.

Marcus is wrong, you are not a cyberchondriac. Okay, yes, maybe you look up symptoms and health-related informa-tion on the Internet, but it's not without good reason. You never look up any symptoms without first experiencing at least a little bit of it physically. You're not a cyberchondriac. And you're not a hypochondriac either.

Okay yes, I know all about hypochondria. I've read all about it. But my mom being sick is not the "contributing cause of my neurosis." In fact, there is no "contribut-ing cause" to my neurosis because I don't have a neurosis originating from . . . contributing causes.

And okay yes, I know what neurosis means. I have Jewish relatives. Plus the word *neurosis* is in almost every article I've ever read on panic attacks, which apparently neurotic hypochondriacs have all the time. But I don't. I also don't obsessively go to the doctor and I don't unreasonably take medicine—well, except for Advil, vitamins, the occasional herbal supplement, and sometimes flu-be-gone tea.

And yes, okay, I do self-diagnose, but that's called doing research. And doing research is important. Research can lead to people feeling better, to cures, to things going away.

I treat my face to a final splash of water and gather my stuff together. Then I book it to government, actually looking forward, for once, to Mr. Harada's mind-numbing oration on checks and balances.

Three outgoing voicemails, six texts, and not one response from Jenna.

I'm wondering if she'll even be at rehearsal today as I head to the auditorium. Maybe she's going to ditch that too.

Nope, there she is, leaning against the side of the stage, chatting with Ryan Paulson.

"So this lady keeps asking me, is the soap gluten-free? And I keep pointing to the words on the wrapper that say *gluten-free* in huge fancy cursive. And she's like, 'Yes, but is it *one hundred percent* gluten-free?' I mean, does she honestly think that Soaptastic secretly fills their gluten-free soaps with gluten?!"

Ryan Paulson is laughing hysterically and saying, "Yeah, like it's this gluten conspiracy."

"I know." Jenna laughs. "Exactly!"

"Hey, stranger!" I chime in, tapping her on the shoulder.

"Hey Izzy, what's up?" Ryan says, still laughing.

Jenna turns to me and then back to Ryan. "So yeah, I can get your aunt a discount. We have this crappy new bar called

Nursery Lime. It's a citrus scent for toddlers. Parents go gaga for it because the shea butter is wild-crafted from Senegal."

"I don't even know what that means." Ryan shakes his head in wonder.

"Hey!" I say a little louder. "What happened to you today? Did you get my voicemails?"

Jenna turns to me again and gives me a glare that I think drops the temperature of the auditorium by a hundred degrees. Ryan frowns at Jenna and then glances at me. Jenna just turns back to him smiling. "It's a shame we discontinued Grape Gatsby, though, 'cause that would be the one I'd recommend."

"Hello? Why are you— Where were you at lunch? Remember the tickets? I was all by myself with no change and—"

"Okay, get ready, people!" Jenna turns and shouts out to everyone. "We're going to start running act two in fifteen minutes!" Then she walks down the auditorium aisle, right past me.

"What is wrong with you?" I'm on her heels, following her out of the theater.

"Nothing's wrong with me. I just don't feel like talking to you right now."

"You don't feel like— Why?"

Jenna stops and turns, her clear blue eyes clouding.

"What?" I practically screech out. "What did I do?"

"What did you do? Like you don't know what you did?"

"I don't! If I knew what I did, I wouldn't have to ask you."

Jenna just shakes her head and walks right past me again. So I follow her around the corner and to the vending machine alcove. Finally she bursts out, "Why did you tell Nate that I wanted to date him? That I wanted to hang out with him? Why would you do that? Why would you say . . . that I—" She stops and swipes a finger against her now wet cheek. But more tears are falling fast, and soon she's rapidly zipping her fingers against her cheeks, one side at a time, like windshield wipers. I feel like I should hand her a tissue or put my arms around her or something, but when I take a step closer, she turns her back to me.

"Jenna, I just thought . . . you liked him . . . and he liked you . . . so I think what I told him, or what I first told Blake was that maybe—"

"Yeah," she says, spinning around, "*you* told *Blake* I wanted to *date* Nate, and he told Nate I wanted to date him, and Nate told *me all about it last night.* He's just sitting there with Jacob while I'm trying to watch the stupid square dance, and he's laughing at me like I'm some idiot, like I'm some sort of desperate, crushed-out— Why would I— You humiliated me!" She folds into herself like an accordion, heaving for breath between sobs.

"What's so humiliating?"

"Why did you have to talk about me with them? Why would you do that?"

"I'm sorry, I just thought that you liked—"

"And Meredith? You're like best friends with her again now? Do you two just sit around talking about me too?

175

Why did you tell her to call me last night? What did she tell you? Did she—"

"What? I don't know why she called you. I—"

"She said you suggested it, that she wanted to . . . Did you talk to her about what I told you about my cousin, about Amy?"

"No. Wait, does she know? She hangs out at those parties too, so maybe she knows someone who—"

"You're so clueless!" Jenna shouts, shaking her head. "How am I supposed to be best friends with someone who's so completely clueless all of the time!" She pushes past me down the hall and through the swinging band room doors. I just stand there, frozen, watching the doors swing.

I'm not sure how long I stand there. A minute? Ten? Finally, I make my way down the hall and back to the theater, but I pass the auditorium and head to the studio instead. It's hard to walk. I feel like my skeleton's been shocked out of my body and then put back in all wrong. When I get to the studio, I can barely turn the knob on the door. It's like I have feet for hands or something.

Eventually I manage to get inside and set up my supplies; not that it matters since I'm just sitting at my table now staring at a pile of finished sketches. Apparently I'm clueless. I guess Jenna did tell me she wanted to boycott dates for the dance, but I obviously wouldn't have tried to set her up with Nate or push her to go out to the party with me if I believed her. If I knew her reasons. Yes, I was distracted and not exactly a great best friend when she told me about Amy.

Still, that doesn't change the fact that she just told me yesterday about something that happened back in September about a cousin I'm not sure she's ever mentioned before. Did she just expect me to figure it out all by myself, that I'd just be magically thinking, *You know what? I probably shouldn't set Jenna up with Nate on the off chance that she hates boys now because her cousin Amy got dumped by a guy after having sex with him.*

So no, Jenna. I'm not clueless. You're just not keeping me . . . well-informed.

I shake away the image of Jenna crying and start to cut and assemble more photos with my mirror fragments when I hear my phone buzzing. I dig it out of my backpack, knocking Pam's now rock-solid baby quiche onto the floor. It's a text from Blake: Pik you up @ 11 tomor!

Okay, I know it's really lame to get excited about a text message, especially one that completely butchers the English language, but so far this text is the only good thing that's happened today. I stare at my phone, blurring out everything else. I even start to smile. But then I catch sight of the empty space on the pottery shelf where Ina's sculpture used to live, and everything I've blurred out snaps back into focus. I flip my phone open again and reread Blake's text, wishing there was a way I could just fast-forward to tomorrow, and erase all of my snapshots from today.

CHAPTER 13

I should have worn a cardigan.

I've tried on six different but basically the same sweaters and it's only ten a.m. I pull off sweater number seven and start rifling through my short-sleeved shirts instead. Because what if it's hot in the museum? I don't want to walk around releasing knit-induced body odor as I point out art to Blake, who will be here in—unghhh—less than an hour.

After battling myself to sleep last night, I missed my alarm this morning and woke up to Leroy using my body as his own personal kitty bed. My stomach's been flipping all morning, but in this good way, like telling me that today is going to be one of those great days; maybe the kind where you end up officially having a date to a dance.

I find a short-sleeved shirt that's not totally wrinkled and throw it on. Then I hear music coming from Mom's room down the hall. Is that . . . *West Side Story*? It's confirmed as I round the corner to see Natalie Wood dance across Mom's mini TV, wearing silly hats and singing about feeling pretty. From the bathroom I hear Mom singing along in her own unique key.

. . . and I pityyyy any girl who isn't mee toooday. La la la la la la la la la.

Mom jumps, turning around quick when she catches me laughing at her in the mirror. "Hey sweetie, good morning. AMC is having a movie musical marathon today. *Tommy* was on earlier."

"Good, Mom." I smile.

" *. . . see that pretty girl in the mirror there—*" She sings out again, gesturing to me with a hand full of lotion. Then she circles the tips of her fingers to her cheeks. She has three different kinds of moisturizers: one for sun damage and revitalizing, one for anti-aging and firming, and one moisturizer for . . . providing moisture, I guess.

Mom fans her face with her hands to dry off her newly applied layer while dancing and now singing backup.

"*. . . who? who? who? who? meeee! such a pretty meee.*" She sashays her hand across her body, accidentally painting her tunic with tinted moisturizer. "Shoot, shoot, shoot!" She sighs, looking down at the mess and then shakes her head and grins at me because I'm laughing at her. I follow her out of the bathroom and lean against the bedpost as she grabs another flowing blouse from her dresser. "You excited for today? Should be fun," she says, quickly taking off her tunic and grabbing the replacement.

"Yeah, I think so." Then I stifle a gasp. I struggle to keep my face still through a brief but disturbing glimpse.

Mom's saying something about the most direct route to Detroit, and the freeway versus Orchard Lake Road. I nod, still seeing her empty bra, her curved, rising ribs, and the bumpy outline of her spine when she bent down to get her blouse.

"Mom," I start, but then don't know quite how to say it.

"What, sweetie?" she asks, leaning closer to her reflection, securing her earrings in place.

"You look so thin. You've . . . lost weight, huh?"

"I don't know. I don't really . . . Do I look it?"

"Yeah, you look . . . Mom, you look *really* thin."

"Oh stop, Izzy." She gives me a quick closed-mouth smile as she shakes her head and walks to the closet. She returns slipping on a pair of high heels.

"I know you're not eating as much and . . ." I stop. The confession that I've read her web post weighs down my tongue.

"No, I know. It's this sinus infection—drainage, I think . . . going to my stomach, nauseating me. But just to be safe I've made an appointment with Dr. Madson, so—"

"Oh, really?" I swallow my confession down. "You have a new appointment with Dr. Madson. Why?" I'm trying to sound casual, as if I don't already know the secrets of LindaSky46.

"He just wants to do some testing, routine stuff, just a checkup. And you know I've been feeling a little under the weather, with this cold, and I've been . . . just . . . having some trouble with nausea so— Oh is that him?" She rushes over to the window that overlooks our driveway, reacting to the sound of a car pulling up. "Nope, false alarm," she declares, now craning her neck around like it's a submarine periscope to get a full view of the driveway.

I join her on Blake Watch at the window. Maybe me going to the DIA today and out to a party tonight isn't such a great idea after all. How long has Mom had this appointment? You can't just make a last-minute appointment with Dr. Madson. You have to schedule it pretty far in advance. And you don't just go see him for checkups or colds either. I'm about to bring this up when Mom squeals, "He's here! That's him!" and we watch Blake pull into the driveway, his little sister, Jillian, in the passenger's seat.

Mom swiftly turns around, giving me a rapid once-over.

"Where's your cardigan? Are you bringing a cardigan? You need to wear a cardigan." She's inches away now, fussing with every single aspect of my appearance at once. It's like she's suddenly transformed into an aesthetic Swiss Army knife, with combs, and glosses, and sprays popping out of her body from all directions.

"I'm taking a cardigan with me, don't worry," I say, escaping from her beauty tentacles and heading down the stairs.

"No, no, put one on now. You can't just walk around all day wearing a short-sleeved shirt," she badgers, following me down the stairs. I grab my cardigan and my coat from the banister.

"And that shirt's wrinkled. Did you pull it off your floor? It looks terrible. This is an event. You really have to be aware of how you present yourself, sweetie."

"I'm aware," I say under my breath as she once again tries

to control every detail of my life and body while refusing to tell me anything about her own.

"Well, you're obviously not aware, Izzy. If you're planning on going public with a—"

"Mom! I'm not going public. I'm just—" And then the doorbell rings, and I stop. Deep breath. I open the door, telling myself that this afternoon I will focus on Blake, who's standing in front of me right now in, oh thank God, just a T-shirt and jeans. And he looks great.

I tried to win points with Jillian right away by letting her stay in the front seat, which I now wholeheartedly regret. I usually don't mind riding in the back, except in this case, where one side is occupied with shopping bags, and the other side, where I'm sitting, is cramp-city, since Jillian's levered her seat all the way back, like she's in a lounge chair or something.

"So we can take Jilly around and check some stuff out, and then drop her off with my mom, and go see that performance art lady, and then, just like hang out? Sound like a plan?" Blake taps his fingers rapidly on the steering wheel while he waits his turn at the four-way stop at the end of my block. He seems even more jumpy now than he did the other night at my house. Maybe it's because I'll be meeting his mom.

"Yup, sounds great," I say, and catch Jillian checking me out in her pulled-down visor mirror. She gives me a toothy grin, and I see her teeth are stained red, probably from the cherry Tootsie Pop she was working on that she's now rested in the cup holder between herself and her brother.

"You remember Izzy, Jills? From art camp?" Blake asks her.

"Nope," she says.

Blake gives me a shrug.

"Well, it was a couple summers ago," I say, shrugging back, "and I wasn't her main counselor, so . . . So Jillian, you're in second grade?" I ask.

"Third," she corrects me, picking up the Tootsie Pop and putting it back in her mouth.

Don't think about the germs, Izzy. Just smile and ask another question.

"And do you like making art?"

"Do you make sculptures?" Jillian asks me.

"Oh, um, sometimes. Mostly I draw and paint, though."

"Are you in any museums?"

"Um, nope."

"How much does your stuff cost?"

"Well . . . I haven't ever sold anything yet."

"You haven't?"

"Izzy's still in school, Jillian. Just like you," Blake tells her. Jillian nods at her brother, contemplating the fact that we're both still in school. Then she pulls the Tootsie Pop out of her mouth and some of her reddish-brown curls get stuck to the candy. *Oh, God.* She drops the hair-covered sucker back in the cup holder and addresses me again through her visor mirror.

"My friend Tiffany's older sister, she lives in New York and her stuff is in places there."

"Wow, that's pretty cool," I say, humoring her.

"My mom likes her stuff that she made, and Tiffany's older sister, the stuff that she made, she sold, and she sold one painting in New York."

"Wow, that's really great," I say, hoping I understood all that correctly.

"One painting buys a whole apartment, did you know that?" she asks me.

"Oh. Well . . . wow. So . . . how old is Tiffany's sister?" I ask.

"She's really old. Like eighteen."

I nod, and see Blake laugh a little to himself.

"Hey Jillian," Blake says to her, "Izzy can do drawings that look real, that look just like the real thing."

"Like a photograph?"

"Yeah, just like a photograph, but she draws and paints them. Isn't that super-cool?"

"Yeah . . ." Jillian says, clearly not impressed.

Blake flashes me a reassuring smile. "Well, I thought that thing you did, hanging up last year, was very cool. I thought they were like black-and-white photographs."

"Thanks."

"Do you know how to use a camera?" Jillian asks. "Can you take real good photographs?"

I shake my head, and then try to turn my grimace into a smile as she puts the Tootsie Pop back in her mouth.

. . .

The new wing of the DIA is amazing. Maybe this is a weird way to describe it, but walking around, you kind of feel like you're in a cinnamon roll. It's this huge round room with all these circles inside circles, each one featuring a different artist. So as you walk, you feel like you keep entering into totally different spaces, even though they're all connected.

Since this is a private opening, and since Blake's mom basically orchestrated the whole thing, a lot of people working there know him. People keep coming up to us every few minutes, from caterers, to security, to guests saying hello, and asking him about school and basketball. And he always introduces me to everyone, saying, "This is Izzy" or "This is Izzy; she's an artist too." Then he smiles at me in this way that amazingly messes with my center of gravity.

After walking through our fourth or fifth circle, and answering what seems like a trillion questions from Jillian about every single piece of artwork, most of them not even to do with the art, like, "What do you think that guy's favorite animal is?" we finally make our way down to the reception area to drop Jillian off with Blake's mom.

Blake has the same thick wavy blond hair as his mom except without the hairspray and the headset. Mrs. Hangry is speed-walking over to us, which you'd think would be hard to do in heels while carrying a clipboard and talking into a portable device. She stops along the way and says something to one of the guys carrying drinks, and then points him in another direction. She tucks her clipboard under her arm and extends her hands out to give Jillian a hug. Then she greets us all in what appears to be one long breath.

"Thank you, sweetie, you're a lifesaver," to Blake. "You having fun?" to Jillian. "Izzy, so glad you could come! So very nice to meet you!" to me.

"Thanks for having me. Everything's really great."

"Oh good." She turns her head, like a security camera, to different points of the room when she talks. "It's been a little hectic, and facilities has dropped the ball on—" Then she stands up on her tiptoes and waves at somebody over my head and turns to Jillian and says, "Remember Miss S. from your Saturday craft class?"

Jillian half nods, busy annihilating a plate of cheese and cookies.

"Deborah, hellooo . . . This all looooks . . . incredible." Miss S. dance-walks over, gives Mrs. Hangry a hug, and then spots me and Blake.

I greet Miss S., still a little shamefaced over my behavior in class yesterday.

"Lovely to seeeee you here." She gives me a shoulder squeeze and asks, "Are you enjooooying . . . the space? Did you see Roriago yet?" Before I can respond, she turns back to Mrs. Hangry. "Deborah, did you tell Izzy about our liiiiiiittle . . . collaboration?"

"Oh, no." Mrs. Hangry's security-camera head turns to me. "That's right—you're a candidate for Italy, Izzy. We just cooked this all up this week and still have to finalize it with the dance committee—but yes, it's very exciting."

"What is?" I turn to Blake, who just shrugs.

"Of course, now we lose a weeeek . . . but I think you'll agree it's worth it," Miss S. bubbles out.

"We lose a week of . . . what?"

"Itaaaaly deadline. Pushed up. Just a week. For the auction!" Miss S. looks at me as if she's just explained everything.

Mrs. Hangry smiles and says, "It's a fund-raiser initiative now for Darfur. All the students' Italy portfolios are being showcased at the dance, and each artist picks one piece to be auctioned off, and then all the money, of course, goes to—"

"Auctioned off? Oh, like . . . Wait, what?"

"Well, it's more like a silent auction, you know, people write their bids, highest wins and— Marcy!" She raises her hands up to signal a tall girl walking by. "Area B seventeen, lighting fixture, replace— So yes." She smiles at me. "We're going to raise a lot of money, I think. I don't know why we didn't connect these dots sooner, but nonetheless . . ."

"Yes, yeeeees," Miss S. adds. "Of course, the winning bidders won't receive their pieces until after your portfolios are juuuudged . . . but yes, all work must be done and set up by the time of the dance, a week earlier, and you're not obligated to participaaate, of course. They are your pieces to do with what you—"

"Yes, but it's encouraged. I'm sure *all* of the artists will want to do their part to raise funds," Mrs. Hangry adds, sending me an enthusiast wink before Jillian tugs at the end of her coral-colored sweater set. "Okay sweetie, we'll wander soon." She pulls a napkin from her pocket and wipes her daughter's chocolate-cheese mouth while telling me, "I'm friendly with a couple of the curators here too, so if all goes well, some of the patrons will come out to the Dance for Darfur auction as our guests, and hopefully they'll be feeling generous."

Miss S. nods and smiles approvingly.

"Wow, well, that's a great idea, that's . . . it's very exciting." Crap. I'm losing a week. Oh, God. I'm losing a whole week. I smile and wave good-bye to them as Jillian tugs her mom away, and Miss S. wanders back into the crowd with an "Enjoy . . . Enjoooy!"

"Okay!" Blake says, repeatedly punching the fist of one hand into the palm of his other, like he's revving up his energy before a big game or something, and seeming more than thrilled to see his family and Miss S. disappear into the crowd. He leads me out of the reception area, first stopping at one of the sweets tables to replace the plate of cookies Jillian devoured. He walks back to me, plate full, shaking his head.

"Why would somebody come here, with all this art around and stuff, and just sit playing on their phone all day?" I turn to see where he's gesturing and realize that what appears to be a woman dressed in all black sitting on a white bench glued to her hand-held device, is actually Juliana Roriago! Which is what I tell Blake, who crinkles his eyebrows together and stares at her some more.

"Well, is she like taking a break or something?"

"No, that's her piece," I say, remembering now some

of what I read about *Plugged In/Plugged Out*. "She's performing. I mean that's . . . her art."

"Izzy, she's sitting on a bench messing around on her phone."

"No, but look," I say, and point to a large screen in the corner of the room about four or five feet away that's projecting a live stream of what looks like some kind of video game.

"Oh, man . . ."

"Yeah, so I think what she's doing is playing—"

"That's Mad Catter!"

"What?"

"On the screen, it's Mad Catter! It's this game where you take these feral cats and you use them as slingshots, like ammo, to knock stuff down."

"Oh."

"Yeah, it's so stupid, but it's really fun, and so crazy addictive. I've busted through to level twenty-two and now I have to wait for them to release more."

"Wow."

"But why is she playing Mad Cattter?" he says, staring at her game on the screen as we walk over to pick up one of her exhibit pamphlets.

"She's been sitting here playing nonstop for almost seventy-two hours now," I tell him.

"Yeah, yeah." Blake nods, now reading from the pamphlet. "Exploring . . . something . . . participate in the cycle . . . death of spirit to birth of instant gratification . . . pushing the confines of the physical body . . . empty rewards, state of un-being . . . no food." He turns back to Juliana Roriago, who, of course, is still sitting on the bench playing Mad Catter. He shakes his head again. "So this is her . . . art?"

"Yeah, well, I guess it's more like an experience. For us . . . too."

"Huh," Blake says, nodding. "So . . . do you wanna stay here and . . . watch her?"

"Um . . . well, yeah, we can."

"Okay. Yeah, sure." He nods, and strains a smile.

"Or no. I mean, that's okay. If you want to keep walking or—"

"Yeah. Yeah, let's just . . . We'll come back, but . . . come on." He grabs my hand and leads me out of the cinnamon roll.

We head down a long corridor of scary Audubon-meets-Andy-Warhol-type bird paintings. Then we go through a couple of doors, passing through what looks like folk art and jewelry, and finally he leads me into a small room full of Buddhist sculptures and painted Japanese screens and scrolls. We're surrounded by so many butterflies and cranes that it feels like we're outside.

"This isn't open to the public yet, so . . ." He walks over to a bench next to a giant marble Buddha and gestures for me to sit down.

"Yeah, nobody in here," I say, sitting down next to him. Then I feel like I need to do something, so I grab a cookie from the plate he's placed on the floor and take a bite.

We sit there on the bench, eating cookies in silence in marble Buddhaland for what seems like so long, I think we've both reached enlightenment. I finally speak.

"So, did you read that she gets a sip of water every time she beats a level?"

"What?" he says, and then I see that he has his phone out.

"Are you playing Mad Catter right now?" I tease.

"No, sorry," he says, finishing whatever he was typing and closing his phone. "So what did you say?" he asks, rapidly tapping his sneakers on the marble floor, the sound echoing in the room. *Taptaptaptap. Taptaptaptap.* "You said she only gets water when she finishes a level?"

"Yup. Kind of crazy, right?"

"Yeah," he says, and then abruptly shifts positions on the bench, almost knocking over the plate of cookies with his foot.

"A couple years ago," I tell him, "she did this piece called *Femme Prick* where she would prick herself with pins repeatedly. If she drew blood, she'd let herself take a sip of water, and if she didn't draw blood, she'd just make this tally mark on the canvas behind her."

"Man that seems so stupid," he says. "Sorry, I don't mean to . . . I know you like her and you know more about this stuff than me, but—"

"No, I get it. It is pretty ridiculous. I guess . . . I just find her interesting, and watching some of her older stuff, the video footage at least, it's kind of cool and I guess a little . . . satisfying."

"Yeah. Wait, like, what do you mean?" *Taptaptaptaptap.*
Taptaptaptap.

"Well, the control she has. The choices she's making to manipulate her body, to take control, or I guess, to let her body take over. I mean, I'm sure our bodies can withstand a whole lot of stuff that we don't even know about, like going for that long without food and—" I stop, thinking now about my mom's body, and how she's not making choices, how she has no control. "And also . . . some of her pieces have other artists in them too, like people painting for long periods of time or—" I stop again because I feel the corset coming back slightly, tightening around my chest.

"You okay?" Blake asks.

"Yes. I'm sorry, it's . . . I'm actually . . . I'm just feeling a little off today."

"Oh," he says, and I can hear in his tone he's taken offense.

"No, no, it's not you," I explain. "This has all been great. It's . . . it's actually my mom, just things are a little off . . . with my mom right now."

He stops his nervous foot-tapping and turns in toward me. "Like what kind of . . . off?"

"Well, my mom . . . she's sick, or she was sick, she is sick and—"

"So not, like, regular sick?"

"No. More like serious sick."

"Oh, man. I'm sorry, Izzy. I didn't . . . wow. That . . . that sucks."

"Yeah. I mean, she's gonna be fine."

"Oh, good. Well, she looks . . . good."

"Yeah, she is good. But then this week I found out that maybe she's not as good, except she's not telling me she's not, so how am I supposed to know that she's not? It's like she can't fit it into her agenda to tell me she's not feeling well. And I'm the one who's there every day and I see her and see that she's not good right now. Like this morning . . . so. . . so . . . I'm the one she should be telling what's going on. Not Pam. Well, I don't even know what Pam knows, but . . . but I don't understand why people just . . . don't tell me things. Why does everyone have to keep all these secrets from me? What's so wrong with filling me in on what's going on when it's going on? It's like, I'm here. I'm right here. But everyone acts like I'm not, or like I can't handle it or something." I look over toward Blake and realize I'm standing up now and have been pacing back and forth between Buddha sculptures.

"Well," Blake says, getting up and walking over to me, "*I* think you're here." He puts his hands on my waist, underneath my T-shirt a little so his thumbs and fingertips are touching my skin. He pulls me in slowly. "You're definitely here."

His hands slide up and his fingers press into my lower back now. The bottoms of his palms are really warm. My lips are at his throat level. But if I stand on my tiptoes, they'd reach his face. Pulled into him so close, just like after we kissed at my house, everything else goes mute. I rise onto my toes and he meets me halfway. We kiss, and my insides rearrange, but in a good way. Then he pulls me in all the way, and moves his lips to my neck. Holy cow in a handbag, am I necking?! And then I feel cold. Which is weird because you'd think our body heat, being pressed up against each other, would keep me warm. But I'm cold. My back is cold. And then I realize that he's lifted up the back of my shirt and is trying to unhook my bra!

Okay, so you know how if something spills near you, you just kind of jump back, like on reflex, to move out of the line of fire? Well, that's what I do when I feel Blake's hand underneath the back of my bra. I jump back fast and say, "Hey! No, no, no."

Hey! No, no, no? Did I just say that? Did I just say "Hey! No, no, no," to Blake Hangry, like he's a naughty little kid?

"Oh my God. I'm so sorry," he says, backing up and then pacing toward the bench. And then he lets out this really loud groan. It sounds like the groan Jenna's dad and his friends make when they're watching the football team they bet all their money on do something stupid.

"I'm sorry," I say, walking over to him. "It's just that . . . I didn't want someone to come in, and we're kind of in the middle of a—"

"No, I'm sorry," he says. "Sorry, sorry, sorry." He repeats it, more like he's trying to get rid of a verbal tick than apologize. "Come on." He picks up the plate of cookies. "I'll take you home."

"Oh. Okay."

I start to follow him out and then stop because *he's* stopped and is checking his phone.

"My mom," he says more to himself than to me without looking up. "Some stupid gift shop crisis and she needs me to—"

"Oh yeah, no, go. I'll stay here. I mean, I'll look around. Maybe I'll go back and look at the new wing some more or . . . watch Roriago or . . . But yeah, I'm fine on my own so . . ." I stop talking, realizing that Blake is still not making eye contact. He's just nodding and looking down at his right foot, which is tapping rapidly on the floor again.

"Okay, cool, I'll find you later," he mumbles as he bolts past me. It's like he can't get away from me fast enough.

Slowly I make my way back to the new wing. I'm trying not to wallow, but I can't help thinking that you have to be one ginormous failure at doing things with guys to literally send them running back to their mothers.

The next forty-five minutes I spend sitting on a really artsy-looking uncomfortable chair across from Juliana Roriago, watching her play Mad Catter, and wishing I could ask her if she's ever mortifyingly rejected a guy while he was trying to unhook her bra in the middle of a museum. Of course she wouldn't answer me anyway, because she metaphorically wouldn't be able to hear me, being so "plugged in." Still, it would be nice if she'd break her artistic fourth wall for long enough to shout across to me, "Yes! Happens to me all the time, Izzy! Hang in there, girl!"

• • •

So far, the drive back from the DIA is remarkably quieter than the way there. It's so silent, I'm actually wishing Jillian and her germy Tootsie Pop were still with us. I guess Blake doesn't really have time to talk to me, being so glued to his phone. At every red light, or any time the car is stopped or going slow enough for him to manage, he's reading or sending something on his phone. Who is he texting so much anyway?

When we pull into my driveway, I realize that fifty whole minutes of awkward car time have passed with only four lousy sentences exchanged between us:

Thanks for today. I really loved the new wing.

and

Good, yeah. No prob.

Then, to my horror, I find myself squeezing my mouth into what I hope looks like a smile and cueing that exchange again as I get out of the car.

Thanks for today. I really loved the new wing.

Good, yeah. No prob.

Unghhh.

I don't even watch Blake pull out of the driveway. I just drag myself back into the house. I bolt the front door closed. Then my phone vibrates in my pocket, and I let out a pleased sigh. Maybe Blake's just more comfortable communicating digitally.

See you soon!!

But it's not Blake. It's Meredith.

I drop my weight back against the front door, and then

suddenly straighten up. Meredith is on her way over. Meredith is on her way over, to fake sleep over, so we can sneak out and go to—oh God—Cara's sister's Becky's boyfriend Phil's cousin's frat party.

CHAPTER 14

I'm invisible.

I wasn't aware until tonight how many combinations of boots, snow boots, and jeans exist. I think Meredith's modeled just about all of them for me by now.

I'm slumped against my headboard, feeling the day in every muscle of my body. I check my phone again, hoping Jenna's gotten back to me. Nope. I've already called her twice. I even asked her if she wanted to come over and just hang out, that I'd ditch going to the party, which I'm thinking I might do anyway.

Jenna's not speaking to me, and my mom's lying to me. Also, it's pretty clear that my plans for a dance double date, or any date at all, are not happening.

Oh God. Blake is going to be at that party tonight. What if it's even more awkward than this afternoon?

"Whatcha think?" Meredith models her latest combination.

"Looks great." I smile and sit up, pretending to fuss with my own appearance in the dresser mirror, making a show of moving the bulk of my hair from one shoulder to the other.

"Do you think your mom will stay asleep?" Meredith asks, frowning at her reflection and then wiggling out of yet another pair of jeans.

"Yeah, she's probably out for the night," I say, moving my hair back to the left.

Mom was sleeping when I got home. Sleeping. At six p.m. When I went to check in on her and tell her Meredith was here, she just sleep-mumbled something about Allissa being out for the night and that there was food in the fridge and have Jenna help herself. I decided it was best, even in her foggy state, not to correct her.

"Wow, good. So, I don't think it's supposed to snow tonight," Meredith adds, grabbing various things from her overnight bag and throwing them into her purse.

"Yeah, that's what I heard too."

Meredith shifts her weight between a high-heeled boot and a ballet slipper. I make an executive decision to split my hair equally on each shoulder. Okay, I should just tell Meredith now. *Sorry Meredith, but I've decided not to go out to this party after all. I don't really want to go without Jenna, and I really don't want to run into Blake. See, I scolded him like a naughty child today when he tried to unhook my bra. So . . . yeah.*

"Boots or flats?" she asks me.

"Um . . . boots." But maybe I *should* go. Maybe it'll actually be fun. Maybe I'm just overreacting and it'll be fine. Great, even. Maybe Blake will apologize. Or maybe I'll apologize first. Or, maybe we'll both apologize at the same time, and then we'll laugh about it. Plus, Mom's already asleep, and it's not like she's going to wake up and have no idea where I am if she checks on me. I left her a note in the kitchen. Which I think, considering her total lack of information-sharing lately, is pretty generous.

"So Karin, Becca's friend, is coming back to Broomington after, and she's the one who's gonna take you home," Meredith informs me, reading off a message from her phone as if it's top secret information she just received from the Pentagon.

"Oh. Okay." Wait, no. No, maybe I shouldn't go. I don't want Mom to worry, especially if she's already not feeling well. Plus, what if after we share a good laugh, Blake just wants to continue right where we left off at the museum? Do I want him to? Yes. Right? Yes. Sure, I was uptight today, but that's because we were smack in the middle of a very public museum with his mom and Miss S. and his sister and all kinds of *strangers* just roaming around. But a public space, a museum space, is different than a party atmosphere. I'm sure I'll be much more relaxed at a party. I hope.

What is wrong with me? I fantasized about that very moment, about Blake taking me to some private, romantic museum spot and holding me close and kissing me. And then it happened. It all happened, and I ruined it.

I watch as Meredith applies a really thick black line to the top of her eyelids. I personally think it looks kind of strange. But then again, what do I know? The last time I tried to put on eye makeup was for my cousin Michelle's wedding and I had to wash it all off before the ceremony even began because I looked—according to Allissa and the rest of our cousins—like a trampy raccoon.

No. I'm not going to go. I'll tell Meredith right now that I'm not going.

"Oh, I almost forgot!" Meredith unzips her overnight bag, rummages around, and pulls out a small plastic bag, which she hands to me.

My eyebrows raise as I take the bag. I peer inside and pull out one of those scoop-necks shirts, like the one Meredith was wearing on Thursday.

"Is this for me?"

"Yeah, I just wanted to say thank you for covering for me. And that . . . I'm glad you decided to come out with us tonight, Izzy."

I unfold the shirt slowly and hold it against me.

"It's gonna look so good! You're wearing it tonight!"

To my surprise I find myself nodding and saying "Okay, thanks."

"And I know you're a little cleavage conscious," she adds, "but I swear it'll look great. And you could pair it with a cute little scarf, if you wanted to, or . . . go ahead, try it on!"

I swap out the button-down I'm wearing for my new scoop-neck and stand in front of the mirror.

"I told you!" Meredith says, looking at me and grinning.

Okay, even though I know this shirt would make Mom's suggestive-detector eyeballs pop right out of her head, I have to admit, it does looks pretty good on me.

"Hey, can I swipe some of this?" Meredith asks.

"Sure." I grimace as she picks up the bottle of raspberry hand lotion my mom got me last week that I think smells like dead flowers soaking in children's cough syrup. "Actually, you can have that if you want."

"Oooh, thanks!"

We make our way down the hall and tiptoe downstairs to the kitchen. Meredith throws her new lotion in her purse, looks at her watch, and then lets out a small yelp.

"Sorry," she whispers, pursing her freshly glossed lips, "but what is that?"

I follow her repulsed gaze to our kitchen table and pick up the ceramic animal skull serving dish.

"It's my mom's," I explain. "One of her clients makes them."

"Oh." Meredith eyes it, then takes a seat at the table, turning her back to the serving dish.

"Mrs. Burk," I whisper-explain, "she's redoing her house, and her husband hunts, and he wants her to use antlers and skulls for decoration," I ramble nervously. "Mom's trying to convince her that their current color scheme doesn't really go with dead things."

Meredith smiles at me indulgently, and I finally shut up.

When we get Cara's text at last, I gesture for Meredith to go out our back entrance. I've mastered the art of closing the sliding back door in silence after years of studying Allissa. I watch as Meredith cautiously cuts across our crusty snow-covered lawn in her high-heeled boots. We make our way to the street, but I don't see any sign of Cara. In fact, the street's completely empty of cars except for a giant conversion van parked across the way.

"That's them!" Meredith rushes toward the van.

"What's up guys, welcome to *mi casa*!" I walk into the van and see Ryan Paulson at the wheel.

"This is a boat." Meredith laughs and walks to the very back to join Cara.

"I know, totally a boat." Cara nods, and waves to me.

The van is huge, with big leather seats and interior lights framing each window like some sort of auto-show Christmas.

"All the seats come out too," Ryan informs us through a huge dimpled grin. "We fit a whole sectional and a flat-screen in here once."

Ryan's dad owns "Just a Man and His Van" moving company. Which technically is fleets of men and their different-sized vans, but whatever.

"Pretty cool," I tell Ryan, sinking into one of the heated leather seats.

"So where's Jenna?" Ryan asks me, leaning forward to adjust his rearview mirror. "Is she not coming out?"

I shake my head.

"Oh . . . okay. Just thought she'd like to see the van and all since I told her we could use it for set load-out."

I nod, and watch as he moves his seat forward as far as it can go, thinking that maybe Ryan's not quite tall enough yet to be a conversion van driver.

"Okay, here we gooooooo!" Ryan shouts out, sounding like a little boy just before an airplane's about to take off, and then in a calmer tone adds, "I've driven this like once before, no worries."

It's really loud at Cara's sister Becca's boyfriend Phil's cousin's frat house. So loud, in fact, that you can't really talk. Which is fine, because I don't really have anyone trying to talk to me. I'm just standing here by myself under a giant poster of dogs smoking cigars, holding a foamy beer in a dirty plastic cup that I have no intention of drinking, and watching people dance. Well, I'm not totally by myself. It's impossible to be by yourself in a living room crammed with people. But Meredith and Cara are gone, off in search of a bathroom, or at least I think that's what they said. I should have gone with them, but by the time I decided to follow, they were already lost in the sweaty, beer-reeking crowd.

My head is suddenly cold. Why is my head cold? Why does my head feel cold and wet? Oh, probably because the tall guy standing next to me is casually using my head as his own personal coaster. Really? I duck out from under the beer and push my way through the crowd until I reach a giant staircase.

"Bathroom?" I ask the girl lean-dancing against the banister.

She points upstairs.

As I'm leaving the bathroom, sore from squatting and

really wishing I'd remembered my hand sanitizer, I see Meredith charging toward me.

"Izzy!" she screams, and throws her arms around me like I've been lost at sea.

"Hi," I say, laughing.

"Oh my God, this party sucks, why do these things always suck? And I lost Cara. Cara!" she screeches down the hall, and then starts opening bedroom doors. "Cara! Cara!"

"Stop," I say, laughing harder now. "She's not in one of those roo—" And then we see Cara, in one of those rooms. She's just sitting on a lone mattress, making a dent in a bag of pretzels.

"What are you doing?" Meredith joins her, giggling.

"I'm bored. Totally bored," Cara says, leaning back on the mattress, which is basically the only "furniture" in the room except for a mini fridge and an alarm clock. I join them on the floor, sitting as close as I can to the edge of the mattress, trying not to think about the stale-beer-dirty-socks-guacamole smell.

"Please tell me you did not find those in here?" Meredith's smoky-lined eyes widen.

"No, kitchen pantry, totally stole them from the kitchen pantry."

"Ladies! Whatcha doing?" Nate strolls into the room and leans against the dirty white wall, Jacob following after him.

"Izzy," Nate talk-laughs at me, eyeing my new shirt. "Bow-chicka-bow-bow!"

Jacob cracks up as if that's the funniest thing he's ever heard and then they both sing together, "Bow-chicka-bow-bow! Chicka-chicka-chicka! Bow-chicka-bow-bow!" and start laughing all over themselves again.

Blake walks in then and leans against the door. "You guys are so loud, what are you—" He stops dead when he sees us. Or sees *me*.

"Hey. Long time no see," I say, in this terrible forced, cheery voice.

Blake doesn't say anything back.

"What's up?" I say again, this time with a little less enthusiasm.

But Blake just stares at me with this expression on his face that I'm pretty sure is identical to the stuffed deer my mom wants removed from Mrs. Burk's living room.

"Oooh," Nate says, pointing at me and then back at Blake. "You guys are so cute. Why don't you two pose together and let me take your picture?" Which for some reason makes him and Jacob burst out laughing.

"Shut up." Blake glares at them and then looks back in my direction, but in this way where he's looking everywhere at once, and never directly at me. It's just like at the museum, but worse now because there are witnesses.

"I need some air and you guys aren't improving the smell in here." Meredith pops up off the mattress. Soon I'm pulled to my feet, feeling like I need something to punch and something to hug at the same time. I make my way past Blake fast, keeping my eyes straight ahead, like he's an accident by the side of the road that I'm afraid I won't be able to stop staring at once I start.

Finally we're outside. I take a deep breath of cold air.

"Mr. Greek?" Cara shrugs at us.

"Yes!" Meredith nods.

"Who?" I ask.

"So much better than pretzels." Meredith laughs, shoving a forkful of feta-covered salad into her mouth.

"Totally." Cara nods, mouth full of a Coney dog.

I smile, leaning forward in the booth at Mr. Greek's, not realizing how much I needed this grilled cheese till now.

"This is always my favorite part of the night." Meredith gleefully holds up her Greek-salad-speared fork.

"Me too, totally." Cara nods again.

"I think we lasted longer at this one than some of the others."

"Eh," Cara says, squirting some more mustard onto her hot dog.

"You guys always end up here?" I ask.

"Yeah"—Meredith nods—"'cause the parties always end up lame."

"Yeah, Becca's lame, totally."

"Your sister's not lame. She just gets so drunk, she doesn't know how lame the parties are."

"You guys never drink at these things?" I ask.

"Well . . ." Meredith fishes an olive out of her salad and

drops it onto her napkin. "I just don't want to end up in a *Babes Gone Bananas* video or something."

"Me too!" I say, and I guess a little too loudly, because it makes Meredith laugh.

"So Izzy," she says after a while, her mouth straightening. "What was that with Blake earlier?"

"Oh. What do you mean?" I'm trying to look casual as if I don't already have Blake's deer-in-headlights face burned into my mental snapshot library.

"What do you mean, what do I mean?" she teases, and then stops, seeing my face, which has betrayed me once again. "Wait, what did he do?" she asks, her thickly lined lids dropping low over her eyes.

"Nothing," I say quickly. "It's more . . . something I did, I guess."

"No, it was probably him, totally all him," Cara says, nodding at me seriously with the beginnings of a chili beard on her chin.

I sigh and then tell them about the DIA, and his sister, and the Buddha room, and the bra fumbling, and me screaming, "Hey no, no, no," and our beyond-awkward ride home.

"Oh Izz Friz," Meredith breathes, which I haven't heard her call me in years, "that's so awful."

"Yeah," I sigh, putting down my grilled cheese.

"You know, he was probably just embarrassed tonight because he tried to get some and he failed. Guys are totally insecure, especially when it comes to bras and stuff."

"Huh," I say, mulling that over.

"All those guys are such douches, total douches," Cara adds.

I scrunch up my face.

"Yeah, Nate especially. I mean, like you don't already know." Meredith rips off a piece of pita bread from our pile.

"Like I don't already know what?"

She looks over at me. "It's okay, Izzy, you don't have to protect her." Meredith nods.

"Yup, yeah, totally, we know," Cara adds.

"I'm not protecting . . . I don't know what you're talking about."

"Okay." Meredith nods at me like I'm a toddler who's successfully Velcro'd her own shoes. "I get it. I won't bring it up again, say no more. It's just, ugh, Nate is just like Jacob. A douche with a capital *D*. Stupid basketball and their stupid initiation crap," she says, her face wrinkling up.

"Oh, you mean like the hazing?" I ask.

"Well, yeah, and their tasks."

"Oh . . . right. Wait, like the underwear?"

"What? No, like tasks. Like Nate's task, to get pictures of me doing you-know-what to him in the girls' bathroom? Not like I would even go into the bathroom with him in the first place. And Nate was so pissed I wouldn't do it. It was kinda funny. Well, until he started telling everyone I *did* do it, and this whole story about how Miss Larper caught us . . . doing that." Meredith pauses, putting down her fork and grinding her teeth on her lower lip.

"Right . . ." I nod, taking this in.

"And people actually believed him! That was the worst part, you know?"

"Yeah," I say.

"Like my mom, I know she knows the truth now, but I still feel like things are weird with us."

"Wow, I'm . . . I'm so sorry, Meredith."

"Yeah, well." Meredith just shrugs and gives me a half smile. "Anyway, point is that Jenna and I, we know first-hand about capital *D* douches."

"What? Oh . . . so, you do know about what happened over the summer? I mean with Jenna's—"

"Ugh, it was awful. And I'm sure she's painted me in a terrible light, but you know it really wasn't my fault. Even though, yes, I still feel somewhat responsible."

"*You* feel responsible?"

"Wasn't your fault, totally not," Cara says.

"Well, I mean, I was the one who kind of set them up, and I thought he liked her, we all did, I think he did, but you know, he screwed up."

"Wait," I say, trying to put it all together, realizing now that Meredith knew Jenna's cousin Amy, and was the one who set her up with the guy in the basement in the first place. "But how do you even know—"

I'm interrupted by my phone buzzing in my coat pocket. I see Allissa's name flashing across the screen. And then my stomach drops down to my shoes. I have five missed calls from my mom. I'm breathing hard, but trying to look calm and not freak out as I listen to my most recent voicemail. At first I can't really understand Allissa because her voice is cutting in and out. Finally I make out what she's saying.

Text! Address! Now! Mom! Flipping! Out! I'm! On! Way! You're! So! Dead!

CHAPTER 15

I'm a bad daughter.

Allissa's driving is even more erratic late at night and when she's angry. I grip the arm rest as she swerves. I haven't said a word since I got in the car, mainly because the first thing she said after I got in was "Don't say a word." But I need to feel things out.

"Thanks for coming to get me. I'm sorry you had to," I start.

"Oh, it's fine," Allissa says with a feigned flippancy. "I was just hanging out with some friends, trying to enjoy *my* weekend, when I get a frantic call from Mom, who's basically about to call *America's Most Wanted*."

"Oh God, so she was mad?"

"Well . . . she was worried. *Now* I'm sure she's mad." Then her voice starts rising, and stays pretty much in that high octave range. "Ugh, first this morning and now this. God, Izzy."

"This morning?" I close my eyes and we drift closer and closer to the highway's guardrail.

"Two hundred and sixty dollars!" she blurts out at dog-whistle pitch.

"Oooh." I drop my head down, and then start shimmying off my coat in the one-hundred-and-five-degree car.

"I got a new charge on my gas credit card, which Mom gave me for *gas*. It's not just like free money for you!"

"I'm sorry. I know. I meant to tell you. I have some of the cash, but . . ."

"And you didn't even get anything good! Sunglasses? Who needs seven pairs of sunglasses? And two art-something neti pots? What the freak is a neti pot?"

"It's for sinus irrigation."

"Oooh, right." She nods and laughs, but in that way where you definitely don't find something funny. "Sinus irrigation."

"It's important to irrigate your sinus cavities."

Allissa flashes me a death stare.

"It's just, Mom's been so congested and coughing. And I wanted to try it too, for myself, but you can't share these things. Do you know how it works? It literally goes all the way up your—"

"No! There's seriously something wrong with you. You need serious therapy. You're always doing this, you're always buying this crap and then I have to cover for you. It's too much this time." She catapults into the driveway. "I'm showing Mom the bill, and then you can explain to her why you bought overpriced glasses and two ugly clay pots that cost more than my nicest pair of shoes!"

I nod, feeling my nose tighten like it does just before I cry.

Allissa miraculously speeds into her space in the garage

without a scrape, and then turns to me and sighs.

"Izzy, just . . . the less you say in there, the better, okay? Just nod a lot and then say sorry, okay?"

I nod at Allissa and then say, "Sorry."

She rolls her eyes and laughs a little. "Good job." And then before getting out of the car, she turns back and gives me a once-over, seeming surprised by her own words when she says, "I like that top."

Mom is sitting at the kitchen table when we walk in. She gets up fast, the pajama pants she's swimming in almost falling down to the floor.

"You're safe!" She runs to me and gives me a huge hug, which I wasn't expecting at all. But then, as soon as she pulls away, her whole body goes stiff and straight, and I know she's morphing into Grandma Iris. Whenever Mom's angry, I mean really angry, she starts talking and acting just like her mother. I could never tell her. But it's pretty freaky.

Now she starts pacing around the kitchen, talking in that ice-cold monotone with the occasional dog-whistle squeak and asking me how I could do this to her, telling me how scared she was, and how angry she is, all the while waving her really bony arms around a lot. Then she stops and leans against the counter to catch her breath and cough. She coughs. And coughs, and coughs, and coughs.

"I knew it. I knew Meredith was still troubled." *Troubled* is Mom's euphemism for "girls who have oral sex on school property."

"No, Mom, she's not," I burst out, forgetting Allissa's

"nod and apologize" advice. "You don't understand. She's fine."

"Fine? Really, well—" And then Mom stops and blinks at me, as if she's willing the image in front of her to change. Her regular voice returns for a moment. "Where did you get that *nafka* top? That is not appropriate for you at all. Did you go out in that?"

"Yes, but it's fine. The top is fine. I don't look—"

"You look inappropriate and—"

"And Meredith is fine. And I'm sorry I went out without asking you, but I left you a no—"

"Did you know that after the whole Meredith incident, Stacy Brightwell lost three clients?" And the Grandma Iris voice is back.

"What? No, Mom, listen—"

"Three! I know because two of them came to me, because nobody wants to hire a woman who can't control her own children; who can't set an example. It's about [cough] trust, and respect, and how [cough] is somebody going to trust me to [cough] reconstruct their home environment if they don't think I can raise children who respect their parents [cough, cough] and themselves?"

I pour Mom a glass of water. She grabs it from me and takes a tiny sip.

"This isn't a large town, girls, so what you do, it doesn't just get lost in the shuffle. It matters [cough] and I'm just so . . . very . . . you're just making things harder than they have to be for me right now, Izzy." She takes another baby

sip of water, moving her fingernails up and down her forehead.

"I'm sorry, I'm sorry." I nod. And I just keep repeating
that, and nodding, feeling smaller and smaller every time I
do.

Mom shakes her head at me and sighs. "I'm heading up."

"Are we still going tomorrow?" Allissa asks quickly and
quietly.

"Oh. Yes." Mom turns back and gives me a serious Iris
look. "Don't think you're getting out of girls' day, and your
haircut. We are going to the mall. We're cutting your hair.
End of story." She brushes past me, pulling up her pajama
pants and coughing.

"Guess she didn't give you a chance to show her your gas
bill," I mumble at Allissa.

"She'll calm down once we get her inside a mall," Allissa
whispers. She gives my shoulder an encouraging squeeze
and follows Mom upstairs.

I lean back against the kitchen chair to sit down, almost
crushing Leroy, who's managed to sleep-balance himself
across it, his belly taking up the whole seat and his arms and
legs dangling off to either side. I scoop him up and take us to
the living room, where I collapse on the cushions, and close
my eyes. Leroy pushes his paws into my thigh and purrs
in my ear while I cry.

CHAPTER 16

I'm finally feeling inspired.

Please don't drop it. Please don't drop it. I repeat this to myself as I attempt to maneuver my now massive map sculpture onto its other side.

I only have about twenty minutes left in the studio before I should head back to study hall to avoid Miss Larper noticing I'm gone. I wish I had longer—who knew Mom's dance decor would be such a great muse?

"Need some help?"

I slowly crane my neck around, both hands clutching the sculpture, and see Ina walking through the studio door.

"Yes, please!" I say, and soon she gently takes hold and helps me flip it around to its unfinished side.

"Thanks," I sigh, smiling. I'm grateful to see Ina smiling back and that the color has fully returned to her face since Friday's disaster.

"What are you doing here now?" I call out to her as she disappears behind her project rack.

"I need to snap some quick pictures so I can work tonight from home."

"Oh. Pictures of . . ."

"New version of the sculpture," she calls back to me.

"Oh," I say again, then pause and look over in her direction again. "Ina, I'm still . . . I just want you to know that I'm still really sorry about what happened last week."

"Yeah." I hear her sigh. "Thanks. I know it wasn't fully your fault. Well, anyway, it was very unfortunate. Yes."

"Yeah." What else can I say? I join her at her table to get a good look at this new sculpture, my eyes widening. "Wow. You kept it! You kept it? How did you . . .? That is very cool."

"Yes, I fished through and saved most of my pieces. I spent the weekend completely reinventing."

"Wow." I walk around it to get the full effect. The sculpture's still really intricate, but it almost looks animated now, like you're watching it break in slow motion. "You know, I actually . . . I think I like this version even better," I say, and then back out of her way as she starts to snap pictures at different angles.

"I'm adding some media now of its different stages so people can experience the journey of it. Well, that is my hope, at least."

"That'll be awesome." I look back at my map, feeling inspired. Ina looks over at it too.

"Your whole portfolio, is it a Darfur theme or just this piece?"

"Oh. Well, no, I think this is just going to be for the dance decoration. It's not—" But I cut myself off. Could this be part of my Italy portfolio? The more work I do on it, the more I like it. I'd have to step up my technique a little, but it might work. I look back at Ina. "Well . . . I'm not sure about this one yet, but . . . yeah, this is my only Darfur-themed piece."

We work quietly side by side at our tables for a couple minutes, me mixing paint for the last area of what might be a portfolio-worthy sculpture, and Ina finishing up her photo shoot. A little while later, as she's on her way out the door, she stops and says, in her closed-mouth way, "Oh and Izzy, your hair looks nice, very sleek now. I like."

"Thanks," I say as my phone starts beeping in my bag.

It's a text from Mom.

Remember to call me before AND after rehearsal. Come right home after!

I deflate a little. Not even a "thanks for breakfast" or a "sweetie" or anything. Mom was still sleeping by the time I got up this morning. She's usually showered, dressed, and made up by then, but I decided not to wake her and instead left a warm cinnamon roll and some eggs in the oven with a Post-it on the oven door: *Breakfast! :) Sorry again about this weekend. Love you, Izzy.*

Not that I thought some lousy eggs and a note would smooth things over, but . . . I don't know.

Allissa was kind of right about Mom's mood, though—it did improve once we got her inside a mall on Sunday. Sort of. She was like a mom Jekyll and Hyde. One moment smiling and laughing with Allissa and the next completely Grandma Iris–ing out on me.

I spent most of the time sitting in a swizzle chair getting attacked by a razor-blade-wielding man in a hot-pink turtleneck sweater who kept saying, "Texturizing layers, giving her the texturizing layers."

I actually don't hate my new haircut. It's not mullet-like or poodle-like, which are two of my biggest haircutting fears. Mom certainly loved turtleneck man's work too. In fact, that was the one time she smiled at me all day—when I answered "I like it" after she asked what I thought of my new hair.

I read Mom's text again and sigh. She's right to be angry. Sneaking out to go to a lame party, such an idiotic move. I check my new messages one last time—no new texts or calls from Blake since Saturday. Either he's not in school today or he's doing a really great job avoiding me. Jenna's not doing so great a job since we practically collided with each other on my way to Spanish this morning. She bolted off fast as soon as I was tackled by Meredith, though, gushing apologies about getting me in trouble and then ogling my new haircut for five minutes.

I put my phone back in my bag and then hear someone coughing. I whip around to see Marcus standing at the door. It's great to see him until I remember that no, maybe it's not.

"Hey, can I . . . can I come in?"

"Yeah, come in. It's not my own private studio or anything."

"No I know, I just didn't want to interrupt or . . ."

"No, it's fine, come in," I repeat.

He walks over to my table and then sets down the paper shopping bag he's carrying with a thud.

I lean forward to peer inside.

"Some of my dad's medical journals," he explains. "Thought you'd like them."

"Oh." I nod. "Thanks."

"So listen," he starts, looking down at the floor, and then across the room at the plaster-dust-covered window. "I'm sure you're still upset about what I said the other day when I implied that you might be . . . focused on being sick because of your mom. You know . . . because of your mom . . . being—"

"I don't really want to talk about it," I say, feeling annoyed already, and then more annoyed because I don't *want to* feel that way around Marcus.

"No, I know, it's just that sometimes when people think they're sick, or want to be sick if somebody they love is—"

"I don't want to be sick."

"No, no, of course not."

"You think I want to be sick?" Now I'm looking at him.

"No, sorry . . . I just . . . I just want to apologize and here I am sticking my foot further into my mouth . . . again. No, I just wanted to say that . . ." He sighs and leans back against a stool. "I'm sorry about Friday, about making fun of those glasses."

"Oh. Well, thank you. I . . . I probably overreacted any-way, so . . ."

"No, no you were right. It *is* stupid not to be open-minded and I tend to not be . . . about some things, but"—he's pacing around the table now—"anyway, it was insensitive of me to— And I just didn't mean to make you feel bad . . ." He stops walking around the table and turns to finally look at me. "Oh wow, that looks. . . Izzy, that looks really good." He comes closer so that I get a whiff of his fresh-soap-boy smell.

"Thanks. I'm not done yet but, yeah, I think it's getting there, and—"

"No, I meant . . . your hair. You got it cut? It looks . . . it looks really good."

"Oh." I clutch at my new layers. "Thanks."

"But yeah . . . no, the sculpture looks really awesome too. You've . . . um, changed it?" Now he's smiling. And it's not his usual nervous smile or the way he smiles when he laughs, but like this nice, face-perfectly-still, slow-growing smile that makes him look kind of older, like handsome.

"Yeah." I nod, then Marcus points to a section of the map and just says, "So . . . green."

"What?"

"Green . . . um, it's . . . a good color." He gestures to that part of the map again.

"Oh. I guess so, yeah."

"No, I mean, it's supposedly one of the most cleansing colors."

I look at the sculpture, and then back at him, getting it. "Yeah, I know."

"Yeah, green is supposed to be good for the pituitary glands and it's supposed to aid in healing infections and rebuilding cells. In fact, there was study in 1978 at this hospital in Georgia and—"

"Okay"—I laugh—"apology accepted."

"Good," he says, still smiling. "Now on to the good news. How would you like to retake your bio quiz?"

"Unghh, yeah right. And what would be the point?"

"I could help you study, for real this time. You need to get your grade up to, what? At least a B, right?"

"Yeah to be eligible for Italy, but Mr. Bayer's not just going to let me—"

"No, see, I was actually talking to him this morning about some of the students who aren't doing so well."

"Oh. And . . . ?"

"I mean, obviously I can't just give you special treatment, but I made a case for some others too who might just need some more . . . attention and—"

"Did you get Bayer to waive that grade? Can I really retake it?"

"Well, he usually only allows study makeups or extra credit for anything below a C minus"—Marcus's smile is getting wider and wider as he talks—"but I got him to include you too so, yes, you can retake it."

"That's great, thank you!" I reach out, giving Marcus a hug, which I don't even realize I'm doing until my arms are already around his neck.

"You're welcome," he breathes out, right into my ear, and I smell that fancy soap again.

"Wait!" he says as I start to pull back. "I think you're stuck."

"What? Oh, sorry!" Some of my newly texturized hair is caught in that sliver of a space where the stems of his glasses meet the frames. "Should I um . . ." I shift a little to the left and feel my hair pull on my scalp. "Ow!"

"Wait, wait, maybe if we, ah . . ." Marcus gingerly takes off his glasses and leans away, just a little bit, though, since we're still connected.

"I don't want to just pull it," he says.

"Yes, no please, don't ruin my perfect hair." I grimace-laugh. Marcus cracks a small smile.

"There!" I say, grabbing the strands near the end and yanking them free. Then I step back a little, realizing that although we were no longer attached, I was still standing close.

"So . . ." Marcus picks out the severed strands and puts his glasses back on. "Anyway, we can find a time to study soon if you . . ." And then he's looking over my head at the door. "Hangry," Marcus says, and the tone of his voice changes to its *hello, good-bye, nice to see you* mode.

"Oh," Blake says, looking at Marcus now. "Sorry, did I interrupt something?"

"No!" we both kind of say at the same time.

"I was just leaving." Marcus nods at me, looks at Blake, and then slowly makes his way to the door.

"So hey." Blake walks over to my table and stands, shifting his weight from one sneaker to the other, not saying anything else.

"Hey. So you're talking to me now? I exist?" I ask, surprised at my sudden nerve.

"No. I mean yeah. Crap." He drops his backpack on the table. "Um . . . listen . . . Izzy . . . Izzy . . ." He repeats my name like it's his word at the spelling bee.

"Yes?"

"I know . . . I should have called or something after the museum, and then I was totally thrown when I saw you at the party. I mean I knew I would see you. I just . . . I don't know what I was thinking—it was like I was brain dead or something. And I . . . well . . . anyway I [mumble, mumble, mumble]," he says, his voice lowering so far, I can't make out anything.

"What?"

"I got you something," he says a little louder, quickly reaching into his backpack to pull out a book, which he sets on the table like he's serving me dinner.

I look down and see *Roriago Revealed*.

"They sell them in the gift shop. I tried to get it signed, but she wouldn't . . . stop playing Mad Catter, so . . . There's pictures in it too," he adds.

I glance up at his face. "Wow, thanks," I say, taking the book and flipping through it. And then Blake asks if we can go somewhere to talk that's not right in the middle of the studio.

"Where?" I ask as I start to put away my supplies.

"Follow me," he says.

I carefully, and somewhat reluctantly, cover up my map and follow him out of the studio.

CHAPTER 17

I shouldn't have opened my mouth.

I should be back at the library right now. But I'm not. I'm not anywhere near the library. I'm all the way across the school in the Rap Room. The Rap Room, the place where kids are supposed to go to "rap out their problems" with our guidance counselor, Mr. Seel. But Mr. Seel is out for the afternoon. Instead I'm here. With Blake. Alone.

We're sitting on the Rap Room futon surrounded by plush pillows. There are posters on the badly painted orange walls with pictures of kids hanging out and doing what all teenagers do: picking up litter at state parks, ladling soup into bowls at homeless shelters, volunteering at nursing homes. There's also one of those charts, where you're supposed to indicate how you feel based on how sad or happy the cartoon faces look. They're numbered from ten down. Number ten is a smiley face with stars for eyes and number one is a frowny face with moons for eyes and lots of tears.

"This place is supposed to be locked when Mr. Seel is out, but it's always open," Blake is telling me, picking up one of the pillows and tossing it quickly back and forth in his hands.

"Cool . . ." I'm trying not to lean too far back on the couch so my head won't touch the pillows, which probably haven't been washed since 1982. I read this article once about a really deadly fungus—the kind that lives in dirty pillows—called Asparagus Fume or something, I forget the exact name, but it killed all these people. Okay, the people the fungus killed were already suffering from leukemia, but I don't want to take any chances.

"So listen, I'm . . . I want to just say . . ." Blake stands up and starts to circle the floor, erratically picking up Rap Room objects, carrying them with him as he circles, and then randomly putting them down again. ". . . I'm sorry about the way the day ended on Saturday. I totally . . . I feel like, I made you uncomfortable. And . . . you know, I guess I was pissed at myself, just for being . . . because I like you. I like you a lot. That's the thing. I do. So . . . that's why this whole thing just totally sucks, you know?"

"Wait—what whole thing? You mean—"

"No I meant . . . me just messing it all up." He falls back onto the couch, not looking at me.

"You didn't mess it all up."

"I didn't?" he asks.

"No." I turn toward him, putting my hand on his arm, stopping him from compulsively zipping the futon cover open and closed. "I mean, I was a little uncomfortable, yeah, but not because of . . . well, not because of you. Just because it was so, you know, public. You didn't mess it all up."

"Really?"

"Yeah," I say.

"And I'm sorry about the party. I didn't mean to ignore you. And I feel so crappy about that. I really should have just . . . spoke!"

"Yeah, that would have been a natural thing to do." I smile.

"Okay so . . . good," he says, finally smiling a little, and then he moves the pillow between us over to the other side of the couch. Which I guess is good, because that looked like the dirtiest of the bunch. But I don't have the chance to think about pillow fungus for much longer because Blake and I are kissing now. It's that nice, soft, organ-annihilating kissing that make my insides get slushy. Then Blake gently pulls my face into his, deepening the kiss, both his hands on the back of my neck. His lips taste like peppermint and French toast. Which is a surprisingly amazing combination.

Finally, he pulls away a little, and I can see his chest moving up and down, like he's breathing really hard.

"You smell good," he says quietly.

"Oh, thanks," I say, realizing I'm breathing hard myself. "My mom uses lavender-scented detergent." Why? Why did I just say that? But Blake laughs, and then he gets this resolute look on his face, like the way those action guys do in the movies right before they decide to parachute out of the plane or leap from one building to the next. Then he leans in to kiss me again and, whoa. This is a powerful kiss. So powerful, it pushes me back against all the fungus-filled pillows so that I'm practically lying down.

"Is this okay?" he asks, pulling away a little and looking at me.

I manage to get out an "Um, uh-huh" before he's kissing me again. And now I don't know what to do. I've never kissed anyone like this, lying down, before. Where do I put my hands? Should I leave them at my sides? Should I touch his hair? Am I still doing this right? Is it bad to think this much when you're kissing someone lying down? Does everyone think this much when they're kissing someone lying down? No, definitely not. Miss S. is right, I think too much. I need to enjoy this. I need to relax. Yes, I need to relax. Maybe I just need to relax my lips. Yes. Okay Izzy, take a deep breath . . . aaaaand . . .

Just as I let my lips soften, Blake opens his mouth.

Gah!

When two people kiss in a movie, both of them open their mouths at the same time. Then they shift their faces to either side simultaneously in a very romantic and sexy kind of way. But Blake and I don't open our mouths at the same time and shift our faces to either side in a romantic and sexy kind of way. No, my neuron receptors aren't working or something and so my mouth doesn't get the message from my brain in time. So when Blake opens *his* mouth, I keep mine shut, and for what seems like an ungodly length of time, Blake Hangry FRENCH KISSES MY FACE!

He finally pulls away and smiles at me. I sit up and discreetly attempt to wipe my saliva-covered face. I want to tell him that I think maybe we should go to class. I don't want to get Miss S. in trouble. Plus I don't want to get face-Frenched again. But I also don't want him to think I'm a prude or no fun. Before I can decide, Blake leans toward me again, this time falling on top of me with both of his outstretched hands landing on my breasts!

I sit up immediately, getting DIA flashbacks.

"Sorry, is that . . . is that not okay?" Blake has a thin sheen of sweat on his forehead.

"No I . . . I just don't want someone to come in," I say. "Public spaces and all that." I laugh weakly.

"Oh. No, no, it's okay," he says, shaking his head back and forth. "The door's locked."

"Oh," I say, "okay, well—" And I want to say more, maybe even get up, but I'm having so many thoughts, it's like I'm physically unable to give orders to my body parts.

And then we're kissing again, and I'm flat on my back again. And then, I don't know if I do it or if he forces it open, but my mouth opens up and my tongue just, kind of, naturally starts moving around. And, oh my God, Blake's hands are underneath my sweater. When did this happen? Oh my God, he's squeezing. He's squeezing both of my breasts over my Lola's Lingerie, double D, grandma bra! He's squeezing and squeezing—and not in a romantic and sexy kind of way either. More like the way a clown squeezes his nose to make it honk. Before I can stop him, he pulls my sweater up and over my head, but he doesn't take it all the way off.

Oh my God, oh my God, oh my God, oh my God, I'm lying down on the Rap Room futon—absorbing deadly fungus spores—with my thick wool sweater pulled tight up over my head while Blake Hangry is . . . Gah! Removing one of my boobs from my bra cup?! I'm trapped underneath my sweater. I'm trapped, and I'm not getting enough fresh oxygen. And I'm sweating now. I'm sweating in my sweater. I need to get up, but I can't. Why can't I get up? I feel like every move I make is in slow motion and every move Blake makes is in fast forward. I need to do something, quick. And then I remember this TV special I saw where this lady took a self-defense class and the teacher said when a "non-armed man" is attacking you to just start screaming and drooling and writhing around like you're having a seizure. Should I fake a seizure? No, I can't fake a seizure. And it's not like Blake is attacking me. I can get up if I want to. Wait, can I? No! I can't get up. I can't get up! He's got one of my shoulders pinned down. It's not my neuron receptors that have me trapped, it's the weight of Blake's body.

I'm really starting to squirm now. I move my legs around. I attempt to sit up. But he doesn't even notice. Or maybe he thinks I'm writhing in pleasure. Oh my God. I open my eyes and quickly close them again—the fuzzies from my sweater feel like they're scratching my corneas. Oh God, I'm going to be the first girl to suffocate *and* go blind while making out with a guy in her high school guidance room. Wait, I feel his weight lift off me for a moment. I spring up, pulling my sweater down from my head. I see

Blake on his cell phone. What? He's on his cell phone?!

"Hey!" he says, quickly looking up from his phone. "I'm sorry, I'm so sorry, I just . . . my brother just texted me about going to one of his practices at State and I wanted to let him know right away that I could because he has to put me on this list . . . anyway, sorry, sorry, sorry," he repeats, shoving his phone back in his pocket.

"Listen," I say, sounding as frustrated as I feel, and trying to shift my body in a way that gets my boob back in my bra. And just as I give up and start to reach my hands in to adjust myself, Blake, who I now notice is actually sweating a lot more than I am right now, puts his arms around my waist.

"No listen—" I start, and then feel him attempting to unhook my bra. "Hey!" I push him back.

"What? What's wrong?"

I stare at him. "We should go to class." I reach for my bag off the floor.

"Oh, okay," he laughs and then leans all his weight on me again, trying to pull my sweater back up and tugging at my bra hooks. I try to push myself up, but he's draped over me and I can't move.

"Stop!" I say, squirming frantically, feeling the itchy futon on my back. And that's when I start kicking. I kick and kick and end up kicking Blake hard in the groin. He falls to the floor with a moan. I sit up, pull my sweater down again, and somehow manage to shout, "I said stop! God!"

"I'm sorry! I didn't hear you." He's clutching himself where I kicked him. "You didn't have to flip out on me!

Jesus, are you trying to kill me?" he says, but not looking angry, just kind of confused, and totally embarrassed lying down there on the floor. And then I start to feel a little confused and embarrassed myself.

"No," I say, "I'm not trying to kill you, I just . . . I just wanted to go to class and—"

"Oh. I thought . . . you were kidding about that."

"Well, I wasn't."

"Okay. Well . . . I didn't hear you say stop before," he says, getting up, and then spits out really fast, "I'm sorry, I just, I thought you liked me and it would be okay if . . . I'm just, I'm just kind of confused here."

"I do like you," I say, starting to feel bad that I kicked him so hard. What is wrong with me? "I'm sorry. Maybe . . . maybe I overreacted," I say uncertainly.

"No, no, no, it's okay. I'm sorry. I didn't hear you. I didn't . . . It's my fault. This is totally and completely my fault. I'm . . ." He pushes his hair out of his face, making it stand up in sweaty points. "I'm such an asshole. God." He picks up his backpack like he wants to throw it across the room. "I'm such a total and complete jerk-douche asshole. I'm sorry, Izzy."

"No, no . . . I'm just— You just— I didn't—" But I can't finish because I don't know what I am or how I feel.

Blake is rubbing the bridge of his nose with both his middle fingers. "Let's just get to class."

"Yes," I say, helping him reassemble the room, and trying to reassemble myself at the same time. I follow Blake outside, closing the Rap Room door behind me, when I hear him say, "Crap!"

I turn around to find him face-to-face with Pam.

"Izzy!" she says, looking more frazzled than usual. I wait for her to tell us that she's taking us to Mrs. Preston's office and reporting us for skipping class and then looking at me with crushing disappointment and telling me that she'll have to call Mom.

"We were just—" Blake says, but Pam interrupts, her eyes on me.

"I just went looking for you in the library. When you weren't there, I thought maybe you went looking for me, that Allissa had already gotten ahold of you."

I blink at her. "What?" I ask, and watch as Blake slinks around the corner and out of sight.

And then Pam tells me about my mom.

CHAPTER 18

I have negative energy.

"Who put the bop in the bop shoo wop shoo wop? Who put the ram in the rama lama ling dong?"

I don't know, and I don't care, and I really don't feel like listening to Oldies 104.3 right now because it just makes my already aching head feel worse. But this is Pam's car and Pam's radio, so I guess I have no choice.

"So . . . how you doing? You okay?" Pam turns to me and lets out a long breath when we're stopped at a red light.

I nod. "Yeah, I'm fine."

"Okay then"—Pam starts digging around in her purse— "still waiting to hear back from Mrs. B. Here, eat a granola bar." She pulls a bunch out and drops them on the seat between us one by one. "I got cranberry, chocolate chip, peanut butter, apple cinnamon . . ." I grab a chocolate chip and hold it in my lap. She waits for me to unwrap and take a bite and then says, "So, if you promise me you won't skip class again to be with your boyfriend, I won't tell your mom about today. Deal?"

I almost choke. "Uh-huh."

Tell my mom about today? How are you going to tell her anything? Who knows if she's even coherent. All we know is that she passed out at a meeting at Mrs. Burk's house. What does that mean, *passed out*? I've messed things up so much with Mom. She's still so angry with me. And, oh God, the mental snapshot she has of me—that terrible mental snapshot of her irresponsible disappointment of a daughter looking all disheveled and wearing a Meredith Brightwell *nafka* top after sneaking out to go to a stupid frat party. What if it's permanent? What if that's the last way she sees me?

I squeeze my eyes shut, trying to squeeze my thoughts away, then foggily turn toward the sound of Pam's voice. She's on her cell now, talking a mile a minute.

"So what you're saying is that Linda passed out, but then she got up again?" Pam is talking to Mrs. Burk, I'm assuming. I turn the radio down and Pam puts Mrs. B. on speaker. It's a little hard to understand her—the speaker is fuzzy and it sounds like she's got a Werther's Original in her mouth—but it's better than nothing.

"Yes, well, she really wasn't looking too peachy when she came over," I hear Mrs. Burk say. There's a slurp-like clacking as the hard candy hits her teeth. "We looked at fabric samples for couches. But she just didn't look like she had a lot of gas in her engine." *Slurp, clack, slurp.* "And then she excuses herself and goes into my bathroom. And I hear her, you know, tossing up her turkey. I mean *really* tossing up her turkey."

Pam tries to interrupt. "Okay, okay, but when did she—"

"So then she comes on out and she says she's gotta jet

'cause she's got the flu. And then she goes to get her things and she just falls on over, I mean right on the ground—the carpet, thank the Lord. And I scream. But then she's sitting up right away. She is sitting up and she is saying that she's fine and just to get her water. But when you toss your turkey and fall, you're not fine. So I say I'm going to call the hospital. And then she gets all mad at me. And I mean she is walking and talking now, but I don't want her moving a vehicle in her state. So I tell her that, and I offer to take her home, but she said to call you." *Suck, slurp, clack.* "So, I hope I did the right thing by calling you."

"Yes, yes, of course! Good that you called. Yes, thank you. We're on our way. Bye," Pam says, hanging up.

"Okay." Pam sets her phone down between us, flashing me an anxious smile. "She's gonna be okay, okay?" Then her features scrunch all the way over to the right side of her face as she mutters, "Hmmm, what was I . . . ? Oh! About today—listen, Izzy, he's a cutie, he really is, but please, just don't let having a boyfriend mess with your grades, okay?"

I choke out a feeble "Yeah, okay."

A boyfriend? Yeah, right. Oh God. There's a Rap-Room-mental-snapshot-slide-show going through my head that I can't turn off. What happened? *Did* I overact? Was it my fault, or was Blake being the asshole, like he said? I feel my face go hot. I can't believe I kicked him in the groin like that. Most girls let guys who are interested in them feel their breasts and more. But not me. I panic and perform spontaneous karate on their genitals.

Why did Blake have to get so aggressive all of a sudden? He *did* get aggressive, didn't he? Or maybe that's the way it should be, all . . . *forceful,* and Blake's just not really good at . . . at foreplay yet. Or maybe he is, maybe he did it right. Maybe he did everything right, and I was just too much of a violent, diseased prude to enjoy it.

But no, he ambushed me. He held me down! And then he totally ignored me when I told him to stop. If you like someone that much, I would think you'd try and be a little more attentive and notice it when you're holding the person down. Or when they're screaming stop.

I have to get out of this car. I just want to get out of this car and see my mom.

"Uh-huh, okay sweetie." Pam's on the phone again. "No, no, we're here now. Are you sure? Maybe you should just continue back and— Okay, okay. No, don't worry. Just drive safe. Okay? Okay . . . bye." Pam drops her phone back into her lap and pulls up to Mrs. Burk's massive brick-paved driveway. "That was Allissa," she tells me. "She's on her way."

We walk up the short set of stairs that leads to a porch, which leads to another set of stairs, which leads to a really unattractive giant brown door with what seems to be gold-plated antler door knockers. Wow, Mom really has her work cut out for her with this job.

When the door opens, we rush toward Mom, who's sitting at an equally unattractive, massive, log-brown kitchen table, reapplying her lip gloss. I have to smile.

"Linda, are you sick? You throwing up?" Pam attacks the seat next to Mom, her kitty cat clock eyes swinging fast. "Should we take you to the hospital? What's going on? Talk to me. You look pale."

Mrs. B. gallops over to us and sets a pitcher of iced tea down on the kitchen island. Her heavily lined, once red lips are a thin crease of worry. She gallops back to the cabinet for cups, her potpourri and barbecue sauce scent lingering over us.

"Did she look this pale when she got here?" Pam calls after Mrs. Burk.

"Well, she's definitely got more color in her cheeks now." Miss B. sets the cups down before continuing to circle nervously around her skull-bowl-covered kitchen island. The animal-themed brooches on her red blazer disco-light the cream-colored walls.

"I'm fine. Much better now. Really, it's fine, Pam." Mom smiles, putting away her gloss.

I stare at my mother, just sitting there in one of her flowy tunic tops, smiling at us as if we've come over to play mahjong. It's like I want to hug her and yell at her at the same time. "We should go to the doctor," I say.

"No, no. No need." Mom waves my suggestion away with both hands and then for the first time since Saturday sends me a smile. "I'm going to Pittsfield tomorrow to see Dr. Madson for testing anyway."

Mom looks at Pam's face and then says, "Please. Please, don't look so worried."

I chew my lip and stare down at Mrs. B.'s orange-and-lime-green kitchen tiles. "Your appointment's tomorrow?" I ask, just as Pam says, "What do you mean testing? Are you eating? You never eat, Linda, you eat like a pigeon on a diet. It's not good."

"I'm fine, Pam." Mom shakes her head at her. "Honestly, I think I'm just really dehydrated today, that's all. But I just drank some water and I feel a hundred times better." Mom goes on talking about her reoccurring cold, and her sinus drainage again.

I don't say anything. I just watch her breezily make it seem like we're the crazy ones to worry about her and her health. And then the corset is squeezing me again. Except this time it feels like there's something filling up my throat too, like I'm breathing in sand. I ask Mrs. B. for the bathroom. I think I might pass out. No, I can't pass out, because I can't go to the hospital, because then they would find some of that Rap Room pillow fungus in my hair, and then they would tell Mom, and then she would find out I skipped study hall to do inappropriate and immoral things with Blake and turn into ice-cold Iris again. But maybe it would be worth it if it would get Mom to the hospital right now. Maybe while I'm in intensive care being treated for nasty pillow inhalation, somebody would take a look at Mom and realize that she needs urgent medical attention too.

Mrs. B. points me upstairs. Her bathroom is bigger

than my entire bedroom. I jump as my cell vibrates in my pocket. *Blake.* I throw my hands over my mouth and swallow hard, trying to keep the contents of my stomach from coming up. I stare at his name flashing across the screen before shoving the phone back in my pocket. I inhale through my sand corset as deeply as I can, and then try to exhale all my Blake thoughts out. I can't think about it now. Something's really wrong with Mom, and I shouldn't be thinking about anything but her right now. Oh God, my chest. It's like I'm breathing through wet cement. I lean back against the wall and try to take a deep breath—but I can't. And the ugly moose painting in front of me looks blurry. Is it supposed to be blurry? *Don't black out, don't black out, don't black out and hit your head on the bathtub.* I repeat this, sliding my body down the wall until I'm sitting on an animal fur bathmat. I lean forward. I drop my head to the fur. I stretch my arms out in front of me, looking, I'm sure, like Allissa does when she starts her yoga videos. It kind of works. I take a shallow breath, start to feel the air pushing through the sand and cement, expanding my ribs. Then another breath, and it goes deeper, moving all the way into my back. I don't know how long I stay down there like that, taking deep breaths on the bathroom floor, but I pop right up as soon as I hear every square foot of Mrs. Burk's ginormous house fill up with a familiarly unpleasant sound.

• • •

I follow the sound to the kitchen—a hiccup, followed by a gasp, followed by a whimper, and topped off with a sob. Oh no, Mount Allissa has erupted.

"Wait, so [hiccup] you [gasp] are just [whimper, sob] dehydrated?"

Allissa loses all control over her body when she cries. Her arms flap around as if she's trying to take flight, and she takes these really shallow breaths that make her shoulders move spastically up and down. Jenna says Allissa has a 1980s-aerobics-class kind of cry. The thought makes me smile, before I remember that Jenna isn't speaking to me . . . Before I remember that my mom's not just dehydrated.

Mom attempts to calm Allissa down while gesturing for me to get all her stuff together. Pam thanks Mrs. B. for everything, and then we slowly make our way down the front stairs. Allissa and Pam are on either side of Mom, holding on to her arms as if she might blow away. I follow behind carrying the rest of Mom's stuff, including a tiny blue trash can that Mrs. B. gave us in case Mom "tosses her turkey again in the car."

"Oh my, it got so dark out already," Mom says, clicking her tongue and looking worriedly at Allissa. "Maybe I should drive?"

"No, no, no," Pam says. "Why don't I just drive you all? Why should Allissa have to drive? You can both leave your cars here and tomorrow—"

"I'm fine! I know how to drive!" Allissa says, jingling her car keys in the air. "My night vision has gotten a lot better."

I have to hand it to Allissa. She drives well under pressure tonight. So far we've managed to stay in one lane at a time. I'm not gripping the sides of the car, thinking every pair of headlights going by in the other direction could lead us to the white light. And she's not even on her cell phone. My phone, on the other hand, is burning a hole through my pocket. I finally take it out and stare at it, dreading my messages.

"Wow, I am exhausted." Mom sighs, leaning her head against the window.

"Well, you just need rest." Allissa is squinting her eyes at the road in a way that makes Mom tighten her seat belt strap.

And then Mom says it's good Allissa's back because she has a coupon for some kind of pedicure she forgot to give her yesterday, but I miss most of the paraffin-filled details because I'm listening to my voicemail from Blake. Or rather, my voicemail from Nate, Jacob, and Blake. A voicemail that makes me want to grab the mini trash can on the seat next to me and make good use of it.

My bedroom isn't that big, but after twenty minutes of speed-walking from one end of it to the other, I'm out of breath. I retreat to my bed and I listen to the message again, probably for the tenth time in a row. Yes, that's Nate Yube's voice: *Hi Izzy, it's Blake . . . um, I was just wondering if you wanted to hang out tomorrow in the Rap Room, and talk! Ahahahahaha!* And then that's definitely Jacob cutting in: *Izzy, I miss you and your—* Then Nate cuts in again: *Gimme the phone, gimme the phone. Izzy, I just want to say thank you for—* But I don't catch the rest because it's all muffled, and then I hear Blake in the background: *Gimme my freakin' phone!* And you can hear all this laughing, and I don't know why I'm listening to it over and over again, because every time I hear it, I just feel worse than I did the time before.

I can't believe it. I can't believe Blake told those guys about today. I mean, he obviously did. How else would they know? Oh God, how *many* of them know? And *what* exactly do they know? What did Blake tell them? Why would he do that?

"Sweetie, you sleeping?" I hear Mom from outside my door.

"No," I say, checking my face in the mirror to make sure I don't look upset, relieved I'm at least in sweetie territory again. "Come in."

"Hey, whatcha doing?" Mom leans against my doorframe in her pair of really loose-fitting pajama pants, sipping from an open bottle of Gatorade.

"Nothing, homework." I look up at her, taking a mental snapshot.

"Allissa and I are going to watch a movie. I'm so tired, but I just can't sleep. You wanna come down?" She puts down the bottle to button her cardigan over her pajama top.

"Okay," I say. "You feeling better?"

"Yes, yes, much. I have to call Gretchen first thing tomorrow, though, and apologize again. I'm so embarrassed."

"You shouldn't be embarrassed, Mom. You got sick. People . . . get sick."

"I know, I know, but I threw up in her bathroom, I fell down in her living room. I knocked over a vase of flowers." She shakes her head, picking up the bottle and taking a small sip. "What a disaster of a day."

"Yeah . . ." I look up at her. "Mom, I really am sorry. I mean about Saturday. I didn't mean to make things . . . worse for you. I'm sorry I did that. It was . . . really stupid."

"I'm sorry too, Izzy, I just . . ." She sighs. "I just worry about you guys so much, and it's exhausting sometimes and—"

"No, I know." I nod. Mom gives me a small nod back and I watch as she concentrates on picking bits of lint off her cardigan with one hand. There's not a chip off her manicure, her makeup is still perfectly applied, and not one hair is out of place. She's such an expert at making herself look good on the outside that, even tonight, after everything that's happened, it's hard to believe that anything could be wrong on the inside.

The movie we end up watching is some really bad made-for-TV movie about an elementary school teacher who falls in love with this gas station attendant who ends up stealing the teacher's identity and threatening to kill all her students. Just as the gas station attendant has broken into the teacher's house for the second time, I start to nod off. When I wake up, the gas station attendant is locked up in jail and the teacher has fallen in love with the detective on the case. I see that Mom's also asleep.

"Hey," I whisper to Allissa, who looks like she might be sleeping too.

"Hey," she whispers back, sitting up. "Should we wake her?"

"No, let her sleep." I cover Mom with a blanket.

Once we've successfully tiptoed upstairs, I say, "Hey, Allissa?"

"What's up?" She stops. The sparkly circles under her eyes from where her glitter eye shadow ran down shine in the dim hallway light.

"Maybe . . . maybe we should have taken Mom to see a doctor today."

"Well, isn't it better if she waits and sees Dr. Madson tomorrow?"

"Yeah, I guess, but—"

"But what?" Allissa sighs.

"Well, okay, so you know I read a lot about PMP online, you know? And I didn't think this particular problem . . . might actually *be* a problem, but then I saw something— read something on my computer that Mom had left— Well, I know the facts vary and, I mean, it's a case by case, I know, but still . . . I think based on what I read that—"

"Izzy, what are you talking about? I don't get what you're talking about."

"I'm saying that it's just that a lot of the people in Mom's web groups, they're not doing well. A lot of them aren't doing well at all and now I think that—"

"No." Allissa puts up a hand. "I don't want to know about any of those people, okay? Just keep all that medical research stuff to yourself."

"But Mom herself wrote—"

"Mom's fine, Izzy!"

"I know she is. But what if—"

"I don't want to talk about this anymore." She whips around and stalks down the hall to her room.

"But we have to talk about this," I say, following her.

"No. *You* have to talk about this, because you *like* talking about this, because you know that Mom relies on you . . . to know all of this stuff, but I—"

"What do you mean Mom relies on me?"

"You know she does. Like this summer? She's like, *Oh you go and live on campus and take that job because Izzy's here, Izzy's going to be my caretaker.*"

"You wanted to stay home and take care of Mom last summer?"

"No, no, I just wanted her . . . to . . . Just forget it."

"Allissa, I don't think Mom chose one of us to— I think she just knew that you had—"

"Whatever, it doesn't matter. Just . . . like . . . I just wish you would stop being so negative all the time. You're such a constant downer."

"What? I'm a what?"

"Have you ever thought that maybe what Mom doesn't need right now is all of your blatant negative energy?"

"Negative energy?" I repeat, feeling like I've been slapped. "What do you mean *my bl—*" But Allissa cuts me off, putting her hand up in front of my face as if she's warding off my bad vibes.

"Please, just . . . forget it. I'm going to bed."

And before I can say another word, she's disappeared into her room, and I hear her bedroom door shut tight.

I wake up later in a sweat to the sound of Mom climbing the stairs. My hands ache and I realize they're clutching my pillow, which I'm holding against my body for dear life. My dream is already sliding away, and I grasp at it, trying to remember.

Mom and I are in the kitchen and I'm helping her peel potatoes. And everything's fine, except when I glance over at her, I notice that her hands look bony. Her whole body looks bony, and she's wearing this hideous neon tunic that's like seven sizes too big. She turns to me and says, "Good job, Izzy," and she squeezes my shoulders. Then my potato and peeler start melting down in my hands. The kitchen walls are closing in on us. The ceiling starts dripping down to the floor. Everything's melting, and I'm wobbling where I stand on a single kitchen tile while Mom and her oversized neon tunic float off in the other direction. I try to grip the countertop to steady myself, but everything keeps moving and melting and Mom's floating farther and farther away. I attempt to jump off my tile toward her, but my legs melt down into my feet. And the worst part is that Mom doesn't seem to care, she's just shrugging her shoulders as she floats away.

I sit up in bed and grab my sketchbook from my dresser, needing to do something physical, to move that mental snapshot of floating Mom out of my head somehow, to get rid of my negative energy.

I once read this article on some website about the power of positive thinking and how it relates to physical illness. There was this therapist/doctor/guru guy, I forget his name, and he said that water molecules are super-sensitive to our emotions, and so because our bodies are made up of so much water, negative thoughts can make us sick, even negative thoughts we get from other people.

Okay, yes, I worry about Mom, and about me, and I guess about things in general, but worrying isn't being negative, it's . . . being prepared. And it's not like Mom's just relying on me to be prepared, and doesn't need Allissa. If anything, she relies on Allissa much more than me; like every time she needs advice about a client, or what to wear, or a billion other little things where I'm sure I'd completely drop the ball.

I grab my phone off my dresser and check the time. It's four in the morning. Then I drop it down again like it grew spikes, remembering that awful voicemail still inside it. Now I have a Jacob Ullman choking-seagull laugh track playing on a loop inside my head. Thinking about tomorrow gives me this terrible, queasy feeling.

Maybe I can switch schools. Or maybe by some miracle I'll finish my portfolio in time, and I'll get picked to go to Italy this summer, and then I'll leave the country and never come back.

CHAPTER 19

I've gone digital.

In Spanish the next day, I try to own the noise.

I read this book once about meditating, and it said that the only way to silence unwanted noise in your head is to accept it and own it. I have no idea what that means, but it's what I've been trying to do all day.

So when I stand up to get a tissue in Spanish and I hear Jacob whisper, "Whew, it's cold in here, just a bit nippley," I try to own the noise, especially since I know there's no way I look "nippley" in a bulky sweater with a T-shirt underneath it and a Lola's bra underneath the T-shirt.

During a pop quiz in algebra, I try to own the noise, even though Aaron Napert is constantly tapping my shoulder, and when I finally give in and turn around, he and rest of the guys in his row start coughing and sneezing the words *tits* and *boobs*.

Okay, so I don't think I've owned even a decibel of noise today. In fact, I feel like I'm living through one of those dreams people have—the one where you arrive at school and realize that you forgot to put your clothes on. Except

I'm definitely wearing clothes today. I'm even wearing my wool ski socks because it's raining and water always soaks through the soles of my shoes. I refuse to wear the rain boots my mom picked out because they have neon-green polka dots and smiley faces on them. Allissa says I could make them look hip if I wanted to, but I don't want to make them look hip. I just want to keep them in my closet. My point is, I'm fully clothed today, thick ski socks, Lola's grandma bra, sweater, the whole shebang. And yet I feel like I'm walking around totally naked with LOOK AT ME AND SNICKER spray-painted across my boobs.

Thank God Mom's picking me up. Today is the perfect day to leave school early. I'm going with her to see Dr. Madson, and I might have to drive her home if they need to do a lot of blood work, which is scary because I've only had my permit for like three months.

At my locker, I check my face in the tiny mirror to be sure I don't have any giant boogers and see a paper bag on the top shelf that wasn't there this morning. It says *Thinking of You* on the outside, and there's a chocolate chip scone inside. When I went to the drama room this morning to tell Jenna that I wouldn't be at rehearsal today, the door was locked, so I just assumed Jenna was still mad. Maybe she still is. Though I'm pretty sure it's her writing.

I'm grabbing a notebook out of my locker when I feel something pointy hit my head. A paper airplane lands at my feet. How mature. I'm about to wad it up and throw it right back at Nate and Jacob, who are standing across from me at their lockers, and making a big deal of acting like they're not paying attention to me at all, when I see that the plane says "read me" on one of the wings. I reluctantly open it up, and there in large, scrawling capital letters is "NICE TITS!!!"

I feel my nose tighten. My chin is starting to tremble. I keep my eyes focused on the contents of my locker, and slowly crumple the paper in my fist. I will not let those guys see me crying over a stupid paper airplane.

Mom's not picking me up for another ten minutes, but I think I should just head outside to wait for her now.

"Hey, Izzy." I see Meredith's strawberry hair out of the corner of my eye.

"Hey."

"Have you seen it?" she says in this weird hushed, detective-like tone.

"What?"

"Well, I haven't seen it yet," Meredith whispers, "but I hear it's pretty bad. Let me know when you see it, I have some theories."

"Meredith, what are you—"

"Crap, chem test! We'll talk later, okay?"

"No, wait—" I say, grabbing my coat and backpack, trying to catch up with her as she jets down the hall and out of sight.

"Delete it! I swear to God!" I hear Blake's voice loud and clear, which stops me in my tracks. "I'm gonna kill you guys! Give it to me!" He's shouting now, jumping up after

Nate, who's holding his phone high above his head.

"No way, dude," Nate says, laughing.

"I erased it, what the hell?" Blake says, getting more and more worked up.

"Jacob sent it to my phone when you were taking a piss." Nate is triumphant. "And I've sent it on to the taskmaster. I did you a favor, dude. You're welcome."

Blake lunges at him and people start to crowd around, waiting for a fight.

"Calm the hell down, Blake! I'm keeping it," Nate says, backing away from Blake.

"Yeah me too. It's sooo pretty," Jacob adds.

"Yeah!" Nate laughs. "It's reeeeally pretty."

Blake actually pushes Nate to the ground then. And when he does, the phone goes flying across the hall and skids into my right foot.

I pick it up. I don't know why I do, it all happens so fast. At first I don't understand what I'm seeing and then, oh my God, gross! I know boys download pictures from the Internet, but I didn't think they kept them as screen savers on cell phones! Then I drop the phone on the ground because my hands are shaking too much to hold it. I recognized something in the picture. The sweater. The fuzzy green sweater above the boob.

I lunge down for the phone, needing to take another look, but Tim Clawson swoops in and snatches it away. "I believe this belongs to us," he says, which makes him and all the senior guys around him laugh.

"Izzy!" I hear Blake calling after me, but I'm already halfway down the hallway, and I don't stop. I'm holding my hands over my mouth and running straight to the girls' bathroom because—

I make it there just in time.

I've never run at this speed, for so long, in my entire life. Still, I can't seem to get home fast enough. I'm getting completely soaked too. Well, except for my socks; my trusty old ski socks.

I want to die. I want to sink into the wet pavement and just die. And then I want to kill Blake Hangry. I want to come back to life and stab him in the head. I want to shoot him. I want to strangle him. I want to poison him. I want him drawn and quartered. I want him to be tortured medieval style, or like that Edgar Allan Poe movie we had to watch for English; something about a pendulum. I want all those things to be done to him, and then I want to die again. Because no matter what happens to him, my boob—my naked, large, disgusting, nasty, ugly boob—will still be saved inside every cell phone of every guy on the varsity basketball team and God knows who else forever.

When I see Mom's car in the driveway, I feel like I might be sick again. But at least she hasn't left yet to pick me up from school. I enter the house through the back door that connects to our laundry room and strip off all my wet clothes. I catch a glance of my reflection in the full-length mirror on the wall and turn my head away. I can't even look at myself.

"Izzy? Is that you?" I hear Mom heading down the stairs and quickly throw on a pair of clean jeans and a sweater from the laundry basket on top of the dryer.

"It's me!" I yell back. "I . . . I decided to walk home!"

"I was just on my way to pick you up [cough]. You should have called. What if we missed each other and—" She stops in mid-sentence when she walks in and gets a look at me. "Oh my God, Izzy, you're soaked! Why [cough] did you walk home in the rain? What were you thinking?"

"I'm sorry. It wasn't raining that hard when I left and . . . I got out of class early, so I just thought I'd walk."

"Okay, well then . . . [cough]. Well, okay. I guess we'll leave as soon as you blow-dry your hair."

"Okay," I say, avoiding her eyes. Then, "You all right?" I ask, because she's leaning against the wall, and even though she's got on her makeup and winter bronzer, she still looks pale. Also, some of the polish on her left hand is chipped. It's miniscule but this is a first and I can't take my eyes off of it. "Mom?"

"Yes, I'm fine. Oh, Izzy, I can't believe you [cough] went and did something like this [cough] and your hair looked so perfect this morning." She sighs.

I tell her I'm sorry again and then head upstairs to quickly blow-dry my hair back to perfection so we won't be late for the appointment with Dr. Madson.

· · ·

"You're beeping again," I tell Mom as her cell phone goes off for what seems like the hundredth time in her purse.

"I know, I know," she says, keeping her eyes on the road. "Will you silence it, sweetie? I can never figure out how to do it."

I reach into her purse and pull out her phone. I see that she has three missed calls from Cathy Mason. *Cathy knows!* Does Cathy know? Maybe she does, and she's already told Mom via voicemail. Or maybe she's told her already, and Mom's just playing it cool, waiting for me to fess up. I search her face, but she just coughs a couple of times and checks her spotless teeth in the rearview mirror.

"Who called?" she asks me.

"Cathy Mason, a bunch of times," I mumble.

"Oh, no. You know what? Hand me my phone, I have to listen to my messages."

"Why? Is everything okay?"

"Actually, no, Izzy. No," she says, shaking her head, "everything is not okay. I've spoken to Cathy Mason already today. Twice," she adds.

I feel like my chest is filling up again, like my neck is the middle of an hourglass, and the sand's just sliding down.

"What's going on?" I manage to get out. But Mom holds up her finger, listening to her voicemails.

It's probably only been about three minutes, but it feels like three years go by before she hands her phone back to me to put away. And now she's shaking her head again, and coughing, and saying, "These kids, these stupid kids."

"Mom, is everything—"

"Izzy, are you aware that pornographic content is being distributed among your entire school?"

Okay. So you know that special power Superman has, where he blows cold air on the bad guys and then they freeze solid? Well, hearing Mom's words turns me into one of those frozen-solid bad guys.

"Pornographic content," Mom repeats, and lets out a long sigh, which freezes me further. "Cathy just confirmed, it's your class!"

"What's my class?"

"I'm sorry, sweetie, I'm just so . . . unnerved. Early this afternoon, I got a call from Jackie Ullman, who got a call from Bari Robertson [cough], who got a call from Jillian Dodgers, whose daughter Wendy called her from school in tears and told her that David Seltzer [cough] forced her to look at a lewd picture! Of a naked breast! That he had on his cellular phone [cough]! And during gym class!"

"Oh . . . my God." Oh God, oh God, oh God. Just crash the car into a tree right now, Mom. It'll be better for everyone.

"I know," Mom says, the perfect line of black under her eyes stretching out as she widens them. "And apparently David was tormenting poor Wendy, asking her if she was jealous, and telling her she had a chessboard chest. Or no . . . a checkerboard chest? I don't know, but—"

"What?"

"Yes! So cruel and immature and—and well, her mother

was so outraged, she called David's parents. That's what Cathy was just calling about, that David Seltzer was called into Mrs. Preston's office, and he said it wasn't his picture, but that it was sent to him, and that, apparently, it's a photo of a girl in your class. Somebody in *your* class, Izzy!"

Don't black out, don't black out, don't black out, just keep talking, keep your voice normal, don't throw up, don't throw up, just breathe. Breathe. Breathe! "So do they um . . . know who it is?" I ask.

"No, not yet. Maybe Meredith Brightwell [cough], one of those types of girls, probably. It's so sad. I feel bad for Stacy."

"What do you mean one of those types of girls?"

"You know what I mean."

"Mom, Meredith isn't one of 'those types of girls.' She didn't even do that in the bathroom with Nate Yube. It was just an awful rumor."

"Is that what she told you?"

"It's true!"

"I'm not saying she's a bad person, Izzy. But those skirts she wears . . . If she lifts her arms too high, her whole factory is exposed. And those heels, I don't know how she walks in them . . . and that red lipstick . . . how her mom lets her out of the house in that *nafka* attire is—"

"Why does that matter?" I ask, my voice rising in volume. "You think she did that in the bathroom just because she wears short skirts?"

"Izzy, lower your voice."

But I don't. "And you think I'd never do something like that because I wear baggy sweaters?"

"No! What? You know I hate those baggy sweaters."

"So you'd rather I wear tighter clothes? Like Meredith?"

"What? No!"

"Because you can't have it both ways, Mom, and it doesn't matter anyway because everything's out there, and—"

"What? What are you saying? What are you yelling about?"

"I just—I don't know. Forget it."

"Well, I can't drive with you [cough] yelling like this. Especially . . . [cough] when I'm not . . . feeling well," she coughs out, digging her chipped fuchsia nail into the fabric of the steering wheel.

"I'm sorry. I . . . well . . . maybe then that's what we should focus on—getting you feeling better, and not some picture of some poor girl who we don't . . . even know."

Mom responds to that by pressing PLAY on the CD player.

My life is sunshine lollipops and rainbows that's how this refrain goes so come on, join in, everybody! Sunshine lollipops . . .

"We just missed the shuttle to Dr. Madson's wing," Mom says an hour later as we pull into the parking lot of the Pittsfield Medical Village and watch a bus pass by our car. "We'll have to wait for the next one."

"Okay," I say.

As we sit in the parked car, waiting, Mom concentrates her gaze on me like I'm a line on an eye doctor's chart. And for a moment I think she knows, I think she knows everything. Then she leans in toward me, pushes a chunk of my hair behind my ears, and says, "They did such a good job with your layers. It's going to grow out really well."

I nod and give her a small smile, concentrating on taking as many mental snapshots as I can right now, while she still thinks I'm not one of those girls.

CHAPTER 20

I didn't know it could morph.

You'd think they'd build a huge medical center, where lots of sad and serious stuff happens, somewhere that's a little sunnier than Pittsfield, Michigan. It's only a couple of hours from home, but the Pittsfield Medical Village feels like another country, where the language is hushed tones and the currency is crisp dollars bills that the vending machines won't spit out.

Dr. Madson has his own floor. It's one big main, circular area with all these hallways going off in different directions. If you looked at it from above, I imagine you'd see kind of like a spider's body, or if you're feeling optimistic, a sunburst. The main area is pretty spacious with a big nurses' station in the center, and clusters of chairs all around it.

I'm sitting in one of those chairs, and I know it's only been a couple of hours, but I feel like I've been at this hospital and on Dr. Madson's rare-stomach-cancer floor for centuries. Mom's still having tests done, or maybe she's already talking with Dr. Madson about the results. I'm really not sure because I haven't heard anything from anybody since the nurse came and took her away when it was still light outside.

So yes, I've had plenty of time to sit here writing horrific captions on all my mental snapshots, going through every single Rap Room moment, and realizing that my ugly, unsupported boob is now immortalized in binary form.

The worst part of it all being, I let it happen.

It's true. I did. When Blake pulled my sweater up, I knew I didn't want to do that and I didn't want to be there. I knew something wasn't right, but I just stayed on my back while Blake took pictures! Pictures that, by now, a *lot* of people have seen, again and again and again, and again and again and *again*. And like me, they probably all said "Ew!" Because even though the reception here is terrible, my phone indicates that I have seven new messages. Seven new *picture* messages. That's right, I've already been sent seven copies of Blake's clear, centered, high-resolution photo of the very worst part of me.

My head, it's seriously going to pop off my neck. It's going to just explode off my body like one of those champagne corks. But obviously, not as celebratory. Are there more photos than the one I saw? Is my face in them? I think my face was underneath my sweater the whole time. Was it? Not that it matters, because all those guys know it's me, and what's to keep them from telling whoever they want? Cathy Mason will find out. She finds everything out. And Pam! Pam saw me leave the Rap Room, wearing that sweater. If she sees it, or if Mom does, they'll recognize it for sure.

I want to run into one of those hospital rooms and gulp

down the first bottle of pills I see, because everyone has seen that picture now, and people will talk, and then they'll all know it's me, and then Mom's going to know, and she's going to be so disappointed. She's going to be so disappointed in me. It will be so much worse than the *nafka* top I wore to that stupid party. It will be so much worse than sneaking out to that party to begin with. It will be more negative energy than her stomach cells can handle. And then she'll never focus on getting better. And it will be because of me.

I'm so stupid.

I'm such a stupid, stupid, stupid person.

Actually, no, I'm not even a person. I'm a task! That's how Blake Hangry has always thought of me. Not that I care what some sleaze bucket thinks anyway. And I hate that I'm even thinking about him right now. It's just upsetting to realize that all the good snapshots of someone in your head were never any good at all. That they were actually terrible.

"Isabella Skymen?"

Suddenly there's a "Hi, I'm Patricia" name tag in my line of vision.

"Isabella?"

"Oh. Yes?"

"Hi there, honey. I just wanted you to know that you'll be able to see your mom in a little bit," she says, giving me this big smile as if she's just told me I'm going to Disneyland. Which I guess is nice. I know it's just her job to be super-friendly, but still it's kinda nice to see someone with a Disneyland smile when you're in a place like this.

"Has Dr. Madson talked to you yet?" she asks.

"No, no one's talked to me."

"Oh . . . okay . . ." she says, looking at her clipboard.

"Is everything okay?" I ask.

"Your mom came in this afternoon . . . right?" she asks more to herself than to me, flipping through her chart. "Okay, yeah. So Dr. Madson's got her set up in room 5112 for the night, and then as soon as he—"

"What?" I shoot up from my chair. "For the night? No, she's not staying here—she's just here for an appointment, a checkup."

The nurse looks at me cautiously for a second and then says, "Okay, um . . . just wait right here for a sec, honey. Let me just see if I can get some more info for you." I watch as she flips through the chart she's holding and heads back to her station.

I don't wait around, though. I grab all our stuff and head to room 5112.

"Mom!" is all I manage to get out when I see her lying in bed wearing one of those hospital gowns and with all these needles in her arms that are attached to beeping machines, which are attached to poles on wheels with plastic bags full of liquid. I'm having flashbacks to the summer. This was just supposed to be a checkup!

"Hi, sweetie," she says, quickly trying to scoot up to a sitting position.

"What's wrong? What's going on?" I move closer to the bed. I want to give her a hug but am afraid I might disconnect something.

"Don't be scared. It's just IVs." She gestures me over. "One for nausea, for fluids, that's all." She smiles and reaches out her arms, and I give her a soft hug and a kiss on the cheek, grateful for the combo of her baby oil moisturizer and perfume after being in Lysol land for so long.

"I just told one of the nurses to get you," she's saying to me. "I think her name was Becky. She's the one who's got on that really awful, orangey lipstick"—Mom pulls back and wrinkles her nose—"but so, so nice." She smiles. "I told her that you might still be in the waiting area and—"

"No, well, this other nurse just told me that you were—"

"And Pam should be here soon, and she's called Allissa, who—"

"Mom, what's going on?"

My mom opens her mouth to say something, but then—

"I completely forgot you wouldn't have your cell phones on in here!" Pam cries, barreling into the room and pulling a large rolling suitcase behind her. "I called both your phones. Izzy, I called yours hours ago. I'm sorry—I forgot what room they told me, and then I forgot the doctor's name, and that stupid shuttle system. Why don't they have a parking structure for this wing? Fortunately I got pointed in the right direction."

Pam parks the suitcase against the wall, gives Mom a kiss and me a shoulder squeeze.

"Oh, yes, that's the one I was talking about. Thank you, thank you, Pam," Mom says, gesturing to the suitcase.

"I think I got everything. At least I hope so. I just took all your makeup. I didn't know what was good and what was crap. So what you don't need, you won't use. I got your good moisturizer, and two hairbrushes. Oh, and I took six pairs of underwear, I hope from the right drawer. That should be enough. We can always get you more underwear; that's not an issue. And I got pajamas, and a robe, and . . ." She stops to catch her breath. "So, any more news?"

More news? I don't have *any* news! And why does Mom need a suitcase and *six* pairs of underwear? And why is it so hot? I take off my sweater; the neck-hole feels like it's strangling me. But before I can get a word in, Mount Allissa erupts into the room, spouting a mile a minute. She's saying something about her exam, and then something about the traffic and how the guy in the minivan had no right to give her the finger since she had plenty of room to switch lanes without signaling. I interrupt because I have no idea what's going on and everything is just chaos.

"Are you staying here overni—?"

"Yeah, why do you need a suitca—?"

"How long are you—?"

"That IV is fluids, and the other is—?"

"You thirsty, you need wa—?"

"I thought this was just a—?"

"Where's the doctor? Who's the doctor? Are you dehyd—?"

"WHAT EXACTLY IS GOING ON?" I practically shout over everyone else.

Mom responds to all the verbal disorder by just raising her arms high in the air. Well, as high as they will go, hooked up to all that stuff. We all stop talking and look at her.

"Pam, would you run out and ask the nurse to get me another cup of ice, please?" she asks. And once Pam has shut the door behind her, Mom says, "Okay, sit. Both of you sit, please. I can't focus with all this movement."

Allissa and I each sit down on a rolling stool and wheel ourselves closer to the bed.

"I don't understand [sniffle] why you're [whimper] here," Allissa sobs out.

"It's okay," Mom says, giving Allissa's hand a squeeze. "I'm just staying here for a little bit because Dr. Madson seems to think I might have a little blockage."

"What?" Allissa whimpers.

"Blockage," I repeat.

"Bowel obstruction," Mom says, like she's saying she has a stuffy nose.

"What's causing [sniffle] this [sob, whimper] blockage [gasp]?"

"Well, it seems that there are some issues with my colon and my appendix, and now some . . . of the stuff has backed up into my stomach, and so I'm a little . . . blocked." I can tell Mom's choosing her words carefully.

"Like gastroparesis," I say.

"Yes . . . well, yes." Mom gives me a quizzical look. "Dr.

Madson seems to think, from the results of my last CAT scan and also my latest tumor markers, that perhaps my PMP may be morphing."

And then it gets so quiet in the room that I swear I can hear the liquid pass through Mom's IVs.

"Morphing? Morphing?" Allissa repeats like a parrot.

"Morphing into what?" I ask.

"Well, he thinks it's possible that I have a faster-growing strain now, or actually, two different strains, so—"

"But that—that doesn't make any sense," I stammer. "It can't just speed up!"

"I know, sweetie. But you know how this disease is . . . it's like trying to predict what the weather will be this same day ten years from now. So even if it *has* morphed and if it *is* growing at . . . at a different rate . . . well . . . listen, nothing's for sure yet, okay? So there's no reason to get worried."

Then Dr. Madson walks in, his shiny silver hair dented as if he just took a hat off. He's wearing a suit, and a stethoscope. He looks more like a businessman playing doctor than a veteran surgeon. He shakes Allissa's hand and then mine as Becky and her orangey lipstick wheel in a vitals cart, telling us they have to run some tests and that we can come back a little bit later.

I barely hear her, though. *No reason to get worried. No reason to get worried. No reason to get worried.* I'm running these words through my head, but they don't make any sense at all.

. . .

"I don't think this chicken is cooked." I hold up my fork, speared with a piece of what the hospital cafeteria claims is a chicken Caesar salad. Worst late-night dinner ever.

Allissa looks up at me from her own soggy cafeteria salad, her sparkly purple eye shadow catching the fluorescent lights and glittering. "Just eat."

This is the first conversation Allissa and I have had in ten minutes. I started the last one too.

"Where do you want to sit?"

"I don't really care, wherever."

So at least our topics are improving.

"I don't want salmonella," I inform her.

She responds by fishing out a baby carrot from her salad and popping it into her mouth.

"I read they wash those things in chlorine." I point at the carrots in the bowl. "There's actually no such thing as a *baby* carrot, did you know that? These are like fake, mutant—"

"Izzy!" She slaps my hand away from her bowl. "Can I please just eat in peace?"

"Sorry." I stab at another piece of chicken with my fork, attempting to gauge if the meat is light pink or white. "I really do feel nauseated, though, my head feels . . . clammy."

"You're not nauseated, you're not clammy, you're not dying!"

"I know I'm not *dying*." I drop my fork, deciding on pink. "But I'm just saying if salmonella isn't treated, then—"

"You don't have salmonella."

"Not yet, but—"

"Izzy!" Every muscle on my sister's face does a vertical stretch.

"What?"

Her fork clatters to her tray.

"I'm so sick of your stupid, dramatic, death, health, crap!" she says really loud and really fast, like she's being timed and has to get out the sentence before the buzzer.

I just stare back at her, feeling my nose start to tighten.

"You're not dying, Izzy. You're not sick. You're fine."

"I know," I manage to get out.

"I'm so sick of you being sick."

"Okay, Allissa. I heard you the first time."

"*Mom's* the one who's sick, *Mom's* the one who's dying."

"Shut up!"

"Well, she is."

I furiously shake my head. "You have no idea what you're talking about. You're—"

"I may not do all your psycho research and know all your medical lingo crap, but I know about PMP. I've read about it too, Izzy. I'm not as big an idiot as you think I am."

"I never said you were! I never—"

"Most people, *most* people at Mom's stage live for like two or maybe four years after their first major surgery, and that's not counting if it like . . . morphs or whatever."

"Just stop talking, Allissa. I don't . . . I don't feel well."

"What? What's wrong with you now? I thought you

liked talking about this stuff." Allissa is practically baring her teeth at me.

"Nothing, I just—" I stop, trying to take a deep breath in. "My chest hurts, it feels like—"

"You're fine! Stop making everything about you. God, I can't handle it anymore. You shouldn't be worried about your chest or salmonella or your thyroid or . . . You should be worried about what's going to happen after, when Mom's gone and we're alone."

"I said stop talking!"

"Like where are you going to live? Probably with Grandma Iris. Or with Dad and Jessica! You're probably going to have to move, and switch schools, and I'm going to have to drop out of college unless Grandma Iris pays for it, which she won't because she'll probably be in debt from Mom's medical bills by that point anyway—"

"STOP TALKING!" I bolt up fast, so fast that I knock into the table and my entire tray clatters to the floor. Suddenly I feel the weight of everyone's eyes on me, every pale-faced patient, worried-looking family member, table of residents. I feel like they're all looking at me and my upside-down tray of undercooked chicken on the floor.

Which I probably should pick up already, but I don't. Instead, I tell Allissa to "have fun cleaning that up," and walk away.

CHAPTER 21

I need to talk to my mom.

As soon as I walk out of the elevator, I feel my phone vibrate. I stop, guessing I should probably take advantage of the fact that I'm standing in a magical spot that actually gets reception. I take a deep breath and open my phone quickly, like I'm ripping off a bandage. *Please don't be another picture message.* It's not. It's a text from Blake that reads Pls cal me! I'll xplain.

Okay, seriously? That's what he writes? He'll "xplain"? I can't believe after what he did to me that he can't even take the time to write out whole words!

I stuff my phone into my pocket and head back to Mom's room, but the door is still closed. So instead I trudge over to the waiting area, and collapse into my same chair. No thanks, Blake. I don't need you to "xplain" anything.

"Hey Izzy." Pam meanders over from the vending machine. "I think I've changed my mind—I'm going to head down to the cafeteria after all. Doctor's still in there and these pretzels aren't getting the job done." She throws me the bag. "Anything good down there?"

I shake my head.

"Okay, well, I'll be right back." She gives my shoulders a squeeze.

I put the half-eaten bag of pretzels down on the chair next to me, my hands and my head still feeling clammy. I need to do something. I look down at the carpeting, which is this pattern of all these interconnecting shapes. I try to trace the pattern with my eyes and find the starting point, but after about thirty seconds I feel woozy and give up. Then I try again, and again, until I'm even more nauseated than I was in the cafeteria. I take a break and eat a stale pretzel and then try again. I'm in the middle of doing another pattern-trace when I'm interrupted by Allissa's heels.

She plops down next to me, practically covering her face with her *Soap Opera Digest*.

"You dropped these."

I turn toward the voice of the pale-faced man sitting across from us. He's interrupted the game of solitaire he was playing on the empty chair next to him, to lean forward and pick up my bag of pretzels from the carpet.

"Thank you." I take the pretzels from him and throw them in my backpack. I see the man still leaning forward and looking at me.

"Hello," he says. He's about Mom's age, maybe a little younger, and wearing one of those shiny neon tracksuits. It makes a loud swishing sound when he moves.

"Hi," I say back. "Um . . . how are you?"

"Oh, I'm okay, for the moment," he says with a sigh. "And how are you tonight?"

"I'm okay . . . for the moment too."

"Well, good. Moment to moment's as far as we can go, right?"

"Right." I nod.

"Got someone in there?" he asks, gesturing to the halls.

I nod again.

"My wife's in there," he says, and points to one of the hallways to our left [swish]. "I'm waiting for them to bring her out so we can take a walk."

"That's good," I say.

"Yeah, it's real good [swish], her walking now. Been rough [swish]. Came out of her second debulking a couple weeks ago . . ."

He continues. "The first one, 'bout two years back, went a lot better. She was walking sooner, not as many complications, but [swish] she's walking a little now, so that's good [swish]. That's real good."

I nod back at him and smile, pushing my lips together tightly, like the harder I smile-push, the better I'll feel.

"Was that your mom?" the man asks, and I realize he's talking about Pam.

"Oh, no, my mom's . . . she's a patient of Dr. Madson's, so—" I cut myself off, hearing my voice jump an octave and crack a little.

"Okay," he says, "well then, I'll keep her in my prayers."

"Thank you." And I really mean it because honestly,

that's the best thing I've heard anybody say all day. He gives me a smile and goes back to his game of solitaire.

A young-looking, frail woman in a hospital gown and bright pink slippers shuffles her way closer to us a couple minutes later, helped by two nurses. She's hunched over a bit, gripping her pole on wheels with both hands. She looks, at most, ninety pounds. Her shoulders are sharp, and her skin looks colorless, like she's wearing one of those Halloween masks where the face is all one shade. She's got three or four different tubes coming from her middle, all emptying liquids into different bags clipped to the bottom of her pole.

She steps closer to us and her lips curve upward when she sees the man in the tracksuit. I guess she's happy to see him, but it's hard to tell because her eyes are kind of glazed over. The man gets up with a swish. He stands next to her and gently puts his arm out for her to grab. She puts her hand on his forearm and leans into him a little bit. "Thata girl," he says.

He nods a good-bye to me and I almost lose it as I watch them inch by, thinking about how if it's true, if it is morphing or has already morphed . . . I open my eyes really wide hoping to dry them out. Then I shut them tight, trapping my tears inside.

I glance over at Allissa, who's acting like she's still reading her magazine, even though her face is wet and she's yet to flip the page.

"I'm going . . . I'm gonna go for a walk," she barely gets out before briskly walking away.

I focus for the next five minutes or so on keeping my eyes dry by opening them really wide and going back to tracing the carpet pattern. Then I hear, "All set in there. You can go back now," as Becky passes me by with a smile, pushing Mom's vitals cart.

I use my palms to wipe away any residual signs of worry from my face and then head back to Mom in 5112. When I get there, I can tell right away that something is really, really wrong.

At first it looks like Mom's just staring out into space, but when I get closer to the bed I see that her eyes are actually very focused, and angry. She's sitting up a little more now too. Actually, she looks like she's about to disconnect herself from everything and literally jump out of the bed.

"Mom, you okay? What's wrong?"

She turns her head toward me fast, and then flashes me a big smile. It's as if someone just pushed an "Izzy's here" button on her face.

"Nothing wrong, sweetie. I'm fine."

"Mom, what's going on?"

"Nothing, I'm just frustrated, but it's fine."

"*What's* fine?" I'm trying to keep the tone of my voice calm.

"It's just Dr. Madson. He's . . . he's being so . . . He just told me that I'm not going to be able to eat for a while, and I have to go on TPN," she says, shaking her head.

"Oh. Wow." TPN is a big deal. It's this liquid nutrition that goes into your blood that people get when they can't eat. You have to hook yourself up to it with a port or an IV.

"No, no, I'll be okay without it. I can still nibble on stuff without getting too sick. I don't know why he has to make things so difficult for me."

"I don't think he's trying to make things difficult. He's—"

"I don't want to be connected to . . . I don't want to carry that bag of stuff with me everywhere I go. I don't need the whole wide world knowing I'm sick."

"I know, but, Mom—"

"It's just not necessary."

"Mom, you *have* to do TPN if that's what Dr. Madson tells you to do," I say, my voice rising in both pitch and volume.

"Izzy, please, I'm fine. Let's not—"

"You're not fine. You're—you're sick."

"Izzy!" Mom says this in the tone of voice she uses when I've said a swear word too loud in public. "Please. I'm sorry I brought it up."

"You're sorry you brought it up?" I repeat, but more to myself. Then I look at her. "You're sorry you brought this up?" I say again, louder.

"Yes, enough!"

"But—"

"Enough, enough, enough!" Mom shouts, punctuating each "enough" with a sharp head shake. My mom doesn't have a "1980s aerobics class" cry like Allissa, or an "I'm going to stay so still, you won't even know I'm crying" cry like Jenna, and she doesn't have an "I'm going to try and trap my tears inside my eyelids for as long as I can" cry like I do. She has a sad puppy dog kind of cry. She cries softly, her mouth pursed together, sniffing in quick inhalations through her nose and then letting out this high-pitched, sing-songy whimper through her mouth.

"Hand me my phone. I have to call Cathy and find out what's going on at school. And I was supposed to finalize the music list this afternoon for the Dance for Darfur DJ, and go through carpet samples for Gretchen and—"

"Mom." I roll my stool closer to the bed and hand her a tissue. "It's okay, please don't worry about all that right now. It doesn't matter."

"No, I need to"—she wipes the tissue under each eye— "find out what's going on [cough] because I need [cough] to handle it."

I don't think Mom takes mental snapshots like I do. In fact, I think she already has her mental snapshots picked out before they even happen, like she needs control over all the images in her head, and how they make up her memories. And I don't think she's ready to let being sick be a part of them just yet, be a part of her yet.

I put my hand on her back because she's leaning forward now like she's trying to cough, but can't quite get anything out. "Are you okay?" I hand her more tissues.

She nods and grabs her bedpan, coughing up into it hard. Then she wipes her mouth with the tissue. But when she tries to speak again, she just starts coughing. I watch her pause to catch her breath, a metallic taste overtaking my mouth. When she breathes in, she makes this low, wheezing rumble, then lets out another huge cough. Another breath in, another wheeze, another cough. And again.

"Mom?" But she keeps coughing and wheezing and spitting up into her bedpan. The sounds she's making are the most awful sounds I've ever heard, ever. It's like I can hear things moving around, trapped inside her chest, clawing to get out.

"You need water?" I push her call button and try hard not to panic. The metallic taste in my mouth is making me feel queasy. I grab her cup of ice chips from the table. "I called the nurse, so—"

"I can't—feel like—I can't—get a breath," she squeezes out.

I run out into the hall shouting, "She can't breathe! She can't stop coughing!" to whoever's close enough to hear. Soon our room is jam-packed with nurses all crowding around Mom's bed. One is clipping something onto her fingers, another's attaching tubes and IVs to a new machine that's being wheeled in, another's paging Dr. Madson, and everything's beeping and buzzing and talking and ringing and crinkling and shoe-squeaking. Now they're putting tubes in her nose, and a mask on her face. Mom's shaking her head back and forth, flailing her arms, and coughing and coughing.

"Okay Linda, I know this is scary," one of the nurses says in a slow, low voice, "but the calmer you are, the easier it will be to breathe, okay? Now try to give me a nice deep breath . . ."

I watch as Mom stops flailing and somewhat surrenders to the nurse's rhythmic breathing. With each steady breath she takes into her mask, the numbers on her machine change with a beep. 90% BEEP 89% BEEP 87% BEEP 88% BEEP. I feel like I should do something, but I don't know what. Maybe I should find out who invented this oxygen-reading machine and strangle them, because the sound of that BEEP is making me want to lop off my ears.

Dr. Madson charges into the room then with Pam and Allissa practically walking on his heels. Since the two of them can't get to Mom, who's entirely surrounded, they rush over to me. Pam starts asking nonstop questions. Allissa's just silent and still, not even aerobics-class crying. As the amoeba-blob of nurses shifts and grows around Mom, Allissa shuffles off to the far corner of the room, her eyes staying on Dr. Madson, who's listening to Mom's chest now. He moves the stethoscope around to different spots, saying things like "Crispy" and "Lungs are crispy on this side."

What? What does that mean? I've never read anything about crispy lungs on the Internet. And I swear Dr. Madson looks worried. That's not good. It's not good when the doctor looks worried. He's saying something to the nurses about Mom's bladder, and drainage, and excess fluids, and there are so many people in this room, there are way too many people in this room. And it's so hot in here, like way too hot. The collar of my sweater is choking me again.

"Right behind you!"

I jump out of the way in time to avoid colliding with

another bed being wheeled past me into the room. Why do they need another bed in here? And I can't understand what anyone's saying. I feel like my ears are connected to a TV remote that keeps flipping through the noise in the room, letting me hear only bits and pieces of people's sentences.

"We're going transfer her over on 'three'—"

"Linda, you're doing great. I'm just going to—"

"It's an NG tube and it might be a little uncomf—"

"This might pinch for just a sec until I—"

"When did she start on the—"

"Ninety-two, ninety-three, ninety-four percent, and now it's at—"

Finally, Dr. Madson gestures for the three of us to follow him outside. He doesn't take us into a private room or his office, but starts talking the minute all three of us get out into the hallway. He talks fast, but in a quiet and even tone. I try to make my remote-control ears stay on him, but I can't seem to do it. I hear *complete obstruction*, and *fluid in lungs*, and *blocked bowels*, and *emergency surgery*, and *laparoscopy*, and *peritoneal cavity*, and *small incision*.

Now they're wheeling Mom away. I don't know where they're taking her. But *emergency surgery* keeps pounding its syllables through my head. And Pam's holding all these papers, and handing them to Allissa and me, and I need to sit down. I lean against the wall, my neck like an hourglass again dumping sand into my chest, faster and faster. Where did they take her? Are they prepping for surgery? We can't even talk to her? There's so much sand. I can't breathe. I manage to stagger over to Pam, who's now sitting on a hall-way bench with her head between her hands. She looks up at me. "It's fine, okay? She's going to be fine," I hear her say distantly.

I nod, try to swallow, tell her I'm going to find a bath-room. Only it's not me who seems to be doing this. It's another girl who just happens to look exactly like me. I watch this girl walk down the hallway, pulling at her collar, and disappear into a single-occupancy bathroom.

When the bolt slides into the lock, my hands fly to my chest and I jolt back into myself. My heart is beating hard. Why is my heart beating so hard? Probably because I'm having a heart attack. My heart is trying to beat through the sand, faster and faster. My chest hurts so much, slicing at my insides. Oh my God, my heart is clogged, I'm having a heart attack! I clutch the sides of the sink and stare into the mirror. My eyes are unnaturally dilated. Oh my God, I'm dying! I need help! I have to get out of here! I have to go get help. No, I need to stay here. Yes, I should stay here because I'm not really dying because that's just ridiculous.

But what if I am? A hospital is the very place people go to die. They either get better, or they die. And right now Mom is not getting better. She's morphing. And she's obstructed. And she's not breathing right. And she's having emergency surgery.

I drop the lid on the toilet and sit down. I'm blacking out, and I don't have enough room in here to get into a good deep-breathing position. I turn myself toward the wall and drop my forehead low against the tiles. Then I crisscross my arms as far as they'll go behind my head and muffle my face between my elbows because I'm starting to sob.

I don't want to die, I don't want to die, I don't want her to die. She can't die. I need to talk to her. I want to talk to her. I want my mom. I want to talk to my mom. I want to see my mom. And I've really messed everything up, and I'm one of those girls, and now it's too late.

CHAPTER 22

I'm scared.

"Izzy!"

My head snaps up. My neck throbs. My shoulders ache. I have no idea where I am. Then I look down and see the ugly patterned carpet, and a flipbook of yesterday's snapshots whizzes through my head. I'm back at the hospital, sitting in the waiting room, because that's where people who don't have heart attacks in bathrooms belong.

We were told Mom's condition was too unstable for surgery last night, and we'd have to wait until the morning to see how she was doing. So I slept on Allissa's dorm room futon last night since her college campus is only twenty minutes away and it didn't make sense to drive me all the way back to Broomington. I don't see how anyone can sleep soundly underneath a ceiling covered in glow-in-the-dark stars and a giant poster of a half-naked male model holding a puppy, even under normal circumstances.

Allissa continues to elbow me awake even though I'm fully sitting up now, my eyes wide open.

"I'm up, I'm up. What's happening?" I ask.

"Pam's in there, talking to Dr. Madson," she says, gesturing down the hall, and then adding, "How do you even nap, Izzy? These chairs are so uncomfortable."

"Well, this sweatshirt kind of doubles as a blanket," I offer.

I'm wearing the only sweatshirt in Allissa's closet that wasn't too small for my chest. It belonged to one of her ex-boyfriends, who I'm guessing was a linebacker. This is the punishment I get for spilling cereal on my sole sweater: an XXXL sweatshirt with "U Got 2 Work 2 Play!" emblazoned across the front in menacing letters.

"What do you think they're talking about?" Allissa asks, staring down the hallway.

I'm about to offer a guess, when we see Pam coming toward us.

"You guys want to see her?" she asks, stopping in front of us with Dr. Madson right behind her.

"We can see her?" I bolt up.

Dr. Madson explains that although Mom had a good night, she's still in the ICU and that they won't be able to treat her fully until she gets her strength back, which could be another forty-eight to seventy hours.

"But then she'll be okay?" Allissa asks, zipping her Bedazzled hoodie and standing up.

"We'll know more in a couple days," is all Dr. Madson says.

You can smell the ICU as soon as you get near it. Fear mixed with hand sanitizer. A new nurse named Anne leads Allissa and me down a bright hallway filled with lots of tired-looking people sitting in chairs against the walls. She takes us into Mom's room, which is really more of a windowless alcove with a bed.

Everything in here is beeping. Each long, clear tube, each metal pole, each bag filled with fluid is connected to something that is beeping, which is somehow connected to the bed, which is somewhere connected to my mom.

"Can we go over to her?" Allissa asks Anne, who's standing next to Mom's bed, hooking up another bag of fluid to a pole. She nods and then says, "She's not totally with it, but I'm sure she can hear you."

Allissa and I venture in from the doorway, slowly making our way to the edge of Mom's bed.

I don't know who that is, but it's not my mom. Her eyes are crusted closed, her skin looks kind of yellow, and her hair is matted on one side. But the scariest part is her mouth. It's all stretched out over what looks like a mini vacuum attachment. Her lips are chapped and cracking, and there's dried blood caked in where the skin has broken.

"That's a respirator," Anne tells us, seeing me eyeing Mom's mouth. "It's just helping her breathe a little bit better so her body can rest."

I nod, and open my eyes wide, then pinch them shut. I feel a clammy hand press into mine, and squeeze Allissa's back.

. . .

I'm standing outside the medical center's main entrance watching Marcus attempt to stop his car, only to be told that no outside cars are allowed to stop here, and that pickups are only allowed at the "pickup parking structure."

That's right, when I got back to the waiting room, Pam hit me with ten very unexpected words.

"Okay, so listen, Izzy. I'm sending you back to school."

Unghh.

So Pam sent Marcus, via Cathy, to take me back to Broomington. So far, it's been ten minutes of Marcus being yelled at by security while circling around a snow-covered island with a "No Pickup/No Delivery" sign on it. Which would be a lot more amusing if it weren't so cold out.

He finally gets the car close enough to the curb to scream out, "Screw this, just hop in!"

"No pickups!" I hear for like the fourteenth time.

"What?" I say, pretending I don't understand while quickly opening the door and practically rolling into the passenger seat.

"Wow, that was . . . intense," Marcus says, illegally speeding off as I fasten my seat belt. "I pride myself on having an excellent sense of direction, but this place is extremely confusing. And that's a completely asinine system they have. For you to take a shuttle to another structure when I'm already here? It defies logic."

"Yeah," I say.

"So, hi." He cuts a glance at me and leans over to give me a side-hug. Or, I hope that's what he's doing because I lean over and give him a side-hug back. And for a nice moment I get something other than hospital smell, Marcus's good, fancy-soap smell.

"I like your . . . sweatshirt dress?" he says as I take off my coat and throw it in the backseat. l look down at my oversized sweatshirt/jeans combo, smile, and say, "Thanks."

We drive for a while, Marcus focusing on finding his way to the highway, and me watching the snow starting to come down again. I'm a little surprised he's by himself, actually. I had figured Jenna would come with him, seeing as the only communication I've had from her was Cathy saying "and Jenna sends her love" when she called to check in on what groceries I needed.

After we've been on the freeway for a few minutes, Marcus says, "So, you're going back to school, but Allissa's staying up in Pittsfield?"

"Yeah." I'm still looking out the window. "Pam said that with my art portfolio due, and dress rehearsals for the play, and exams, and helping your mom get stuff together for the dance, that it's more important for me to back in Broomington than at the hospital. And Allissa's school is so close, so . . ."

"So your mom is . . . ?"

"Not strong enough to have surgery, I guess."

"Oh, okay." Marcus nods. "Well . . . I'm thinking good thoughts for her."

"Thanks, Marcus."

And that's the last thing I remember saying before hearing, "Izzy? Izzy, we're here."

I lift my head up off the side of the window and stretch my arms up in the air.

Marcus comes to my side of the car and opens the door. "Madame," he says, and does one of those fake flourishes while holding out my coat.

"Wow, what great service," I say, stepping out.

"So"—Marcus closes the car door and helps me shrug into my coat—"you okay?"

"What? Yeah, I'm fine. I'm . . . pretty good."

"Yeah?"

"Yeah," I say, leaning up against the side of the car. I look at Marcus and wonder for a second if he's seen the photo. Just the thought of it is so exhausting that it's easy to push it away.

"Okay," Marcus says, leaning back against the car now too. And he's just close enough now where if I wanted to, I could tilt my head to the side and let it rest on his shoulder.

"Well, good. As long as you're . . . good," Marcus says.

"I am—I'm good. I mean, I'm just—well, I'm kind of . . ." I close my mouth and straighten myself up. But then Marcus slips his arm behind my back and kind of pats it gently, and when he brings his hand up to my shoulder and gives it a little squeeze, it's like something inside me unhinges, like I'm one of those camping tents with the cheap poles that keep popping out of place, and I collapse.

Marcus pulls me into him, close.

"I'm scared for her," I say into his chest. "I'm kind of . . . just . . . scared."

He wraps his arms around me tight and lets me cry.

CHAPTER 23

I don't want to talk about it.

I know it seems cowardly, but I've been hiding out in the bathroom stalls between classes, and coming out only after the bell rings. I just don't feel like talking or seeing anybody. I slip into my classes late, just after they've started. I don't get in trouble either, because Pam has already talked to all my teachers about Mom. So when I walk in, they all just nod and give me these encouraging smiles, as if they're impressed I'm even upright.

"There you are!" Meredith manages to cut me off before I can make it inside the art room. She cocks her head to the side, her ponytail falling around her shoulder, and gives me the smallest of smiles.

"Izzy." She says my name like it's the title of a very sad, serious movie. "How are you? How are you feeling?"

"I'm fine, I'm feeling"—empty, defective, like something inside me is disconnected—"fine."

"You up for doing some set painting?" she asks, because I guess technically I'm supposed to be at rehearsal right now.

I shake my head and tell her I'm just going to stick around the studio tonight and get some work done.

She nods and reaches her arms out, giving me a double shoulder squeeze, and then before walking away, says something about how she's here for me, if I need to talk.

That's what a lot of people have been saying to me, that they're "here for you if you need to talk." Which is nice, but some of these people I don't even talk to under normal circumstances, so I'm thinking it would be strange to use them now, like as a therapist. And how would they react if I said, "You know what? Yes, I'd love to talk," and then sat them down and told them how I looked at my hairbrush this morning and saw that it had an unnaturally large amount of my hair in it, and how for a split second I thought that it must be because of the progeria, that I'm losing my hair as I prematurely age. But then, right as I was about to look up "teenage hair loss" on Symptomaniac, this voice popped into my head, and she said, *Come on, Izzy. You know that's a normal amount of hairbrush hair,* and I answered myself, in my head, *I do? How can you be sure?* and there was no answer, and it was hard, but I walked away from the computer and continued getting ready for school. You'd think I'd feel better, that voice telling me that I'm fine and not sick. But I don't. I just feel lost.

I throw on my smock, grateful nobody else is here tonight, and grab one of my half-finished paintings from the rack.

"Hey."

I look up to see Jenna peeking her head around the door, and then turn my eyes to my canvas. The familiar gesture—poking her head in like that—now just feels bizarre to me.

"How are you?" she asks, walking over. "How's your mom?"

"The same," I say.

"Oh. Okay. Well, I guess that's . . . good?"

I shrug and start adding some white to my beige mixture, still not able to get Mom's skin tone quite right.

Jenna sets her Post-it-note-plastered binder on the table, unsticking her sleeve from it, which is covered in bits of different colored gaffing tape.

"So . . . we're in tech week and . . . it's pretty crazy. I was hoping to see you at rehearsal, but—"

"Nope," I say. So this is the reason she finally drops by, because she needs me at her play rehearsal.

"Listen, Izzy," Jenna says, and she's close enough now that I can hear her breathing. When I still don't turn around, she hoists herself to sit on the table and dips a tiny paintbrush into some of my blue paint. "I'm really sorry about blowing up on you and being so . . . dramatic lately. I've been totally overreacting about everything." She brushes blue paint onto her pinky fingernail. "And I don't even know why I got so upset about you trying to fix me up with Nate. It's not a big deal. I mean, I just . . . I'm not interested in him, but that's no reason for me to go to crazyland, right?"

I nod and shrug, keeping focused on my canvas.

Jenna paints another nail blue, and then smiles at me again.

"You're wasting paint," I say.

"Oh. Sorry."

"My mom's in the hospital." I fully stop what I'm doing and look at her.

"I . . . I know," Jenna mumbles, slinking down from the table. "I've been thinking about you and—"

"People who hardly know me are coming up to me left and right, and you're supposed to be my best friend and you don't even—"

"I've been thinking about you this whole time!" Her eyes and mouth widen simultaneously.

"Great. Thanks for the thoughts."

"I've been . . . I've been wanting to talk to you, to tell you that"—she pulls a long piece of yellow gaffing tape off her elbow, coiling it between her thumb and index finger— "well, you know that I think organized religion is structured societal brainwashing, but I'm still praying for your mom. I am. And I told my mom to tell you—"

"Why didn't you just tell me yourself?"

"I don't know." She shifts her gaze from her twisted tape to the studio's paneled ceiling. "I guess I was just embarrassed about . . . I was so awful to you, and confused and . . . and I didn't want it to stress you out even more, hearing from me. But I wanted to call you. I wanted to tell you that—" She flicks the tape to the floor, leaning her upper body back and turning her palms out like she's under arrest. "God, Izzy I'm sorry. I'm not good at this stuff."

"What stuff? Being a good friend, being a decent person?"

"You know"—her hands and eyelids drop—"you're not good at this stuff either."

"What's that supposed to mean?"

"I try to talk to you, I've tried to talk to you so much."

"What?" I get out through clenched teeth.

"All last summer and you just kept . . . blowing me off."

"I did not. I— That's not true." I turn back to the painting, shaking my head.

"Yes you did." She hops back onto the table, gesturing at me with my tiny blue brush. "I tried to see you, and I asked about your mom all the time, and tried to get you to talk about it, just even . . . a little bit, but you just totally isolated yourself, and you kept saying how busy you were with your portfolio, but—"

"Well, I was."

"Yeah, but you could have at least just come out with me *one* night or—"

"Well, going to U of M and drinking at some frat house with a bunch of your writing group friends was kind of the last thing I wanted to do after a day of taking care of my mom!"

"Well . . . fine, but . . . we didn't have to go up there, we could have—"

"No, it was always 'so and so's having a party, and this guy's gonna be there, or that guy's gonna be there.' I don't even know who you were hanging out with. I guess with Meredith and all them, and your cousin, who I didn't even know about until last week! I didn't even know you had a cousin Amy until *last week!*"

"Just forget it, I'm sorry I brought it up, I don't . . . I don't want to talk about the summer anymore."

"Well, clearly you do, because you're— Give me that." I grab the brush from her hand, which is shaking so much, she's splatter-painted her shoes.

"Listen"—she shifts her weight onto the table again, looking down at her now black-and-blue boots—"can we just—" Then she stops and looks over my shoulder. "What are you doing here, Marcus?"

"What?" he says, poking his head through door and taking off his headphones. "What?" he says again.

"You're supposed to be going over light cues with Derrick?"

"Well, when Derrick is done humping Emily Belfry in the lighting booth, I'll go ahead and do that," he tells Jenna. And then to me: "Hey, how's um, how's it going? Any news?"

"Nothing new," I say, giving him a smile.

"I looked for you in the choir room and thought maybe you'd be set painting."

"No, I'm actually . . . um, not working on the play anymore," I say.

"Oh. Why?" Marcus says, turning to Jenna.

"She's busy with her portfolio and her mom and everything, duh," Jenna answers, springing off the table.

"Oh. Right. Yeah, so I just wanted to see how you were doing, and drop this off for you." He pulls a pint of strawberry ice cream out of the bag he's carrying.

I smile. "All for me?"

"I figured you could use it."

"I really could," I say, taking the pint from him.

"Well"—Jenna claps her hands together loudly—"that was . . . nice of you, Marcus. Enjoy your ice cream, kids. I . . . have to go . . . remove Derrick's tongue from Emily's mouth, and you know, finish the run-through and . . . so . . ." She grabs her binder, flashes Marcus her special Cathy smile, totally avoids my gaze, and bangs out the door.

"Sorry . . . I'm not interrupting your art . . . flow or anything, am I?"

"No, it's already been interrupted. Have a seat." I open the pint of ice cream and fish a plastic spoon from the bag.

"So my mom talked to Pam, and she said your mom has some kind of digestive problem?"

"Yeah." I shovel the strawberry into my mouth. "Blockage."

"Hmm . . . you know, the stomach, it's weird, it's actually, it's kind of like the heart."

"Oh. Huh. What do you mean?"

"Well, it's not totally like the heart, but it has electrical waves that make it contract. And I guess after we eat something, our stomachs contract like two or three times a minute, grinding up all our food and then sending away all the stuff that it . . . doesn't need. So when someone has blockage or stomach problems, I think it means that for whatever reason, there's something that's messing with their electrical waves, so that their stomach doesn't contract, and so then all the food inside can't go . . . where it's supposed to go."

"Uh-huh," I say, shoveling in more ice cream.

"But with your mom," Marcus continues, "I think some of that mucus you were talking about is probably . . . mucking things up too."

"Right. Probably," I say, turning back to my canvas, not really wanting to think about my mom's abdomen and her mucus right now. I just want to find out when she's going into surgery and get back to the hospital to see her.

"It's just that last week, after you told me more about what your mom has, I looked some stuff up."

"You did, huh?"

"I was curious. Also, I figured you might want to talk about it more because . . . well, because what she has is rare, and so there's probably not a lot of people to talk about it with . . . and I just figured if you wanted to talk about it . . . ever, you could, with me."

"Thanks," I say. I hear Marcus shift his weight behind me, but he doesn't say anything more.

"So . . . I should probably get back to work." I gesture to my canvas. "I have a week less to finish everything now, and I have to do some of Mom's prep work for the dance too and—"

"If we even have a dance," Marcus says, sounding relieved for something else to say.

"What?"

"Mrs. Preston still wants to cancel, but my mom and her whole PTO crew are torn, I guess because of all the work they've put in, and it being a fund-raiser. They're meeting with Preston tomorrow, or no, day after tomorrow, I think, to try and work something out, I guess."

"Why would they cancel? What are you talking about?"

"Because of . . ." He clears his throat and says at a barely audible level, "Boobgirl."

"What?"

"I'm sorry, that's what everybody is calling her, it's terrible. But yeah, if nobody comes forward, then—"

"They're going to cancel a dance just because of one . . . stupid picture?"

"Well, it's basically gone viral. It's been e-mailed to me at least thirty times already."

I clench my teeth. "Really? Wow. Really."

"Yeah. It's gone around the whole district. So I guess the pressure is on to . . . punish somebody . . ."

"Huh," I say.

"Anyway, if the dance does happen and you and Blake want to go with us, Meredith said that—"

This makes me wheel around, and suddenly my face is on fire, so I turn quickly to face my canvas again. "Oh. I didn't know you were going with—"

"Oh, yeah, yes I am. Meredith asked *me,* actually." He laughs, but it sounds more like he's got something caught in his throat.

"Wow."

"Yeah, I think after helping her out with her photos, she was just grateful that—"

"That's great," I say, putting the ice cream down on the table and starting to mix the already mixed paint on my palette. "I'm . . . I'm not sure what our plans are, but . . . sounds like fun."

"So is that something new?" Marcus asks, moving so he's next to me and gesturing toward my canvas.

"Yup."

"It's really good," he says, studying the painting. "Must be hard for her."

"Who? Meredith?" I ask.

"What? No, um, for your mom," he says, walking closer to the canvas, "losing control of her body like that because . . . you know . . . she's always so . . . put together."

"Oh. Yeah. I guess so," I say, angling the canvas a little more in my direction. "It's not done, I'm still in the middle of . . . I'm really just . . . just painting."

"Oh, and you're using some of the medical journals I got you," he says, pointing to the small stack at the end of the table and smiling.

"Yeah, yeah, some of the pictures are pretty cool."

"This one"—he picks up the magazine at the top of the pile—"has this really interesting article in it, this study about love and feelings and how—"

"A *study* about love and feelings?" I glance at him.

"Well, yeah. It's about how it's basically the result of some feel-good biological union between some peptides and some cells. Just a chemical reaction; a . . . generic addiction."

"What is?"

"Love."

"Oh," I say, mixing some colors, deciding to change Mom's skin tone slightly. "Wait, so then why do we love certain people and not others?"

"What?"

"If it's so generic, why do we love some people and not—"

"No, I think it just depends," he explains, "on how chemically attached you are to them."

"But aren't we all chemically attached to everyone?"

"Um . . . I guess kind of." His eyes go unfocused as he thinks about this.

"And if love is something so . . . generic," I say, "then shouldn't all people be at the same generic level of love to each other and therefore replaceable? I mean, different people have different relationships with other people that produce their own unique chemical reactions, right? What's so generic about that?"

"No you see . . . okay, yes, you can have different relationships with different people, but that doesn't necessarily mean you have more love for them. Is that what you're saying?"

"No . . . I'm just trying to say that . . . Wait, so you think all people are replaceable?"

"No," he says. "But, well, maybe in a biological sense, I mean, we're all just a bundle of—"

"You think . . . that my mom is replaceable? Like if something happened to her and she was gone, I wouldn't miss *her*, specifically?" I ask.

"What? No. No, no, no, that's not what I'm saying," he says, blinking, "but technically . . . I mean chemically speaking—"

"Wow, well, thanks for this heartwarming chat, Marcus, but I have to get some work done."

"Wait, what's wrong?"

"You," I say, "you're wrong. I didn't even want to talk about any of this—my mom, her stomach, the stupid dance, and that stupid photo, and chemicals, and the biological definition of love. And then you just start talking about how my mom—how you think my mom is replaceable!" I drop my paintbrush, barely even knowing what I'm saying.

But apparently Marcus knows exactly what I'm saying, and to him it all translates to "Get out of my studio and leave me alone."

Which, he does.

CHAPTER 24

I was picked.

"I'm beginning to think you should juuuust . . . set up a cot and sleep here, Izzy." Miss S. walks toward me slowly from her office, setting down a towel, a really large wooden vintage picture frame on top of it, and a hammer on the table next to me.

I'm at the studio for the second night in a row.

"This thing is such a space sucker." She runs her long fingers against the ridges of the frame and then hands me a pair of safety goggles. She puts on a pair herself over her glasses and then picks up the hammer and takes four powerful whacks at the frame, splitting it at the corners.

"Sorry," she says as I wince at the noise and remove my goggles.

"So, how's your mom?" she asks simply, propping her goggles on her head and picking off bits of wood from the towel.

"I just got off the phone with Pam," I tell her, adding some more red to Mom's lips. "She's still pretty knocked out, but Pam says she's getting stronger. She's going to call when they put her on the surgery schedule." We both turn and look at my cell phone sitting on the table like it's a bomb that could go off at any second.

Miss S. sits down on the stool next to me. She reaches her hands up to the top of her head, and then into her pockets, and then claps them together kind of like a seal, which she does when she's trying to remember something.

"You're wearing your glasses, Miss S."

"Ah," she says, smiling, tapping at her frames, "yes I am. So, can I look at this for a moment with you?"

We take a second and both just stare at my canvas. Then she turns to me.

"I think this is really good, Izzy." Her voice goes quiet.

I turn to her. "Really?"

"Yes. And it's not far from being . . . remarkable."

"Thanks, it's . . . I mean, it's not finished yet."

Miss S. glances at my canvas and then back at me again. "You are so good at capturing the shot, you know what I mean? You're technique iiiiiiis . . . your brush is like a camera, click, click, click." She smiles and pushes the shutter down on the air camera she's holding.

"A camera?" I concentrate on rolling a wad of dried paint between my thumb and forefinger.

Miss S. bends over the table, resting her elbows on it and turning her head to me. "What I'm trying to saaaaaaay . . . is that this is *really* good work." She turns her head back to the painting and slowly nods at it, like it just talked to her or something. "She looks liiiike . . . a perfect snapshot. So . . . real."

"Yeah, she does." I smile, but it feels sad.

"But she's not, right? Just paint and canvas. I thiiiiiink . . . that's one of my favorite things about art. You're free to move all your snapshots out of thiiiis . . . reality"—she sweeps her palms across the room—"into this one"— she puts one palm on the top of my chest, the other on my forehead, then presses her hands together with a small smile, and adds, "Thaaaat's remarkable."

I nod, staring back at the Mom on my canvas. Then we hear the doorknob make a soft clang as it touches the wall.

"I'm sorry, I didn't mean to interrupt, I was—"

"No wooorries . . . Mr. Hangry, come in." Miss S. gives my back a quick rub and then heads out through her office.

I tighten my grip on my brush and tell myself that, although tempting, turning around and stabbing Blake's eyes out with the end of a paintbrush won't solve anything.

"I thought I'd find you here. We're on break from rehearsal. Wow, that looks . . . really good," he says.

I whip around. "Don't comment on my painting. You don't—you don't know if it's good or not good."

"Okay, I know you're mad. I mean, of course you're mad, but—"

"I'm not mad. I'm actually just . . . I thought you were—"
He starts to say something but I cut him off. "I thought you were human, when in fact you're not. You're spineless. You're a . . . *testosteclone*," I spit out, stealing Jenna's word, but thinking she'd approve.

"A what?"

"A . . . a lemming! You're a lemming!"

"Listen, I want to explain how this all . . . I mean, it wasn't supposed to . . . I didn't mean for it all to go down like that, and—"

"You didn't mean for it to 'go down like that'? Wow, well, that makes everything better. That makes it all okay then." I turn back to my canvas.

"I'm sorry, okay? I tried to get rid— Listen, I have this plan, this story. I'll start this rumor that it was just some girl, some girl from Lakewood Prep or something, and—"

"What? No! Please don't bother." Ugh, why should I let Blake think he can fix this, that he can just start some rumor, foist it off on some other girl, and make it all okay?

"I'll handle it, okay?" I say. "I'll decide what to do. I'll figure it out." And I will. I've decided. I'm going to just march into Mrs. Preston's office tomorrow—I've already made the appointment—and shout, *"Blake Hangry! Blake Hangry is your man! Punish him, but don't cancel the dance."* Then she's going to look at me and say, *"And how do you know that, Izzy?"* And I'm going to say *"Because it's me, Mrs. Preston. Boobgirl is me."* It will be simple enough. Yes. I don't need Blake to save me from being Boobgirl. Which, the more that I think about it, really seems like a pretty minor problem to have right now.

"No, really, Izzy. I don't mind." Blake's still talking, his voice rising slightly. "I'll start the rumor about this other girl and then everyone will think—"

"I said don't bother. You got what you needed, now just . . . please just leave me alone."

"Izzy, I'm sorry, okay? I didn't want to get involved with you, but I had to. I didn't want to involve you in any of this, but—"

"Oh, well, I'm so sorry you *had* to get involved with me. I'm sorry you *had* to hang out with me, and lie to me, and use me and—" I cut myself off, bolting across the studio under the guise of needing to fill my tub with more water.

"Come on," he says, slumping down onto one of the stools. "That's not what I meant. I like hanging out with you. I wanted to hang out with you. That's why those guys picked you, because they knew how much—"

"I was *picked*?" I turn back to him, holding my newly filled tub, the water rippling in my shaking hands.

"No! Crap. Yes. Okay, yes, you were, but—"

"What do you mean I was *picked*?" I ask, walking slowly toward him.

"You were, but only because I liked you, that's why. They knew I liked you, so that's why they picked you, and I had to get them that picture. But afterward I swear I—" But he doesn't get to finish. I'm hearing *"had to get them that picture"* and seeing the Rap Room, and my boob, and my sweater, and that cell phone picture—they fill up my whole head. It's like I'm some sick mental snapshot copy machine spitting out copies and copies of that picture until I can't see, and the next thing I know Blake is drenched from head to toe in paint water.

"Woo! Way to go, Izzy!" someone shouts. I turn to see Meredith and Cara standing at the studio door, which I realize now was open. Cara blows her bangs out of her face, takes a sip from the can of pop she's holding, and remains standing there, gawking at us as if she wants us to push PLAY on the movie we've paused. Meredith steps in and says, "Why don't you go clean yourself up, Blake. Not that it would help."

Blake slowly lifts both arms and runs his hands up his face and then over the top of his head, squeezing the murky water from his hair. Then he stomps his feet on the floor, one after another. But not in an angry way, more like his legs are heavy, like it's an effort to just pick them up and plunk them back down again.

I'm breathing hard and holding the empty water tub up in the air with one hand, like it's a gun that accidentally went off. Blake looks like he's about to say something, but then turns around and walks out of the studio, dripping a trail behind him.

"Listen, um . . ." My tongue fumbles around in my mouth as I try to say something to the girls, to explain. "I'm turning myself in tomorrow, okay? So . . . don't worry about the dance. I—"

"No, no, don't do that! Why?" Meredith says.

"Totally, don't do it." Cara shakes her head back and forth as she starts to mop up the floor with paper towels.

And then the table starts buzzing. I pick up my vibrating phone.

"Pam! Hi, what's going— What? Right now. Is she—? Uh-huh. Okay, well what should I— Okay, are you sure?

Are you sure I should—? But— Okay. Okay, I will. Thanks. Bye."

"What's up?" Meredith asks.

"They're going to be prepping Mom for surgery, tomorrow night, and then she's scheduled for the next morning."

"Oh my God," Meredith says, taking Cara's can of pop from her and handing it to me as if it's a bouquet of flowers. "Are you going down there? You need us to find you a ride?" she asks.

"No, no. Pam said that she'd just be unconscious anyway and it would make more sense to wait to come when she's . . . awake," I explain, taking a sip.

"Well, we can keep you busy at dress rehearsal tonight, get your mind off things," Meredith says.

"Totally." Cara bobs her head.

"Oh, I . . . I really should just stay here and work. I still have a whole new piece I have to start and—" I look down at the puddle of paint water on the floor, feeling my nose tighten, my eyes sting.

"Ugh, Blake is like so the last thing you needed right now," Meredith says, throwing up her arms. Then she reaches both her hands out to me, and this time, instead of a double shoulder squeeze, she gives me a great big bear hug.

In the movies, when a girl does something like pour a tub of water over a guy's head, or slap him across the face or something, it's a happy moment; a moment for the soundtrack to kick in. The music would swell, the girl would nod her head and smile at her posse of friends, and then the film would freeze on a shot of them all high-fiving as the credits role. Or maybe the girl would be alone, and she'd just look down and smile at the dejected guy, and then saunter away to the theme music, her hips swinging in slow motion.

I'm pretty sure if the movie ended with the girl hugging and crying ugly-face into her ex-best friend's hair, people would want their money back.

CHAPTER 25

My lightbulb's on.

I'm still in the art room, and I'm having a staring contest with a blank canvas.

I decided to start on my last piece, since tonight and tomorrow are maybe all the time I have left. But it's been over an hour and I've done nothing. Absolutely nothing. What a waste.

I pull off my smock and head down the hall toward the back entrance to get some air. The front entrance is closer, but that's right near the theater and I don't want to mingle with the dress rehearsal still going on.

Even though I'm in just a thin T-shirt and jeans, it feels good to be outside. Well, for a quick moment at least, until a gust of wind blows by that's so strong, it zips up and under the bottom of my shirt, making my shoulders shudder.

"You know, it's winter out here!"

I look up and see Marcus slowly driving up to me from the student parking lot, shouting out his window. He stops in front of me, and leans his head out farther.

"I'm heading to pick up pizza for rehearsal. Wanna ride with me?"

I look toward the back entrance doors and then at Marcus, tapping his fingers on the steering wheel, wearing a nervous smile. I walk over to the passenger's side and get in.

After two minutes of silence mixed with some "Is the heat on too high?" and a little "Feel free to change the radio station," I start to regret it.

"So . . ." I finally say. "It's . . . freezing out."

"Yeah," he says.

And silence.

"My mom's having surgery, day after tomorrow," I finally say.

"Oh"—Marcus nearly jerks the car to a stop at a yield sign—"well, that's great! I mean . . . that she's strong enough."

"Yeah."

He nods. I nod. Then silence again. We arrive at a red light.

"So listen, Izzy." He leans forward and turns down the already low radio. Then he kind of laughs and sits back. "I feel like I'm always saying this to you," he says, looking up at the ceiling of the car and then over at me. "But I'm really sorry. I mean, I'm really sorry I . . . went off on a tangent about . . . all that stuff," he finally gets out, looking back at the road. "It's just, well . . . when I'm scared, or when I'm upset about something, I . . . I find it comforts me to tackle it with . . . well, the facts, kind of."

"Okay . . ."

"Yeah 'cause . . . you know, with computers, the stuff I do, and science, well for the most part, there's really not a whole lot of room for . . . subjectivity. It's like 'this' is the way something is, and 'this' is the outcome that will result, because of 'these' specific things. Knowing that, having that logistical, uh . . . structure, makes me feel better. But I didn't even think about how that might not be, um . . . the kind of stuff that makes *you* . . . feel better."

I nod and tell him that that makes sense, also wondering, what *is* the kind of stuff that makes me feel better?

"And that stuff about your mom and chemicals and . . ." He accelerates through the green light now. "I just get excited about new things I read and I just ramble. I have this habit of letting whatever's in my head just pop out before I get a chance to . . . filter it. And so, sometimes what comes out ends up being . . . well, being . . ."

"Hurtful? Rude? Insensitive?" I offer, but with a smile.

"Well"—he smiles back at me—"those weren't the exact words I was going to use, but, yeah, sometimes. I just . . . didn't mean to upset you like that, especially this week."

"Thanks," I say as we pull into the Ramano's parking lot, which is pretty filled up. I offer to run in, so Marcus shrugs off his coat for me to wear and tells me the cash is in the front pocket.

As Vinnie Ramano Junior impressively packages up the three large pizzas, two orders of breadsticks, and liters of pop for me to carry, I think about what Marcus just said, about saying whatever it is that pops into your head without filtering it first, and what a foreign concept that is for me.

Marcus pulls up the car to meet me and pushes the passenger-side door open. I set the pizzas down on my seat and put the rest of the bags in the back, moving the shopping bags there out of my way and onto the floor.

"You do some recent shopping at Babies in Toyland?" I ask him, putting the warm pizza boxes on my lap and closing the door.

"What?" he pulls out of the lot, his car already fully smelling like garlic and oregano.

"The shopping bag in the back, from Babies in Toyland?"

"Oh, yeah. Yes. I mean, not for me—something I had to pick up for my mom."

I raise my eyebrows at him.

"No, no, it's a gift," Marcus explains, "for our cousin Amy. It's her birthday next weekend, and so—"

"It's for Amy's birthday? Is your cousin . . . is she having a baby?"

"A baby? Is she *having* a baby? What?" And then Marcus starts laughing so hard, he has to take off his glasses because his eyes are watering.

"Marcus . . . what's so funny?"

"Well, my three-year-old cousin having a baby is kind of hilarious. No, actually," he says, not laughing anymore, "it's kind of disturbing."

"Oh. Oh, I'm sorry I thought, I thought we were talking about your other cousin Amy, the older one. I guess on your dad's side?"

And that's when Marcus tells me that they only have one cousin named Amy, and that she's turning three tomorrow.

I'm waiting for him to say *Just kidding*, or *Happy, excessively early April Fool's Day*, but he doesn't. So I ask again, just to be sure I heard him correctly. I make him repeat his answer like three more times, until I'm sure he thinks I'm either crazy or hard of hearing. And suddenly, as we near the school, I feel like one of those cartoon characters with the lightbulb popping up over its head. Mine's dimly lit, but it's there.

The theater is a complete madhouse. I've never seen so much pandemonium take place while listening to four-part harmony with twang. At the end of the act, Marcus holds up the pizzas. Soon chaps-wearing boys, can-can girls, and Southern belles swarm him from all sides.

"Don't eat in your costumes!" Jenna shouts, hopping down from the stage and shaking her head. She stops when she sees me standing next to Marcus, handing out pizza.

"You're here." Jenna breaks out into a huge smile.

"I am," I say, opening up a pepperoni box to a crowd of drooling cowboys.

"Do you want to help out, or are you just hanging? You can just hang, but if you—"

"No, I'll help. Or hang . . . whatever," I say.

She grabs a plate and loads a couple slices on it. I get some napkins and follow her out of the chaos. We walk into the choir room and see Ryan Paulson standing on a chair, finishing up some foliage painting.

"Hey," he says, jumping down, eyes on Jenna, "how's it going? I'm almost done here, how's it looking?"

"Great," Jenna tells him. "Pizza's here."

"Oh cool. Did you get some? Do you want me to get you a slice? Izzy?" he asks.

"We're good," Jenna says, looking down at the plate of pizza she's holding.

"Oh, yeah right." Ryan makes a goofy, "I'm so stupid" face and then just stands there, bouncing from one foot to the other, looking up at Jenna.

"So . . . you should probably go get some before it's gone." Jenna waves him out, shaking her head and laughing a little. "He's like a worker bee jumping bean."

I laugh and then tell her the set looks great.

"Thanks. It's almost done. We're kind of behind, though." She walks around the piece Ryan was finishing, looking amused. "He thinks he's Rothko or something. It's just a tree. I keep telling him one shade of green will do."

"Well." I smile. "We all need to express ourselves."

"Izzy!" Meredith spots me as she's walking by. "I'm so glad you're here!" She rushes into the choir room, holding what looks like one of our cafeteria's napkin dispensers.

"We ran out," she explains, "and pizza hands plus costumes . . ." She shakes her head.

"Good thinking," Jenna says. Then quietly, "Thanks."

"You're welcome." Meredith smiles and turns to me.

"Okay, so I've been thinking about this a lot, and I don't think you should turn yourself in tomorrow. I know you're planning on it, but I don't think you should."

"Oh, oh no, Meredith—" I stumble around for the right way to tell her to keep her mouth closed, while Jenna stops mid pizza bite and gapes at Meredith as she continues spilling my beans, getting more and more animated and energetic as she goes.

"I just don't think you admitting to being Boobgirl will make anything better. Why should you do that? Don't do it. I'm sure they won't cancel the dance, and if they do, oh well. It's not your fault. It's Blake's fault. And you shouldn't feel guilty. Right? Jenna, you agree, right? Will you please help me convince Izzy not to go Preston tomorrow? It's just so not worth it!"

Jenna doesn't respond. In fact, I think she might be choking on her pizza. Finally she coughs, swallows, and gasps out, "You're Boobgirl?" It sounds like she's asking a question and making a statement at the same time. "Why didn't you say something? Oh my God!" She puts her pizza down on the chair next to her and starts zigzagpacing around the room. "Here I am going on and on about the play and the set and you're Boobgirl? *You're Boobgirl.* I have to sit down."

"No! That's wet!" Meredith screeches, stopping Jenna from getting brown paint all over the back of her pants. Which would be hilarious for a second and then just really unfortunate.

"Wait a minute, you didn't know?" Meredith asks Jenna. "How did you not know?"

"Yes, Meredith. Thank you. Why didn't I know?" she shrieks, then says in a softer tone, "So . . . you told Meredith, and not me?"

"No, she found out by accident."

"How come you didn't tell me? I mean, I know that we've been . . . Oh my God! This is so huge. I didn't even know . . . you were . . . doing anything with Blake. You . . . you haven't told me anything."

"Well, you didn't tell me anything about last summer until last week. And you lied about it," I counter pointedly.

"I . . . what are you talking about?" Jenna gets up slowly and walks toward the set, hiding herself behind a Rothko green tree.

"I know about Amy!"

"What?" Meredith's looking at us both now like we're the walls of some maze she's stuck inside of. "Who's Amy?"

"Jenna's cousin, who had sex with the capital *D* douche last summer. Only it wasn't—"

"Your cousin had sex with Nate Yube too?" Meredith sits down now, taking this in.

"No, no, no." Jenna paces a full circle around the foliage. "There's no cousin Amy, I mean, there is, but . . . never mind."

"Nate Yube?" I turn to Jenna. "What does she mean . . . Oh." Oh! "Well . . . right . . . so then it's true. You were . . . it was Nate Yube?" I ask, the lightbulb over my head growing brighter. "Wow. Wow, so is there anyone else you were secretly dating last summer that you decided to not tell me about? Ryan Paulson? Jacob, maybe?"

"See? This is why I don't tell you these things, because you're so . . . judgmental."

"Judgmental?"

"Yes. You're . . . Your tone, you're judging me."

"No," I say, turning toward her, "do whatever, with whoever you want. Date the whole basketball team. I dated Blake, if you can call it that. But when you lie to my face about it—"

"I was going to tell you the truth. I started to a million times, and then . . . I don't know, the whole Amy lie just came out. And it was so much easier because then I could tell you what happened, and you'd still . . . want to be my friend . . ." She trails off.

"You think . . . You thought I wouldn't want to be friends with you anymore . . . because of that?"

"No. But, I don't know. Maybe."

I chew my lip and look down at my slice.

"I thought," Jenna continues, "I thought that's why you and Meredith weren't friends, because she was *that* girl."

"I'm sorry," Meredith whispers, who we now realize has relegated herself to a corner of the room, and is just standing against the wall trying to make herself scarce. "I should go."

"Oh, crap. No, *I'm* sorry," Jenna says to her. "I didn't mean it like that, I—"

"It's okay, I get it." Meredith nods. "I should get this to

the theater anyway," she says, picking up the napkin dispenser and walking out of the choir room.

"I should go apologize." Jenna looks toward the door. "She's been nothing but nice this week, trying to make amends, and I feel like I should—"

"Did you think . . . ? I mean, you thought I wouldn't want to be friends with you anymore . . . because you had sex with Nate Yube? I can't . . . I can't believe you thought . . . that's really what you think of me? Really?"

"No, I just . . . I don't know. I'm sorry I lied. I wish I hadn't and I wish you had told me about Blake because I feel like I could have maybe— Oh my God, that picture. Are you really going to turn yourself in?"

"I have to. I just . . . I already made the appointment. By one p.m. tomorrow I will officially be Boobgirl."

Jenna just shakes her head, and for the first time in as long as I can remember, she seems tongue-tied.

"I should get back to the studio," I say, picking up my uneaten pizza slice and throwing it in the trash, then heading for the door.

"Hey, Izzy," Jenna calls. I turn and she opens her mouth, and then closes it, and then opens it again and then just sighs and says, "Don't paint Leroy."

I shake my head, fighting a smile. "Oh, didn't I tell you? I'm working on a whole Leroy collage. It's pictures of him mixed in with garbage and I'm calling it . . ."

"Kitty Litter!" Jenna finishes for me, which was the phrase on Mrs. Kerns's sweatshirt today. Only it was a cat garbage man that looked nothing like Leroy. We laugh, and it feels easy again.

"Good luck tomorrow," she adds, and smiles.

"Thanks," I say. I head back to the studio, appreciative of Jenna's well wishes even though I know good luck won't make Boobgirl go away.

I step away from my Mom canvas, stretch my arms up over my head, and shake out my wrists, which are starting to feel a little numb. I wonder if it's something to do with my circulation or if it's maybe some kind of clot. Then that *"You're fine!!!"* voice bellows into my head again, and I stop myself from flipping through my mental Symptomaniac archives of illnesses with blood clot side-effects.

I shake my wrists out again and pick up a couple vintage picture frame pieces that Miss S. left lying on the table. *They're probably just asleep. But what if they aren't?* I shake them out again. Okay, if I still have wrist tingles in ten minutes, I'll worry.

Every time something like this happens now, I remember what Marcus said the other day about me *wanting* to be sick. And okay, I know wanting to have a heart attack sounds even more messed up than feeling like you're having one when you're not. But if I really was sick like that, then at least Mom could concentrate on something about me that's potentially fixable and not out of my control, like the way my body looks when I walk. And then she and I could be sick together; we could be in the hospital room together right now, and then maybe she wouldn't be so ashamed about it all, and about me.

I squirt some paint from the almost empty bottle of yellow and mix it with some water. I back away from my canvas and see Mom's perfect snapshot face staring back at me.

I'm sorry I'm not with you right now, but Pam told me to stay here, I think at her.

Relax, Izzy, she says. *I'm fine. Get your work done. Why waste your time idling around a dreary hospital with your comatose mother when you have so much to do!*

I guess you're right, I think at her, and then zigzag the end of the wooden shard across the canvas, cracking her into pieces.

CHAPTER 26

I am photogenic.

I look at my reflection in the mirror. My keypad is indented in my cheek. I guess sleeping on my cell phone wasn't a good idea.

I get out of the shower ten minutes later and have two new voicemails. I almost drop the phone hearing Allissa's voice, but then relax after she says, "Status quo, nothing new to report." Then Cathy Mason's voice keeps me company while I walk to school.

"Hello, Izzy. It's Cathy. Cathy Mason. Hope you're eating breakfast. Pam said to get you the whole wheat English muffins, so that's what I got. Yum. So let me get down to business here. I e-mailed you a dance checklist. Check your e-mail. It should be in your e-mail by now. Subject is 'dance checklist.' So most of it is self-explanatory. But honestly just peruse it, if you see something you can do, or want to do, do it and let me know. If not, no worries. No stress. I'm going to take care of finalizing and e-mailing 'Ray Ray the DJ' the inappropriate song list. And I'll keep you posted this afternoon on how it goes with Mrs. Preston. But don't you worry

your head about that smut. Okeydokey. Love and light to your mom, and talk soon-ish."

I walk through the school parking lot but feel like turning right back around. I keep going, though, repeating my mantra: *Show up, tell the truth, and it's over. Show up, tell the truth, and it's over.*

By the time I get to my locker, I feel like I'm in one of those dreams again, except not the one where you go to school naked. In fact, I don't know what I'd be wearing or not wearing when I go to school in this dream; I just know that people would be acting super-duper strange. Like all the girls would be huddled together in little clumps whispering and giggling. And not in their usual clumps, either. These are, like, mixed-up clumps — girls standing around with girls they would ordinarily never stand around with.

I get to my locker and, as I'm pulling out my Spanish book, I see Meredith reflected in the mirror on my door. She's leaning against her locker with Cara down the hall and also . . . Jenna? Meredith's waving her arms around a lot, and Jenna's writing stuff down in a notebook and nodding. Then Cara and Jenna scatter in different directions. Meredith stays at her locker, though, furiously typing into her phone.

I'm about to head over to see what's up when I feel someone tap me on the shoulder. I turn around and see Ina standing behind me.

"Hi," I say.

She grins at me wildly and then gives me a thumbs-up and says through mostly closed lips, "I'm in! Are you in?

Hope you're in too!" and then slouch-sprints away.

Okay. What?

Then in Spanish when I'm heading to the front of the room to give my oral presentation using the subjunctive, Sara Ronaldson, in her cheerleader uniform, pats me on the back and says "Rock it" like she's revving me up before a big game or something.

And by the time I book it out of English to Mrs. Preston's office for our appointment, two more people have given me a grinning thumbs-up, and this freshman girl I don't even know fist-punches me in the shoulder. What the hell is going on? Why is everyone being so . . . *nice* to each other?

When I get to the lobby, I see a crowd of girls lined up outside the main office. Oh God, maybe I'm too late. Maybe the dance has already been canceled. But then why would everyone be acting so happy about it?

"Try and stay in order, please, and keep your chatter to a minimum." Assistant Principal Kippley is walking through the line, handing girls what look like little slips of paper, like at the deli in Farmer Jack's. When I get closer to him, he hands me one too. It says *60*.

"What's this?" I ask.

"Your number," he says, dismissing my puzzled face and walking away.

"Mr. Kippley," I shout over the babbling hum of girls, trying to follow him toward the office without losing him. "I'm Izzy Skymen." I tap him on the back. "I have an appointment with Mrs. Preston right now."

"What? Oh. You do? Hmmm. Izzy . . ." He sighs. "Well, yes . . . hmmm. Well . . . let me see if she can still take you." He pushes a button on his phone, looks around the lobby with a grimace, and says, "Jeanine, I have Isabella Skymen— No, no, she has an appoint— Yes. No. I don't think that's the case. Okay, will do." He slips his phone back in his suit pocket and gestures for me to follow him inside.

I take a seat on the bench outside Mrs. Preston's door. Thirty seconds later the door opens up and I hear Mrs. Preston say, "And are you sure you want to go on record with this information, Miss Belfry?" Wait, what is Emily Belfry doing in Mrs. Preston's office? Go on record with what?

"Yup, I'm sure," Emily says, and her magazine-ad face breaks out in a huge smile when she walks out the door and sees me on the bench. I don't think I've ever seen her teeth for that long.

"Isabella, come in."

Mrs. Preston adjusts her suit skirt and gingerly takes a seat behind her desk. She tucks a strand of short, curly hair behind her ear and pulls a tissue out from the dispenser on her desk. She's only about forty-five, but the perfume she chooses to overspray herself with ages her by about thirty years. She takes the tissue in her hand and uses it to dab across her upper lip. Then she lets out a long sigh and smiles at me. The skin around her eyes crinkles at the sides, which makes her liner lines look really off. It hasn't been proven yet, but we're all pretty sure Mrs. Preston has her eye makeup tattooed on. To draw eyeliner of the same angle and thickness, and produce the same blue-green blend on the lids every single day . . . it's just impossible.

"So Isabella, good to see you," she says, looking down at what I'm assuming is my file. "How is your mother? We're thinking of her, of course, and you."

"She's um . . . the same," I say.

"Well . . . yes. So, I have to say you're a breath of fresh air today. A break from the masses," she says with a tattooed-makeup crinkle-smile.

I smile back at her, not quite understanding what she means. Then I look behind me at the door, which seems really far away right now. What am I doing here? Why did I think this would make things better? Why didn't I just let Blake lie for me? Why am I taking the blame for this? What does that solve? What was I thinking? Tell the truth and it's over? Yeah, it's over for *me*.

No, no, I have to do this. I have to be the one to do this, not Blake.

"So," I say, taking a deep breath, "what I wanted to talk to you about was the cell phone picture."

"What? Oh . . . oh no, really? *Really?*" She lays both her hands flat on her desk and is leaning forward, looking at me, her black pupils taking over her light blue eyes.

"Um . . . yes, I . . . See, that picture is actually of me."

"You know what?" Mrs. Preston jumps up from her chair, shaking her head, and raises both hands in the air as if signaling to the heavens that she gives up. "I give up!"

she actually says, shaking her hands. "I give up! I give up! I give up!"

Uh, not quite the reaction I expected. "Excuse me?" I say, slowly rising from my chair.

"Isabella, I'm disappointed in you."

"I'm sorry I . . . I just thought I should come forward so that—"

"Kippley!" Mrs. Preston screams into the buzzer. "Miss Skymen is one of them. Put her on the list. All right," she says to me, opening up her door, "so like all the rest, I now have to officially ask you, are you sure you want to go on record with this information, Miss Skymen?"

"Um, yes . . . Wait, the rest?"

"Mrs. Preston, it was me! I'm the girl in the picture. It was me," Angela Rodriguez screeches, shooting up from the bench.

"For the love of all that is sane." Mrs. Preston shakes her head. "No offense, dear," she says, taking a long look at Angela's flat freshman chest, "but that's just not possible."

"No, it was me. I'm your girl," Angela says, nodding her head up and down.

Mrs. Preston sighs, dismisses me with an outward wave, and leads Angela into her office with an inward wave. Then she shouts to Mr. Kippley, who's standing by the main entrance looking around like it's infested with mice. "Ten more minutes and that's it!"

I float out of the main office like I'm on one of those moving walkways. I make my way past the waiting line of girls, which goes all the way through the main entrance, past the cafeteria, and down around to the study alcove hall, until suddenly Meredith, Cara, and Jenna grab hold of me, and like a bunch of ants seizing a large piece of food, they drag me to the drama room.

"Okay, what just happened?" I ask, falling into a nearby desk.

"That was . . . amazing!" Meredith says, giggling and opening up a celebratory pop that she cheers into the air, spilling some on Cara's head. "Mrs. Preston looked like she was about to commit herself when I told her," she adds. "Classic."

"Totally, so classic." Cara bobs her head in agreement.

"Well, she can't blame anyone now," Meredith says, clapping her hands together, "right?" She turns to Jenna, who's standing by the door, nodding and darting her eyes around the room as if this is the first time she's been here.

"Wait . . . you guys . . . you did all this?" I ask.

"Jenna masterminded it." Meredith giggles, still sounding a little out of breath from our sprint to the drama room.

"You did?" I turn to Jenna.

"We strategized after you left rehearsal last night," Jenna explains with a sly smile.

"Yeah." Meredith beams, her eyebrows practically touching her hairline.

"Wow. So . . . wait, everyone knows?"

"No, no, the other girls don't know who, they just know to confess," Jenna says quickly.

"Oh," I say, still taking it all in. "I— Wow. Thank you, guys. This is— Wow, thanks."

"So I'm thinking the dance is still on," Jenna adds.

"Oh"—Meredith turns to Jenna—"my mom said we can use her display panels from her showroom, but we have to transport them."

"Perfect. Ryan said we can use his van."

"Just a Man and His Van," Cara says in a deep voice, imitating Ryan's dad's commercial. There's a pause, and then we all laugh. Cara smiles. "Is he in our group?"

"Oh . . . I don't know . . . I guess we could ask him to be." Jenna shrugs.

I must look confused, because then Meredith says to me, "We're screwing the whole date thing, going as a group instead."

"Oh."

"Marcus was cool about it," Meredith adds.

"Uh-huh, totally cool." Cara nods.

"I mean, he's like obviously so into you, anyway."

"Yup, totally. Totally into Izzy." Cara nods. Which makes me spit a mouthful of pop across the room, and which makes everyone, including Jenna, burst out laughing again.

"What? He's not in . . . What are you talking about?" I look over at Jenna, who's now half smiling, rolling her eyes, and wiping up my spit take.

"Oh please," Meredith says, "it's like . . . the way he looks at you when he's not talking to you."

"What way?" I practically screech.

"I don't know, it's like . . ." Meredith's eyes roll up as she searches for the words.

"Like he wants to marry you and have a hundred babies and live in a little house and be your boyfriend and husband and everything and stuff," Cara bursts out, which is the most I've ever heard her say at once.

"What are you, like five?" Meredith pokes her in the ribs as we head out of the room, giggling past the line of girls that Mr. Kippley is unsuccessfully trying to disband. That one sentence loops through my head as we walk: *The way he looks at you when he's not talking to you.* But then the chaos in the lobby cuts through.

"Ladies, if you're confessing to the viral picture, the matter is now—"

"But Mr. Kippley, it was me!"

"It was me too!"

"Why are we doing this, again?"

"So Boobgirl doesn't get suspended, duh."

"I can't believe some stupid guy actually sent that."

"What if we get in trouble?"

"We won't—there're too many of us."

"I don't know . . ."

"What if Jason sent your picture around?"

"Jason's my boyfriend!"

"But what if he did?"

"I would kick him in the balls."

"If I had those boobs, I'd send the pictures around myself."

"Sara, that's not the point!"

"Jenna? Izzy?" We turn to see Cathy Mason charging toward us. Cathy always takes giant steps when she walks, the kind of lengths you would need if you were climbing up stairs two at a time. Meredith and Cara disappear into the clump of girls being escorted back to class, while Cathy cuts Jenna and me off at the pass. She taps her right hand against the dance binder she's pressing up against her chest, the charms on her multicolored bracelet swinging.

"What are you two doing out here? Are you a part of this madness?"

"No, just heading to class." Jenna flashes an angelic, made-for-Cathy smile.

"Oh, good. I'm just in such a state. It's one thing after another. How are we supposed to get a message across that this behavior is unacceptable if there's no punishment? But we can't punish a hundred-plus girls, now can we?"

"No, we can't." Jenna grins and then shifts to a straight face. "It's a shame."

"But, you know, I am relieved, actually, because now we can get down to business, because I said to her, I said 'Jeanine, all these girls shouldn't be punished for lending their innocence to one marked lamb,' right? Right, Izzy?"

"Um . . . right, yes, Cathy."

"Bathroom stalls, teachers' lounges," she says, as if she's

listing porn titles. "Make it legal and get a room. *I* had a room. One sacred, matrimonial room."

"Mom!" Jenna yelps as I turn my head aside to swallow my smile.

"Well anyway"—Cathy points her index finger in the air at no one in particular, her charms clinking against the bracelet—"we aren't forgiving or forgetting, we're just moving in a forward direction."

I look at Jenna, then back at Cathy, and nod solemnly.

"Mom, we gotta get to class."

"Yes," I add, "but I'll take care of my dance list now that it's . . . still on."

"Yes, yes, okay. Do what you can, dear. Jenna and I will take care of it. Oh, that reminds me, here." She extends her arm to Jenna, which has three shopping bags hanging off it like she's a rolling rack. "I brought the twine and the rest of the supplies to make the donation card trees. Can you start that tonight, please?"

"Yeah, I'll take care of it." Jenna grimaces, transferring the bags to her arm.

"Love to your mom." Cathy kisses her hand at me and waves us off.

Jenna and I round the corner and head down the much quieter hall to our lockers.

"Thanks again for today. That was . . . it was pretty amazing."

"It was pretty fun, wasn't it?" Jenna grins. "I was all broad strokes, rallying the troops, and Meredith was awesome at organizing. You know, she's not so . . . bobbly . . . all the time."

"Yeah, I know."

Jenna balances the bags with one hand and opens up her locker with the other.

"Izzy, I'm sorry that . . . I'm sorry I didn't do anything to . . . I feel like with you I could have maybe seen this all coming or—"

"Well, I think you kind of did." I cut my eyes to her. When she doesn't say anything, I go on. "But maybe I wouldn't have listened anyway. It *was* . . . Blake."

"Yeah." She nods. "It's just that I gave Meredith a hard time about not knowing about Jacob, and for being *that* girl with Jacob . . . when really it was me. I'm *that* girl."

"No. You're not. I'm not either. And neither is Meredith. There's really no such thing as *that* girl."

"When we were figuring this all out last night, I didn't really think it would work. I thought there's no way everyone's doing this. But they did."

"I know." I shake my head and laugh. "Emily Belfry?"

"Right? She was amazing. She designed the mass e-mail."

"Wow."

"Yeah, it's crazy. Seeing everybody today made me . . . I don't know, I guess it made it . . . not okay, but . . . you know. Better." She makes room in her locker for the dance supply bags. "Not that it's ever going to be okay, what happened with Nate. But . . ." She slams her locker door. "Do you know what I mean?"

"I think so . . ."

"'Cause I did this for you. I did. I just didn't realize until it was all happening, how . . ." She glances at me and trails off, this weird look on her face.

"What?"

"Well, I guess it was good for me too. I needed it too, I mean." Then she grabs my arm, hauling me down the hallway. "Man, I wish you could have seen Mrs. Preston's face when I told her it was me." Jenna laughs. "I definitely caught her staring at my T-shirt, comparing my baby chesticles to your pixelated lady curves."

"Oh no!" I laugh. "Poor Mrs. Preston."

"You know, it actually *was* a really good picture of you. You're very photogenic."

I shake my hands in front of my face, palms out, like trying to erase what she just said.

"I mean it. You *have* seen it, obviously."

"Briefly. Just once. I've deleted it from my in-box like twenty times already."

"No, no, you have to take a good, long look at it. Own it," she says, fiddling with her phone. And then mine starts beeping.

"Jenna!" I say, seeing she's just sent me the picture.

"Save it. Make it your screen saver."

"You're hilarious," I say, holding my phone now like it's contraband.

"What is going on over there?" Marcus passes us by, shaking his head.

"Free pizza outside Preston's office," Jenna ad-libs.

"What? Really?"

"You better hurry!" Jenna shouts.

"You're so mean." I shake my head, watching Marcus take off down the hall, and then realize that Jenna's watching me watch Marcus. We stare at each other silently for a second before Mrs. Kerns walks by us and says, "Hello ladies" in a Mice Skating sweatshirt. Then, for the first time in days, I let myself really enjoy a full-out, totally obnoxious, belly-snort laugh.

Twenty minutes have passed and I've gone as far as covering my blank canvas in shades of gray. Whoopee. Way to go, Izzy. I can hear singing through the walls, and debate just giving up on this last piece and watching another dress rehearsal instead.

I stare at the gray plane before me. *No. Come on. Just paint something. Anything.* I wipe my hands down my smock, and in a pathetic attempt at procrastination, I slide my phone on again to check my messages. Of course it's the same as it was ten minutes ago, just one unread picture message from Jenna.

I set my phone back down and rip off a new paper towel. I dip it back into my gray. I swirl my hand around the canvas, darkening and thickening from the bottom up. Then I squeeze out some yellow and blue onto my palette. I'm trying to get this specific color that's snap-shotting around in my head. I mix some more color in, and then add some white, then I mix, and add, and mix, and add, and then abruptly stop, dropping my brush down so quickly to my side that paint splatters all over my blue jeans. But I don't care. I'm transfixed by this color. I put my palette down, backing away from the canvas as if it's about come alive or something.

I wipe off my hands and slide my phone on again. I try and keep my hand steady, but it's already starting to shake a little. I manage, though, to open up my latest picture message. And there it is: my boob, my bra, and my fuzzy green sweater.

I don't know how long I stay staring at it, but I know it's long enough where the picture starts to lose its context. The subject starts to blur into the background, the planes merge, and it no longer looks like a boob, a bra, and a sweater, but just pixels and colors and shapes and shadings and dark and light and greens and pinks and reds and oranges and whites and browns and yellows.

I flip my phone upside down and stare some more. I turn my phone on its side, and stare some more. I zoom in. I zoom out. I zoom back in. Then I get out my sketchpad.

CHAPTER 27

I think it's beginning too.

The waiting area on the surgery floor is a lot nicer than the one on Dr. Madson's floor. It's got bigger chairs and more privacy, not being smack in the middle of everything, and there's a bunch of private rooms to go into if you want to be alone. One of them even has a fancy, super-loud, instant cappuccino machine in it.

"Gin!" Pam says, throwing down her cards while taking a bite of her tuna sandwich. "Again?" I shake my head and lift one of Allisa's magazines off her body. She's passed out with her earbuds blaring, so I don't think she'll mind. I look at some pictures of a bunch of girls all wearing the same color dress, and then start reading an extremely engrossing article about the kinds of things celebrities do that "real" people do too.

I try to occupy my mind with this useless information, like how many face cards I have in my hand, or the name of a celebrity grocery store in a city I don't live in, where I can buy the best gluten-free food. That fact led to me treating myself to a Symtomaniac fix about celiac disease, and gluten intolerance, which actually did help pass the time.

I'm about to drop Allissa's magazine back on her body when she bolts up, now wearing her earbuds like a necklace. "What? What? What happened?"

"Nothing. No news."

"What's taking so long?" she says groggily, opening and closing her mouth, like she's registering the post-nap taste in her mouth.

"I'm sure we'll hear something soon," Pam says. "It probably takes some time afterward to . . ."

"Bring people out of anesthesia," I conclude, handing Allissa a piece of gum.

"Oh God, not again. I really don't need to hear those kinds of words right now, Izzy."

"What words?"

"Words—medical words, like . . . *anesthesia*."

"Anesthesia?" I ask. "The word *anesthesia* bothers you?"

"Stop saying it!"

We all stare down the hall toward Dr. Madson's office, and then back at each other.

"Allissa," I finally say. "You know what anesthesia is, right?"

"Yes, Dr. Izzy." She hops up. "I need coffee."

"Sorry," I say, following her down the hall and into the cappuccino machine room, "I just don't understand why that's a scary word. I mean, yes, it's dangerous when not administered correctly, and Mom is really thin, but it's not like—"

"Okay, stop." Allissa grabs a cup and pushes the button on the machine. "Why do you have to go there all the time?"

"I don't know," I say over the gurgling, whirring, and hissing. "So I won't . . . go insane, I guess."

"Well, hearing all those details, all the time, kind of makes *me* go insane, okay?"

"Yeah, okay. I know." I grab a cup for myself, thinking about Marcus trying to talk details with me the other day.

Allissa takes a sip of her instant cappuccino, makes a blech face, puts the cup down on the side table, and takes her phone out of her pocket.

"Which one of these do you like better?" She passes me her phone, which has a picture of two identical objects that I think are called credenzas.

"Um . . . the black one."

"Izzy, they're both black."

"Oh, sorry . . ."

"I have to finalize for Stacy what we want for the attic."

"Oh." I take another look. "The one with the silver handles."

"Yeah, you're right. The other one is 'tacky, tacky,' but that one is 'classy tacky,' you know?"

"Yeah," I lie, and take a sip of my—barf—cloudy, coffee-flavored sugar water.

"I know Mom's birthday's not for another couple weeks," Allissa says, flipping through more pictures of furniture on her phone, "but I want to have this done for her, or nearly done soon. 'Cause she'll want to work when she gets out of here, right?"

"Yeah."

"So . . . you think she'll like it?" Allissa asks.

"What, the attic? The new furniture? Yes. She's gonna flip out."

"She went gaga over your painting last year." Allissa slumps down on the chair next to the machine. "She still brags about it to people. And what did I get her? A stupid pair of earrings."

"She loves those earrings!"

"Eh."

I sit down next her.

"I'm really sorry I charged those things to your card," I tell her now.

"It's okay, I didn't . . . I won't rat you out. I guess you were just trying to help Mom."

"Well, it doesn't matter. Nothing I do, or did, really helped. I mean, I know facts and stuff, but who cares. It doesn't . . . It didn't help her."

"Izzy, there's nothing you could have done. I mean, what could you have done?"

"I don't know, something! I heard her coughing, and I knew she wasn't eating, and then I saw she posted in her chat room, and . . . She told me about her appointment with Dr. Madson before she told you and Pam, but I never said anything . . . *useful*, and now she's—"

"It wouldn't have made any difference. Don't make yourself more crazy than you naturally are." She gives me a small smile. I smile back and take another sip of my cappuccino.

"I'm not . . . I'm not moving away if anything . . . if she . . . you know . . ."

"No, of course not, we're both staying here. You'll come live up here with me," she says matter-of-factly, and I guess I look skeptical, because she adds, "I mean, once I get out of the dorms and get my own place."

I smile at her, nodding.

"I'm so sick of being here," she gasps out, drop-folding her upper body forward like a marionette. She pops back up, and then marionettes her neck over the back of the chair. She looks absolutely exhausted. But, at the same time, still kind of great. She's managed to inherit that Mom gene that makes even a T-shirt and sweatpants look perfect. But I know underneath, like I do with Mom, that it's not.

I soon nudge her upright because Pam's marching over to us with Dr. Madson right behind her. He looks more like a real surgeon now, in scrubs and one of those fancy masks around his neck. Pam has an "I'm crying, but it looks like I'm laughing" kind of cry. She's holding one hand to her stomach and the other to her mouth while leaning back and shaking her shoulders up and down.

"What is it? What's going on?" I stand up with Jell-O legs, and put a shaky arm around her.

Twenty years go by, but finally Pam gets out, "She's . . . she did good!"

I drop my shoulders down and lean into Pam's side.

• • •

A nurse named Carlos has led the three of us into the recovery room, where he's telling us that Mom's a "happy camper right now."

Which I think is think code for "super-drugged-up."

". . . Pepse, gimme Pepse, wanna Pepsi," Mom's mumbling when we arrive. Which I think is a good sign, that she's talking now.

"Hi, Mom," I say, trying to sound cheerful.

She opens her eyes a little and squints at me. "Izzy, Izzy, Izzy," she says, but kind of all together like it's one name.

"Yeah? Hi, Mom," I repeat.

Pam and Allissa both step around to the other side of the bed and say hi, murmuring encouraging words. Mom mumbles out their names and then says, "Whacha'll doin'?"

"Um . . . nothing much," Allissa says.

"'Kay, well, gimme Pepsi."

"Linda, everything's going to be okay. Okay?" Pam says.

"Okeydokey," Mom mumbles. "Donlehem put me underneath withow cuttin' my hair off."

"What?" Allissa says.

"I need a cut before they put me underneath it 'cause my hair's very irregular and s'not very regular. Is it regular?"

"Looks . . . pretty regular to me, Mom," I assure her.

"Your hair looks great," Allissa chimes in.

"I gotta go underneath now so see you ssslater, 'kay?" Mom mumbles.

"Linda, you've already gone under. It's over now, okay?"

"No, no, no, it's the beginning, it's all the beginning," Mom insists.

"No Mom, it's all over. It's over." Allissa reaches for her hand.

"Yes, it's over Linda, it's all over," Pam says.

"It's all beginning. And I wanna wear my pink sweater. Not the Pepto-pink one. The other one. 'Kay? Donlehem do anything to me till I ge'my pink sweater on."

"Okay, Linda, whatever you say." Pam is smiling.

Then Carlos comes in again and tells us that Mom needs her rest. We kiss her good-bye while she continues to mumble something about Pepto-pink, her skin tone, and a Pepsi.

We leave the room, and I know Mom might have been really loopy in there, but I think she was right. I think it's all just the beginning too.

CHAPTER 28

I'm not sorry.

"So that's why I'm using scented candles now," Pam says, finishing up this story about how Tootsie—her ginormously fat cat—won't stop eating the potpourri in her bathroom and keeps throwing up lavender-smelling vomit.

Allissa almost spits up her tea, she's laughing so hard, and next to me at the kitchen table, Cathy Mason looks so disturbed that I'm surprised she hasn't excused herself to the bathroom yet. I laugh-snort some milk out my nose, and even Mom, who hardly ever finds bodily function humor funny, cracks a small smile when she says, "Oh, Pam, that is absolutely disgusting." She reaches for her wheely pole. "Okay," she says, "who wants another piece of cake?" She slowly gets up from her chair, and we all turn and watch her rise. Walking on her own is a development as of yesterday, and it makes us all a little nervous.

"Linda, sit yourself back down," Pam says.

"It's my house and I'll serve cake when I want to," Mom replies, shuffling and wheeling her way over to the kitchen counter. Mom's only been home three days, but yesterday the visiting nurse who changed her PIC line said she's acting as if it's been three weeks.

"Linda, you look so good," Cathy says.

"Eh," is Mom's reply.

I've been trying to keep her beauty routine up, but I'm not very good at it. I blow-dry her hair for her in the mornings, but I don't have the skills with the round brush to get it into her usual stiff yet buoyant shape. And her hair's a lot thinner than mine, so if I take too long, random chunks end up looking creased or waving in the wrong direction. Her makeup is on as usual, though she still has some cuts on her lips, and the skin around her eyes looks a lot looser now since she's lost more weight.

She takes the plastic lid off the giant cake that Cathy brought over and says, "Mmm, it smells so fresh." Then Cathy apologizes, again, for being the dunce who brought food to a woman who can't eat. Mom says, "Hush," and picks up a huge knife to start cutting more slices for everyone. It's pretty impressive, since one of her arms is pretty much useless, still hooked up to her TPN pole.

Allissa and I help carry the cake plates back to the table. I pull a giant piece of wallpaper trim off Allissa's back on the way. Mom hasn't been able to do stairs yet, but after the work Allissa and I did today, she won't even recognize the attic when she sees it.

I should have spent today at the studio, but it's been really nice having everyone here and hanging out. Since Allissa has midterm exams coming up, and Pam was needed back at school, I've been mainly on my own with recovery duty at home this week.

". . . And so the whole thing overall was really very impressive," Cathy says, finishing up her *Oklahoma!* review. "Although the kiss at the end between that cowboy and soprano girl was way too long. And I'm pretty sure I saw tongue! Which I think is a tad inappropriate, especially for that time period."

"Hmm," Mom says, as if she's seriously contemplating a French kiss's historical accuracy.

I missed seeing the play, since opening night was Mom's first night back home. She kept mumbling, "If it's important to you, go," every time she'd half wake up on the couch. And I'd respond by telling her the truth, that it wasn't, and that it had always been more Jenna's thing than mine anyway.

Jenna actually called me from the opening night cast party and confirmed that Emily Belfry and Ben Roswin did indeed French throughout the entire curtain call. When Marcus called me later that week to check in, he added that he's now had to take over lighting duty because apparently Derrick, who was not so happy about all the stage Frenching, decided to have trouble "finding Emily" with the spotlight during her big musical numbers.

"Well, I'm sorry we missed it," Mom says now. "But I can't tell you how thrilled I am to finally be getting out of the house tomorrow."

"Are you sure you're up for going?" Pam asks.

"Yes! I can walk, so I can go. That was the deal. And we get to see Izzy's portfolio!" She turns her head to me, smiling.

"Yup," I reply, nodding back at her.

"Pam said your Darfur sculpture is already on display, right in front of the lobby window," Mom says, "and that it made her cry."

"It did, it really did," Pam says, mid cake binge.

"Yes, yes, they brought it out after the show last night. It's very large," Cathy chimes in, "but lovely. Large and lovely."

"Thanks," I say. "That's . . . what I was going for . . ."

Allissa stifles a laugh, and Pam gives me a wink.

"So are you ready? Everything all set?" Mom asks.

"Almost," I say.

"They should really give you a circumstantial extension, but I guess now"—Cathy stops to lick a bit of frosting off her thumb—"with the auction and all, they can't."

"Nope," I say, shaking my head.

I thought Mom's first two days back home would be pretty productive for me, since the nurses said she'd mostly sleep. But then Cathy was always calling to talk dance stuff. She wasn't really asking me to do things, she was just kind of venting out loud about what needed to be done, like paint/ decorate thirty centerpiece vases, design the donation box, and make signs, signs, signs. A sign for the donation table, a sign for the food, additional no-smoking signs by the bathrooms, a sign telling people where to donate, a sign telling them where to place their auction bids, and, of course, a sign thanking them for their donations/auction bids. I did help her a little with those, since I had some paints and foam boards at home. And then yesterday when I finally got a chance to open my sketchbook and start thinking about how I wanted to organize my display, Mom randomly decided she wanted me to bring all of her clothes downstairs to her. Not just the ones hanging in her closet, but all of them. Then from her position on the sleep sofa, she directed me on proper pile placements, making ones for "keep," "Goodwill," "garbage," and "alterations," all while changing her bandage dressings. So yeah, I've gotten no portfolio work done at all this final week.

And it looks like I'm not going to get anything else done tonight either, because right after everybody leaves, when I finally have a moment of time alone with my sketchbook to select the drawings I want to include, my cell phone buzzes and I see a "nails/sofa bed assembly, please?" text from Mom. I'm so glad she took my cell phone suggestion, because texting is way less annoying than that awful tiny crystal bell Grandma Iris made her use over the summer.

I find Mom leaning up against the living room door, staring at her reflection in one of her tiny compact mirrors

"How am I supposed to go out in public with this?"

"With what?" I ask, bending down to pull out her sofa bed.

"With this face. And this stupid pole."

"Well . . . we could make the pole an accessory," I suggest, arranging her pillows how she likes them and stacking the rest in a pile on the floor. "We could decorate it. Make it look festive."

"Very funny," Mom says, laughing, and then quickly re-grimaces, catching her reflection again. "I'll be an embarrassment to you like this tomorrow. You'll be showing off your art, and people will say, 'Well, where's the mother?' 'Oh, she's the one in the corner who looks like an aging zombie.'"

"You do not," I say, "and I don't think zombies age."

Mom just shakes her head at me and sighs.

"You don't look like a young zombie either. You look great."

Which is true. She does look great, especially for someone who had a respirator in her mouth less than a week ago. Still, I know that by her standards, her appearance must seem horrifying.

"So," I say, getting her nail kit from the kitchen drawer and filling up a bowl of warm water, "you want to still do this, or are you too tired?"

"No, no, yes, let's do it," she says, holding out what she's been calling her "hospital claws."

She sits down on the sofa bed, and I pull up a chair beside her, laying out my supplies. I grab her hands into mine and assess the damage.

"Wow, dangerous," I tease.

"I told you."

I dunk one of her hands in the bowl of water and keep hold of the other. Her nails might need filing, but her hands are still soft, and they smell like her baby oil moisturizer. I squeeze her hand a little as I file, just to make sure she's really here, sitting in front me, and not still lying in some hospital bed, or worse.

"You can round them. Or square them. Whatever's easier, just make me human again," she says, shifting on her cushion so her PIC line's not pulling. "So," she says, stopping her pole fidgeting and looking right at me now. "Mrs. Preston called me this afternoon."

"Oh, why?" I ask, focusing on gently pushing down her cuticles.

"Just a 'get well' courtesy call," she says, still eyeing me.

"That was nice of her."

"Yes, it really was. She also wanted to let me know that your name has officially been cleared, and that your actions won't be going on your permanent record."

"Oh." I pause, mid file. "My actions won't be going on my . . ." I'm repeating what Mom said, sincerely trying to comprehend.

Then she says, "Izzy!" and pulls her free hand out of the water and gestures at me with it, as if she thinks I'm playing dumb or something.

I catch her runaway hand and attempt to towel it off, saying, "What? What did I do?"

"I know," is all Mom says.

"You do?"

"Yes."

"I can explain," I start.

"Yes, can you explain to me why you, and apparently every other girl in Broomington, confessed to being the subject of that obscenity?"

"*Oh.* Um . . . well . . ."

"Why would you put yourself in that position, tarnish your name and—"

"I didn't. I mean, you said it's not going on our records—"

"That's not the point, Izzy."

"We all did it, Mom, it was the only way to—"

"Just because everyone is shooting up needles of cocaine doesn't mean—"

"Mom that's not—" I take a breath, realizing it's not the right time to correct her on her drug analogies.

"What then? Explain this to me."

I feel the weight of a thousand different words on my tongue. So many different combinations, so many ways I can tell my mom the truth.

"Well, first of all, no girl sent that picture. It was a boy who did it. And how would you feel if . . . I mean if that was me, in that picture? If some boy sent it around and it was a picture of me? Wouldn't you want all those girls sticking up for me and protecting me?"

"I . . . I don't know. I never thought of it like that, as . . . protecting. But I still think that whoever it is needs to be punished. There obviously needs to be some sort of disciplinary reaction to that . . . behavior."

"Right, sure, but . . ." I start on Mom's primer coat, trying to keep my hand steady. "But . . . I'm sure she'll be punished enough by . . . I mean, once her mom finds out, she probably won't even really love her in the same way and—"

"No . . . no, I don't think that's true. You don't just stop loving people, especially family, just because of . . . just one thing they do."

"But what about with you and Grandma Iris—"

"Your grandma and I . . . we still love each other. We're just bad at . . . being around each other, that's all."

"Well, Mom. I don't want *us* to be bad at being around each other."

"We're not." Mom pulls me in closer to her with her half-painted hand. "Now let's move on to more important matters, like what are you wearing tomorrow? What about that dress we got you, with the pretty flowers? Do you have shoes for that?" And she starts in on how many people will see me standing there at the dance tomorrow next to my work, and how some might even take pictures of me, and something about patterns versus solids and horizontal lines being the devil.

"This is what I'm talking about!" I finally cut in, catching Mom so off guard, her hands flinch away from mine. She quickly steadies them, though, to protect her wet nails, and rests them stiffly on her lap.

"What do you mean, what you're talking about?"

"You. Wanting me to look . . . how you want me to look! I hate that dress with the flowers. I hate it! And if I don't look absolutely perfect for pictures, then . . . well, I don't care. But I know you do, and that clearly you're unhappy with the way I look all the time. But I can't do anything about it, or do anything about how people see me and . . . it's just that every time you . . . look at me, I . . . I just feel so terrible about . . . everything about me sometimes."

Mom's looking at me like English isn't her first language.

"Izzy," she starts. "I'm not . . . I'm not unhappy with how you look all the time. I . . . oh sweetie no, no, no, I just . . . I just want you to look your best."

"Yeah, but . . . my best according to you."

"No. Sweetie . . . I hate that you feel terrible about . . . I just . . . I don't know what to say. I'm sorry."

"No, Mom. I'm sor—" I'm about to apologize, but then I stop, because I'm not sorry. In fact, I feel like that's what I always say to people, "I'm sorry, I'm sorry." It just comes out "I'm sorry" even when I'm not, or I shouldn't be. I take a breath and instead just say, "Okay, thanks."

I finish up with her nails and by the time I come back into the room to plug in the mini fan, she's passed out. Leaning against the back of the sofa bed, hands still slightly outstretched on her lap. Even my phone buzzing against the coffee table doesn't wake her up.

I head upstairs and see a text from Jenna. Miss you! Sculpture KICKS ASS!!! I smile, hoping those are the types of comments I get from the Italy reviewers too. Well, not in those exact words maybe.

I've been trying to figure out why Jenna didn't just tell me about what happened last summer. And I'm thinking now, maybe it's the same reason I didn't just tell my mom tonight about what happened with Blake. Was Jenna afraid of disappointing me, the way I'm afraid of disappointing my mom? But like Mom said, you don't stop loving someone just because they do something that surprises or even disappoints you. Maybe facts and formulas comfort Marcus, but I think that article he read was totally wrong. You don't love chemical reactions or particles or neuron receptors. You love whole people. Including the parts you didn't know were there, and the parts you're waiting for them to become.

CHAPTER 29

I've got girl-balls.

I don't mean to sound conceited or anything, but my sculpture really does look kick-ass.

You can see Meredith's photos and the mirror sections reflecting off the window when you pull up to the school's circular driveway. Which I'm doing right now, and very cautiously, since this is only my third time driving with my permit, and since the car is filled to the brim with dance supplies and folding tables and chairs that could easily fall and wreck my carefully wrapped artwork. No big deal, no pressure.

"So, you have your bag with your change of clothes?" Mom asks for like the eight hundredth time.

"Yes, don't worry, I won't be wearing these sweats."

"No, no, it's fine. Just checking," Mom says. She pulls down the passenger's-side mirror and checks her face one last time.

"You look great," I assure her, especially proud of myself for having evenly round-brushed her hair.

Mom smiles at me, and then nervously looks out the window as I'm trying to pull up to the curb without driving over it. As soon as I stop the car, a barrage of ladies surrounds it from all sides. They're opening doors, taking out the tables, helping Mom out, grabbing her wheely pole, asking me how to handle my artwork, popping the trunk, handing off folding chairs. I feel like I just stopped at a NASCAR pit stop. Once I see that Mom and all of our stuff is in trusted hands, I park the car. And by park the car, I mean that after three attempts, I pull an Allissa and decide our car deserves to take up two spaces.

"Ryan, watch yourself there, make sure those are locked in plaaace . . . ?" I hear Miss S. say as she guides some boys in setting up the display panels. She waves wildly when she sees me, and then dance-walks over to my pile of canvases and books.

"Whacha think?" she asks, quickly swinging her body toward the display panels, her braids and twisted hair boomeranging around her head.

"Looks good," I say.

She calls a couple of the guys over to help me move my stuff to the studio and then pats me on the back and says, for only me to hear, "I'm proud of you." Then to everyone else, "One hundred and twenty minutes until show tiiiime . . . !"

I thought two hours would be more than enough time, but I didn't count on being so distracted. Everyone's already like six steps ahead of me, and so I'm spending a lot of time helping people move their stuff over to the display area. But I still have to mount and frame *Viral* and arrange all my sketches and smaller drawings in binders. Then I have to move everything out there, display, and label.

When I get back from my third trip to the panels, my hands a little cut up from carrying Ina's new scrap sculpture, I see Meredith and Marcus waiting for me in the studio.

"Oh my God, is it that late already?"

"No, we're here early," Meredith says. "Hi!"

"Oh. Sorry. Hi," I say, leaning in to give them each a hug and then realizing that I'm sweaty, and dusty, and covered in paint and they look like freshly showered movie stars.

"Air hug," I say, pulling back. "Wow, you both look fantastic."

They really do. Meredith is wearing this little red dress that makes her legs look like they go on forever and ever. Her strawberry blond hair is in loose curls, and up in one of those fancy ponytails. She's wearing this sparkly green eye shadow that makes her eyes look huge, and her lipstick is the exact shade of her dress.

And Marcus, wow. Marcus looks really good in a suit.

"We just saw your mom," Marcus says, smiling. "She looks great."

"Yeah. She's doing good," I say, staring back at him and nodding and—unghh—acting like a complete bobble. "I . . . I heard closing night went really well."

"It did," Meredith says. "Jenna definitely missed you, though."

"Is she here?" I ask.

"She's with my mom, trying to calm her down," Marcus says, looking around the studio. "So where's Blake?" Marcus asks.

"Oh. Um. I d-don't. Know," I stutter, probably sounding like a robot malfunctioning. "We. Didn't. Um. We're not . . ."

"Izzy dumped that loser, please," Meredith rescues me. "Such old news," she adds, as if Marcus should know everything about it.

"Oh," Marcus says, "sorry, I wasn't aware that you—"

"Man, I feel like . . . such a bum." I change the subject, looking myself up and down in Miss S.'s office mirror. "And I still have so much to do, I don't even know if I'll have time to—"

"No, you look perfect," Marcus says. "I mean . . . you look like . . . the perfect way you should look for someone who's showing off their . . . artwork."

"Yeah . . ." Meredith agrees, looking at Marcus with a slight laugh. "It's so cool you used my photos. I'm totally a part of your portfolio!"

"Yes"—I nod—"thank you! They were perfect."

"Oh, my God!" we hear, and then turn to see Ina slack-jawed and staring at *Viral*. It's only the second time I've seen her mouth open that wide.

"What? What's wrong?" I say.

"Izzy Skymen," she says, her eyes still on my canvas, tilting her head to the side, "you've got some huge girl-balls!"

"Girl-balls?" Marcus repeats, furrowing his eyebrows as Ina walks past us carrying a stack of sketchbooks.

"It's, like, a feminist way of saying that Izzy's got balls," Meredith explains.

"Oh," Marcus says, still looking a little perplexed, "but, logistically speaking, I mean from a feminist standpoint, that doesn't really—" But he's cut off by Meredith erupting into giggles.

"That is so cool!" she says to me, nodding at my canvas and grinning.

"Oh yeah," Marcus says, taking a look himself. "It's really pretty. What is it, like a field with . . . what is that, like a . . . strawberry?"

"Come on," Meredith says, pulling Marcus away from the painting, holding her chest, she's laughing so hard. "Izzy has work to do."

I know it's my artwork that's displayed behind me, but I feel like I'm the one mounted up on that panel, and everyone's ogling and analyzing and scrutinizing me. Or maybe I just feel self-conscious because I'm at a huge fancy school event in my paint clothes. Ugh, I can't believe I didn't have time to change. But by the time I was filling out all my description cards, the DIA people were already arriving and asking me questions and I've had no break to even run a comb through my hair. And I almost died when Mrs. Preston came over and started examining my latest piece from about three different angles. She kept saying how beautiful it was and how much she loved that shade of green and how it complemented the pink colors so nicely. Though I seriously thought at any minute she would stand far enough away, at that particular angle, and suspend me from school right then and there. But no, she just patted me on the back and said, "Well done, Izzy."

"Just ten more minutes . . ." Miss S. says, "of mingling with the common folks, and then you're freeeeeeee . . ."

Great, maybe I can sneak off and change before Mom sees me. Pam said she was stuck inside, manning the donation tables, but that she'd be out here pretty soon.

"Oooh, and here's Izzy's!" Cathy exclaims, doing her two-stairs-at-a-time march over to my display with Jenna trailing behind her, holding a donation box. Cathy starts at the far end of my table, sifting through some of my sketchbooks, while Jenna looks at the canvases behind me.

"Awesome," she says, her eyes doing an initial perusal.

"Thanks." I give her a hug hello.

"Looking hot, Izzy!"

I roll my eyes, and tell her I didn't have time to change. Then she whispers, "Nope, was talking about *that*," and points to my canvas.

"Oh," I say, shaking my head, "right."

"So what do you think?" Jenna asks, modeling her silk camisole-skirt combo with an open safety-pin back.

"I like it!"

"I made it!" Jenna exclaims, doing a twirl.

"Too much skin, but resourceful nonetheless," Cathy chimes in, motioning for Jenna to move along.

"It's a sleeveless ensemble—shoulders don't count as skin," I hear Jenna say as Cathy drags her off to the next display.

"Wow," I hear, and I know that voice. Reluctantly, I turn to see Blake standing at my table. He's wearing dark jeans and a blazer, and his tie's knotted a little too short, but he pulls it off. He's standing farther back from me than one would normally stand to have a conversation.

"I'm not going to . . . throw water on you," I finally say.

"No, I know," he says, but doesn't come too much closer. "So, am I . . . am I allowed to comment on your stuff?"

I really want to just icily ignore him, but the way he's fidgeting with his tie, and tapping his hand rapidly on the side of his leg . . . well, he looks pretty miserable as it is.

"Yeah, I guess." I raise my chin a little, looking over his head.

He walks over to the start of the display and checks out my innards canvas. "This is so freaking awesome," he says like a boy watching a gruesome scene in a horror movie.

"Thanks," I reply politely.

"So, how come you're the only who looks like . . . not dressed up?" he asks.

"'Cause I'm the only one who didn't have time to get ready," I say.

"Oh. Right." Then he makes his way around the corner to the end of the display. "I like this one a lot too. What's it called?" he asks, leaning in closer to read the description card.

"*Viral*," I say.

"Oh. So is it a cell . . . or a . . ." Then he tilts his head a little, and his eyes get so wide, I feel like they're about to merge Cyclops-like into the center of his forehead. "Oh my God," he says. I see the tops of his cheeks start to flush.

I stay very still now, looking him right in the eyes as he turns to me.

"Wow," he says, shifting his weight from one foot to the other and wiping his face on the inner sleeve of his blazer. Then he leans in closer to me. "I want you to know, and I know you don't want to hear it, but I . . . I deleted it right away. I didn't send it. I . . . Jacob found it in my temporary . . . It doesn't matter. I just— I wasn't going to use it and I . . . I wish I could get some of kind of . . . do-over and . . . I wish I could do it all over, that's all," he says, letting a long, slow stream of air escape his lungs, like a deflating balloon.

I nod once, not really knowing why. It's not a bobble-type nod, though, like I'm flustered and don't know what to say. It's more like, I'm acknowledging he said something, but not sure it's even worth a response. Then I see my mom, shuffling her way over to us from across the lobby. I excuse myself, leaving Blake there, and go to meet her.

CHAPTER 30

We're all in the snapshot.

Mom's trying to pick up speed as she shuffles closer, her wheely pole rolling faster than her body is able to go, her eyes looking up at my pieces on the panel like a finish line.

"Look at all this!" She flings out her free hand when she finally arrives at the start of the display. "It's so exciting!" she gushes, turning away now from the panels and looking at me. "And look . . . at you . . . you're . . . in your paint . . . clothes," she says, now fully looking me up and down. Then she sees Blake shifting from side to side behind me, like one of those toddler toys that never fall over.

"Oh, hello, Mr. Hangry, don't you look nice," she says to him. And then to me, "I can come back if you—"

"No, no, Blake was—"

"I was just leaving," Blake says, and nods good-bye to us both. We watch as he speed-walks back toward the gymnasium.

"I'm sorry, did I interrupt something. Are you two . . . ?"

I shake my head in a way that I hope implies that no, Blake Hangry and I are not anything at all.

"Well . . . look at you!" Mom says again, taking in my entire ensemble.

"I didn't have time to change, Mom. I guess I'm the one embarrassing you," and I'm about to add *I'm sorry*, but I catch myself.

"No, no, it's . . . Listen, everyone is coming up to me and telling me how talented you are, and how much they love your stuff! And I'm sorry it took me so long. I was stuck at that donation table forever. Jenny Hartigan said she was just going to the bathroom, but on her way back she stopped at the dessert table and started yapping with Mrs. Seltzer, as if I didn't have anywhere to be," she says, shaking her head. "It's not like her daughter has any art on display," Mom adds.

I laugh and take Mom's arm, walking her to the start of my portfolio. She leans back and feigns fright when she sees the innards canvas and then asks me a ton of questions. Mostly logistical, like what I used to get that texture, or how I got that effect. She smiled approvingly when I point out the nail polish. Then we turn the corner and when she sees *Morphing Mom,* the tips of her fingers on her free hand fly up to her lips.

I turn and watch the profile of her face as she stares straight at the canvas. Which, I now realize, is practically screaming at her, *"You're sick, Linda! And we all know it!"*

I didn't mean for this painting to scare her, or make her feel bad in the least. I guess it was just something in my head that I needed to get out. But now that I see the way Mom's looking at it, I want to put it all back inside.

"Mom—" I'm about to apologize, not knowing what else to say, but she cuts in.

"No, no, no," Mom says, a slight whimper escaping from her lips. "It's perfect, it's just perfect."

"Just a couple more minutes," Miss S. says, bounding toward me, "and then you're freeeeee . . . ! Oh hello, Lindaaaaaaa . . ." she says, seeing Mom. "You look wonderful. So aren't you just burstiiiiiing . . .?"

"Yes, yes, I am," Mom says. "I am so proud of her."

Then a group of freshman boys crowds around my display, ogling my final canvas.

"That's the one!"

"Looks like a scoop of ice cream."

"No, no man, it's somebody's butt cheek."

"No, no, dudes look. It's a TIT! It's just one HUGE TIT!"

I press my sneakers into the tiled floor, hoping the pressure will help keep me on my feet. Mom turns her head fast, like Leroy when he hears the can opener, and shuffle-wheels herself up to my last painting. Miss S. is walking over to the boys.

"No, gentlemen, it is not 'just one huge tit.' It is a landscape of nurture-dom . . ."

The boys look at Miss S. like she's talking to them out of a fourth head while my mom regards the canvas, tilting her one head in various directions.

Miss S. continues to talk to the boys as if she has their rapt, art-loving attention.

". . . As you can see from the trajectory of Miss Skymen's

wooork . . . ? This last piece is saying something that is both broad and finite about the vital role of the maternal figure in an angst-filled, war-wrought humanity . . ."

My mom turns to me now, looking at me as if I'm some sort of optical illusion she can't quite figure out. Then she turns her attention to Miss S., who's still waxing philosophical on my *Viral* painting.

"It's not just a tit, boys, it is an ample *teat*, a lone faucet from which the milk of human kindness driiiiips . . ." she concludes, shooing away the boys and smiling after them as if she just changed their lives. Then she turns to Mom and says, "I just love how Izzy went from a literal war landscape with that sculpture, to a visceral internal human guts landscape, to a figurative battle of mortal existence, to this glorious mountainous, primal nourishing landscape of maternity!"

Wow. I wish I wrote *that* down in my portfolio description.

"Oh Izzy," Miss S. says, pushing her glasses down to the tip of her nose and giving me a dramatic stare. "Italy, here you come!"

We watch as Miss S. dances away to the next display, and then Mom turns her attention back to the canvas. Then she turns to me. And then back to the canvas. And then back to me. And then back to the canvas. It's as if she's watching a very slow, invisible tennis match or something.

"Linda, we have a dessert table crisis," Pam announces, springing over to us, holding a plate full of brownies and cookies. She goes on to explain that Debbie Belfry hid all of Nancy Freel's brownies behind the sign, telling another mother that they tasted like cardboard, and that now Nancy has thrown away an entire tray of Debbie's lemon squares. "Food-wise you're really not missing out, Linda," Pam adds. "Debbie's right, the brownie's are dry like desert sand."

Mom reluctantly turns her attention to Pam and her dance duties, and tells me to go inside and enjoy myself. And then she's gone.

I make my way to the dance, detouring to pass my map sculpture. I walk around it, stopping to catch my shattered reflection in the mirrors, and am satisfied when, at the right angle, it reflects myself flanked with Darfur teens on one side, and Meredith's Broomington High candids on the other.

I finally get inside and weave through our cafeteria tables, covered now in different shades of pink fabric. They've all been pulled back and set up in two semicircles around the dance floor. Each one is adorned with a festive pink painted vase holding Cathy and Jenna's donation card tree bouquets. I'm pretty sure Mom didn't approve this idea, giant donation index cards mixed in with her carefully chosen floral arrangements, but I guess it's the cause that counts.

The brick wall in the back flashes with the light from the DJ booth—a folding table, some strobe lights, and a laptop—and from Meredith's pictures, the ones I didn't end up using in my sculpture, which are playing as a slide show on all of three flat screens typically used for school announcements. The room really does look amazing, and the donation/auction table looks pretty crowded too.

"Congratulations," Pam shouts, speed-walking past me, like she has a fire to put out.

"What?" I shout back.

"I heard there were three silent bids on your ice cream painting! Woo!" she shouts, before bounding out the door. I look back at the auction table but can't really make out anyone in the crowd. I continue scanning the room, catching sight of Blake.

I stare at him standing against the flickering brick wall with Nate and Jacob and can't believe I ever felt sorry for him about what a rough time he was having with basketball hazing, or for being such a "nice guy" stuck with such immature, obnoxious friends. Ha. Maybe some of Blake's friends and all those senior guys think it was a pretty awesome thing for him to do—completing his task and taking that picture. But they didn't see the way he acted in the art room yesterday, or come to think of it, how weird and uneasy he was in the Rap Room, and even at the museum. If he really didn't want to do it, if he knew it was wrong, then the fact that he went through with it actually only makes it worse.

I know I might not have a whole basketball team full of friends, but at least I have one or two who care about me enough to defend me, and stand up for me, and risk getting in trouble for me. Which is more than I can say for Blake.

I spot Jenna on the dance floor with Meredith and Cara

and make my way over to them, grabbing one of Mrs. Freel's cardboard brownies on the way and deciding to avoid the bowl of festive pink punch.

No one on the dance floor is really dancing, just kind of standing around talking and occasionally moving to the beat.

"Where's your 'date'?" I ask Meredith, making quotes with my fingers since technically they came as group. Meredith turns to me, still giggling with Cara over the fact that Ray Ray the DJ keeps looking over at them and winking.

"I think he went looking for you." She smiles, and then on cue Marcus walks up to us and says, "Hey, I was just looking for you," which makes us all, well, except Marcus, crack up.

Then Ray Ray the DJ says he's going to "slow down this joy ride" and Cara drags Meredith over to stand closer to the DJ booth. Soon everyone starts coupling off. Even Jenna, who's dancing with Ryan Paulson and sort of adorably stooped over his shoulder, not seeming to mind their height difference.

"Hi," Marcus says from behind me.

"Hi," I reply, turning around so we're face-to-face and I'm seeing again—wow—how great Marcus looks in a suit.

"So . . . did you hear about that really cool exhibit that's opening in Detroit next week. *Body Parts*?"

"Oh yeah, heard about that! It's supposed to have like over three hundred specimens, and dissected organs and stuff."

"Yeah, they put the body parts in this vacuum chamber to preserve them and— Wait, why are we slow dancing by ourselves?" He laughs, and I realize that we're both standing across from each other swaying to the music.

"I don't know!" I start laughing too, but then stop when he steps closer and puts his arms around my waist. I can feel his chest moving up and down as I lean against it and relax my arms around his neck, swaying with him to the music.

"So . . ." he says now, but kind of more in my ear, "you want to go see it sometime?"

"What?"

"*Body Parts,*" he says, and I feel the warmth of his palms pressing against the back of my sweatshirt. "Or is that a weird thing to do for a date?"

"Oh." I turn my head in. "Yeah. I mean . . . no, it's not." I shake my head, which is so close to his now our lips are practically touching. "It's not a weird thing to do for a—" and then our lips *are* touching. He crisscrosses his arms around my waist and pulls me into him closer. I close my eyes, and breathe him in as my head just naturally tilts to the side and everything inside me loses density.

I don't know how long we kiss, but I think about three whole spinning century-seconds go by before we pull away a little. Marcus laughs. It's a nice laugh. "Okay, good."

"Good." I smile and let my head rest on his shoulder.

Two slow songs later and I'm practically floating out of the cafeteria. I didn't see Mom by the donation table and I'm heading to the bathrooms, wanting to make sure she's okay.

Then I spot her back where I left her, staring at my display.

"Hey," I say.

"Hello, sweetie." She remains staring up at my *Viral* canvas. Then she turns to me. "Look at you," she says almost more to herself than to me.

"I know, I look awful."

"Oh, no, no. You look very pretty," she says.

"Right." I shake my head. "I doubt that's what you think."

"No . . . I—listen I know I'm not the easiest to please regarding . . . presentation and well . . . perhaps . . . perhaps I do need to broaden my scope when it comes to thinking I know the way you girls should look, and . . . I just don't want you to ever think that I'm truly unhappy with how you . . . I mean, even now sweetie, right now . . . I think you do look . . . *very pretty*." She smiles, and leans closer to brush one of my paint strands up and behind my ear with her good hand.

"Thanks." I smile back at her.

I stay close to her side, both of us now looking up at my *Viral* painting, tilting our heads at the same angle.

"You know, my range of motion and strength are getting pretty good now," Mom says, keeping her eyes on the canvas.

"Oh . . . well, that's great, Mom."

"I couldn't even use both arms for carrying the other day, but just this morning I was actually able to open the dryer, empty it, and everything."

"See, I told you if you just did those stretches gently, you'd—"

"Such a pretty shade of green," she cuts in breezily, pointing at the canvas. "Which reminds me, you shrunk some clothes."

"Oh . . . Oops."

"No, it's okay. It was mostly your things, and nothing that nice really. Might have to throw out a couple of your sweaters, them being so tiny now and all. Especially that green sweater. Such a pretty shade of green." She looks at me and then back at the green in the canvas. "But I think we should definitely throw that one out, yes?"

"Oh. Um . . . yeah." I smile, staring at Mom still fixated on *Viral*. "I really . . . I hate that sweater now anyway."

"I thought so," Mom says, nodding her head. "So . . . my Izzy might be going all the way to Italy, huh?"

"Yeah," I say. "Maybe. Maybe not."

The truth is, I don't know if now's the best time to go off to Italy for a whole summer. I don't even know if I got the scholarship anyway, but it's just that I have the whole rest of my life to be off, traveling on my own. But how many more summers will I get to spend here with my mom?

"Well . . . I'm very proud of you. And I think this piece I splurged on"—she gestures back to the *Viral* canvas—"is going to look great in my new office."

I turn to her, feeling my eyes widen and soften as I smile and say, "Yeah, I think it will too."

Mom shuffles in closer and wraps her free arm around my waist.

I know she's waiting for me to pull away and give her my

"please stop embarrassing me on school grounds" look, but instead I turn in and wrap both my arms around her waist. I think she's surprised at first, me hugging her like this in public, and in the middle of my high school. But then she loosens up and wheels her pole forward so she can partially wrap her other arm around my back. I press into her gently so as not to hurt her stitches, and she squeezes me back tightly with her good arm.

I'm wishing everything could pause somehow and we could stay together like this for a long, long time. I don't focus on taking a really good mental snapshot of the moment, though, because I know as soon as I do, it will be too late, it will be over already. And really, no mental snapshot will ever be good enough. It's like tracksuit man said—moment to moment is as far as you can go sometimes. And I'm thinking right now, it's the best place to be.

Acknowledgments

Many, many thanks—in no particular order . . .

To Jessica Garrison, for her indispensable insight, guidance, answers, questions, and patience. Thank you for finding me and then letting me find my story; to Lauri Hornik for believing in Izzy from day one; to Maggie Olson, Greg Stadnyk, Jason Mercier, and Kristin Smith for their jacket design and art expertise; and to Kathy Dawson, Sarah Creech, Regina Castillo, and everyone at Penguin Young Readers for their hard work and enthusiasm.

To my NYC comedy family, the stand-ups, the storytellers, the improvisers, the music makers, the wig-wearing character slayers—for letting me belong, and always inspiring me to create and play.

To all my New York offices (diners, coffee shops, bars with outlets): specifically Galaxy Diner, Carroll Gardens Classic Diner, and Fortunato Brothers for letting me stay and refilling my coffee.

To Benson Barr for his much needed guidance at the start; to my agents, Kelly Harms Wimmer, who got this Izzy car running; and Christina Hogrebe, whose patience, support, gentle prodding, and know-how got it to the finish line; and to everyone at Jane Rotrosen.

To Marc Pattini, for giving great pep talks, listening to my symptoms, putting his headphones on when I asked him to, and letting me ramble it out; and my Pittsburgh second family for so many years, Art, Nancy, Dana, and Dave.

To my crazy posse of loving Jewish relatives spread throughout fourteen states, specifically Suki and Dewey Loselle, for giving me a Connecticut home away from home and constantly keeping my belly full; and my partners in Raf-crime, Stacey Graff and Brian Raf, and my Raf-in-laws Jon Graff and Kelly Raf—thank you for keeping your Chicago and Portland doors open.

To my dad, for his wisdom, for worrying but never doubting, and for continuing to tell me to do what I love; and my mom, for singing to her kugel, banging on pots and pans, and for being classy, witty, selfless, brave, and full of love right to the end.

Mindy Raf is a writer, comedy performer, and musician based in Brooklyn, New York. She is a graduate of the University of Michigan, and grew up in a suburb of Detroit right around here (visualize the bottom of your left thumb). Mindy has written for CollegeHumor, VH1, TNT, The Daily Comedy Network, and was a contributor to the *My Parents Were Awesome* anthology. She continues to perform stand-up and music across the country.

Visit Mindy at www.mindyraf.com